THE COMPLETE SIMON IFF STORIES

THE COMPLETE SIMON IFF STORIES

Aleister Crowley (1875–1947), as an occultist, writer, mountaineer, philosopher, poet, secret agent, magus, libertine, prophet and mystic. He was an influential member in several occult organizations, including the Golden Dawn, the A.∴A.∴, and Ordo Templi Orientis (O.T.O.), and is best known today for his occult writings, especially *The Book of the Law,* the central sacred text of Thelema. He gained much notoriety during his lifetime, and was infamously dubbed "The Wickedest Man in the World." He claimed to be the re-incarnation of Dr John Dee among others, lived in England from 1875 through 1947. He is the author of several Weiser Books titles, including *Book of Thoth, Diary of a Drug Fiend, Magick, Book of Lies, Book of the Law and 777 & Other Qabalistic Writings.*

The yellowbacks... classics of popular fiction

The yellowjackets or yellowbacks were a great series of bestselling adventure and crime thrillers that had its origins in the mid to late 19th century following on from the 'penny dreadfuls'. They virtually began the mass market revolution of the early 20th century with a clear standard format and imprint/series livery (what would today be called branding). Hodder & Stoughton published the yellowjackets in two main series with series run dates of: 1923-1939 and later 1949-1957.

As the tagline ('where thrillers really began') on the back cover implies, the imprint and series focused on thrillers that were the bestsellers of their time. This current reissue or retro revival if you will, brings back many of these masterpieces, now classics in their own way and extends it further by including key titles from that period that were either great crime or thriller or even general commercial fiction (including sub-genres of noir, horror, gothic, romance, westerns, etc.) influences of their time. There are some perennial favourites and many rarities either lost or not easily available being revived in the current series. Writers and characters ranged from adventure heroes like Bulldog Drummond, Allan Quatermain, Richard Hannay or the Saint through thriller grandmasters Edgar Wallace and E. Phillips Oppenheim, crime and mystery maestros like Patricia Wentworth, GK Chesterton, Agatha Christie and the Detection club, to western and swashbucklers like Zane Grey, Max Brand, Captain Blood and even romance or general fiction classics like Hermina Black, Denise Robins, Marie Corelli or Stella Morton. These were books that had storytelling at their heart and always entertained.

The yellowbacks had both hardback (with varying design elements) and paperback (which built the series look) versions with the latter still carrying the imprint 'yellowjacket'. The current reissues pay tribute to both and use an amalgam of elements from both editions while retaining the complete yellow (or 'mustard-plaster') livery with the author's name in blue beveled type with a 'simulated emboss' effect and a white outer 'outline', and the book title in black. These reissues retain the distinctive size of the original mass market paperback and follow the three main category variations—the thrillers (crime, westerns, mystery, adventure) had blue lettering for the author's name, while Romance and softer general fiction had red; and other categories like humour had green.

For more detail and a full list of titles visit https://www.hachetteindia.com/home/yellowbacks

THE COMPLETE SIMON IFF STORIES

Aleister Crowley

HODDER AND STOUGHTON
YELLOW JACKET
hachette

The Complete Simon Iff Stories
First published in 1917–1918 in the New York publication *The International* under the pseudonym Edward Kelly

1

The texts in these editions in most cases have been reprinted as is, with minimal editorial changes and by and large no bowdlerizing for political correctness; though in some editions, a few words and phrases considered archaic, or those considered offensive now, along with archaic punctuation may have been modified in places to make the text more accessible to today's readers. The narratives, language, beliefs, social mores and/or cultural depictions, in these volumes are a reflection of their times and must be viewed as such. They may also contain certain cultural, racial and gender prejudices and stereotypes that may be outdated or clearly wrong then and wrong today; but their removal would be tantamount to claiming these prejudices never existed. The Publisher does not endorse or support those depictions or stereotypes; and these books have been made available for a discerning audience that will read it for entertainment value and a chronicle/record of popular fiction of past times.

Cover design by Priya Singh adapted from the original classic yellowjacket by Hodder & Stoughton.

Cover illustration by Ishan Trivedi.

Series note: Some of the books in the series (unless otherwise credited) may have cover or inside illustrations from the original yellowbacks or early editions, and while full restoration has been attempted, some images may be grainy or faded due to the condition of the original material. The end notes or bonus material or blurb details may have been sourced from the public domain or free use publications such as Wikipedia and attribution is hereby made also allowing similar free use reproduction from here. Sources requiring further specific attribution may write in and further detailing and/or corrections shall be made in subsequent printings/editions.

Reprint specifications may be subject to change including but not limited to finishes, paper, colour sections.

ISBN: 978-93-5731-222-6

Hachette Book Publishing India Pvt. Ltd.
4th & 5th Floors, Corporate Centre,
Plot No. 94, Sector 44, Gurugram - 122 003, India

Typeset in Electra LT STD 10/12.5 pt by Manipal Technologies Limited, Manipal

Printed and bound in India by Manipal Technologies Limited, Manipal

MIX
Paper from responsible sources
FSC™ C043100

CONTENTS

Simple Simon

1

The Scrutinies of Simon Iff

THE BIG GAME

1

Dick Ffoulkes was in good practice at the criminal bar, and his envied dinner-parties, given to few and well-known friends, were nearly always held in his chambers in Lincoln's Inn. They looked out on one of the pleasantest green spots in London.

There was a brooding of fog on the first December night of 1911, when Ffoulkes gave a supper to celebrate his victory over the Crown in the matter of the Marsden murder.

Marsden was a wealthy man, and had no enemies. The police suspected a mere protégé of his unmarried sister, who was his only heir; he might thus benefit indirectly; no other motive could be found. The boy – for he was barely twenty – had dined with Marsden on the night of the murder, and of course the police had finger-prints by the dozen. Ffoulkes had torn their flimsy web to rags, and tossed them in the air with a laugh.

All his guests had gone but one, his oldest friend, Jack Flynn. They dated from Rugby, and had continued their inseparability at Balliol. They had read together for the bar, but Flynn, after being called, had branched off into the higher journalism.

The Marsden case had stirred England profoundly. Slight as was the motive attributed to Ezra Robinson, the suspected boy, there was no other person with any motive at all; faint as were the clues which pointed to him, there were none at all to point elsewhere.

Besides these considerations, there was apparently no physical possibility of any other murderer. Marsden had unquestionably died of a thrust in the heart from a common carving-knife, which was identified as the one which had been sent up with the dinner. Unobserved access to the suite was impossible, a floor-clerk being continuously seated in full view of the only door to the whole apartment. The only person known to have been in the room, after the table had been cleared by the hotel servants, was the accused. And even Ffoulkes had not dared to suggest that the wound – a straight drive from above and behind – might have been self-inflicted. Nor was there any motive of robbery, or any trace of search for papers. But there was an undoubted thumb-print of Robinson's in blood on the handle of the carving-knife, and there was a cut on his left hand. He had explained this, and the presence of the knife itself, by saying that it had slipped as he was carving, and that he had run into the bathroom to wash and bind the cut, leaving the knife on the wash-stand.

The only point clean for the defence was the medical evidence, which put the time of death some two hours later than the departure of Robinson. This coincided with a temporary failure of the electric current all through the hotel. Ffoulkes suggested that the old man, who had drunk a good deal of wine, had gone to take a bath before retiring, seen the knife, remembered his old skill as an amateur juggler, ample testimony of which was forthcoming, and started to play at catching the knife. The light had gone out while he was throwing; he had dodged maladroitly, and the blade had chanced to catch him between the shoulders.

The opposite theory was that Robinson had returned to fetch his cigarette-case, which was in fact found in the room by the police, passed the floor-clerk and slipped into the suite in the short spell of darkness, seen his opportunity and seized it, making off before the light was restored. He had not been able to give a satisfactory account of his movements. His story was that he had left Marsden early on account of a severe headache, and had wandered about the streets trying to obtain relief; on the other hand, no one in the hotel would swear to having seen him after his ostensible departure. The floor-clerk had testified to a considerable commotion just at the time of the failure of the electric supply; she had heard noises apparently in several rooms; but this might well have been the normal confusion caused by the sudden darkness.

Flynn had been of the utmost service to Ffoulkes in the case. He had performed a weekly miracle in avoiding a spell of prison for contempt of court; for every week he had returned to the charge. There were long articles on miscarriages of justice; others on the weakness of circumstantial evidence where no strong motive was evident; others again on strange accidental deaths. He quoted the case of Professor Milnes Marshall, who slipped and fell while setting up his camera in Deep Ghyll on Scawfell. He was on a gentle slope of snow, yet he made no effort to recover himself, and rolled over and over to the edge of a precipice, at whose foot he was found dead, smashed to a pulp. This happened in full view of several other climbers. This accident was contrasted with that of Arthur Wellman on the Trifthorn. He fell eight hundred feet, and yet only hurt himself by cutting his leg slightly with his ice-axe.

A hundred such parallels were at the service of Flynn, and he hammered them into the head of the public week by week, while scrupulously avoiding any reference to Marsden. As the courts had no idea, officially, of the line of the defence, they could say nothing. But Flynn moulded the opinion of the public soundly and shrewdly, and in the end the jury had acquitted Robinson after a bare quarter of an hour's deliberation.

Ffoulkes' guests had complimented him on the ingenuity of his theory of an accident, but the lawyer had not been pleased. 'That was a frill,' he had replied: 'the real defence was Absence of Motive. Grant the police their theory of Robinson's movements; put the knife in his hand, and a certain getaway – which he had not got, mind you; the light might have come on any second – but allow everything, and then ask yourselves: "Why should he stab the man?" There was no quarrel; his marriage with Miss Marsden was not opposed; on the contrary he risked that marriage by a mix-up of this sort; yet we are to suppose that he did it on the mere chance that there would be no fuss, and that his fiancée would have twelve thousand a year instead of four. Why, a sane man would hardly kill a rabbit on such motive!'

But now the guests were gone; Ffoulkes and Flynn lit fresh cigars, and settled down for an honest talk. At the elbow of each stood a bottle of the Green Seal '63, one of the soundest wines that ever came out of Oporto. For some time they smoked in silence.

'This is capital wine, Dick,' said Flynn presently.

'Ah, *cher ami*, it is only ten years older that we are. We are getting to the port and portly stage of life.'

'Well, there are thrills left. This has been a great case.'

'Yes. I'm glad you stayed. I thought you might care to hear about it.'

'Hear about it!'

'Yes, there were interesting features.'

'But we need hardly recapitulate.'

'Oh, I don't mean what came out at the trial.'

'No?... I suppose nothing ever does come out at a trial!'

'Just as nothing ever gets into the newspapers.'

'All right. Spit it out. I suppose Robinson did it, for a start.'

'Of course. There was an accident in it, but one of a different kind. When the elevator put him out on Marsden's floor, he was amazed to recognise an old flame in that very prepossessing floor-clerk Maud Duval. They had been members of some kind of devil-worship club, and one of their games was cocaine. Robinson's a perfect fiend, by the way; we had to smuggle the stuff in to him all the time he was in prison, or he'd have gone crazy. Well, the old passion lit like tinder. They had lost each other somehow – you know how such things happen – both had made desperate efforts to renew the link, but in vain. So he told her his plans in ten words. Her answer was equally sweet and to the point. "Kill the old man – I'll cover your tracks; marry the old girl; and meet me at our old trysting-place at midnight a year from today. We'll find a way to be rid of her. Don't risk another word till then." Great and successful criminals have always this faculty of firmness of character and promptitude of decision. The rest of the story is short. The knife incident was intentional; for Robinson had brought no weapon. He left the hotel openly at nine-thirty; came in again by the bar entrance, went unnoticed to the mezzanine floor, and thence to Marsden's floor, thus avoiding the notice of the main office. The failure of the electricity had nothing to do with it – happened twenty minutes later. He walked in, killed the old man, and left as he had come. Pretty bold? Only cocaine. So now he's off to marry old Miss Marsden's money.'

'I begin to see some sort of motive! Maud is what they call "some peach" across the Straits of America.'

'Yes; a perfect devil, with the face of a baby, and the manners of the *jeune fille bien élevée*. Just such a woman as you are a man, Jack, you old scoundrel.'

'Many thanks. I think your own morals – in this case – have been a trifle open to criticism. I suppose it's your fifteen years of law.'

'No; it's being under the influence of dear old Jack, with his fifteen years of journalism!'

'Stop rotting! I'm a bit staggered, you know, straight. Let's have another bottle of port.'

Ffoulkes went to the buttery, and returned with a couple. For ten minutes neither spoke.

'I've a damned funny feeling,' said Flynn at last. 'Do you remember the night we put the iodide of nitrogen in the Doctor's nighties?'

'By the soft leather of this chair, I do!'

'Yes; we caught it! But it's the spirit, not the flesh, which goads me now. I've loved skating around the judges, these last weeks. The best thing in life is the feeling of escape. It's the one real thrill. Perhaps that's why I've always been so keen on solitary climbing and big game shooting.'

'I always preferred fishing. My thrill comes from proving my intellectual stamina or subtlety.' There was a pause.

'What do you think of murder, anyhow?' suddenly blurted out the journalist.

'The most serious crime, except high treason, known to the English law.'

'True, O wise judge! But what is it morally?'

'An art, according to that ass Wilde.'

'When I write an essay on it, I shall treat it as a sport. And between you and me, that is why I have never written one.'

'Why?'

'Why, old intellectual stamina and subtlety, because if I ever do take it up, I don't want some fool to fix me up with a motive. But after your story of tonight, I don't mind telling you; if I'm caught, I'll brief you! Observe, O man of motives, the analysis. Man is no longer killed for food, except in distant countries, or in rare emergencies such as shipwreck.'

'He is only killed nowadays for one of two motives, gain or revenge.'

'Add love.'

'That's psychopathic.'

'Well, we're all psychopaths; it's only a term of endearment in common use among doctors.'

'Get on!'

'But there's the greatest motive of all – adventure. We've standardised life too much; and those of us who love life are more and more driven to seek adventure in crime.'

'Or journalism.'

'Which is only one of the meaner crimes. But you needn't talk; the practise of law is the nearest thing we have to man-hunting.'

'I suppose that's true.'

'Of course it's true. But it's a mere pheasant-shoot, with all your police for beaters. The game hasn't a chance. No. The motiveless murderer has the true spirit of sport; to kill a man is more dangerous than to follow a wounded gaur into the jungle. The anarchist goes after the biggest game of all: but he's not a sportsman; he has a genuine grievance.'

'Your essay on murder will make some very pleasant reading.'

'But doesn't it attract you too, with your passion to prove your mental superiority to others? Think of the joy of baffling the stupid police, fooling the detectives with false clues, triumphantly proving yourself innocent when you know you are guilty!'

'Are you tempting me? You always did, you know.'

'Anyhow, you always fell!'

'*Cher ami*, for that alone I could forgive you everything!'

'Sarcastic to the last!'

'You have me to thank that we usually escaped the consequences!'

'Pride, my poor friend!'

'Truth, comrade in misfortune!'

'No. Seriously. I'm crazy tonight, and I really am going to tempt you. Don't prove it's my fault, blame your own good port, and also certain qualities in your own story of the Marsden case. One or two little remarks of yours on the subject of Miss Maud Duval—'

'I knew something would come of that.'

'Yes, that's my weak point. I'm absurdly feminine in vanity and love of power over – a friend.'

'Now I'm warned; so fire ahead. What's the proposal?'

'Oh, I haven't thought of that yet!'

'You big baby!'

'Yes, it's my bedtime; I'll roll home, I think.'

'No, don't go. Let's sober up on coffee, and the '48 brandy.'

'It's a damned extraordinary thing that a little brandy makes you drunk, and a lot of it straightens you out again.'

'It's Providence!'

'Then call upon it in the time of trouble!'

Ffoulkes went in search of the apparatus. Jack rose lazily and went to the window; he threw it open, and the cold damp air came in with a rush. It was infinitely pleasurable, the touch on his heated, wine-flushed face.

He stood there for perhaps ten minutes. A voice recalled him to himself.

"*Café noir*, Gamiani!'

He started as if he had been shot. Ffoulkes, in an embroidered dressing gown of black silk, was seated on cushions on the floor, gravely pouring Turkish coffee from a shining pot of hammered brass.

At one side of him was a great silver hookah, its bowl already covered by a coal from the fire.

Jack took a second dressing-gown that had been thrown across his chair, and rapidly made himself at ease. Then he seated himself opposite to his friend; bowed deeply, with joined hands upon his forehead, and said with mock solemnity: 'Be pleased to say thy pleasure, O most puissant king!'

'Let Scheherazade recount the mirific tale of the Two Thousand and Second Night, wherein it is narrated how the wicked journalist tempted the good lawyer in the matter of murder regarded as a pastime and as a debating society!'

'Hearing and obedience! But I must have oh! such a lot of this coffee before I get wound up!'

As it happened, it was two hours before Jack deigned to speak. 'To use the phrase of Abdullah El Haji i-Shiraz,' he began, 'I remove the silken tube of the rose-perfumed *huqqa* from my mouth. When King Brahmadatta reigned in Benares, there were two brothers named Chuckerbutty Lal and Hari Ramkrishna. For short we shall call them Pork and Beans. Now Pork, who was a poet and a devil of a fine fellow, was tempted by the reprobate Beans, a lawyer, whose only quality was low cunning, to join him in a wager. And these were the terms thereof. During the season of the monsoon each was to go away from Benares to a far country, and there he was, feloniously and of his malice aforethought, to kill and murder a liege of the Sultan of that land. And when they returned, they were to compare their stories. It was agreed that such murder should be a real murder in the legal sense – an act for which they would be assuredly hanged if they were caught; and also that it would be contrary to the spirit of sport to lay false trails deliberately, and so put in peril the life of some innocent person, not being the game desired to fill the bag. But it must be an undoubted murder, with no possibility of suicide or accident. The murder, moreover, must be of a purely adventurous nature, not a crime inspired by greed or animosity. The idea was to prove that it would be perfectly safe, since there would be no motive to draw suspicion upon them. Yet if either were suspected of the mamelukes, the *sbirri*, the janissaries, or the proggins, he should take refuge with the other; but — mark this, O king! – for being so clumsy he should pay to him a camel-load of gold, which in our money is one thousand pounds. Is it a bet?'

Ffoulkes extended his hand. 'It's a bet.'

'You're really game?'

'Dying oath.'

'Dying oath. And now, O king, for I perceive that thou art weary, hie thee to thy chaste couch, and thy faithful slave shall doss it on the sofa.'

In the morning Ffoulkes said, over the breakfast-table, 'About that bet.'

'It's on?' cried Flynn in alarm.

'Oh, yes! Only – er – I suppose I need about another seven or eight years of law; I stipulate that – what is thrown away – shall be as worthless as possible.'

'Certainly,' said Flynn, 'I'm going to Ostend.'

'Good for you. Newspaper accounts shall be evidence; but send me the whole paper, and mark another passage, not the one referring to the bet.'

'O intellectual subtlety and stamina!'

'Have some more coffee?'

'Thanks.'

An hour later each, in his appointed lighthouse, was indicating the sure path of virtue and justice to the admiring English.

2

The Trinity sittings were over. Sir Richard Ffoulkes – for the King's Birthday had not left him without honour – was contemplating his wig and gown with disgust. On the table before him was a large leather book, containing many coloured flies; and he had just assured himself that his seventeen-foot split cane was in good order. In fact, he had been boyish enough to test the check on his Hardy reel by practising casts out of the window, to the alarm of the sparrows. It was the common routine for him on the brink of a holiday, but it never lost its freshness.

Then there came back to him the realisation that this was to be no ordinary holiday. He was pledged to do murder.

He went over to the mirror, and studied his face steadily. He was perfectly calm; no trace of excitement showed in his keen features. 'I have always thought,' he mused, 'that the crises of life are usually determined by accident. It is not possible to foresee events with mathematical accuracy, and in big things it is the small things that count. Hence the cleverest criminal may always make some slip, and the clumsiest escape by a piece of luck. Let me never forget the story of the officer at Gibraltar who, focusing a new field-glass, chanced to pick up a shepherd in the very act of crime. On the other hand, how many men have got clear away through stupid people disturbing or destroying the clues: from Jack the Ripper downwards! But it is the motive that counts. Where that does not exist, the strongest clues lead nowhere. For our surest faith is that men's actions are founded upon reason or upon desire. Hence the utter impossibility of guarding against lunatics or anarchists. I should hardly believe the evidence of my senses in such a case as this: Suppose the Master of the Rolls dropped in to see me, and in the course of a perfectly sound conversation, broke up my fishing-rod without explanation or apology, and, when questioned, calmly denied that he had done so. Who would believe my story? Hence I think that I could walk into the Strand, shoot a perfect stranger in the crowd, and throw away the gun, with no danger of being caught, provided only that the gun could not be traced to me. The evidence of those who saw me fire would be torn to pieces in cross-examination; they could even be made to disbelieve their own eyes.

'From this I draw these conclusions as to the proper conditions for my murder: First, there must be no conceivable reason for the act; second, there must be no way of tracing the weapon to my possession. I need not trouble to hide my traces, except in obvious matters like blood; for it is exceedingly stupid to attempt to prove a false alibi. In fact, there is no bigger booby-trap for a criminal (*pace* the indignant ghost of Mr Weller, Senior).

'My plan is therefore a simple one: I have only to get hold of a weapon without detection, and use it upon an inoffensive stranger at any time when there happens to be nobody looking – though this is not so important.'

He returned to his fishing tackle. 'It's rather a big bet, though,' he added; 'there's more than a thousand pounds to it. I think I will be pretty careful over details. Practice may not be quite so simple as theory!'

However, the first part of his programme turned out to be delightfully easy. It was his custom to train during the holiday by taking long walks, on his way to the lake or river where he fished. He detested motor-cars. As luck would have it, during the first week, as he tramped a lonely road, his eye was caught by an object lying on the ground. It was a heavy motor-spanner, evidently left behind by some chauffeur who had had a breakdown. His mind instantly grasped the situation. There was no one in sight. The spanner was already rusted, had lain there some days. Any of a hundred people might have picked it up. It could never be traced to him. He had never possessed such a tool in his life; besides, the pattern was common. He thrust it quickly into his pocket. When he got home, he packed it away carefully in his travelling cash-box, a solid steel affair of which there was but one key, which never left his chain. 'Now,' said he, 'the problem is to find the inoffensive stranger. I had better leave Scotland. Everyone in Scotland is offensive. Also, in the matter of motive, our common humanity urges us all to kill Scotchmen. So goodbye, land o' cakes!'

Further meditations were in this key following: since he was to kill with the spanner, certain precautions must be taken. It must be a very clean kill, with no outcry or struggle. At the end of his cogitations, he decided that the victim had better be asleep. His legally trained mind had snapped its last link with the idea of adventure or sport; his motto was 'safety first.' His attitude to his projected crime was simply that of preparing a brief: he wished to meet every contingency; the atrocity of his proceedings was invisible to his intellectuality. Reason is perfectly amoral.

It was on his way from Edinburgh to London that the brilliant idea occurred to him. He would kill old Miss Marsden! She was now Mrs Robinson, by the way, for she had testified to the faith that was in her by marrying her protégé directly after his acquittal. Ffoulkes knew the house well; he had stayed there several days while working up the case. It was a lonely place, and the old lady was a fresh-air fiend, and slept on the veranda, winter and summer. She was perfectly friendly, had paid most liberally for the defence. Everything was in his favour. Even if Ezra happened to see the murder committed, his tongue was tied; indeed, he stood the strongest chance of being arrested for it himself. The servants slept far away from the veranda, at the other end of the old rambling house; there were no neighbours, and no dogs. His presence in the vicinity would excite no remark, for there was good dry-fly fishing in the streams. He would rent a cottage in the district for the second half of his holiday, walk over the downs – five miles or so, nothing to him – one moonless night, do the job, and walk back. A thousand to one that no one would know that he had ever left his cottage.

On this plan he acted. The only additional precautions suggested themselves to him on the spot: he cultivated the vicar assiduously, playing chess with him every evening, and he feigned a considerable devotion to that worthy gentleman's only daughter. It will be well, he thought, to seem to have my mind well occupied with the pleasures of a simpler chase. Further, the villagers would see nothing in a lover taking long walks by nights, in case he were seen leaving the cottage or returning to it.

A last refinement shot across his mental horizon when he began to calculate the time of the new moon. She would be just a week old on the anniversary of the Marsden murder.

That would be the night for the job; the clever-clever novelist-detectives would fabricate a mystery of revenge in connection with the date. Ezra, too, would be away to meet Maud. There was, of course, a possibility that poignancy of memory would keep the old lady awake on that particular night; but he must chance that.

Things turned out for him even better than he had hoped. Three nights before the proposed crime the vicar mentioned casually that he had met young Robinson – 'the charming lad whom you defended so brilliantly' – motoring to London, called away suddenly on business. He expected to be back in a week or ten days. No, Mrs Robinson was not with him; 'she is slightly ailing, poor lady, it appears.'

When the great night came Ffoulkes made his master-stroke by proposing to the vicar's daughter. He was obviously accepted, and the young people, after dinner, went gaily arm-in-arm through the village, and received the congratulations of the few belated travellers in that early-to-bed-and-early-to-rise corner of the planet. But Ffoulkes had the spanner in his pocket, and after bestowing his fiancée at the vicarage, went, deviously at first, then swiftly and directly, over the downs. Luck followed him to the last: he found his victim fast asleep. A single blow of the spanner, which he had wrapped in a paper bag to deaden the sound, smashed in the skull; he made his way home without being seen or heard by anybody.

Two days later he wrote to Flynn, with a cutting from the local paper.

'My dear Jack, here's a terrible sequel to the Marsden murder. It is now clear that there is some family feud connected with the fatal date. Probably an affair going back a generation. Shocking, indeed, even to a hardened lawyer like myself; but you see how right I was to insist that there must have been a strong motive for Marsden's murder. Shall we ever know the truth? It sounds like an Arabian Nights' tale.'

A month later he returned to London; he had had no answer from Flynn, and supposed him to be still away on his holiday.

There were no arrests, and no clues, in the matter of Mrs Robinson. The spanner, which Ffoulkes had dropped by the veranda, served merely to suggest a tramp, who might conceivably have been a chauffeur gone to the bad. But the mystery was deepened by an amazing development: her husband had disappeared completely. There was no question of his complicity in the crime, for on the previous evening he had dined with the British Vice-Consul in Marseilles, and it was physically impossible for him to have returned in time to commit the murder.

The obvious deduction was that whoever hated the Marsdens had included him in the schedule.

'Well,' soliloquised Ffoulkes in his chamber, 'at least I shall not lose that thousand pounds. But now I've got to edge away from Miss Bread-and-Butter-and-Kisses. Ugh!'

3

When you have dined at Basso's, which is the summit of human felicity, you should avoid too sharp a declension to this vale of tears by taking a stroll along the quays to the old quarter on the west of the Bassin. There you will find streets almost worthy to rank with the Fish-market at Cairo, and decidedly superior to even the best that Hong Kong or Honolulu or New Orleans can produce. In particular, there is an archway called by initiates the Gate of Hell, for it forms an entrance to this highly fascinating and exceedingly disreputable district.

Under this archway, on the night of the exploit of Sir Richard Ffoulkes, stood a young man, quietly dressed in the English style, though with a trifling tendency to over-indulgence in jewelry.

He glanced at a watch upon his wrist; ten minutes before midnight. He then took a little bottle from his pocket, after a quick inspection of the vicinity. From the bottle he shook a few grains of powder on the back of his hand, and drew them into his nostrils. Next came a moment's indecision; then, swinging his cane, he walked briskly out of the archway, and paced up and down a strange little square of green, set there as if somehow hallowed by great memories. After a little while he returned to the archway. This time it was tenanted. A girl stood there. She was dressed in plain black with the extreme of modesty and refinement; but the piquancy and vitality of her face, and the lustre and passion of her eyes, redeemed the picture from banality.

There was a long look of recognition; the girl reached out both arms. The man took them in his own. For a minute they stood, feeding on each other, prolonging the delicious torture of restraint. Then slowly they drew together, and their mouths met in an abandoned kiss.

It would have have puzzled them to say how long the embrace lasted; but at its truce they saw that they were not alone. Close to them stood another man, tall, elegant, slim, almost feminine in figure, as he certainly was in the extremity of the fashion which tailored him. Nor was there wanting a touch of rouge and powder on his cheeks. His thin, white hand was lifted to his nostrils, and the lovers perceived that he was taking advantage of the darkness to indulge in cocaine.

The new-comer spoke in silken tones. 'Forgive me,' he said in softest French, 'but it gave me pleasure to be near you. I saw monsieur here a few moments ago, and knew that he was one of the elect. And mademoiselle, too? May I have the honour?'

The girl smiled. 'Among friends,' she murmured charmingly, and raised the back of her hand towards him. He saluted it with his lips, and then shook out a generous supply of crystal poison from a snuffbox in amber and emeralds that dated from the great days of Louis XIV.

The girl turned her eyes full upon him, almost ardently. 'I haven't touched it,' she said, 'for ever so long. By the way, excuse me, won't you, but aren't we all English?'

'I am,' said the exquisite. 'I'm an actor on a holiday. Won't you come to my rooms? It's only a garret, or little better, but I have plenty of the Snow of Heaven, and we could have a wonderful night.'

'Let's go!' said the girl, pressing her lover's arm. He hesitated a moment.

'Three's company,' urged the other, 'when they all understand.'

'It would be perfect,' chimed the girl, 'and it would suit us – in other ways,' she added, darkly.

'Yes, the scheme has points,' admitted the younger man; 'thanks very much. We'll come. What's your name? Mine's Herbert Aynes. This lady – we'll call her Mab, if you don't mind. There's an injured husband in the offing, you know; that's one reason why we have to be careful.'

'Certainly, prudence before all things; but I've no troubles; call me Francis Ridley.' They linked arms, and strolled gaily along the main street of the quarter, enchanted by the colour and the chiaroscuro, by the hoarse cries in all strange tongues that greeted them on every side, even by the weird odours – for when people are lit by love and adventure and cocaine, there is no place of this whole universe which is not sheer delight. Presently, however, they branched off, under Ridley's direction, and began to climb the steep streets on their right. A minute later they entered an ancient doorway, and after three flights of stairs found Ridley's dove-cote.

It was a charming room, furnished, as if for a woman, with all bright colours and daintiness. On one side of the room was a divan, smothered in cushions; on the other a hammock of scarlet cords hung from the rafters. Ridley went to the window and closed the shutters.

"*Madame est chez elle!*' he announced gallantly.

'What a wonderful place!' laughed the girl. 'However did you find it?'

'Oh, it used to be a house of assignation.'

'Used to be!'

And this time all three laughed in unison.

4

The reopening of the courts found Ffoulkes enormously preoccupied. For the past two years several influential newspapers had been accusing Ministers of the Crown of the grossest kind of robbery. They had bought and sold stock, it was alleged, manipulating the prices by using their positions to announce that the government had or had not decided to make contracts with the companies involved, and subsequently denying the rumours when they had taken their profits. The attack had been so persistent that the accused ministers had been forced to desperate measures. They had started a prearranged libel action against a newspaper in Paris for reprinting one of these articles; but people still asked why they did not prosecute one of the sheets that were attacking them in London. Unhappily, not one of these was to be bought; each, carefully sounded, announced its intention to fight, and redoubled its venom.

It was at last decided to attempt a criminal prosecution of the weakest of its enemies, a paper edited by a man personally unpopular, and to bring every kind of indirect pressure upon the court to secure a conviction.

Of course the law officers of the Crown were unavailable for the prosecution; and the choice of a leader had fallen – at the last moment, when their own counsel suddenly declined to go on with the case and returned the briefs – upon Ffoulkes.

He had thus only a month to assimilate what really required six; but if he won, he could be sure of office next time a Liberal Government was in power.

So he worked day and night, seeing nobody but the solicitors and witnesses employed on the case.

He had no news of Flynn but a telegram from Berlin, saying that he would be back in a month, and that there was 'nothing to report as yet.' This amused Ffoulkes hugely; it would be great if Flynn failed to bring off his murder. However, he had no time for trifles like murder these days; he had to get a conviction for criminal libel; nothing else mattered.

But when the case came actually into court he saw it to be hopeless. His opening was masterly; it occupied two days; but on the second day he sent word to his clients during the lunch hour that it was no good to go on, and that he felt forced to take the measures previously agreed upon. These were simple: near the conclusion of the speech he managed to blunder into disclosing a flaw in the procedure so obvious that the judge could not possibly overlook it.

His lordship interrupted: 'I am afraid, Sir Richard, that you have no case. If you will refer to *Jones v The Looking Glass*, you will see that it has been expressly laid down that—'

An elaborate legal argument followed, but the judge was inexorable. 'You must redraw your plea, Sir Richard. The case is dismissed.'

The docile organs of the government condoled with the great counsel for losing an 'already won case' on a technicality; but Ffoulkes was sorry he had ever touched it. He would go to the club and play a game of chess. Flynn would be there later; he had returned to London that morning, and telegraphed his friend to make it a dinner at the Empire.

In the lounge of the club was only one little old man, who was known as a mathematician of great eminence, with a touch of the crank. He had recently finished a pamphlet to prove that the ancients had some knowledge of fourth-dimensional mathematics, that their statement of such problems as the duplication of the cube implied an apprehension of some medium in which incommensurables became tractable. He was especially strong on Euclid's parallel postulate, which has not only been unproved, but proved unprovable. He was also a deep student of Freemasonry, whose arcana furnished him with further arguments on the same thesis.

This old man, whose name was Simon Iff, challenged Ffoulkes to a game of chess. To the surprise of the lawyer, who was a very strong amateur, he was beaten thrice in very short games. Iff then took off a knight, and won a fourth game as easily as before.

'It's no good, sir,' said Ffoulkes; 'I see you are in the master class.'

'Not a bit of it,' replied the old man, 'Lasker can beat me as easily as I beat you. He really knows chess; I only know you. I can gauge your intellect; it is limited in certain directions. I had a lost game against you most of the time; but you did not make the winning continuations, and I knew that you wouldn't and couldn't.

'Let me tell you something, if you'll forgive a senior for prosing. There are two ways to play chess. One is a man against a man; the other is a man against a chess-board. It's the difference between match and medal play at golf. Observe: if I know that you are going to play the Philidor defence to the King's Knight's Opening, I do not risk being forced into the Petrov, which I dislike. But in playing an unknown quantity, I must analyse every position like a problem, and guard against all possibilities. It takes a great genius and a lifetime's devotion to play the latter game. But so long as I can read your motive in a move, so long I can content myself with guarding that one line. Should you make a move whose object I cannot see, I am compelled to take a fresh view of the board, and analyse the position as if I were called upon to adjudicate an unfinished game.'

'That's exceedingly interesting. It bears rather on my game, law.'

'I was about to venture a remark upon that point. I was fortunate enough to be present at the trial of Ezra Robinson, and I cannot compliment you too highly on the excellence of your defence. But, as you will be the first to admit, his acquittal was no solution of the question, "Who killed Marsden?" Still less does it tell us who killed Mrs Robinson exactly one year later.'

'Do you know the solution?'

'No; but I can show you on what lines to attack the mystery.'

'I wish you would.'

'I may be tedious.'

'Impossible. You have beaten me so abominably at chess that I am all on fire to learn more from watching the working of your intellect.'

'Intellect is our weakest weapon. This world is run upon "inflexible intellectual guiders," as Zoroaster put it, but it was "the will of the Father," as he also explained, which laid down those laws which we call laws of nature, but, as Kant has shown, are really no more than the laws of our own minds. The universe is a phenomenon of love under will, a mystic and poetic creation, and the intellect only stands to it as mere scansion does to poetry.'

'It is at least a charming theory.'

'It works, Sir Richard. Let us apply our frail powers to this Marsden mystery. Let us take the second murder first, because it is apparently the more abstruse. We have no clues and no motives to mislead us. True, Robinson had a strong interest in his wife's death – yet not only does he prove an alibi, but he vanishes forever! If, as we might imagine, he had hired a knave to do the job, he would have kept in sight, pretended decent grief, and so on. Of course, as has been suggested, he may himself have come to some sudden end; but if that be so, it is a marvellous coincidence indeed. No! We are forced to believe him guiltless, of this second murder at least. Consequently, having eliminated the only person with a motive, we are thrown back upon the master's way of playing chess, pure analysis.

'Now then, let us look at this second murder again. What is the most striking fact about it? This, that it was committed by a person with a complete contradiction in his mind. He is so astute that he leaves no clue of any sort; there has not even been any arrest. If he did the first murder also, it shows that he is capable of turning the same trick twice. In short, we see a man of first-class mind, or rather intellect, for we must assume a lack of moral sense. A man, in fact, with a mind like your own; for since this afternoon's exploit, I imagine you will not claim to be scrupulous.'

'You saw through the trick?'

'Naturally; you knew you had no case, so you preferred to lose on a foul, and claim a moral victory.'

'Good for you!'

'Well, this same first-rate intellect is in another respect so feeble that the man takes pleasure, or finds satisfaction, in arranging his crime on a significant date. He must be the sort of man that takes precautions against witches on Walpurgis Night!'

'Jove, that's a good point. Never struck me!'

'Well, frankly, it doesn't strike me now. There are men with such blind spots, no doubt; but it is easier for me to think that the murderer, with plenty of nights to choose from, chose that one in particular with the idea of leading people astray, of playing on their sense of romance and mystery, of exploiting their love of imaginative detectives stories!'

'If so, the point is once more in favour of his intellect.'

'Exactly. But now we are going to narrow the circle. Who is there in whose mind the date of the first murder was so vivid that such a stratagem would occur to him?'

'Well, there are many. Myself, for example!'

Iff began to set up the pieces for another game.

'We must eliminate you,' he said, after a few moments of silence; 'you lawyers forget your cases as soon as they are over.'

'Besides, I had no possible motive.'

'Oh, that is nothing in the case. You are a rich man, and would never do a murder for greed; you are a cold-blooded man, and would never kill for revenge or jealousy; and these things place you apart from the common run of men. Still, I believe such as you perfectly capable of murder; there are seven deadly sins, not two; why should you not kill, for example, from some motive like pride?'

'I take pride in aiding the administration of justice. My ambition is a Parliamentary career.'

'Come,' said Iff, 'all this is a digression; we had better play chess. Let me try at Blackburne's odds!'

Iff won the game. 'You know,' he said, as Ffoulkes overturned his king in sign of surrender, 'whoever killed Mrs Robinson, if I read his type of mind aright, has left his queen *en prise*, after all. There is a very nasty gap in the defences. He killed the woman from no common motive; he has therefore always to be on his guard against equally uncommon men. Suppose Capablanca dropped into the club, and challenged me to a game; how should I feel if I had any pride in beating you? There may be someone hunting him who is as superior intellectually to him as he is to the police. And there's a worse threat: he probably took the precaution of killing the old woman in her sleep. He could have no conscience, no remorse. But he would have experience in his own person that such monsters as himself were at large; therefore, I ask you, how does he know, every night, that someone will not kill him in his sleep?'

Ffoulkes called the waiter, and asked Iff to join him in a drink.

'No, thank you,' returned the old man, 'playing chess is the only type of pleasure I dare permit myself.'

At this moment Flynn came into the club, and greeted both men warmly. Iff had written many a glowing essay for the Irishman's review. He wanted both to dine with him, but once again Iff declined, pleading another engagement. After a few moments' chat he walked off, leaving the two old friends together.

They dined at the club, and pointedly confined the conversation to the libel case, and politics in general. With their second cigars, Flynn rose. 'Come round to Mount Street,' he said. 'I've a lot to tell you.' So they strolled off in the bright autumn weather to the maisonette where Flynn lived.

5

They made themselves at ease on the big chesterfield. It was a strange room, a symphony of green. The walls were covered with panels of green silk; the floor was covered with great green carpet from Algeria; the upholstery was of green morocco; the ceiling was washed in delicate eau-de-Nil with designs by Gauguin; and the lamps were shaded by soft tissues of emerald. Even the drinks were of the same colour: Chartreuse, the original shipping, and créme de menthe and absinthe. Flynn's man brought cigarettes and cigars in a box of malachite, and set them down with the spirits. Flynn dismissed him for the night.

'Well,' said Jack, when the man had gone, 'I see you got away with it all right.'

'I had a scare this afternoon. Old Iff made rings round me at chess, and then proceeded to develop a theory of the – exploit – that was so near the truth that I thought for half a moment that he had guessed something. Luckily, he's just an old crank in everybody's eyes; but, by Jove, he can play chess!'

'Iff's one of the biggest minds in England; but the second-raters always win in London.'

'Well, what about your end of the bet?'

'Oh, there's no news yet. But they'll find the bodies next week when my tenancy of the place expires.'

'Bodies!'

'Two. You see, I went after your friend Ezra Robinson and the fair Duval. I knew from you of the appointment on the anniversary of the murder, but not the place; so I had him shadowed from the day of the bet. I took a room in the old quarter of Marseilles, when I found that he had stopped there. I got myself up as Francis Ridley, whom you may remember in certain amateur theatricals.

'I got them along to make a night of it, and filled them up with cocaine, while I took – mostly borax. Then when we got to the stage of exhaustion and collapse, I unslung a convenient hammock that hung in the room and told them what I meant to do. And then I hanged them by the neck until they were dead, and may the Lord have mercy on their souls! Next day I crossed to Algiers, went down to El Kantara and shot moufflon – I'm having a fine head mounted especially for you – then I came back through Italy and Germany. That's all!'

'I say,' cried Ffoulkes, shocked, 'that's hardly in the spirit of the bet, old man. I don't see any moral turpitude involved!'

'You wretched hypocrite,' retorted Flynn, 'it was deliberate murder by both French and English law. I don't see what you can want more than that. You ought to be ashamed of yourself, with your legal mind!'

But the lawyer was not satisfied. He began to argue, and ultimately turned the discussion into what was as near a quarrel as such old friends could ever contemplate. In fact, Ffoulkes saw the danger, and went home at an unusually early hour.

Flynn dismissed the matter from his mind, and passed the night in composing sonnets, in French, to the honour of the green goddess – absinthe.

6

A month later. Flynn had been unusually busy, and saw little of his friends. Twice he dined with Ffoulkes, but the latter was more moody and irritable than ever. He had lost three important cases, and seemed altogether out of luck. His looks reflected his worry as much as his manners. Flynn asked him to come to Paris for a week's rest; he refused; Flynn went alone.

Returning to London, he called at the chambers in Lincoln's Inn. They were shut up. He went on to the club, hoping for news.

Almost the first man he saw was an old college friend, a judge, the very man to have the latest tidings. Probably Ffoulkes had been in court that day.

'Hush! It's terrible,' said the judge, and drew Flynn into a corner of the lounge. 'They had to take him away yesterday. He had persecution mania, a hopeless form, I'm afraid. Hadn't slept for a month. Said he was afraid of being murdered in his sleep! These things are too bad to talk about; I'm going home. Brace up!'

The judge rose and went; but when Flynn came out of the stupour into which the intelligence had thrown him, he found Iff seated at his side.

'You've heard? Isn't it awful?'

'No,' replied Iff, 'not more so than the fact that two and two make four. Which in a sense is awful indeed, and according as you are for or against the tendency of the universe, is encouraging or terrifying. But it is fatal and inexorable. Perhaps to say that is to say enough!'

'Explain what you mean.'

'A little while ago,' replied the old mystic, 'he came here to play chess with me – you remember; you were there, the day of your return. Well, I mastered his mind; I saw its limitations; I mapped its roads; I measured its heights and depths; I calculated its reactions. I beat him easily, at odds. We then began to talk of the Marsden mystery, and I analysed the mind of the man who killed Mrs Robinson – a mind like his own. I showed that the coincidence of dates was probably a deliberate false trail. I then asked who would be likely to think of such a point, who would have vivid reason to think of that date. I was speaking in perfectly general terms; no suspicion of him had crossed my mind. He instantly suggested himself. I knew how he played chess, so I knew that he must have had himself in view subconsciously, that he must be trying to put me off the scent by boldness. It was just the same type of tactics as choosing the anniversary of the first murder. From that instant I knew that he was guilty.

'A moment later he confirmed me. I suggested that a man like himself might kill for such a motive as pride; and he replied that he took pride in the administration of justice. Now after that libel action, and coming from such a man, the English hypocrisy, which might have been natural in a lesser man, was a complete confession. Therefore I determined to punish him. I knew there was only one way: to work upon his mind along its own lines. So I said to him: "Suppose the murderer realises that there are intellects superior to his own? And – how will he sleep, knowing that there are people who will murder others in their sleep without reasonable cause?" You know the answer. I suppose that I am in a sense the murderer of his reason.'

Flynn said nothing, but his eyes were streaming; he had loved Dick Ffoulkes dearly, and a thousand memories were urgent in his heart and mind. Iff seemed not to notice it.

'But the murder of Marsden is still a mystery. Ffoulkes can hardly have done that.'

Flynn sat up and laughed wildly. 'I'll tell you all about that,' he cried. 'Ezra Robinson did it, with the help of the floor-clerk. They were to meet on the anniversary of the murder. I tracked them down, and I hanged them with these hands.' He stretched them out in a gesture of agony. The old man took them in his.

'Boy!' he said, '– for you will never grow up – you have perhaps erred in some ways – ways which I find excusable – but you need never lose a night's sleep over this business.'

'Ah!' cried Jack, 'but it was I who tempted my friend – it was a moment of absolute madness, and now I have lost him!'

'We are all punished,' said the old man solemnly, 'exactly where we have offended, and in the measure thereof.'

THE ARTISTIC TEMPERAMENT

1

Jack Flynn was the centre of a happy group of artists. They were seated upon the terrace of the Café d'Alençon to drink the apéritif; for although November was upon Paris, the Sun still remembered his beloved city, and fed it with light and warmth.

Flynn had come over from London for a week to see the Autumn Salon, and to gossip with his old friends. The conversation was naturally of Art, and, like the universe itself, had neither beginning nor end, being self-created by its own energy, so rolled easily through the aeons in every combination of beauty.

But half of beauty is melancholy, a subtle sub-current of sadness; and on this particular occasion it was visible, giving a grey tone to the most buoyant rhapsodies. The talkers were in fact subdued and restrained; each spoke gaily, yet stood upon his guard, as if there were some subject near his consciousness which he must be careful not to broach.

It was a curiously distinguished group. Two of the men wore the Légion d'Honneur; the elder of the two, who looked more like a soldier or a diplomat than a painter, seemed to be the object of constant solicitude on the part of the younger, whose ruddy, cheerful ironic face was like a picture by Franz Hals – but a Franz Hals in the mood of Rabelais. He seemed particularly anxious lest the other should say something unfortunate, but he should really have been looking round the corner, for there was where the danger lay.

Round that corner, all arms and legs, came swinging the agile body of no less a person than the mystic, Simon Iff.

His first greeting was the bombshell! 'Ah ha!' he cried, grasping the hand of the elder of the two décorés, 'and how's the dear old sea?' For the person addressed happened to be famous all over the world as a marine painter.

The younger man sprang to his feet. 'Just don't mention the sea, please, for a few months!' he said in Simon's ear.

It was unnecessary. Even in the general joy at the return of an old friend, Iff's quick apprehension could not fail to detect a suppressed spasm of pain on every face.

The mystic turned and greeted the man who had interrupted him with honest gladness; then his other hand shot out to Flynn.

'I've been out of the world all summer,' he cried, shaking hands all round, 'in a hermitage after my own heart. Fancy a castle dating from the crusades, on the very edge of a glacier, and every practicable route barred against the world, the flesh and the devil, in the shape of tourists, *tables d'hôte* and newspapers!'

'You look thirty!' declared one of the men.

'And I feel twenty,' laughed the magician; 'what do you say to a little dinner at Laperouse? I want to walk across the Luxembourg to a feast, as I've done anytime these fifty years!'

As it happened, only two of the party were free: Major, the young man with the button, and Jack Flynn.

After some quiet chat the three strolled off together, arm in arm, down the Boulevard Montparnasse.

When they reached the Avenue de l'Observatoire, they turned down that noble grove. Here, at all hours of day and night, is a stately solitude. Intended for gaiety, devised as a symbol of gaiety by the most frivolous age of all time, it has become by virtue of age the very incarnation of melancholy grandeur. It seems almost to lament that eighteenth century which fathered it.

Before they had passed into this majesty more than a hundred yards, the mystic said abruptly: 'What's the trouble?'

'Haven't you really seen a paper for six months?' countered Flynn.

'Of course I haven't. You know my life; you know that I retire, whenever I am able, from this nightmare illusion of matter to a world of reality. So tell me your latest evil dream!'

'Evil enough!' said Major, 'it doesn't actually touch us, but it's a narrow escape. We only heard the climax three days ago; so it's a green wound, you see.'

'Yet it doesn't touch you.'

'No; but it touches Art, and that's me, all right!'

'Will you tell me the story?'

'I'll leave that to Flynn. He's been on the trail all the time.'

'I was even at the trial,' said Flynn.

'Come, come,' laughed Iff, 'all these be riddles.'

'I'll make them clear enough – all but the one. Now, no interruptions! I have the thing orderly in my mind.'

'Five, four, three, two, one: gun!'

'The place is a small rocky islet off the west coast of Scotland, by name Dubhbheagg. A few fisher-folk live there; nobody else. There is one landing-place, and one only, even in calm weather; in a storm it is inaccessible altogether. Overlooking this quay is a house perched on the cliff; an old stone mansion. The proprietor is one of our sacred guild, and spends most of his time in Central Asia or Central Africa or Central America or Central Australia – anything to be central! – and he lets the house to anyone who is fool enough to pay the price.

'This summer it was rented by the president of the Royal Academy.'

'What's that?' said Iff, sharply.

'The Royal Academy,' explained Flynn, 'is an institution devised by divine Providence for the detection of British Artists. It brings them into notice by ostentatiously rejecting their works. The president is Lord Cudlipp.'

'Wasn't he a Joseph Thorne, or some such name?' asked Simon Iff.

'Thornton, I think. Ennobled thirteen years ago,' corrected Flynn.

'It was Thornley,' insisted the sculptor, Major.

'Yes, Thornley; I remember now. I know him slightly; and I knew his father before him; an M.P. and a biscuit manufacturer,' exclaimed the mystic.

'A pity the son didn't follow the father,' murmured Major. 'I feel sure that his biscuits would have been delightful!'

'You're interrupting the court,' protested the editor. 'To proceed. Here we have Cudlipp in the Big House of Dubhbheagg, with a man and wife to cook for him, both old servants, with him thirty years. There are also his son Harry, his daughter Eleanor, her companion-maid, and – a man from the Quarter!'

'This Quarter?'

'Up in Montrouge his studio is, I think, one of those lost cottages with a garden in the middle of a block of houses. Well, this man, or rather boy, he's not twenty yet, is, or wants to be, a marine painter like Cudlipp—'

'God forbid!' groaned Major.

'Shut up! The boy's name is Andre dé Bry; he's half French, half English, I believe, a pretty hot combination.'

'So I've noticed,' remarked Iff, as they turned into Lapérouse, crept up the narrow stair, and found a table by the window in the Salle des Miroirs.

'Harry and Eleanor were born seventeen years ago, twins—'

'Which is dead?' interrupted Iff. The others stared.

'Excuse an old man's vanity!' laughed the mystic. 'I really have to show off sometimes! You see, I know Jack's passion for precision of language. He wouldn't say the simple thing, "They are twins," or "They are seventeen years old," and he wouldn't say "They were twins," or "were seventeen years old," so I knew that one, and one only, was dead.'

'I hope your acuteness will continue through dinner,' laughed the editor. 'We need it. Now, then, to business. Cudlipp had sort of adopted André de Bry, used him to prepare his bigger canvasses, and so on. De Bry had fallen in love with Eleanor. She returned his passion. De Bry was hopelessly poor – no, not hopelessly, for he had a rich uncle, who had a fad of independence. He wouldn't give André a farthing; but if the boy succeeded in making himself a career, he promised to leave him every penny he had. The family is noble, much better than Cudlipp's; so the boy was not a bad match for Eleanor, and, contingently, a very good one. He and Harry were perfectly good friends. There was, in short, no element of disagreement worth notice. The days passed pleasantly, either in painting or fishing, and the evenings in games. One can hardly imagine a more harmonious group.

'On the 18th of August the yacht, which supplied the island with stores from the mainland, called and left provisions for the party. To avert false conjecture from the start, I may say that it is absolutely impossible that some mysterious stowaway could have landed from the yacht and hidden somewhere on the island. The police subsequently went through the place with a fine-tooth comb. It is thirty miles from the nearest land, is barely a quarter of a mile in its greatest length, has neither a cave nor a tree on it. So don't talk about that! Well, the yacht weighed anchor on the afternoon of the 18th; that night a storm came up from the Atlantic, and raged for a whole week. It is physically impossible that anyone should have landed on the rock during that period. Furthermore, the Big House stands on a quite unclimbable pinnacle – I'm a rock climber, as you know, and I went to see it, and there's not a crack anywhere. It was only connected with the rest of the island by a wooden bridge of the cantilever type; and the violence of the wind was such that on the second night of the storm it carried it away. This was inconvenient for them, as will be seen; but it simplifies the matter a good deal for us. Well, on the 25th the storm abated, and the fishermen were about to put to sea when they observed Lord Cudlipp on the edge of the cliff, firing his shotgun. Seeing he was noticed, he signalled and shouted to them to come up. He met them, so far as he could, at the chasm where the bridge had been. 'There has been murder done here,' he said shortly, 'take this message and telegraph it at once.' He flung a stone to them, with a paper wrapped about it. The telegram asked for the police; also for a gang of men with materials to build up the bridge. The following noon relief arrived.

'The rest of the story needs little detail. It is as astonishingly simple as it is perplexing. The naked body of the boy Harry was found on the morning of the 23rd in the big room used by the other men as a studio – Harry and Eleanor took not the slightest interest in art. Death had been caused by a small deep wound in the femoral artery; a pen-knife might have made it. But there was no blood; and at the postmortem was revealed the utterly astonishing fact that there was no blood in the whole body – when I say no blood, I mean, not enough for a rabbit! It had been systematically drained. I need hardly tell you that the whole island went wild with stories of vampires and witches; I won't bother you with that sort of rubbish.

'But the horror of the circumstances cannot be easily matched. Imagine to yourselves that lonely crag, itself a monument of desolation, towering from sea to sky, bleak, bare, barren and heartless as sea and sky themselves. Such a place has always bred strange stories – and strange crimes.

'But think of the feelings of the people in the house, one of them certainly a murderer!

'However, the police were easily able to narrow down the possibilities. The boy had been chloroformed or otherwise rendered unconscious, without doubt, for there could have been no struggle. The wound was clean, and obviously inflicted by someone with first-rate anatomical knowledge. It was, too, a highly civilised crime, so to speak.

'This really restricted the field of enquiry to the two painters. Common sense excluded the father, whose main hope of an illustrious line was thus cut off. On the other hand, de Bry was a doubtful character. In Paris he had been accustomed to frequent the lowest haunts – the sort of place one finds in these little streets about here – and as a matter of fact, he was usually called the "Apache" as a sort of nickname. But no one had ever heard of anything very definite, except an alleged duel with knives in a shop off the Boulevard St. Germain called Tout à la Joie, a low drinking cellar. This came out in court later, and sounded nasty, though it was proven that he had been attacked without provocation, and the police had not even arrested him. Still, a man so ready with a knife – it impressed the jury badly, I could see that.

'To cut a long story short, they arrested André. He refused to enter the witness-box; he had no story to tell; nor, indeed, had any of the others. Harry had gone to bed alive; he was found dead in the morning. No quarrel anywhere. No motive for anybody.

'The jury was out for twenty-four hours; they came back with that joy which only Scotland offers to its jurymen – the Verdict of the Sitter on the Fence: "Not proven." They all thought he did it, but they couldn't make up their minds to hang him; so there was the way out. Therefore, André de Bry is at large again; and, by the same token, I came over on the boat with him.

He was muffled to the eyes, but I knew him. So he's probably within a mile of us at this minute.'

'What do you think of the story?' asked Major, a little anxiously.

'Oh, I agree with the natives,' replied the mystic, laughingly, to the astonishment of his hearers. 'Excuse my referring to the fact that I'm a professional Magus – still, you should not be surprised if I tell you that I hold to the theory of vampires and wehr-wolves and sirens and the rest of the dear creatures!'

'Be serious, master!' urged Flynn, using a title which he knew would put the mystic on his honour.

'My dear lad, I believe this murder was done by someone whom none of them knew to have been there.'

'But how could he have got away?'

'Vanished whence he came.'

'A haunted house? Damn it, something in your tone makes my blood run cold.'

'Well,' slowly answered the mystic, 'possibly, in a sense, a haunted house.'

Major called the waiter to bring another bottle of Burgundy.

'Have you really formed a theory about the case?' asked Flynn. 'To me it's absolutely beyond reason.'

'Beneath it, beneath it! Ah well, no matter! As a fact, I have not made up my mind. How can I, till I've seen this chap's pictures?'

'You think there was some motive of jealousy?' snapped out Major.

'I don't think at all till I've seen them. Look here! Do you know his work?'

'No; he hasn't shown anything. He's an absolute kid, you know. But Tite saw a thing of his in some studio or other, and Tite said it was damned bad. So I dare say it's pretty decent stuff.'

'Where's his studio?'

'Don't know,' answered the sculptor. 'I'll find out tonight, if you're really set on this. May I call for you in the morning? We'll go up together; perhaps you'll let me make it *déjeuner* – you'll come, of course, Jack – as I've been shouting for Burgundy at your dinner, you shall shout for Claret at my lunch!'

'I'm at Bourcier's, 50 rue Vavin, as always,' said Simon Iff. 'The best house, and the best people, in all Paris. Come round at nine.'

'Right. Meet me there, Flynn. It's a great hunt, the truth!'

'With a hunter like Simple Simon, you'll find it so,' said Flynn, enthusiastically.

2

The next morning saw the three friends tramping it up the Boulevard Raspail, past the great calm glory of the unconquered Lion de Belfort, along the busy Boulevard de Montrouge, and so to the very hem of Paris, the *fortifs* dear to the Apache. Here they turned west, and came presently to an old wine-shop, through which lay the entrance to the studio of de Bry.

He was already at work in his little garden; an old man, leaning on a spade, was posing for him.

Major advanced and offered his card. 'Monsieur de Bry! I feel sure you will pardon me. I am a Sociétaire of the Beaux Arts; I have heard that your work is excellent, and I am here with two friends of the most distinguished reputation to ask the honour of looking at it.'

'Mr Major!' cried the boy, as he put his brushes down in his eagerness – at first he had not recognised the great man – 'indeed, the honour is altogether mine. But I've nothing worth seeing, I assure you.'

Major introduced his friends. De Bry, telling the model to rest, led the party into the studio. With infinite diffidence the boy began to show his work.

In a few minutes Major, with his hands thrust deep into his trousers' pockets, and his head thrown back, was reduced to utter silence. Simon Iff, who was watching him as well as the pictures, smiled his grimmest smile. The editor, inured to small talk by his profession, made the conversation.

'It's all beginnings,' said the boy, 'but this is more what I've tried for. I did it in the summer.' The mystic noticed with a darkening face that he seemed to speak of that summer as if it had held nothing but a holiday.

The canvas showed the rock of Dubhbheagg amidst the breakers. It had been painted from a boat on a clear day. The sky was blue; a flight of wildfowl gave life to the picture. But the rock itself was more vital than the birds. It seemed the image of some great lost God of solitude, eternally contemplative, eternally alone. It was more melancholy than Dürer's masterwork, or Thomson's interpretation of it. And de Bry had not used the materials of melancholy, or images of death; he had merely painted a rock just as it was when he saw it. Yet he had made it a creature of cosmic life, as significant and vital as the universe itself – and as lonely and inexorable.

Simon Iff spoke for the first time. 'Is that picture for sale?' he asked.

'Yes,' said the painter, rather eagerly. They noticed that he looked ill.

'Probably hasn't had a meal since that damned affair,' thought Major.

'How much?' very stiffly from Simple Simon.

The painter hesitated. 'Would you give me fifty francs for it?' he asked timidly.

The mystic rose to his feet, and shook his stick in the boy's face. 'No, you damned young scoundrel. I will not!' he roared. 'How dare you ask such a price?'

The boy shrank back; he expected that the old man would strike him.

'Do you know who I am?' thundered Simon. 'I'm the chairman of the Art Committee of the Hemlock Club! That's the trouble with you artists; you're blacklegs, every one of you. Offering a thing like that for fifty francs and pulling down the price of everything but the old Masters! Answer me straight now: how much is it worth?'

The boy was too taken aback to reply.

'Have you ever seen a worse thing offered for ten thousand francs?' asked Simon, cynically.

'Oh yes!' he stammered at last.

'I'll give you fifteen thousand. Here's a thousand on account; I'll send a cheque for the balance this afternoon. Send the picture to Simon Iff, 50 rue Vavin. And, if you've nothing to do, come and see me as soon as the light fails this afternoon. Yes, bring the picture around in a fiacre. About 5, then!'

He thrust a big thousand franc note in the boy's hand, and withdrew stormily from the studio.

The others followed him; but Major stopped a moment. 'Did you like my bust of Rodin?' asked the sculptor. The boy was still too bewildered to do more than nod. 'I'll send you a bronze, if you'd care to have it. And come and see me, any time you care to, and particularly any time you need a friend.' De Bry grasped the offered hand in silence.

The others had reached the street when Major caught them. 'I hope you don't mean mischief by that boy,' he said to Iff. 'I seem to smell a trap. For heaven's sake leave him alone! He's the biggest thing since Turner; if he keeps on growing, the planet won't hold him.'

'My mind is quite made up,' returned Simon Iff, coldly. 'If the lunch is still on, suppose we take a taxi. If you don't mind, we'll have a private room at the Café de la Paix. We shall need to go rather deeply into this matter.'

3

Simon Iff would not talk at all of anything but old times in Paris until after lunch, when the decks were cleared of all but the three Cs – coffee, cigars and cognac. Then he cleared his throat.

'As you have heard me say about a million times, Jack, "Do what thou wilt shall be the whole of the Law." Failure to observe this precept is the root of all human error. It is our right and duty – the two are one, as Éliphas Lévi very nearly saw – to expand upon our own true centre, to pursue the exact orbit of our destiny. To quit that orbit is to invite collisions. Suppose it to be my illusion to think it my will to pass through that closed window. I bump my head; I cut my face; I finally make a mess on the boulevard. Or I think it my will to steal my neighbour's watch. I am caught; police-court, prison and general disaster. Merely the result of my ignorance in regard to my true destiny. Failure in life and especially criminal failure: collision. Then where is the original collision? In myself. There is a conflict between my conscious will and my unconscious will, between the sophisticated babble of reason and the still small voice of the soul. Poe had quite an idea of this, with his "Imp of the Perverse"; Ibsen, the greatest of all realists, a more detailed conception, with his "troll"; but both imagined that consciousness was right and the Inner Light wrong. Now that is a mere assumption, and we mystics, who know that Light, know better. It is the first task of every man who would not only be himself, but understand himself, to make the union or harmony between these two perfect. Now of course most men, so far as the main path of their lives is concerned, never find these two forces in conflict, never become aware of them at all. The troubles of genius are principally due to a recognition of this truer Light, and of its apparent incompatibility with the conscious will, or perhaps of a realisation that they cannot execute their will, because of the pressure of circumstance upon them. Hence the well earned celebrity of the Artistic Temperament. Frequently we observe that the artist, unable to fulfil himself in his art, turns to vice of one kind or another. It is as if a sculptor, in a gesture of impatience with his Venus, dabbed a handful of clay on her nose, and made her look like an elephant!'

'If you knew how often I've done just that thing!' laughed Major.

'Well,' continued the mystic, 'to come to the murder of this boy Harry—'

'I see where you're driving,' broke in Jack Flynn. 'And as I'm sure you noticed the perfect nonchalance of de Bry when he showed us that picture, you are going to prove that he did it unconsciously, or at least that it's all so natural to him that he has no sense of it.'

'You would find out what I am going to prove if you would let me do it,' said Simon, in some ill-humour. Major had felt ashamed of himself for smiling; he was genuinely concerned about his great new artist.

'To come to the murder of this boy Harry,' repeated the magician, 'we notice two things. First, the general surroundings. Storm, isolation, the wild weird atmosphere of the Scottish Highlands – enough to send any man, with an original touch of madness, over the line. Second, the nature of the murder itself; it is in perfect keeping with the setting. Its details are elaborate. It is not an ordinary murder, but the murder of – a – I can't find the right word.'

Major broke in grimly: 'The murder of a great mind gone wrong? Of such a mind as conceived, and such a hand as executed, those masterpieces? Oh my God!'

'Your interruptions will not alter the facts of the case, or my deductions; pray let me proceed! Besides, there is still one step to take before we arrive at any such conclusion. I want you to remember a peculiar fact about the French Revolution. Here we find a whole set of people, educated, intelligent, complex, and above all humanitarian, who suddenly indulge in wholesale massacre. This, like the crime we are discussing, was a perverse crime. It was not at all in accordance with the general will of the Revolutionists, which was simply Social Justice.

'But they had been thwarted for generations; thwarting was in their blood, as it were; and when they came to action, they became perverse. Thus – I beg you to believe – it is not merely the artistic temperament which produces these horrible crimes; it is simply any temperament which is suppressed long enough. It is more usual to find this manifested in artists, because they are advanced people who understand pretty well what their will is, who suffer more keenly, in consequence, from the thwarting of that will, especially as they usually perceive only too keenly the fact that it is the errors and stupidities of other people, people who have strayed far from their own orbits, that cause the thwarting in question. I will ask you to consider the case of a man who makes friends of spiders. Oh, you say, that is after he has been in the Bastille for twenty years. Precisely. He may have been a very bad man; he may himself have thwarted his own fundamental impulses of love; but the complete suppression of that instinct for so many years results in its peeping out at last, and taking an unnatural form. There are plenty of similar instances which will occur to you. In the case of the French Revolution, we must also consider the question of atavism. Humanitarian as the leaders were, their forefathers had been inured to fire and sword since the dawn of the race. It was the primitive tribal passion that broke out in them, after centuries of suppression. So you get the same phenomenon in both the man and the race.' Simon paused.

'That boy,' said Major, 'has one of the greatest souls ever incarnated on this planet, and I won't believe he did it.'

'Your courage is splendid,' replied Simple Simon, 'but your beliefs do not invalidate the conclusions of science. *E pur si muove.*'

'Is that all?' asked Flynn.

'For shame, Jack,' cried the mystic; 'I have hardly begun. But I perceive that the light is failing; we had better end this conversation in the presence of André de Bry.' Major paid the bill; and they went across Paris to the old magician's little studio in the rue Vavin.

It was a small room, and very simply furnished; but the paintings and sculptures would have made the fame of any museum. Each was the gift of a master to Simon Iff.

'We shall wait for the young man,' said the mystic, as they seated themselves. 'You will see that I have no difficulty in forcing him to confess.'

'I'll never believe it,' insisted Major.

'Don't believe it till you hear it!' was the abrupt retort.

4

A quarter of an hour elapsed; then the slim figure of the boy appeared. In his arms was the picture.

Simon took it and placed it upon the mantel. Major was right; there was nothing in the room to equal it. The magician went to his desk, and wrote out a cheque for fourteen thousand francs, which he handed to the young painter.

'If you would sign this receipt?'

De Bry complied.

'Do not go!' said Simon. 'I have much to say to you. You really like the picture? You think it worthy of you?'

'I wouldn't have sold it if I didn't.'

'Yet you were in sore straits? You were denying yourself food to pay your model?'

'I shouldn't have sold it to you if I didn't think it mine.'

'That too is worthy. But now, sit down. There are others to consider in this matter. I am going to ask my friends to remain absolutely silent while we talk.'

'I know what you are going to say,' said the boy. 'I think it unnecessary and cruel.'

'Wait till I have done. It is not only necessary and kind, but it is very urgent.'

'I can't refuse the first man who has appreciated my work.'

'Listen while I tell you a story. Many years ago I knew a man named Thornley, a wealthy manufacturer of biscuits. He had one son, Joseph. He asked me one day to recommend a tutor for the lad. I told him of a clergyman named Drew, a man of deep scholarship, great culture and intense love of art. He worked on the ambition of Joseph Thornley, and the boy, after a year's tuition from Drew, decided to be a painter. The tutor died suddenly; but the boy's ambition remained. He persuaded his father to let him go to various art schools, where he studied incessantly with the most praiseworthy diligence.'

'Damn it!' roared Major, 'he had no more capacity for art than this chair I am sitting on!'

'I asked you not to interrupt,' returned Simon mildly. 'I never said he had! To continue. Backed with ample wealth and influence, and fortified with determination to succeed, Thornley's career was one long series of triumphs. Although primarily a marine painter, he also did other work, notably portraits. His picture of the King in the uniform of a British Admiral caught the public taste more than any other of his efforts. It was in that year that he was not only elected to the presidency of the Royal Academy of Arts, but raised to the peerage with the title of Baron Cudlipp. His only sorrow was the death of his wife two years after the birth of his children.'

The magician turned to André.

'Good! Now – how did you spend the week of the great storm?'

'Billiards, mostly,' stammered André, taken by surprise. 'Chess, too, and some card games. I sketched of course, nearly all day. Eleanor had some needlework. Poor Harry was very bored; he did nothing much.'

'And Cudlipp buried himself a good deal in anthropology?'

'Yes; he had Frazer's *Golden Bough* all the time—' The boy broke off, and stared. 'How did you know that?' he said, aghast.

'A little bird told me,' said Simon lightly.

All of a sudden Major sprang to his feet. 'Then Cudlipp killed his son,' he shouted. 'Oh! Simple Simon, what a fool I've been!' And he suddenly broke down in spasm on spasm of sobs.

'I promised these gentlemen,' said Simon, taking no notice of the outburst, 'that I would force a confession from you this afternoon. I think this is the moment. Come, we are all attention.'

'I certainly cannot hear this senseless slander against my protector without—'

'Hush!' said Simon. 'I told you this matter was urgent. I meant what I said. You must catch the nine o'clock train for London.'

'Why?' said the boy, defiantly; 'who are you to say this?'

'I am a person who is going to put a letter in the post in an hour's time; and you had better arrive before the letter.'

'I don't understand.'

'I was explaining to these gentlemen at lunch that all crime was the result of conflict; that perverse crime, in particular, was caused by conflict of the conscious and unconscious wills.'

'Don't you see?' said Major, mastering himself, 'it couldn't be you. You were supremely happy: you had the girl you loved; you had found yourself as an artist. But Cudlipp had thwarted his own inner will all his life; he was meant to bake biscuits; and he had forced himself to do those eye-destroying horrors. But – go on, master! – I still don't see the whole story.'

'I haven't told you all the facts yet. Cudlipp's family was originally Armenian, for one thing, the offshoot of some old Babylonian tribe. Then there was *The Golden Bough* with its detailed description of various savage rites, especially the sacrifice of the first-born, an idea, by the way, which the Jews only adopted at third or fourth hand from older and autochthonous races. Then the newspapers were filled with long arguments about the Hasidim and ritual murder, the trial of that man somewhere in Russia – can't think of his name, begins with a B – was on at this time. Well, when the suppressed genius of the man for baking biscuits – which may be a passion like another – when that broke out, probably under the strain of the long storm, and the wildness of the whole scene, and possibly some sudden realisation that this boy here could paint, and he himself never could, why, then his brain snapped. The recent impressions combined with some far strain of atavism, and he resolved upon the murder.'

'I still can't see why murder,' said Flynn. 'Why should not this biscuit-baking genius go into the kitchen and bake biscuits?'

'I want you to recognise the fact, you dear good simple soul, that madmen are a thousand times more logical than the sane. The conclusions of normal men are always balanced by other considerations; we criticise our ideas of proper tailoring, for example, in the spotlight of our cheque-books. The madman doesn't. He wants clothes; he thinks of nothing else; so he goes down to Savile Row and orders a dozen sable overcoats and thirty dress suits. It's much more logical, if logic were all!

'So Cudlipp reasoned something like this, as I imagine: "I've wasted forty years trying to paint when I ought to have been baking biscuits; now I must make up for lost time." How to do that? The madman's reason finds it easy. The connection between gold and copper coins is an arbitrary one, isn't it? Yes. Well, if I haven't got a barrow-load of coppers, I can give you a fistful of sovereigns, and it's just as good. The whole idea of primitive magic (which he had been reading, remember!) rests on arbitrary substitution. The king must die every year, or the sun won't come back – there's an arbitrary connection, to begin with, though it's based on false reasoning, or rather on correct reasoning from false observation. Now the king doesn't want to die; so he takes a criminal, labels him king, and kills him. Everyone is happy. So this man seeks to satisfy his genius, suppressed for forty years, in a night. Surely it must be through some monstrous act of violence and horror! That is madman's logic. Then, as I said before, some ancestral memory in the subconscious self influenced his recent impression, and that gave the form to the idea. It is also conceivable that he had a real purpose, thought that the sacrifice of the first-born might enable him to become a painter. Gilles de Retz murdered over eight hundred children in his endeavour to make gold. But of this theory I have no evidence. However, the rest stands.'

André de Bry listened with white lips to this speech.

'Now will you confess?' asked the magician, with mild persistence.

'I don't see why I should.'

'Because you are still looking at the past. Can't you foresee the future?'

'Ought I to kill myself?'

'Be serious, sir!' reprimanded Simon. 'I see that I must tell you more. So far, I have told you how I know that Cudlipp killed his son, and how he came to do it. You may or may not know why he did it, but you must know that he did it, if only by a process of exclusion. Then – what will he do next?'

The boy began to smile. 'Oh, Eleanor is with an aunt,' he said; 'she's safe enough.'

'Now we begin to confess, indirectly,' continued Simon. 'But what will he do? Is he conscious of his act? You see, I must know all. I was already sure that you would never have left Eleanor in danger. But there are other problems.'

'I'm beaten,' said André. 'I'll tell you all I know.'

'Good.'

5

'It was I who discovered the body of poor Harry; for I had risen with the first light, intending to paint. I needn't go into the events of that day, much; it was all suspicion, perfectly hellish. I haven't your reasoning powers, Mr Iff, and I didn't think he had done it, particularly. He pretended to suspect me, of course. We can see now, thanks to you, that his whole life has been one long hypocrisy, that he has been pretending to be an artist, just like any other fraud. His deadly earnestness about it only made it worse; I see that now. But I didn't see it then; to me he was just a bad painter, and I looked no deeper. Well, by dinner-time our nerves were all on edge; Eleanor's, naturally, more than any. After dinner I said I would go to bed, meaning to snatch an hour's sleep, and then to watch Eleanor's door all night. I had told her to have her companion in her room – the poor old lady was glad enough to have company, you can imagine.

'Eleanor's manner to me had been strange beyond words; but I only thought that it meant that she suspected me. However, when I said I was going to bed, she jumped up: "Do play me a hundred up first!" she cried; "I'll go mad if you don't." We went into the billiard-room together. She closed the door, and put her back to it. "Andre," she cried, "I've been insane about this all day, but I'm in a fearful position. Only – I can't let you go to bed. I must tell you. Papa did it." I caught her in my arms, for she was falling. In a moment she recovered. "Last night," she went on, "I woke with frightful dreams – and I found my nose was bleeding. I lit my candle, and got up to get water. Then I knew suddenly that something was wrong with Harry. I always have known; it's the twin sympathy."'

'Damnation!' interrupted Simple Simon in a fury, 'I'm getting old. I ought to have known that she knew.'

'You've done well enough, sir,' said André; 'it's been like a miracle to me to hear you. Eleanor went on: "The moment my nose stopped bleeding I took my black kimono, and went down to Harry's room. The door was open. I slipped in. It was dark. At that instant I saw the studio door open." (They were right opposite, Mr Iff.) "I knew there would be all kinds of trouble if I were caught wandering about the house at that time of night. I kept still. I could see through the crack of the door. Papa was silhouetted against the light in the studio. He had a wash handbasin, carrying it carefully. I heard him give a short harsh laugh, and say aloud: 'Now I begin to live.' He went down the little corridor by Harry's room." (It leads to a pepper-box turret. Harry's room has a window on to that corridor.) "I went to the side window. I saw papa throw the basin over the cliff. Then he went back, and down the main corridor to his room. I felt for Harry in his bed. He wasn't there. I found matches. The room was empty. I went into the lighted studio. I saw Harry at once, and knew he was dead. I fainted. When I came to myself I was in my own bedroom. I must have walked there without knowing. A few minutes later, I suppose, the alarm came. Forgive me; I ought to have told you before; you must have suffered fearfully. But—" I stopped her. "It's best, I think, that you have told me now," I said, "we must save him. We must be on our guard, and do nothing." We noted Cudlipp's conduct. It became clear that he would hide his crime to the end, even to letting me be hanged for it. I told her that I would never speak to her again if she interfered, that I would die for the honour of her family. I made her swear by her dead mother. I doubted at first if he were aware of what he had done, but his manner left no doubt. For instance, he made no enquiry into the mystery of the basin missing from his room, and never spoke of it in court. So we knew.'

'You're a very noble and very wrong-headed young man,' said Simon; 'you don't really think we can leave things as they are, do you? Observe what is happening now. The explosion in the man's brain once over, habit has resumed its sway. He's the hypocritical bourgeois once more – but with the memory of that most fearful deed to lash him. If I know anything of men, it will prey upon his mind; and we shall have either another murder, or, more likely, suicide. Your sacrifice and Eleanor's will be useless. This is what has to be done: you and I will go to London together tonight. In the morning we will confide in two alienists. We will all go to Cudlipp House; the doctors will certify him insane; he must consent to our terms. He must put himself in the charge of a medical attendant and a male nurse, and he must go away with them, so that he never returns.

'The newspapers will be told that the shock of recent events has undermined his health, and that he has been ordered a complete change of scene.

'We shall then go to Eleanor, and tell her what has been done; you will marry her here in Paris; I will arrange with the Consulate for secrecy; and you will yourself seek a change of scene for a year or so. You, Major, will supply him with money if he needs it; you can get rid of some of those canvasses, I suppose?'

Major nodded.

'And you, Flynn, will invent a way up those cliffs, and a story about a maniac vampire, ending with his confession and suicide, to round it off nicely; we must clear this lad of that ghastly "not proven" business.'

'That is a job,' said Flynn, 'which I shall most thoroughly enjoy doing. But now you must all come and dine with me; we have no time to lose, if we mean to catch that nine o'clock train.'

6

Two years later a certain pretty French countess was enthusiastic, at the Salon des Beaux Arts, over the six South Sea Island pictures of a new Sociétaire. 'André de Bry?' she said to her escort, the great sculptor Major; 'isn't that the young man who was accused of poor Bibi Sangsue's last murder?'

'The maniac vampire? Yes, the fools! As if anyone could mistake Bibi's handiwork!'

'Truth is certainly stranger that fiction; Bibi's career sounds like the wildest imagination. Doesn't it?'

'It does,' said Major solemnly. 'But perhaps you knew him?'

'At one time,' murmured the Countess, writh a blush and a droop of the eyelids, 'at one time – well – rather intimately!'

'I,' said Major, 'knew only his father and mother!'

OUTSIDE THE BANK'S ROUTINE

He thought he saw a Banker's Clerk
  Descending from the bus:
He looked again, and found it was
  A Hippopotamus.

1

It was a sunny Saturday in April at Prince's Golf Club at Mitcham, and Ian Macpherson, London manager of the Midlothian and Ayrshire Bank, had the honour at the seventeenth tee. Unfortunately, he was one down. His opponent had been playing wonderful golf; and the Scotsman thought his best chance was to scare him with an extra long drive. It came off brilliantly: the ball flew low, far and true, up the fairway. Normally, he calculated to outdrive his opponent twenty yards; but this time it looked as if it might be fifty.

The other stepped to the tee. 'No!' he said to the caddy, 'I'll just take a cleek.'

Macpherson looked round. This was sheer insanity. What in Colonel Bogey's name possessed the man? Was he trying to lose the game?

The cleek shot lay fully eighty yards behind the drive. They walked after their balls, Macpherson still wondering what was in the wind. His opponent might still have reached the green with a brassie for his second, though it would have been a wonderful shot. Instead, he took a mashie and played a long way short.

'What ails the man?' thought Macpherson. 'He's fair daft.'

He came up with his ball. Should he take an iron or a spoon? 'Never up, never in!' he decided at last, still wondering at his opponent's actions, and took the spoon. 'I must spare it,' he thought. And so well did he spare it that he topped it badly! Thoroughly rattled, he took his iron for the third. The ball went clear over the green into a most obnoxious clump of whins. The other man chipped his third to the green, and Macpherson gave up the hole and the match; also a half-crown ball, which hurt him.

By the time they had played the bye, he had recovered his temper. 'Man!' he said, 'but you're a wunner. An auld man like ye – an' ye keep your caird under your years, A'm thinking.'

'Yes,' said his opponent, 'I'm round in eighty-one.'

'It's juist a meeracle! Tell me noo, for why did ye tak' your cleek to the seventeenth?'

'That's a long story, Mr Macpherson.'

'Ye'll tell me o'er a sup o' the bairley bree.'

They sat down on the porch of the club, and began to talk. 'When we stood on that tee,' said the old man, 'I didn't watch your ball; I watched your mind. I saw you were set on breaking my heart with your drive; so I just let you have it your own way, and took a cleek. As we walked, I still watched your thinking; I saw that you were not attending to your own play, how to make sure of a four, but to mine, which didn't concern you at all. When it came to your second, your thoughts were all over the place; you were in doubt about your club, took the wrong one, doubted again about how to play the shot – then you fluffed it. But I had won the hole before we ever left the tee.'

'I see.'

'If you want to win your matches, play as if it were a medal round. You have all the keenness; and the disasters don't hurt you, which gives confidence. But of course, if you can read a man's psychology, there are even surer ways of winning. Only be sure not to let your opponent get the psychology on you, as happened this afternoon.'

'Ye're a gran' thinker, sir. I didn't quite get your name; I wish ye'd dine wi' me the nicht.'

'Iff,' said the old man, 'Simon Iff.'

'Not much If,' muttered Macpherson, 'aboot your wurrk on the green!'

'But I'm afraid I'm busy tonight. Are you free Monday? Come and dine with me at the Hemlock Club. Seven-thirty. Don't dress!'

Macpherson was enchanted. The Hemlock Club! He had a vision of Paradise. It was the most exclusive club in London. Only one scandal marred its fame: early in the eighteenth century, a struggling painter of portraits, who had been rejected by the Academy, was black-balled by mistake for an Archbishop of York, whom nobody wanted. They made it up to the painter, but there was no getting rid of the Archbishop. So the committee of the club had dismissed all its servants, and filled their places with drunken parsons who had gone to the bad; in a month the Archbishop withdrew with what dignity remained to him. They had then hung his portrait in the least respected room in the club. To consolidate their position, and arm themselves against counter-attack, they passed a rule that no man should be eligible for membership unless he had done something 'notorious and heretical,' and it had been amusing and instructive to watch bishops attacking cardinal points of their faith, judges delivering sarcastic comments on the law, artists upsetting all the conventions of the period, physicists criticising the doctrine of the conservation of energy, all to put themselves right with the famous Rule Forty-Nine. Most of these people had no real originality, of course, but at least it forced them to appear to defy convention; and this exercised a salutary influence on the general tone of Society.

On the walls were portraits and caricatures of most of the club worthies, with their heresies inscribed. Wellington was there, with his 'Publish and be damned to you!' So was a great judge with that great speech on the divorce law which begins, 'In this country there is not one law for the rich, and another for the poor,' and goes on to tell the applicant, a working tailor, that to secure a divorce he needed only arrange to have a private act of Parliament passed on his behalf. Geikie was there with 'I don't believe that God has written a lie upon the rocks'; Shelley with 'I had rather be damned with Plato and Lord Bacon, than go to Heaven with Paley and Malthus'; Byron with 'Besides, they always smell of bread and butter'; Sir Richard Burton, with a stanza from *The Kasîdah*:

> There is no God, no man-made God; a bigger, stronger,
>   crueller man;
> Black phantom of our baby-fears, ere Thought, the life of
>   Life, began.

Swinburne was there too, with 'Come down and redeem us from virtue'; and a host of others. There was even a memorial-room in which candles were kept constantly burning. It commemorated the heretics whom the club had failed to annex. There was William Blake, with 'Every thing that lives is Holy'; there was James Thomson, with

> But if you would not this poor life fulfil,
> Lo, you are free to end it when you will,
>   Without the fear of waking after death. –

There was Keats, with 'Beauty is Truth, Truth Beauty'; John Davidson, with a passage from the 'Ballad of a Poet Born':

> 'Fill high the bowl! We are the scum
>   Of matter; fill the bowl;

Drink scathe to him, and death to him
Who dreams he has a soul.

Aubrey Beardsley, Ernest Dowson, Beddoes, Crackenthorpe, were all represented. They had even Victor Neuburg, with 'Sex is one; go now, be free.'

There was in this room a votive tablet with the names of those who had been invited to join the club, and refused; notably Whistler, below whose portrait of himself was his letter of refusal, which he had sent with it: 'I could not possibly consent to meet people of my own kind; my friends tell me it is very painful.'

King Edward VII, also, was in this group, with the letter from his secretary:

> His Majesty commands me to inform you that greatly as he appreciates the good wishes and loyalty of the president and members of the Hemlock Club, he cannot possibly take an oath declaring himself a Republican, or a Jacobite, as he understands is necessary to comply with Rule Forty-Nine.

There were many other curious rules in the club; for example, a fine of a guinea for failing to eat mustard with mutton; another of five pounds for quoting Shakespeare within the precincts of the club. The wearing of a white rose or a plaid neck-tie was punishable with expulsion; this dated from the period when it was heretical to be a Jacobite but dangerous to display it.

Many other customs of the club were similarly memorial: the Head Porter was always dressed in moleskin, in honour of the mole whose hill tripped the horse of William III; members whose Christian names happened to be George had to pay double the usual subscription, in memory of the club's long hatred of the Four Georges; and at the annual banquet a bowl of hemlock was passed round in the great hall, decorated for the occasion as a funeral chamber; for it was always claimed that Socrates was the real founder of the club. There was a solemn pretence, every year, of a search for the 'missing archives of the club.' On November the fifth there was a feast in honour of Guy Fawkes; and on the eleventh of the same month the Lord Mayor of London of the year was burnt in effigy.

Such is the club to which Macpherson suddenly found himself invited. He felt that now he could marry; he would have something to boast of to his grandchildren!

2

But, as things chanced, Macpherson nearly missed the dinner after all. He would have called off anything else in the world. But he couldn't give up that! However, it was a very sorry Scotsman who appeared at the door of the club.

In keeping with the general eccentricity of the place, the entrance to the club was mean and small, almost squalid; a narrow oaken door, studded with iron. And no sooner had he reached the great open space within than the Head Porter called him aside, saying in a whisper, 'Excuse me, Sir, but the Hanoverian spies are everywhere. Allow me to relieve you of your neck-tie!' For Macpherson had worn the tartan of his clan all day. He was accommodated with a selection of the latest neckwear. This trifling matter subdued him most effectively; he felt himself transported to a new strange world. It did him good; for to the very steps of the club he had been obsessed by the calamity of the day.

Simon Iff received him with affability and dignity, offered him a cigarette, and proceeded to show him the club. Macpherson was intensely awed; he was in a kind of private *edition de luxe of* Westminster Abbey. He resolved to put on all his panoply of Scottish culture. At the memorial chamber he exclaimed aloud: 'And all our yesterdays have lighted fools the way to dusty death. Out, out, brief candle!' He was enchanted with the Whistler portrait. 'A true Scot, Mr Iff.' he said. 'He was a man, take him for all in all, we shall not look upon his like again!'

'True, very true!' replied Iff, a trifle hastily.

Before Aubrey Beardsley the Scot grew more melancholy than ever, 'For he was likely, had he been put on, to have proved most royally,' he cried. They came to the portrait of Keats, a Severn from Sir Charles Dilke's collection. 'I weep for Adonais – he is dead!' said the banker.

'Thank Heaven!' murmured Iff to himself, hoping that all would now be well. But his luck was out: he brought the next blow upon himself. 'Some have doubted the autograph of Thomson here,' he said.

Macpherson was determined to shine. 'Never fear!' he said, 'that's the man's fist. Do we not know the sweet Roman hand?' And he added: 'I am but mad nor'-nor'west; when the wind is southerly, I know a hawk from a handsaw.'

Iff groaned in spirit. He was glad when the memorial chamber was done.

They came to the gallery of club members. Here the banker unmasked his batteries completely. Before Shelley he said that he, 'like the base Indian, cast away a pearl richer than all his tribe'; he recognised Pope with eagerness as 'a fellow of infinite jest'; he said to Byron, 'The sly slow years shall not determinate the dateless limit of thy dear exile'; he apostrophised Swinburne, 'Not marble, nor the gilded monuments of princes shall outlive this powerful rime'; of Burton he sighed, 'A great traveller; mebbe the greatest, save Davie Livingstone, that we ever had; and now he's gone to that undiscovered country from whose bourne no traveller returns.' Before Bishop Berkeley, he said: 'That was the fellow who thought he could hold a fire in his hand by thinking on the frosty Caucasus or wallow naked in December snow by thinking on fantastic summer's heat.' He dismissed Wellington with an airy gesture. 'Seeking the bubble reputation even in the cannon's mouth,' he said; but, feeling this to be rather severe, hedged with the remark that he frowned 'as once he did when in an angry parle he smote the sledded Polacks on the ice.'

Simple Simon decided to take his guest to dinner without further delay, to induce him to feed heartily, and to enter, himself, upon a quick-firing monologue.

'I am in a light, French, effervescing mood tonight; I will drink champagne,' he said, as they took a seat at the table where, as it was darkly whispered, Junius had composed his celebrated letters. 'We have a wonderful Pommery.'

'I'm with you,' replied the banker, 'though, for my part, I need it to relieve my mind. 'Tis not alone my inky cloak, good mother, nor customary suits of solemn black, nor windy suspiration of forced breath, no, nor the fruitful river in the eye, nor the dejected 'haviour of the visage, together with all forms, moods, shows of grief, that can denote me truly: these indeed seem, for they are actions that a man might play: but I have that within which passeth show; these but the trappings and the suits of woe.'

Some of the men at the next table – that at which Clifford, Arundel, Lauderdale, Arlington and Buckingham had formed their famous Cabal – began to laugh. Simon Iff frowned them down sternly, and pointed to the Arabic inscription on the wall – it had been given to Richard I by Saladin – which reads in translation, 'He that receiveth a guest, entertaineth God.'

'I am sorry you should be troubled on this particular night,' he said to the Scotsman; 'it is the pride of the members of this club to make their guests happy; and if it be anything within the power of any one of us to amend, be sure that we shall do our best. But perhaps your misfortune is one in which human aid is useless.'

'I will not bother you with my troubles, Mr Iff,' returned the banker; 'on the surface, it's a purely business matter, though a very serious one. Yet the onus is of a personal nature. How sharper than a serpent's tooth it is, to have a thankless child!'

'Well, if you like to tell me about it after dinner—'

'I think it would interest you, and it will comfort me to confide in you. I do not wear my heart on my sleeve for daws to peck at; but on the other hand, why should I sit like Patience on a monument, smiling at grief? But till dinner is done, away with sorrow; we will talk in maiden meditation, fancy-free, and tell black-hearted fear it lies, in spite of thunder.'

'Then let me tell you something of the history of this club!' cried Simon desperately, and he began to rattle off a combination of legend and fancy, mingled so happily with fact, and touched so elegantly with illustration, that Macpherson quite forgot his culture, and became the plain Scottish man of business, or rather the ambitious boy again as he was thirty years before, when he had first set foot on the ladder that was to lead him to one of the highest positions in the financial world.

When the waiter presented the bill, Iff marked a 19 in front of a printed item at its foot; the waiter filled in £95, and made the addition. Iff scribbled his name.

The figure caught the trained eye of the banker. 'Excuse me!' he cried; 'it's the rudest thing possible, but I would like to see that bit o' paper. I'm just that curious, where there's money.' Iff could not refuse; he passed the bill across the table.

'Nineteen Shakespeares!' exclaimed the Scot. 'Ninety-five pounds sterling! What 'll that mean, whateffer?'

'Well, I didn't mean to tell you, Mr Macpherson; it's not very charming of me, but you oblige me. There is a fine of five pounds for every Shakespeare quotation made in this club – and of course, as your host, I'm responsible. Besides, it was well worth the money. The men at the next table have not had such a lovely time for years. Simple Simon, as they call me, won't hear the last of it for a while!' But the Scot was stunned. He could only keep on repeating in a dazed way, 'Ninety-five pounds! Ninety-five pounds! Ninety-five pounds!'

'Don't think of it, I beg of you!' cried Iff. 'I see that it distresses you. I am a rich man, and an old one; I shall never miss it. Besides, the fine goes to a most worthy object: the Society for Destroying Parliamentary Institutions.'

'I never heard of it.'

'Indeed! it is very powerful, I assure you. It carried through Payment of Members; it has greatly enlarged the Franchise, and is now working to have it extended to women.'

'I thought ye said Destroying Parliament.'

'Just so. These measures are directed towards reducing the whole thing to a farce. Already the power of Parliament is a thing of the past; authority is concentrated in the cabinet – nay, in a camarilla within the cabinet, and even this camarilla is very much in the hands of permanent officials whose names the public never hears.'

'D'ye ken, I can hardly believe mv ain ears.'

'When the public demands a law which those in authority don't like, they either block it in the Commons, or throw it out in the Lords, or get the judges to interpret it so as to mean nothing at all, or the opposite of what it was intended to mean.'

'Losh!'

'You're a banker. Would you submit your bank to popular management, interference by people who don't know the first principles of the business?'

'It wad be the shutters up in just one se'nnight!'

'Nor will we intrust our country to people who know neither law, nor history, nor geography, nor commerce – except in their own petty trade – nor foreign affairs, not so much as whether our interests lie with those of our neighbours or clash with them; nor any other of the arts necessary to government.'

'Weel, weel, but these are strange sayings. But I doot ye're richt.'

'Let us have our coffee in the lounge, and you shall tell me all about your troubles. I feel I've bored you with all my talk about the club.'

They walked into the lounge and took a seat in the low window which overlooks St James Park.

'See the palace!' said Simon Iff. 'The Foreign Secretary is with the King tonight. His Majesty was anxious about the ultimatum to Russia.'

'Russia! She's our ally!'

'Last night war was thought a certainty. This morning a way out was found. How would it do to let that cat out of the bag, with the Press howling for blood? The price of Democracy is eternal Hypocrisy!'

Macpherson was by this time completely overwhelmed. He felt himself among the Powers. He thought of Paul caught up into the seventh heaven, and hearing things not lawful for men to speak.

'Now, then, your little private grief,' said Simon, when the waiter had brought the coffee, a box of Upmanns, and two great Venetian glasses, milky with threads of gold, in which was the special club brandy from the cellars of Frederick the Great of Prussia.

'It's a serious situation, Mr Iff,' began the banker, who, once on familiar ground, grew confident, lucid and precise.

3

'My bank, as you know, is situated at the corner of London Wall and Copthall Avenue. The chief officials are three: myself, Fraser, who came with me from Edinburgh, has worked with me for fourteen years, and Fisher, who has been with me for two years only. Both men are steady in every way. Fisher, for example, though a young man, has already managed to purchase the house in which he lives at Tooting Beé; a charming though compact detached residence with a garden, which he spends most of his leisure in tending. He won a prize in the *Daily Mail* Sweet Pea competition, and his roses are wonderful. An extremely promising young man.

'Next week is Easter. At this time there is a very great demand in Paris for English banknotes; this year we are sending no less than twelve thousand pounds in tens and fives. On Friday, this sum arrived from the Bank of England; it was checked, made into a special parcel ready for transmission today, and stored in the safe.

'I had noticed some unusual commotion in Fraser during the whole of this past month; on Friday I asked him its cause. He replied that he was in love, having recently met Miss Clavering, a customer of the bank, by the way, with an average monthly balance of some five to seven hundred pounds. I wished him good luck. He was to take her to the Earl's Court Exhibition that night, he said.

'So much for Friday. On Saturday I reached the bank at a quarter before nine, as is my custom. I saw Fraser disappear into the bank as I approached it. He did not go to his desk, but was waiting for me to enter. He had his hand to the side of his head. The face was decidedly swollen, and the eyes injected. "Mr Macpherson," he said, "I had to come down; I've not missed a day since we came to London; but I'm in agony of neuralgia; I've not slept all night." He jerked the words out with evident difficulty. "Go right home!" I said, "or why not run down to Brighton for the week-end, and let the sea wind blow the poison out of your system?" "I will that," he said, and was gone. Fisher, by the way, had entered the bank and heard this conversation, or all but a few words.

'On Saturday the bank closes at one o'clock; but several of the clerks stay behind to finish the week's work. I myself leave at noon, or a few minutes earlier, in order to attend a short conference in connection with our American business. The banks concerned each send a representative. I had intended to go to a matinee last Saturday, but the brightness of the day tempted me to Mitcham, where I had the pleasure of meeting you.

'Now let me tell you what occurred after I had left the bank. A few minutes only had elapsed when Fraser appeared. "I'm going to Brighton on the one o'clock train," he told Fisher, who was, of course, surprised to see him; "but I'm worried to death. I've got it into my mind that the Paris parcel was not put into the safe." Together they went and opened it; they could not have done it separately, as Fisher had the key, and Fraser the combination. The parcel was duly found. Fraser took it up, looked at it, noted the seals, and replaced it. "That's all right," he said with relief; "see you Monday." "So long," said Fisher, and Fraser went out.

'Now, sir, the story becomes bizarre and uncanny in the extreme. We'll suppose that the Paris package has been tampered with, as turned out to be the case. Then you'll imagine at least that we'd hear nothing of it until Monday; perhaps not until the packet reached the bank in Paris. Instead, the plot goes off bang! Bang! like the scenario of a moving picture.

'I return from golf to my rooms in Half Moon Street. I find Fisher waiting for me. Fraser had wired him from Brighton to be at my place at once, and wait. The message was so urgent that he could not disregard it. There is a telegram for me on my hall table. From Fraser. "Absolutely certain Paris parcel has been stolen. Formally request you make sure." Nothing for it but to go down to the bank. Sure enough, the package is a dummy. We warn the police, public and private. By Sunday morning evidence is tumbling in like an avalanche.

'Fraser was seen at one o'clock at Euston. He bought a return ticket to Edinburgh, and paid for it with one of the stolen notes. He was in no hurry, and bothered the clerk a good deal trying to get some kind of holiday ticket that the railway didn't issue. He talked of his old mother in Edinburgh; hadn't seen her for two years. The clerk recognised his photograph at once; remembered him specially, because he had given him his change a shilling short, and, discovering the error immediately, sent a porter to find him; but he could not be seen. This in itself struck the clerk as curious.

'He was recognised in the luncheon-room of the Old Ship Hotel at Brighton, at a time so near that of the Euston incident that he must have jumped into a high-power car after buying the ticket, and broken the speed laws every yard of the way to Brighton. He is known in the hotel; besides, Murray, of the City and Shire Bank, saw him and spoke to him. Fraser said, "I'm going back to London. I'm sure there's something wrong at the bank. I dreamed it three nights running.'

'At dawn on Sunday Fraser's body, horribly mangled, was found at the foot of some cliffs near Ilfracombe – another long drive. His letters and papers were found on the body, and about eighty pounds of the stolen money.

'I had this news about 11.30. Ten minutes later the telephone rang. It was Fraser's voice, without any question. "I'm worried about the Paris package," he said. "I hope you don't think me quite mad. Do tell me you went to the bank, and found all well." I was so amazed that I could not speak for a moment. Then I saw that the question was one of identity, first of all. I asked him a question which it was most unlikely that anyone else could answer: who was paying teller at the bank when he first joined it, and where did he live? There was no answer. Ten minutes later the bell rang again. "They cut us off," he said, and then gave the reply correctly.

'By this time I began to believe myself insane. "Where are you?" I cried, "I want to see you at once." Again the telephone went dead. Two hours later the front door bell rang. It was Fisher. "Has he come?" he cried. Fisher said that Fraser had driven to his house in a big touring car very early that morning, and called him out by honking. "I can't stop," he had said. "I'm on the track of the stolen money. Meet me at Macpherson's at two.'

'I forgot to tell you that enquiry at Fraser's rooms showed that he had left about six on Friday, saying that he would be out until late. He had not returned, so far as the landlady knew; but he had a latchkey. However, his bed had not been slept in.

'I waited with Fisher until three o'clock. There was no Fraser, and no further word of him. I had telephoned the police to trace the calls I had received, and obtained the reply that no record had been kept. The operator fancied that it was some exchange in Southwest London; but enquiries at those exchanges produced no result.

'About one o'clock on Monday morning two cyclist policemen, returning from the patrol of the Ewing Road, heard an explosion in front of them. Turning a corner, they came upon a powerful car, its lights out, its identification marks erased. In this car was the body of Fraser, the bowels torn out by a shot from a heavy revolver, one of the bank revolvers. In the pockets were a signed photograph of Miss Clavering, a watch, a handkerchief, six hundred pounds of the stolen money, and some loose gold and other coins. I saw the body this morning; it was undoubtedly that of Fraser. But the doctors said he had been dead since Sunday afternoon!

'This was at eight o'clock; I went to the bank at nine; among my mail was a telegram from Fraser. "Everything all right now. Consider the incident closed." The police brought me the original, which had been handed in by Fraser himself, apparently, at a nearby office in Cornhill; it was in his own handwriting.

'There's the case so far. Man, it defies the imagination!'

'No, no!' replied Iff briskly, 'it defies the conventions of the routine of banking business.'

4

Macpherson opened his eyes in amazement. He did not in the least comprehend the point of view.

'Let me try to make this matter clear to you.'

'Clear!'

'Like all mundane matters, its complexity is illusion. Let us begin at the beginning. The soul of man is free and radiant, like the sun; his mind light or dark as he happens to be illuminated by that soul. We call this night; but it is only that we are in the shadow of the earth itself; the sun is shining gloriously, I make no doubt, in China.'

'I don't see how this bears on the robbery and murders, Mr Iff.'

'Exactly. Which is why you are only Mr Macpherson of the Midlothian and Ayrshire, instead of Lord Macpherson, pulling the financial strings of the whole world. Observe: you know all about banking; good. But you make the mistake of not seeing that banking is only one of the smallest fragments of knowledge needed by a banker. Your acquaintance with Shakespeare is a good sign – yet I feel sure that it has never occurred to you to put that bit of your brain to work on the rest of it. The cleverest banker I know is passionately devoted to the Russian ballet; Nijinsky pirouettes before him; he translates Nijinsky's legs into the movements of the gold supply, and out comes a scheme to shake the world.'

The Scot shook his head. 'I ken the mon ye mean; but it's juist an accident.'

'There are no accidents in this world. There are only ignorances of the causes of certain events.'

'Oh ay! that's true. Davie Hume said that.'

'I see you're a scholar, Mr Macpherson. Now do let us try to use these qualities to explain the problems which at present beset you. To begin: You are puzzled by the complexity of the case. To me, on the other hand, the fact simplifies it at once. I perceive that the entire drama has been staged by a highly-coloured and imaginative mind.'

'Fraser's mind was as prosaic as his own ledgers.'

'Precisely. Fraser is clearly an entirely passive agent in the whole business. Note, please, how Mr Someone Not Fraser has obsessed you with the name Fraser. Even when Fraser's body is found dead, you somehow feel that he is responsible. In other words, Mr Someone has shouted Fraser at you till your ears are dinned.

'Now let us look at the facts in detail. Practically everything you have told me is an Appearance of Fraser, like a ghost story.

'Either he is there or he writes or telephones. He's the busiest man in England all this week-end. He has two of his own corpses to play with, and his wire this morning leads you to hope that he is still alive.'

'I loved that lad like my own son.'

'Yes, yes; but you must forget that for a moment; or rather, you must detach yourself from it, and regard it merely as one of the facts in the case.

'Now let us recapitulate the Appearances of Fraser. Check me as I go, please.

'One. At the bank at nine on Saturday. Anything suspicious?'

'Well, yes, now you say so. I can imagine a personation, aided by the neuralgia. But I had no suspicion at the time. And if it were not Fraser, why did he come?'

'To prepare the minds of the others for his visit number two.'

'But they were surprised to see him.'

'Just what he wanted, perhaps. Yet I'm not sure. He may have done it merely because that it was unlikely that he should do it. The man's prime intention was to confuse and bewilder your mind.'

'He did that!'

'Number Two. Sure that was the real Fraser?'

'No; but Fisher didn't doubt it.'

'Fisher's mind was prepared by your recognition of him earlier in the day. Or – wait a minute. That may be merely what clever Mr Someone wants us to think. Wait a moment.'

There was a long pause.

'If that were so,' continued Simon Iff, 'it would look as if Mr Someone were trying to make things easier for Fisher. Has Fisher acted naturally throughout?'

'Perfectly. He's an exemplary man for a subordinate position.'

'Yet he grows roses. That's a suspicious trait. Rose gardening is a devilish pursuit!'

'Ye're joking, man.'

'Oh, a Scotsman can see a joke when there isn't one there! However, to go on to Number Three. Vision of Fraser at Euston. Now that was certainly not Fraser.'

'Why not?'

'He didn't count his change. You tell me he's the most accurate man you ever had.'

'Never made an error or so much as an erasure in ten years.'

'You see! If that man were walking in his sleep he'd still get his figures right. It's part of his being.'

'I think you're right.'

'Note too that he does everything, not too unusual, to get the clerk to remember him. In fact, we might think that he took the short change on purpose to attract notice. It would strike Fraser to do such a thing. So he may have been Fraser after all.

'Number Four. Brighton. Again the identification is very doubtful.

'Number Five. Ilfracombe. Here the corpse is certainly not Fraser's; yet all pains are taken to make us think that it is his.'

'But that's so silly, when he is going to bob up again a few hours later.'

'All done to keep you happy during the week-end! Number Six. The first telephone call.'

'That was his voice. He spoke as if in pain, as on the Saturday.'

'Still doubtful, then. Number Seven. The second telephone call.'

'It's most improbable that anyone else could have got the information. He could have no idea that I would ask.'

'But he might have got it from Fraser in the intervals between the calls.'

'And why should Fraser give it, if he's not in the game?'

'Ah!'

'But I'm dead sure of his voice. On the Saturday I might have doubted; I was not paying attention. But this time I was concentrating my whole mind on the question of identity. And, ye ken, identity's a question of constant and primary importance to a banker.'

'I agree with you. Number Eight. Fraser at Tooting. Here we have only Fisher's identification, which we suspected once before, though there's no reason to do so in either case. Yet we note that Fraser makes an appointment which he does not keep; nor does he refer to it in his telephone call. Number Nine. Fraser's corpse again, this time the real thing. No doubt possible?'

'None. The face was quite uninjured. I knew every freckle by heart.'

'And no disguise possible, of course. It would have been easy to blow away the head; so Mr Someone Clever wanted you to find him. Yet the doctors say the man had been dead twelve hours?'

'Nearly that; an hour more or less.'

'I wonder if Mr Clever thought that might have been overlooked. You see, I'm sure it wasn't suicide, though it was made to look like it. I'm sure this last scene – for I shall dismiss Number Ten, this morning's telegram, as an obvious fake; the wire was written out long beforehand – this last scene was most carefully stage-managed. And what is the significant article, the one thing to attract our attention? The picture of Miss Clavering!'

'I can't see the bearing of that, on any theory.'

'Luckily, I've got no theory, so far. Let's boil down these facts. The only visions you are sure of are not visions at all. You *heard* Fraser on Sunday morning; but so far as you can be absolutely certain, he has not been *seen* alive since Friday night.'

'That's so, by heaven!'

'Did he ever meet Miss Clavering that night?'

'No; she had made the appointment with him, as it chanced, in the bank itself, where she called on Friday morning to draw a hundred pounds. She looked ill, and I remarked on it. She replied that she had drawn the money for the very purpose of resting over Easter at Ostend. But she did not go. That afternoon, shopping in Bond Street, she slipped on a banana skin, and twisted her ankle. A doctor took her to her house in John Street. Her servants had been given a holiday from Saturday to correspond with her own, and she allowed them to go as if nothing had happened; a nurse is with her, and prepares her food. The doctor calls twice daily. Of course she was the first person whom we questioned. It is extraordinary that Fraser should not have called there that evening.'

'Perhaps he was prevented. No; no one has seen him, to be positive, since the dramatic features began, later than Friday evening, or perhaps possibly after he left the bank.'

'That's so; and there's nae doot o' it.

'But he was seen after leaving the bank on Friday; a man answering to his description hired the big touring car in which his body was found this morning, at an hour very shortly after he left me. Otherwise he has not been seen, as you say.'

'Yet infinite pains have been taken to show you the man, dead or alive, here, there and everywhere.'

'But some of those are unreasonable. This morning, for instance, and the corpse at Ilfracombe.'

'Yes, my poor pragmatic friend, that is the point. You would have analysed purely rational appearances; these were beyond you. The strange atmosphere of the case bewildered your brain. It's probably the same at Scotland Yard.

'Observe how you were played on throughout. Why alarm you so early, and so elaborately? Criminals always prefer the maximum time to make their getaway. This thing was planned from long before – and probably, if you had refused to be frightened about the money, the whole scheme would have miscarried. Note that Mr Clever does not begin to alarm you until after Vision Number Two, when doubtless he changed the package for the dummy. Stop! What was the size of the package?'

'Pretty bulky; about a cubic foot.'

'Then I'm an ass. Oh dear! Now I must begin to think all over again.'

'If he changed it before Fisher's eyes, Fisher must be in the plot. Yet that would compromise him hopelessly. Besides, that must have been Fraser, now that I come to think of it. He had the combination.'

'Oh, that doesn't matter, as I see it. I've been rash and foolish, but I see the whole thing now, I think. Others besides Fisher would have noticed if Fraser had carried a parcel, or a bag, in or out?'

'Yes: I asked that. He had nothing in his hands; and his light overcoat was buttoned tight to his very slim figure, so he couldn't have concealed it.'

'Thank you. Everything is perfectly clear now. But I don't want to tell you; I want to prove it to your eyes. Let me call at your apartment at 9.30 tomorrow morning, and we will settle this business together. Can you keep the morning free?'

'Oh yes! Fisher can do all that is necessary at the bank.'

5

The next morning Simon Iff was punctual to his appointment. 'Our first business,' he told Macpherson, 'is one of simple good feeling and good manners. Miss Clavering must be in a terrible state of mind. We will call and tell her that Fraser has been cleared, and condole with her upon his loss. Would you telephone and ask for an appointment?'

Macpherson did so. The answer came that Miss Clavering was still asleep; on her waking, the message would be given. Where should she, the nurse, telephone? Macpherson gave his number.

About twenty minutes later the nurse called him. 'Could you be here at ten minutes before eleven?' she said. Macpherson agreed.

'Splendid!' cried Iff, when he hung up the receiver; 'of course, I wish she could have made it twelve minutes instead of ten. We may be a little late at the bank.'

The Scot looked at him to see if his mind were not sick; but his whole face was so radiant, his eyes so alight with mischievous intelligence, that the banker could not fail to divine some signal triumph. But he was none the less amazed. What information could the man have gleaned from the mere time of a quite commonplace appointment?

Simon Iff was exceedingly punctilious in pushing the bell at Miss Clavering's to the minute. They were admitted at once. The girl, a tall, slim, languid beauty, Spanish in type, with a skin of extreme pallor, was lying on a couch. She was dressed very simply in black; her mind seemed exhausted by the grief and pain through which she was passing. The nurse and doctor, kneeling at the foot of the couch, were in the act of dressing the injured ankle. It was probably adorable in normal times, but now it was swollen and discoloured.

The first consideration of Macpherson and his friend was to express sympathy. 'Is it a bad sprain?' they asked the doctor.

'I have a feeling that one of the small bones is displaced; I have asked Sir Bray Clinton to step in; he should be here in a few minutes.'

'Perfect, perfect!' murmured Iff; 'if the case goes ill, it will be from no lack of care.'

'Everybody is charming to me,' lisped Miss Clavering faintly.

Macpherson then proceeded, as arranged, to exonerate Fraser from guilt; though he said that he had no idea of the real culprit, and it was the most bewildering case he had ever heard of.

'We know the principal party concerned, though,' chirped Iff. 'He is a Chinaman, we are sure of that, though we don't know his name; and there's not the least chance of arresting him. In fact, one can hardly say that he is guilty.'

Macpherson turned open-mouthed upon the mystic. 'A Chinaman!' he gasped.

'Well, now you mention it, I don't really know whether he was a Chinaman after all!'

Macpherson thought it best to hint that his companion was a little fanciful.

At that moment the bell rang. 'That will be Clinton!' said the doctor.

'I'm so charmed with your calling,' sighed the girl, in evident dismissal, 'and I'm so relieved that at least Mr Fraser died an innocent man.' She covered her face with her hands for a moment; then, mastering herself, extended them to her visitors, who leaned over them, and departed with the nurse.

On the doorstep stood Sir Bray Clinton, to whom both Iff and Macpherson extended hearty greeting.

'Now,' said Iff, as they turned down the street, 'that pleasant duty off our minds, to the bank, and prepare for sterner work!'

6

'It is a cold morning,' said Simon Iff, taking a chair in the managerial room, 'at least, to so old a man as I. May I have a fire, while we are waiting? And would you please be so good as to ignore me for a while; I will tell you when all is ready'

Macpherson grew more bewildered every moment, for the day was very warm; but the authority of the Hemlock Club still weighed upon his soul. He was a snob of snobs, like all Scotsmen who barter their birthright of poverty and independence for England's sloth and luxury; and he would almost have jumped out of the window at a request from any member of the aristocracy. And the Hemlock Club thought no more of snubbing an Emperor than a child of plucking a daisy.

Half an hour elapsed; Macpherson busied himself in the bank. At the end of that time Iff came out, and brought him back. 'I should like,' he said, 'to have a few words with Mr Fisher.'

Macpherson complied. 'Shut the door, Mr Fisher, if you please,' said the magician, 'we old men fear the cold terribly. Take a seat; take a seat. Now I only want to ask you one small point connected with this case; it is one that puzzles me considerably'

'I'm entirely baffled myself,' returned Fisher; 'but of course I'll tell you anything I know.'

'There are really two points: one you may know; the other you must know. We will take them in that order. First, how did the doctor come to miss his appointment on the Ewing Road? Second, how long—'

Fisher had gripped the arms of his chair. His face was deathly.

'How long,' pursued the mystic, inexorably, 'is it since you fell in love with Clara Clavering?'

Macpherson had bounded to his feet. He compressed his Scottish mouth with all his Scottish will.

Simon Iff went on imperturbably. 'I think perhaps you do not realise how critical was that failure of the doctor to materialise. Knowing the moment of Fraser's murder, everything becomes clear.'

'I suppose this is what you call the third degree!' sneered Fisher. 'I'm not to be bluffed.'

'So you won't talk, my friend? I think you will when we apply this white-hot poker here to your bare abdomen.'

Fisher faltered. 'That was terrible!' It was the cry of a damned soul.

'*Was* terrible, you'll note, Mr Macpherson,' cried Simon Iff, 'not *will* be. Come, Mr Fisher, you see I know the whole story.'

'Then you had better tell it.'

'I will. You'll remember, Macpherson, I told you that I saw in this whole plot the workings of a creative mind of high colour and fantasy; possibly on the border of madness. So I began to look for such a mind. I did not need to look for clues; once I found the right kind of mind, the rest would fit. I began to suspect Mr Fisher here on account of his rose-growing activities; but I soon saw that he had too many alibis. Fraser, with a mind like a Babbage calculating machine, was out of the question from the start, although he had just fallen in love – which sometimes works some pretty fine miracles in a man!

'The only other person in the circle was Miss Clavering herself, and I made an opportunity to see her. I saw, too, that she was not very much in the circle; she appeared accidentally and quite naturally. I thought that such an apparent comet might be the Sun of the system of deception.

'I was delighted when I was given an exact time, not a round hour or half hour, for the interview; it suggested an intricacy.

'I arrive at the house; I see a perfect stage picture; an undeniable swollen ankle, which is also an undeniable alibi; and, in case anyone did doubt the ankle, there was a witness above all suspicion, Sir Bray Clinton, on his way to see it. Could I doubt that Miss Clavering was awake when Macpherson first telephoned, and used the interval to make a date with Clinton and the doctor? Only we must not be there for the interview; Clinton would ask when the accident happened. It would not do to tell him "Friday," when the other doctor had deliberately dislocated the foot, as I was sure, on Monday, after Vision Number Ten of poor Fraser.

'But how does it happen that Fraser writes and telephones just as Miss Clavering dictates? Here we touch the darkest moment of the drama. He was evidently a puppet throughout. It is clear to me that Miss Clavering, disguised as Fraser, hired the big racing car; that she met him on Friday night, chloroformed him, took him to the house of Fisher here, and kept him in durance.

'On the Saturday she and Fisher play their appointed roles. Vision Number Two is devised to make it appear that Saturday noon is the moment of the robbery, when in reality the parcels had been exchanged long before.'

'I never packed the notes,' said Fisher. 'I put them away in my bag and took them home with me on Friday night.'

'Good boy! Now we're being sensible. Well, to continue with Saturday. Miss Clavering has a corpse in her car – and this made me suspect a medical accomplice – goes through her tricks, and returns to Fisher's house. They then proceed to put pressure on Fraser. He resists. Miss Clavering resorts to the white-hot poker. How do I know? Because care was taken to destroy the abdomen. Under this torture Fraser wrote the telegram which was later handed in by Clara; then he was set to telephone to you, Macpherson, with the implement of torture ready in case he should make a mistake. Yet he kicked; they had to ring off, and have a second orgie of devilment before he would give the answer you required. It was useless for him to give a false answer; his best chance of help (as they probably showed him) was to convince you that it was he. Directly this is over, Fraser is murdered. It would really have been safer to wait till the last moment—'

'Of course it would. You don't know all, though you must be the devil to know what you do. But Fraser had aortic regurgitation; he died while still speaking to you. We had meant him to say a great deal more. That was where our plan broke down.'

'Still, it was a good plan,' returned Simon Iff cordially. 'And the rest is simple. The car is left on a lonely road, with Fraser in it, an evident suicide. And the doctor was to drive past; he was in waiting, after firing the shot into Fraser's abdomen, for the lights of the patrol or whoever should come up; and he was to certify that the shot had caused death. Why should anyone suspect anything else? Perhaps the doctor would offer to take it away in his car, and lose time in various ways, until the hour of death was no longer certain. Now, Fisher, why didn't he do as arranged?'

'Clara was full of morphia up to the neck. She did it all, plan and execution, on morphine and hysteria. Oh, you don't know her! But she broke down at that moment. She was in the car with Leslie; she had a fit of tearing off her clothes and screaming, and he had to struggle with her for an hour. When she came to, it was too late and too dangerous to do anything. When I heard it, an hour later, I knew the game was up. I knew that Fate was hunting us, even as we had thought we were hunting Fate! The two accidents – Fraser's death and her insanity – were the ruin of all! God help me!'

'So she took morphia!' cried Macpherson. 'Then was that what you meant about the Chinaman?'

'Good, Macpherson! You're beginning to bring your Shakespeare into the bank!'

'But you – how did you know about it?'

'I was ten years in China. I've smoked opium as hard as anybody. I recognised the drama from the first as a mixture of opium-visions and sex-hysteria.'

'But I still don't see why they should play this mad and dangerous game, when it would have been so simple just to steal the money and get away'

'Well, first, there was the love of the thing. Secondly, it was exceedingly shrewd. The important point was to cover the one uncoverable thing, the theft of the money. Left alone, your business routine would have worked with its usual efficiency. You would have traced the Paris package minute by minute. Instead of that, you never gave it one thought. You were out on a wild goose chase after Fraser. She took you out of the world you know into the world she knows, where you are a mere baby. I could follow her mad mind, because I have smoked opium. You might try that, too, by the way, Macpherson, if the Russian ballet doesn't appeal to you!

'And now, Mr Fisher, I wish you to answer my second question. I have reasons for inclining to acquit you, in part; for giving you a chance. The man I mean to hang is Dr Leslie. He is one of a common type, the ambitious money-loving Scotsman, clever and handsome, who comes to London to make his way. They become women's doctors; they seduce their patients; they make them drug-fiends; they perform abortions; and to the extortionate charges for their crimes they add a tenfold profit by blackmail. These men are the curse of London.'

'It's true; I think he ruined Clara with morphine. I feel sure she was a good girl once.'

'Tell us of your relations with her.'

'I met her a year ago. Her fascination conquered me at once. Oh, you don't know her! She could do anything with us all! She could tantalise and she could gratify, beyond all dreams. She was a liar to the core; but so wonderful, that even at the moment when reason declared her every word to be a lie, the heart and soul believed, as a nun clings to a crucifix! I was her slave. She tortured and enraptured me by day and night. At this moment I would kill myself to please her whim. She has delighted to make me do degrading and horrible things; she has paid me for a week of agony with a kiss or a smile; she—'

The boy gasped, almost fainted.

'Are there such women?' asked Macpherson. 'I thought it was a fairy-tale.'

'I have known three, intimately,' returned Simon Iff: 'Edith Harcourt, Jeanne Hayes, Jane Forster. What the boy says is true. I may say that indulgence in drink or drugs tends to create such monsters out of the noblest women. Of the three I have mentioned, the two latter were congenitally bad; Edith Harcourt was one of the finest women that ever lived, but her mother had taught her to drink when yet a child, and in a moment of stress the hidden enemy broke from ambush and destroyed her soul. Her personality was wholly transformed; yes, sir, on the whole, I believe in possession by the devil. All three women ruined the men, or some of them, with whom they were associated. Jeanne Hayes ruined the life of her husband and tore the soul out of her lover before she killed herself; Jane Forster drove a worthy lawyer to melancholy madness. Of their lesser victims, mere broken hearts and so on, there is no count. Edith Harcourt made her husband's life a hell for three years, and after her divorce broke loose altogether, and destroyed many others with envenomed caresses.'

'You knew her intimately, you say?'

'She was my wife.'

Macpherson remained silent. Fisher was sitting with his head clasped in his hands, his body broken up with sobs.

'Now, Macpherson, we are going to compound felony. I'm glad there was no murder, after all. I want you to let me take Fisher away with me; I'm going to put him with a society of which I am president, which specialises in such cases, without cant or cruelty. Its aim is merely to put a man in the conditions most favourable to his proper development. This was a fine lad until he met the woman who destroyed him, and I know that such women have a more than human power.

'It will be your business to put Miss Clavering in an asylum, if you can catch her, which I sorely doubt. But I think that if you go warily, you may catch Leslie.'

It turned out as he had said. Clara had scented mischief, with her morphine-sharpened intellect and her hysteric's intuition. She had persuaded Sir Bray Clinton to send her down to a hospital of his own in the country – and on the way she had seized the soul of the chauffeur. They disappeared together, and there was no word of her for many a day. But Leslie had suspected nothing in the visit, or had laughed it off, or had decided to bluff it out; he was arrested, and sentenced to penal servitude for life.

Fisher justified the good opinion of Simon Iff; but his spirit was broken by his fatal love, and he will never do more than serve the society that saved him, with a dog's devotion.

Macpherson followed the old mystic's advice; he is today the most daring, although the soundest, financier in London. Two nights ago he dined with the magician at the Hemlock Club. 'I've brought Shakespeare into the bank,' he said, laughingly, to Simple Simon. 'But I'll keep him out of the club, this time!'

'Oh well!' said Simon, 'to spend too much time in studies is sloth; to use them too much for ornament is affectation; to make judgment wholly by their rules is the humour of a scholar; they perfect nature, and are themselves perfected by experience; crafty men condemn them, wise men use them, simple men admire them; for they teach not their own use, but that there is a wisdom without them and above them won by observation. It's well worth five pounds!'

'But,' objected Macpherson, 'that's not Shakespeare; that's Bacon!'

Simon Iff did not permit himself so much as the antepenumbra of a smile. 'William Shakespeare wrote the works of Francis Bacon; that is one of the Official Beliefs of the Hemlock Club.'

'For the Lord's sake!' cried the banker. 'I'll never live up to this club. Man, it's a marvel!'

'Well,' answered the magician, sipping his wine, 'you might try a course of William Blake.'

THE CONDUCT OF JOHN BRIGGS

Simon Iff bounded into the Hemlock Club. He was by all odds the oldest member of the club; but today he had the elasticity of a boy, and he was so radiant that some people would have sworn that they actually saw flashes of light about his head. He bounded up the great stairway of the club two steps at a time.

The porters relaxed their solemnity, for the man's exaltation was contagious. 'So Simple Simon's back from one of 'is Great Magical Retirements again. I wonder wot in 'Eving's name 'e does.'

'I wisht I knew,' replied the other. 'The old boy's ninety, if 'e's a dy.'

In the lunch-room the atmosphere was certainly in need of all the exhilaration it could find. There were only a dozen men present, and they were talking in whispers. The eldest of them, Sir Herbert Holborne ('Anging 'Olborne of the criminal classes) was neither speaking nor eating, though his lunch lay before him. He was drinking whiskey-and-soda in a steady businesslike way, as a man does who has an important task to accomplish.

Simon Iff greeted them with a single comprehensive wave of the hand. 'What's the news, dear man?' he asked his neighbour. 'Are you all rehearsing a play of Wedekind's? Oh, a steak and a bottle of Nuits,' he added to the waiter. 'The old Nuits, the best Nuits, for I must give praise to Our Lady of the Starry Heavens!'

'You do not appear to require the stimulus of alcohol in any marked degree,' observed Holborne, in his driest manner.

'Stimulus!' cried Iff; 'I don't take wine to stimulate. It is because I am stimulated, or rather, fortified, that I drink wine. You must always drink what is in tune with your own soul. That's the Harmony of Diet! It is stupid and criminal to try to alter your soul by drugs. Let the soul be free, and use what suits it. Homeopathic treatment! So give me green tea when I am exquisite and aesthetic like a Ming vase; coffee when I am high-strung and vigilant as an Arab; chocolate when I am feeling cosy and feminine; brandy when I am martial and passionate; and wine – oh, wine at all times! – but wine especially when I am bubbling over with spiritual ecstasy. Thus, my dear Holborne, I fulfil the apostolic injunction, "Whatsoever ye do, whether ye eat or drink, do all to the glory of God!" Every meal is a sacrament to me. That's the simplicity of life! That's why they call me Simple Simon!'

The outburst brought his fellow-clubmen out of their apathy. One of them remarked that, while agreeing with the thesis, and admiring the force and beauty of its expression, it was unseasonable. He wished to tone down the exuberance of the old mystic, for the sake of the general feeling.

'Why, what is wrong?' said Iff more sedately. 'Not that anything is ever really wrong; it's all illusion. But you evidently think there's a great deal amiss; and' – he looked round the table – 'Sir Herbert seems to be at the bottom of it.'

'I will ask you to spare me,' spoke the judge; 'this morning I was compelled to perform the most painful duty of my career. Tell him, Stanford!'

'Why, where have you been?' said James Stanford, a long lean lantern-jawed individual who filled the Chair of History at Oxford University.

'Oh, I've been everywhere and nowhere,' replied Simon. 'But I suppose a historian would take the view – an utterly false and absurd view, by the way – that I have been sitting in my oratory at Abertarff, meditating, for the last two months. I have heard nothing of the world. Are we at war with the Republic of Andorra?'

Stanford leaned forward across the table, while the rest kept silent.

'You remember Briggs?'

'Knew him well at one time; haven't seen him for ten years or so.'

'Well, this morning Holborne had to sentence him to death for the murder of his nephew.'

'I say, Holborne, that's a bit thick,' ejaculated Iff, rudely. 'Just because you dislike the way he ties his neck-ties, to go and fit him out with a hemp cravat!'

'I am in no mood for your stupid jokes, Iff,' retorted the judge, severely. 'I had no course but to give effect to the verdict of the jury, which they gave without leaving their seats.'

'But your summing-up must have been a masterpiece of imbecility!'

'There was no defence, nor could be. Look here, Iff!' the judge broke out hotly, 'I thought you knew men. Can't you see I'm all broken up over this? I knew Briggs intimately; I was exceedingly fond of him; this has been the shock of my life.'

'Oh, well!' returned Iff, 'it is done now, and the best thing we can do is to forget it. Listen to what happened to me at Abertarff! One of those nasty skulking tramps came round and set fire to my barn. Luckily the stream was flowing at the time – as it does all the time – but, seeing the danger, it directed its course against the fire, and extinguished it.'

'Another miracle of Simple Simon!' sneered one of the younger men, who knew the old man chiefly from his reputation as a magician.

'Young man!' replied Simon, 'I drink to your better understanding – and your better manners. (Waiter, bring me another bottle of this Nuits!) I shall need much wine.' He fixed his small oblique eyes terribly on the offender. 'The difference between you and me is this,' he continued. 'I don't believe the silly story I have just told you; whereas you all do believe the silly story Stanford has just told me.'

'Come, come!' said Stanford, 'it is stupid to talk like this. You haven't heard the evidence. You're simply defending Briggs because you think you know him; because you think you know that he wouldn't have done such a thing.'

'Oh, no!' said the mystic, 'all men are capable of every kind of evil intention. But some are incapable of carrying such intentions into effect, just as a paralytic cannot walk, although he may desire infinitely to do so.'

'There was no difficulty about this murder. It was a quite plain shooting.'

'If you'll tell me the facts, I'll prove to you how you are wrong.'

'I wish you could, damn it!' interjected Holborne. 'Stanford has made a very special study of this case. He has been in court all the time, and he has verified every piece of evidence by independent research.'

'My university asked me to watch the case,' explained Stanford. 'As you know, I am a barrister as well as a historian. Briggs, of course, was at Magdalen with me, though I never knew him well. The Vice-Chancellor begged me to leave no stone unturned to discover a flaw in the procedure, or in the case for the Crown. I failed utterly.'

'Have you your notes with you?' asked Holborne. Stanford nodded. 'Suppose we adjourn to the smoking-room? They will take some time to read.'

'This is a lovely piece of luck,' remarked Iff, as they filtered into the adjoining room. 'I come back from my isolation, fairly bursting for distraction, and I walk right into the heart of a first-class fairy story.' But he was quite unable to communicate his

baulks, Peter, I hope I shall be there to do his work for him." There was thus the greatest possible animus.

'Four. Financial relations of the parties.

'The Briggs Family Settlement disposes of the sum of ninety-four thousand pounds. From one-sixth part of this Briggs drew an income; Clark, on the death of his parents, was entitled to a similar amount. The balance was held in trust for the next generation; that is, if either Briggs or Clark had children, the fund would be divided among these on their attaining majority. If Briggs died without children, the income would accumulate with the bulk of the fund in expectation of heirs to Clark; but if Clark died first, Briggs, as sole survivor of the earlier generation, would enjoy the income at present paid to Clark in addition to his own. Thus Briggs would find his income doubled if Clark died, while, if Briggs died, Clark could only benefit indirectly through his children, if he ever had any. Thus we see that Briggs had a strong financial motive for the murder; whereas Clark would gain nothing whatever. Nor had Clark any other motive for killing Briggs: on the contrary, he was always hoping to conciliate his uncle, and get him to help him, both directly in a financial way, and indirectly through his influence. The bearing of this will be seen later, when we touch upon the actual circumstances of the crime.

'Briggs had been making some elaborate experiments in connection with aircraft, and was in great need of money. Eight months earlier he had mortgaged his house, down to the Old Red Sandstone. This emphasises the motive for the act.

'Five. Conditions immediately antecedent to the murder.

'Clark had been staying in the neighbourhood, and had pestered his uncle intolerably. On one occasion he had come into the laboratory while the professor was eating his lunch. The butler, who was present, says that this was exactly two weeks before the murder. He remembers the date, because it was a Sunday, and lunch had been late, owing to his having been over the moor to church.

'He swears that he heard the professor say the following words: "Mark me, Peter. At the house I don't mind so much; but if you come bothering me here, I shall most assuredly have recourse to assassination." With that he had risen, gone over to his desk, taken up the revolver, and tapped it, nodding his head repeatedly. The boy, thoroughly scared, had slunk out of the laboratory.

'Six. The day of the murder.

'This was a Sunday. Briggs had again passed the night in the laboratory. The butler had gone over to church, leaving his wife at home. She heard the clock strike twelve, the signal for her to prepare lunch. Immediately afterwards she was startled by the sound of a shot; but she was not particularly alarmed, as small explosions frequently occurred in the laboratory.

'This fixes the moment of the crime within one or two minutes, and the medical evidence confirms it.

'She expected her husband to return at 12.15; he did not do so. She went out to look for him, and saw him driving towards the house with another man, who proved subsequently to be the vicar of the parish. Reassured, she returned to her kitchen.

'The butler, with the vicar, drove to the house, took out the horse, and went over together to the laboratory.

'This is what they saw. The professor was stooping over the body of Clark. He was apparently in deep thought, and seemed undecided as to what to do. The men were shocked into silence, and had the fullest opportunity of watching the actions of Briggs.

'He remained motionless for some little while; ultimately he laid down his revolver, which was still in his hand, and picked up a Browning automatic, which was firmly grasped in that of Clark. This was done with the evident intention of representing the death of Clark as the result of suicide.

'This latter weapon, although loaded, had not been discharged; the Webley had been fired recently, and the empty shell was still in the chamber; as appeared later. It was a Webley bullet which killed Clark; it had been fired from a very close range, estimated at two yards by the experts.

'The vicar now interrupted by a shocked exclamation. Briggs remained intent upon the automatic, looking at it as if it were some strange new object.

'The professor looked up as the two men approached him. He waved a hand. "Go away! go away!" was his only remark.

'The vicar sent the butler to fetch the police and a doctor; he himself remained on guard. Briggs went over to his desk, put the automatic on one side, and buried his head in his hands. It was clear to the vicar that he was stunned by the realisation of what he had done.

'But the vicar made a supreme effort. He went over, put his hand on his shoulder and shook him roughly. "Man," he cried, "Don't you realise what you have done?" Briggs answered: "By God, you bet I do." This is the only intelligible remark that has been drawn from him. A plain confession. Then silence.

'Seven. Subsequent events.

'It has proved impossible to rouse the professor from his apathy. He has made no defence of any kind. He remains crouched and inattentive; when addressed he merely repeats: "Go away! go away!" He would not even plead when brought into the court; he said nothing when he was sentenced this morning.

'The reason for this course of conduct is evident. He is a man of the acutest intelligence, and realising that he was caught practically in the act, is relying for escape upon simulation of dementia. We investigated the point on his behalf, supplying him with writing materials as if it were part of the prison routine. After a short time he seized on them with apparent eagerness. Here is what he wrote: "Revolve – gyre – explode

– balance – soul – wings – action and reaction." Under that he drew a thick line. The rest of the sheet is covered with abstruse mathematical formulae, evidently intended to impress us still further with the idea of madness; but although they are unintelligible to the mathematicians to whom they have been submitted, they are, wherever they can be understood at all, perfectly correct. He is certainly not insane. With great shrewdness, on the contrary, he has chosen just the one chance of saving his neck.'

Stanford paused.

'Is that all?' asked Simon Iff.

'All?' cried Holborne. 'Could any case be more complete? Two strong motives for murder, one of them urgent. Expressed intention to commit it; caught in the act of endeavouring to set up a defence; confession of the crime immediately afterwards; a subsequent attitude compatible only with the simulation of insanity. There isn't a link missing.'

'No, but I think there's a missing link!' snapped Simon Iff. 'In heaven's name, where are your brains, all of you? Look here; let me repeat that story, word for word, only instead of "Professor Briggs" let us say "the cabbage," or "the antelope," wherever his name occurs. You wouldn't suspect them, would you? And I assure you that Briggs is just as incapable of pulling a gun on a man as either of those! It simply would not occur to him to do it.'

'My dear man,' said Holborne, 'we all appreciate your attitude, I assure you; but facts are *chiels that winna ding*'

'Ah, facts!' cried the mystic, with as near a sneer as he ever allowed himself. 'Now look out, Stanford, I'm going to pump lead into you! You promised me two things: to give me all the essential facts, and to give me nothing but the facts. You are doubly perjured, you lost wretch!'

'Come, come, I say! I think I've given you an absolutely full and fair account.'

'No: omission number one. You don't say why he resigned from Owens College.'

'Yes, I do; he wanted to prosecute his experiments with less distraction.'

'Just half the fact; I happen to know that he was forced to resign.'

'What?'

'They simply could not get him to lecture. Either he would not go down to the classroom at all, or else he would forget all about the class, and start hieroglyphics on the blackboard!'

'What has that got to do with it?'

'Why, the problem is the man's mind. You say nothing about his mind. You don't even tell us the most important thing of all; which is, what is he thinking of at this moment?'

'Wondering if he'll dodge the noose,' put in the young man who had previously laughed at Simon Iff.

'Oh, no!' flashed back the mystic, 'with death so near him, he must be thinking of really important things – perhaps even of you! That would at least explain his dejection,' he added musingly. 'Having crushed it, let us pass on to my next point. You actually permitted yourself to draw deductions which are quite unjustifiable. You say that he exchanged pistols with the corpse, evidently to set up a defence of suicide. Evident to whom? You see, you fatally neglect the calibre of Briggs' mind. To me, it seems much more likely that he was quite preoccupied with some other matter. You judge him by yourselves. You assume that he killed Clark, and then argue "But if I had killed Clark, I should be thinking solely of how to escape." I say that if he did kill Clark, two seconds later his mind would have returned to the problems on which it had previously been at work. You men don't understand concentration: Briggs does. Besides all this, if he was going to put up the suicide theory, why not do it? He did not know that they had seen him change the weapons.'

'Hang it all, he confessed to the vicar.'

'That was my next point; he did nothing of the sort. He told the parson, emphatically, that he realised what he had done. But what was that? No word of any murder! The question is what he did do, and what he is doing now.'

'You're super-subtle,' said the judge. 'I wish you were right, but there's nothing in it.'

'Stick to the point! What does his whole attitude, from the very moment of discovery, indicate? Simply this: that he is busy.'

'Busy!' It was a general shout of derision. 'Busy! with his throat in a noose! Busy!'

'I ask your pardon, Stanford,' said the magician quietly; 'you are the historian here, and I beg you to correct me if I have my facts wrong. At the siege of Syracuse—'

'The Siege of Syracuse?' The company became hilarious, despite themselves.

'I forget who conquered it; it doesn't matter; but whoever he was, he gave orders that the great geometer Archimedes should be spared. The soldiers found him drawing figures in the sand, and asked him who he was; but he only said: "Get away! Get away! I'm busy!" And they killed him. Waiter! let me have another cigar and some more coffee!'

The judge was a little impressed. 'This is an amusing theory,' he said, 'though I'm damned if I can believe it. How do you propose to develop it?'

'Will you help me?'

'You bet I will.'

'Well, I want a copy of that jargon of Stanford's about "wings"; and I want five minutes alone with Briggs in the condemned cell.'

'Here's the paper,' said the historian.

'I'll get you an order from the Home Secretary this afternoon. I'll go now. If you can do anything, all England will have to thank you.' This from 'Anging 'Olborne.

'Oh, I can't do anything; but I think Briggs can.'

'Ah, you think he's shielding someone!' put in the objectionable young man for the third time.

Simon Iff lit his cigar with deliberation. 'I shall certainly be obliged to you,' he replied with studied courtesy, 'if you will recommend me some of the lighter types of sentimental detective fiction. Time often hangs heavy on one's hands in London, for one cannot always be certain' (he rose and bowed to the young man) 'of enjoying such very entertaining and illuminative conversation.'

'Look here, Iff,' said Holborne; 'come with me, and we'll see the Home Secretary right away.' They left the room together.

Two hours later, Simon Iff, armed with authority, was in the condemned cell. The professor was seated on the floor, his head sunk deeply on his breast, his hands playing feverishly in his long sandy hair.

The old mystic went close up to him. 'Briggs!' he cried aloud. 'I'm Iff. You know me! I won't keep you a moment; but this is damned important.'

The professor gave no sign that he had heard. 'I thought not,' said Simon.

The magician proceeded to insert his thumbs under the armpits of his old friend, and began to tickle him. Briggs wriggled violently, but only murmured: 'Get away!'

'I knew he was innocent,' said Simon gleefully to himself. 'But I see there is only one way to get him to talk.'

He sat down very positively in front of his victim, and began to recite from the paper in his hand: 'Revolve! Gyre! Explode! Action and reaction! Balance! Soul! Wings!'

Briggs looked up suddenly, savagely.

'You'll never do it!' went on the magician. 'You thought you did; but you didn't, and you never will. It's hopeless! Revolve – gyre – explode!'

'Damn you; get out!' said Briggs.

'Taking G as 31 point 2,' continued the torturer, 'and pi as 3 point 24156, and *e* as—'

Briggs sprang to his feet. 'You can't! You're getting it all wrong. Curse you! Curse you!' he yelled.

'You'll never do it! You'll never do it!' went on Simon implacably. 'Sin *theta* plus Cos *theta* equals twice the root of minus eight! You'll never do it! You'll never do it!'

'Are you the devil come to torture me before my time?'

'Good. No. I'm Simon Iff. And all I want to know is – how long do you need to finish your problem?'

'Oh, get out! Get out!'

'Seven times six is forty-four, and—'

'Get out!'

'Log one plus *x* equals *x*, minus half *x* squared plus a third *x* cubed plus—'

'Minus, you dolt!' shrieked Briggs. 'For God's sake, stop! You're putting me all out!'

'Some people are going to disturb you very soon by hanging you.' He squeezed the professor's windpipe till he gasped. 'Tell me how long you need to finish the problem, and I'll go, and I'll see you have all you need, and no disturbance.'

'A month, six weeks. Oh, go, there's a good fellow!'

Simon Iff went out without another word. He had an appointment to meet 'Anging 'Olborne for dinner.

'Well, I had to put him to the torture,' said the magician; 'but I got him to say one rational sentence. Now I want you to trust me in this. Get the execution postponed for a month. Don't disturb old Briggs. Let him have anything he calls for, in reason; he'll need little. As soon as he talks rationally again, you and I will go and see him in the cell. I can promise you this thing is going to clear up like a day in spring. April showers bring May flowers.'

Just five weeks later Holborne telephoned to Simon Iff to come round to his house. 'Briggs has woken up,' he said; 'for the last week he has been working with drawing materials which he had asked for. Suddenly he swept the whole thing aside and looked up at the warder. "Who the devil are you?" he said. "And where's the lab gone?" They rang me up at once. Let's get down.'

They found Briggs pacing his cell in a rage. 'This is an outrage!' he cried when he saw his friends, 'a damned outrage! I shall write to *The Times*!'

'You'd better talk to us first,' said Holborne. 'I may say that all England has been waiting to hear from you for some months.'

'I should say so,' retorted Briggs; 'and you may go and tell them that I did it! Alone I did it!'

'Are we not talking at cross purposes?' suggested the mystic mildly. 'Our mundane minds are preoccupied with the small matter of the murder of Peter Clark. And I don't think you did that.'

'Who? I? Of course not. Don't be so silly!'

'Well, you were there. We should really be grateful if you would tell us who did do it.'

'That fool Marshall, of course.'

'Marshall?' said the mystic.

'The farmer down by Saffield. Peter had seduced his wife. He tracked the boy up here – I mean up there; I can't realise this isn't my lab, you know, just yet. Followed him into the lab. Peter drew an automatic. Marshall got my Webley, and fired while the boy was hesitating. Then he threw down the gun, and went out.'

'Don't you think you might have explained this before?' said Holborne. 'Do you realise that you've been convicted for murder? If it hadn't been for Iff here, we'd have hanged you a fortnight ago.'

'How could I?' said Briggs irritably. 'You don't understand.'

'Well, explain later. We'll get you a free pardon as soon as possible. I may tell you that Marshall fell down a quarry the same night as the murder. He must have been half insane. But we never connected his death with your case. Anyhow, I'll see to it that you get out by tomorrow, and we'll celebrate it at the club. Perhaps you would make us a little speech, and tell us what you've been doing all these months.'

'All right. But I've got to see Williams right away'

'Williams!' said Simon Iff. 'So that is what it was, was it? I'll tell him today to come right down and see you; and we'll have him up to the dinner tomorrow, and we'll all live happy ever after!'

Two days later Briggs was on his feet at a great and special gathering of the Hemlock Club. Simon Iff was on his best behaviour, except that he would drink only tea, saying that his mood was exquisite and aesthetic like a Ming vase. Briggs, as the guest of honour, was seated on the right of the president of the club, on whose other hand sat Rear-Admiral Williams, a trusted member of the Secret Committee of Public Defence, which is known to just a few people in London as a liaison between Navy and Army, and a background to both.

The professor was no orator, but he did not lack encouragement.

'I want to thank you all very much,' he said. 'Of course we can't tell you just what this thing is, but Admiral Williams has been good enough to say that it's all right as far as he can see, and that ought to be good enough for us all. He's a jolly good fellow, Williams, and I wish we had a few more like him. I mean I'm glad we've got a lot more like him. Oh hang it! that's not what I mean either. I'm no speaker, you know; but anyhow I thought you'd like to hear just how I came to think of this damned thing.

'You see, I was working that morning – just finished verifying Mersenne's statement for p equals 167, rather a tricky proof, but awfully jolly, so my mind was absolutely clear and empty. Well, here comes the Watt and the Kettle business. That poor devil

Marshall runs in after Peter, right on his heels. Peter draws; I didn't notice particularly. Marshall gets my Webley and fires. I see it revolve and explode. See? Two ideas, revolve and explode. Nothing in that. Well, then Peter stays on his feet, quite a while, though he was dead. So I thought of reflex balance; you know, the automatic dodge in our soles; it goes wrong when you get locomotor ataxia. Then he gives a gasp, and puts his arms out, like wings; and then I thought of his soul flying away. Nothing in that. Well, then, Marshall throws down my Webley by the body and runs out. I picked up the gun, because its proper place was on my desk; I'm a man of precision in such matters; but to get to the desk I had to cross Clark's body, which should not have been there at all. It brought me up with a jerk. I stood by it, I dare say for a long time.

'Now here's the funny part. I was thinking, or rather something inside me was thinking, for I don't know to this minute who was thinking, or what. The next thing I remember, I was picking the automatic out of Peter's hand; and my mind clove to the contrast with the revolver, the way in which recoil is used to reload and recock the Browning.

'Then all the pieces of my mind flew together. I became conscious of an idea. I would make a duplex rotating engine to act as a gyroscope, with a system of automatic balances, operated by the recoil of the explosions in the engine. In other words, I had the idea for a self-balancing aeroplane, a true mechanical bird. When the vicar asked me if I realised what I had done, I naturally replied: 'By God, I should think I did,' or something of the sort.

'After that I got more and more absorbed in the details of the problem – can you wonder that I could think of nothing else? I remember nothing but a great deal of irritating talk around me, though with long intervals of most blessed silence. Then I woke up to find myself in the condemned cell!

'I want to tell you all how much I appreciate your kindness, and I thank you all very much.'

He sat down suddenly, exhausted and embarrassed. 'I hope I said the right thing. I'm such an ass,' he whispered to his neighbour. But the applause reassured him.

A little later the president turned to the old magician. 'I'm sure we are all keenly interested to hear how Mr Iff solved this case, and saved his friend – our friend – and helped him to do this great thing for England. I will call upon him to say a few words to us.'

Iff rose rather awkwardly. 'I'm afraid of boring you,' he said; 'you know I'm a bit of a crank, with theories about the tendencies of the mind.'

'Go on! Go on!' came from every quarter.

'Well, it's like this. If we get full of alcohol – any of us – too often and too steadily and too long, we begin to see rats and serpents and such things. We don't see horses and elephants. That is, our minds are machines which run in grooves – narrow grooves, mostly. We can't think what we like, and how we like; we have to think as we have been taught to think, or as our whole race has been taught to think by aeons of experience. So I know that there are certain ways of thought in which a given man cannot think, however obvious such ways might seem to another man. For instance, imagine a man of high lineage and education and wealth. By some accident he is stranded penniless in a far city. He is actually starving. He revolves the situation in his mind. He exerts his whole intelligence to meet the problem. But what does he do? There are thousands of ways of making money. He could get a job at the docks; he could obtain relief at a charitable organisation – no such method occurs to him at all. He does not look through the want advertisements in the papers. His one idea is to go to his consul or some person of position, explain his situation, and make a highly dignified loan. Perhaps he is too proud even to do that; ultimately it strikes him to pledge his jewelry. A thief in a similar position is equally limited; he looks about him merely for an opportunity to steal.

'Similarly, an Alpine guide will despair and die on a quite easy mountain if it be unfamiliar. It is the flower of biological success to be able to adapt oneself to one's conditions without effort. The whole of human anatomy is in accord with these theses. The brain is merely a more elaborate thinking machine than the rest of the body. The spinal cord thinks, in its own fashion. Even such simple organs as those which operate digestion have their own type of thought; and narrow indeed is the groove in which they move. A bee, inclosed in an empty flower pot, held against a window pane, will beat itself to death against the glass, though it could escape quite easily at the other end, if it were only capable of thinking outside its groove; similarly, the alimentary canal is so convinced that its sole duty is peristaltic action that it will insanely continue this movement when rest would save the man attached to it from a lingering and agonising death. We are all highly specialised and not particularly intelligent machines.

'In the matter of crime these remarks are peculiarly applicable; outside quite obvious things like picking pockets, you have merely to describe a crime to the police; they will tell you that five or six men only, in a city of as many millions, could have done it. Swindling has as much individuality and style as writing poetry – and it is infinitely more respectable! But I digress.

'With regard to this case, I knew at once that however much our friend here might have wanted to get rid of his nephew, it simply was not in him to do it. It is not a question of his moral outfit, but of his mental equipment.

'But much more interesting than this, which is, or should be obvious to us all, is this point: How did I manage to communicate with the man, absorbed as he was in some world beyond ordinary ken? I found him quite insensible to direct appeal. His situation? He did not know that there was any situation. I tickled him. His body responded automatically, but his mind was wholly disconnected by an act of his very highly trained will, and was merely conscious of an irritation and disturbance.

'So I determined to talk to his mind on its own plane. I knew from the so-called confession to the vicar that he was acutely conscious of having done something. I suspected that something to be of the nature of the solution of a problem; and by his continued abstraction, I knew that he had only got a general idea, and was at work on the details. So I told him that he would never do it, again and again. I knew that he must have had many moments of despair. It woke him up; the voice of his particular devil – we all of us have one; he always tells us to give up, that it's hopeless, that we shall never do it – that voice became material in mine; so he responded with curses. But that was not enough; to rouse him further I began to attack his mind by quoting mathematical formulae incorrectly. I knew that must upset his calculation, confuse him, rouse him to contradiction.

'The plan succeeded; he had been deaf – physically deaf, to all intents and purposes – to all other remarks; but to an attack on the fortress in which he was shut up he was bound to reply. I forced him to come to terms by refusing to stop the torture. He was distracted, upset, uncertain whether two and two still made four. In this way I made him tell me how long he needed to finish his work; and it was then easy to arrange a reprieve to allow him to finish his work.

'I'm sorry; I hope I have not bored you.' And he sat down abruptly.

NOT GOOD ENOUGH

'It seems a very interesting case,' interrupted Simon Iff.

'Well, sir,' replied the Assistant Commissioner, 'not at all, from your standpoint; there's no psychology in it. There seems little doubt that Haramzada Swamy killed the girl; he may have had one of fifty reasons, though robbery was evidently one of them. There are certainly some curious features in the affair, but none that would be of any interest to you.'

'You make me feel so fiery and martial,' returned Iff, 'that I shall certainly order some brandy. I hope you will join me. I originally interrupted your remarks in the hope that you would tell me all about the case. I have theories of my own.'

'If I may adopt your theory of drinking – which it gave me much pleasure to hear at the Hemlock Club – I am feeling narrative, and a pot of beer and a churchwarden is about my style.'

It was a summer afternoon. The place was the lawn of Skindle's at Maidenhead. The Assistant Commissioner of Police, Roger Broughton, had motored over to lunch with a friend, Jack Flynn, Editor of *The Emerald Tablet*, an advanced high-class review. They had found 'Simple Simon,' who had rowed up the river in a skiff outrigger from his summer cottage at Henley, lunching on the lawn in a peculiarly naïve, yet sumptuous, manner.

'In summer,' he explained to them, after the first greetings, 'meat heats the blood. I am therefore compelled to restrict my diet to foie gras and peaches.'

'But foie gras is meat.'

'The animal kingdom,' said the mystic, 'is distinguished, roughly speaking, from the vegetable, by the fact that animals have power to move freely in all directions. When therefore a goose is nailed to a board, as I understand is necessary to the production of foie gras, it becomes *ipso facto* a vegetable; as a strict vegetarian, I will therefore have some more.' And he heaped his plate.

The new-comers laughed; no one ever knew when to take the magician seriously.

'What's the drink?' asked Flynn. 'It's a new one on me.'

'This is a Crowley Cup No. 3,' he said. 'So named after its discoverer. Take a large jug, the larger the better; half fill with selected strawberries; cover the fruit with Grand Marnier Cordon Rouge; ice carefully; fill up with iced champagne, the best obtainable. Stir the mixture; drink it; order more, and repeat. A simple, harmless and wholesome beverage.'

'A temperance drink, I suppose?' queried Broughton, laughingly.

'Certainly,' replied the magician; 'in my recent journey to America I was careful to obtain an exact definition of what was and what was not alcoholic. Drinks which contain less than forty per cent alcohol come under the general heading of the Demon Rum; their sale is restricted in every possible way, and in many states prohibited altogether. Drinks containing more than forty per cent of alcohol are medicines, and are sold in the drug stores without restriction of any kind.'

'But that champagne reduces the percentage, surely?'

'Champagne forms no part of the drink; it is used merely to dilute the medicine itself.'

Broughton, who knew Iff but slightly, looked bewildered, and appealed mutely to Flynn, who knew him well. 'You mustn't laugh or cry,' said he; 'you must just let your brain expand, and try to get the point of view.'

'You mustn't think I'm laughing at you, Mr Iff,' apologised Broughton; 'we don't forget your masterly work in the case of Professor Briggs.'

So lunch proceeded; it was only at the end, as it were by accident, that Broughton had mentioned the murder which had stirred London a few days earlier.

Broughton, having been accommodated with the primitive refreshment indicated as harmonious to narrative, began his story.

'Ananda Haramzada Swamy is a Doctor of Philosophy of the University of London. He is thirty-three years old, and has a wife, to whom two children have been born—'

'By a previous marriage? I asked because of your phrasing.'

'It's a long story, and has nothing to do with the case. Haramzada Swamy – let us call him the Swamy for short – is a Eurasian; and curiously enough, it is his father that was black, a Tamil. The mother was an Englishwoman.'

Simon Iff pursed his lips.

'He is a man of loose morals,' continued the Commissioner, puffing at his long pipe, 'and rents an apartment, or rather a bedroom with bathroom attached, on the fifth floor of St. Noc's Mansions, near Hyde Park. This room is a mere assignation chamber. It is furnished only with a divan, a wardrobe and a small cupboard full of liquors and tobacco. The room is, however, sumptuous in the Oriental style, and the walls are covered with obscene pictures and photographs. He allowed no one to enter, naturally enough, but used to send his wife weekly to dust it.'

Simon Iff could not restrain another gesture of disgust.

'The whole block of apartments is "under the Rose," as it were; but – please note this – although in a general way we ask no questions as to the doings of the inhabitants and their visitors, we maintain a correspondingly strict supervision of them, on the watch always for anything outside what I may call honest, straightforward immorality.'

'I see,' said Iff, thoughtfully.

'The last masked ball of the season took place at Covent Garden on the first Saturday in July. Haramzada was present, and won a prize for the magnificence of his costume, that of a Persian prince of the 15th century. I may mention that he was a critic of art, as well as of philosophy. He left on the arm of a masked lady, who had not competed; no one had seen her face. They went direct in a taxi to the Swamy's flat. This was about 3 A.M.; the time is uncertain. It may have been much earlier. A few minutes before five, however, and this time is accurate within ten minutes, Haramzada was seen, in his ordinary day costume, creeping down the stairs, stealthily and swiftly. The lift man only saw him by chance. He had gone up to the fifth floor on a ring, only to find no one there. Irritated, he left the lift, and looked over the stairs, just chancing to see the Swamy as he crossed the hall. He supposed, naturally, that the lady was with him.

'Now comes the hand of Providence. It was the custom of that wicked elevator attendant to search the rooms of the tenants, when he was sure of their absence, and not too likely to be caught off duty; his hope was to find what he has since described to us, in a burst of candour, as "perks"; *videlicet:* any small objects of value which seemed to him unlikely to be missed. So he pulled his lever, and went up to the fifth floor, opened the Swamy's flat with his master-key, and entered. The light was switched on.

'The body of a nearly naked woman lay before him. Blood was pouring from a wound in the head; but life was perhaps not extinct. Daniels, as the man was called, acted quickly and properly. He called a doctor on the telephone, describing the nature of the wound, and then notified us. He then had a messenger sent for the man who would normally have relieved him at seven o'clock, so that he might remain on guard.

'When our men arrived, a minute before the doctor, we found Daniels trying various primitive methods of first aid.

'Detective-Inspector Brown took in the situation at a glance. While the doctor attended the wounded woman, he telephoned headquarters, and a general alarm was sent out for the apprehension of the Swamy.

'At 5.45 the doctor, who had been working energetically to restore consciousness to the victim of the outrage, pronounced life extinct. Daniels was dismissed, but two minutes later he reappeared with the news that the Swamy was in the street outside.

'Brown flung open the window, and cautiously looked out. The Swamy, with his coat collar turned up, and his slouch hat pulled well over his face, was approaching the door in a very furtive manner. Brown determined to give him a free hand. He telephoned down to the other porter to go up to the ninth floor, so as to give the Eurasian his chance to enter unobserved. The door of his flat was closed, and the party awaited developments.

'Unfortunately there was no place where our men could hide. The wardrobe would only have concealed one man. In a few minutes the steps of the Swamy were heard coming up the stairs; a key was pushed into the lock; the door opened; our men seized him. The creature collapsed, mentally and physically, in their arms. It was actually found necessary to apply restoratives. The wretch had evidently counted upon ample leisure to dispose of the body.'

'Why had he left the place at all?' This from Jack Flynn.

'Evidently in order to dispose of the proceeds of the robbery. Doubtless he has some safe cache. Well, to continue. When he came to, he was arrested and cautioned. He said, however, that he knew nothing about the matter at all; denied that he knew the woman, or of her presence. Charged at the police court with the murder, he reserved his defence, and was remanded for a week. The same day he wrote out a long rambling statement which I can only call fantastically feeble. The following week he was committed for trial. He then issued another statement, entirely contradicting the former, and endeavouring to explain it away. It is, however, as contrary to ascertained fact as the earlier effort. I expect the truth is that the animal is almost mad with fear. He had probably arranged a safe way of disposing of the body, which was upset by the chance of the early discovery of the crime.

'The murdered woman was identified by her husband on the afternoon following the crime. As you know, it was old Sybil Lady Brooke-Hunter, a leader of the smart set, fast, alcoholic, a plague to her old husband, who should have divorced her ten years ago. She haunted every shady rendezvous in London in search of adventure—'

'Well, she found one all right!' put in Jack Flynn.

'She did. That night she was wearing over ten thousand pounds' worth of jewelry, like a fool, as she was. It has all disappeared. Daniels noticed that she was wearing it when she entered St. Noc's Mansions.

'The curious part of the case is her husband's attitude. He refuses to believe that she was ever guilty of an indiscretion in her life; insists that her wanderings in London were purely philanthropic, that she must have been drugged or chloroformed or hypnotised or what not. He is an old man of Puritan views: "if I believed her guilty of so much as a flirtation," he said to Brown, "I would thank God that He had punished her!" And he's the only man in London who doesn't know what she was. She was a barmaid, you remember, as common as the bar she served, when he married her. Lord, but there are some fools about!'

'Is that the story?' asked Simple Simon, quietly.

'I think that's everything. We haven't found the jewelry. There's no reason to suspect any other man in the case. The facts are all against Haramzada Swamy, and his six-cylinder double-action lying doesn't help him.'

'How was she killed?'

'There is a large open fireplace in the room. He had caught up the poker, and brained her. It was lying by the body, with blood on it.'

'So you rest your case there?'

'All right, my lord!'

'Oh no! I'm for the defence,' said Simon Iff. 'Here are some facts quite incompatible with the theory that Haramzada Swamy committed the murder. Only last month I happened to be reading his book on Buddhism.'

Jack Flynn threw a laughing glance at the Police Commissioner, as much as to say, 'now the fun begins.'

'In this book,' pursued the mystic, 'he conclusively proves himself innocent of this murder. I will not distress you with the details, but the main argument of the book is that the Buddha was a hedonist, that he called pleasure the greatest good. This argument is based on one fact only: this, that the Buddha declared everything to partake of the nature of sorrow – which is just one-third of the truth – and that his whole system is therefore devoted to the escape from this Everything.

'But pleasure has nothing to do with this. Sensation is only the second of the *skandhas* in Buddhist psychology; at the very second gate on the path, pleasure and pain must be recognised as illusions, and rooted out of the mind. Why, desire in any form is the very cause of all sorrow and evil in the Buddhist system.

'Now, gentlemen, we are none of us Buddhists; we may dislike Buddhism very much; and we may call it too abstract, too remote, too barren, too bitter, too ascetic, too formal, too metaphysical, too almost anything you please. We may abuse the Buddha as an Atheist, as a nominalist, as a rationalist, as a sceptic; no one can do more than argue the contrary. But if we represent the Buddha as a high priest of pleasure, and his religion as a religion of pleasure, we should be shut up in an asylum – or, if not, realise that we have given ourselves away. For there is only one type of sane man who can fail to recognise the elevated morality, the self-abnegation and nobility, the lofty compassion, the almost unthinkable passion for renunciation, which mark Buddhism. To this day the *bhikkhus*, or rather *pongyis*, of Burma, where alone the true canonical doctrine has been preserved free from corruption, are men of the most exalted virtue. They are often ignorant by our standards; but of their sincerity, their purity, their general morality, there is only one opinion. Even the missionaries, whose one chief task is to slander the people among whom they live, have failed to destroy the reputation of these noble men. I lived among them myself for three years; I might have joined their ranks, had I felt myself worthy to do so. My lord and gentlemen of the jury, I confidently leave the fate of my unfortunate client in your hands.'

'Heaven help me!' cried Broughton, 'he's never mentioned the murder at all!'

'Ah that's what you think – and what I think,' laughed Flynn; 'but in reality he has torn your case to pieces!'

'If you're not convinced of his innocence,' retorted Simple Simon, 'I really despair of human reason. However, let us get a few fresh facts. What, besides this book on Buddhism, which I have dealt with so effectively, do we know of his antecedents?'

'As it happens,' said Jack Flynn, 'I can tell you a lot. It's an ugly story, too, and I'd hang him on that alone, if I were judge and jury. It's not evidence – like what the soldier said – but this being a psychological investigation, it is pertinent. Broughton has told us how he might have done the murder; I will prove to you that he was just the sort of man who would have done it. And I am assuming that the little lecture on Buddhism was intended to prove that he was the sort of man who would not.'

'Precisely,' said the mystic.

'Well, he had a side to his nature which he did not put in his book.'

'Impossible,' said Iff. 'Men's books are always artistic images of themselves. Of course, this thing has no creative genius at all, and he's a hopelessly bad critic, absolutely incapable of discerning greatness, just as a fly, whose time-sense is extremely rapid compared to ours, cannot perceive movement in a body which travels more slowly than about a yard a minute, or as an amoeba could not understand generation or even gemmation. But, such as his mind is, he must put it into every page he writes.'

'I'm going to show you he has a criminal mind.'

'We're listening,' acquiesced the old magician.

'When he was at the University of London, there was a small scandal, which rather shows the man's quality. He made friends with a man, who confided to him the secret of a love-affair with a woman of the streets. Haramzada Swamy tracked the girl, and tried to buy his friend's letters to her, to blackmail him. The girl was loyal and told her lover, who horsewhipped the Eurasian soundly. Shortly after taking his degree he married an Englishwoman. I should like here to make the point that she was a sex-degenerate.'

'I agree.'

'I agree.'

'She was quite crazy about him – "too fond of her most filthy bargain" – and they were happy for a while. Then the snake entered Eden in the shape of a little music-teacher, another degenerate, again a case of heredity, for she was marked with Hutchinson's Teeth. You know what that means?'

Both men nodded gravely.

'The Swamy and his wife were great on preaching Free Love. The snake – and she had the temper of a Russell's Viper! – agreed entirely. A few weeks later she became Haramzada Swamy's mistress. She was so passionate and jealous that she resolved to upset the marriage; this decision was confirmed by necessity, for she became *enceinte*, and the Swamy, who hated the idea of children, showed every sign of throwing her off. She actually had the nerve to go to his wife with her story! After various violent scenes, a divorce was decided upon. The Swamy, who has no will of his own, was seized upon by the music-teacher, and never allowed to stir a foot, under penalty of other tempests, until the divorce was granted, and she dragged him to the registrar's. With amazing cynicism, they had a wedding breakfast, with cake complete, and the baby playing on the floor!

'The Eurasian now had more freedom; he got an appointment in India, and on one excuse or another managed to leave his wife and child behind. Arrived in Hindustan, he set up a harem of dancing-girls, and was happy. But the necessity of a periodical remittance to the fair Florrie soon began to prey upon his mind. He determined to bring her out; for one thing, an English wife might do him some good socially, for of course he was an outcast from both English and native society; for another, it would be cheaper to keep her in India than in England; for another, perhaps, the climate might kill both wife and child, and put an end once and for all to the expense. As it happened, one of his best friends, a full-blooded Indian who also had a taste for white women, and so did not mind mixed marriages and their results so much as his stricter countrymen, was returning to India. He put his wife in charge of this man. On the voyage she promptly seduced him. When the husband became aware of the fact, some six weeks after they landed, he made some mild protest, but did nothing. In fact, they travelled about together, all three, for some months. But the woman was absolutely shameless, caressing her lover even in front of the servants, and the contempt of these – all true Indians are extremely moral and decent, even to prudishness, whether they are polygamists or not – the contempt of the servants became so marked that even the Swamy could not stand it any more. He insisted on a separation. In vain the wife implored her lover to take her with him; he had too much sense for that. It was ultimately agreed that his child – for she was again pregnant – should be treated by Haramzada as his own; and she was to go back to England with her husband.

'Two years later found them in New York. Florrie picked up another lover, greatly to the relief of the Swamy, who hated paying for her dinners. This man, however, insisted on her playing the game: a straight divorce, a straight marriage and no more foolishness. Haramzada gladly agreed. But just at this moment it was discovered that Florrie was not so penniless as had been supposed; a rich uncle wrote, offering to make her his heir, his only son having been killed in France. The Swamy instantly altered his whole position. He went back to his wife, pleaded with her, begged her forgiveness, played on her pity – ultimately got her to waver. She was now again with child by the new lover. All this time, however, Haramzada was carrying on an intrigue with a German girl, the regular Broadway type. At this moment of sham reconciliation the uncle died. Haramzada resolved on a masterstroke. During her previous pregnancy the sea-voyage had come near to causing one, if not two deaths. He hated his wife most bitterly – of course, such a creature is utterly incapable of love for anybody; he was her heir, and besides, her life was heavily insured. So he insisted on her going to England to see her children, and attend to the estate left by her uncle. She became dangerously ill, and miscarried; but she lived. The Swamy then hurried over to join her. What was his chagrin to find that her uncle's money was left in trust for her children, so that he could not touch more than a small necessary income?

'He was in great financial straits; robbery and murder were certainly in his heart. Can we be surprised that his hand followed suit? It only needed the opportunity; and the other night he evidently had it.'

'You have failed utterly,' replied the mystic with some scorn, 'to grasp the mind of the thing. All because you will not read his book on Buddhism! He had no opportunity to rob and kill. Any other, yes; but not he. Consider all his acts. We find extreme meanness, selfishness, cunning, the most ignoble attitudes throughout, never a glimpse of anything vertebrate. This is all in accordance with his view of Buddhism. He had a thousand "opportunities" to kill his wife in India. But not what he, Ananda Haramzada Swamy, calls opportunities. He won't put his neck in a noose; not he! He hopes that the Indian climate may kill her; he hopes that the sea-voyage may kill her. But he won't do more in the way of murder than say: "Darling, do come out; I'm so lonesome," or "Darling, do go to England; I'm so anxious about the sweet babies." He's cold as a fish, but he's never brutal, and he's a coward to the bone.'

'That's rather cute,' said Flynn. 'Now you mention it, I'll do another lap. I got this story from Florrie's lover No. 3, by the same token. You wouldn't blame him for talking. I've known him twenty years, and he was all broken up – just in that state when one has to tell someone or burst. He told me how he left her. When she went back to the Swamy he cut off short, and she's been plaguing him ever since to take her back. He won't. Well, one day he had slapped her gently for impudence. She was going to try to make a slave of him, as she had of her yellow and black men. She said to him: "If only Ananda had beaten me I would have loved him always." So evidently he never had.'

'What was your friend doing in that galley?' asked Broughton.

'Oh, he's a crank. Saw good in her and wanted to save her. Damned fool! But of course he knew that the only way was to be like a rock – never to yield an inch to any of her gusts of passion. If the Swamy had not murdered their baby I think he might have won.'

'I agree with your estimate. Your friend's quixotic,' said Simon Iff. 'My interest is in schools, not in hospitals. To let the degenerates drop out is the true kindness – certainly to the race, perhaps even to them.'

'To get back to the point,' said Broughton. 'You still hold the Swamy innocent?'

'I do. Buddhism is a religion of the most dauntless courage. The whole force of the universe from all eternity is challenged by him who would become an *arhant*, as they call what we call saints, only it's more than that. The saint has God on his side; the would-be *arhant* has nothing but himself and the memory that there was once a man who won in that incalculable struggle. Yet you suggest that the man who not only fails to appreciate this courage, but even to perceive it, is brave enough to kill a woman with a poker, and even to return to the house where her corpse lies. If he had killed her, by some chance, he would have fled – fled, fled to the darkest corner of the earth!

'No, sir, Dr Haramzada Swamy did not kill that woman!'

A newsboy ran across the lawn. 'Extry! Extry!' he shouted, 'full confession by the Injun!'

Broughton and Flynn jumped for the paper; Simon Iff only poured himself another glass of brandy.

Flynn's professional eye first caught the paragraph. 'Textual!' he exclaimed gleefully, and began to read aloud.

'As everyone knows,' the confession began, 'Lady Brooke-Hunter was notorious for her immoralities.'

Iff chuckled, and rubbed his hands.

'She had become old and unattractive. I met her at the Covent Garden ball. She begged me to pass the night with her.

I took pity on her, and consented. A little before five o'clock she said she must go home. I remarked, as she rose, upon her obesity, and suggested, out of pure kindness, a way to remove it by practising Indian clubs. I illustrated some exercises with the poker. Suddenly I had a dizzy fit; the poker slipped out of my hand and struck her on the temple. Horrified, I rushed out to find a doctor; but in my bewilderment I could not do so. Then I bethought me of the telephone, and returned home to use it. To my surprise I found the police in the flat. Daniels must have stolen the jewels.'

Broughton gave a great shout of laughter. 'I don't believe a word of it,' he roared. 'Nor will the jury.'

'Nor do I,' said Jack Flynn. 'Disgusting! Look how he throws all the blame on everyone else. All but the deathblow – and that's an accident. Dizziness! No, sir, he had that poker by the business end all right!'

'I don't altogether believe the story myself,' murmured Simon Iff, in a rather deprecating manner. 'He never struck that blow. I'm humbled over this thing, gentlemen; I can't see the truth. And what's more, I can't see why that Eurasian can't tell the truth; I'm sure he could save his neck if he did. I can only think of two possibilities: one, that to tell the truth would disclose some other crime, some meaner crime, some vileness possible for him; two, that, somehow or other, he doesn't know the truth himself. Or is it that he's incapable of truth as such? Confound it, I've been so keen to argue with you that I've not put on my thinking cap!'

'I tell you what,' interjected Flynn. 'Write me an article on the case; once the man's condemned, as he will be, I can print it. And see if you can get a reprieve on the strength of his book on Buddhism!'

'You shall have the copy tomorrow. It's time I paddled up to Henley. So long!'

The old man went down the lawn to his skiff. He was not as straight as usual; and as he pulled off, the others thought his figure an incarnate Note of Interrogation.

Not long afterwards the case was tried. Haramzada Swamy was found guilty, as the whole country had anticipated. The next day the article by Simon Iff appeared in *The Emerald Tablet*.

'I am no orator, as Antony was,' it began. 'I come not to praise Caesar, but to postpone his burial'; and went on to recapitulate in a precise and logical form the arguments already advanced on the lawn at Skindle's. The wife of the condemned man had delightfully given permission for the publication of her nauseating story. In her own eyes she was a heroine. The article ended by saying that murder depended upon three things: will, capacity and opportunity; that in this case all three were apparently present, but that the type of murder was one of which Dr Haramzada Swamy was incapable. 'I'm not saying this to flatter him. But he is incapable of it. A snake may bite you as you walk unwarily in the jungle or across the *jhil*.' (Simple Simon delighted in exotic words.) 'But a snake will never kick you. I would stake my life that Dr Haramzada Swamy is innocent of the murder for which he has been condemned to death. HE IS NOT GOOD ENOUGH. If he is hanged, it will not be, perhaps, altogether a miscarriage of justice. But it will be an error of law.'

The publication of this essay threw England into convulsions of merriment. Their beloved crank had surpassed all his previous efforts. Even the little clique of his admirers were compelled to represent this article as mere sublimity of paradox.

A week later came another explanatory confession from the Swamy, equally unavailing as it was unconvincing. A week before the date set for the execution he broke down altogether, made 'true and full confession of deliberate murder,' disclosed the place where he had hidden the jewels, which were duly recovered, and was received into the Roman Catholic Church.

Reconciled thus with his Maker, he strove to obtain the pardon of his fellows; but the Home Secretary 'declined to interfere' in a voice that destroyed a reputation for suavity of manner that he had been forty and three years in building!

At the appointed moment Ananda Haramzada Swamy, Doctor of Philosophy, suffered the extreme penalty of the law.

Jack Flynn was playing billiards with Simon Iff in the Hemlock Club. 'You must be pretty fed up,' the editor remarked. 'I don't want to rub it in; but that final confession must have made you feel pretty sore!'

'Not a bit!' replied the mystic cheerfully, 'it's all of a piece with the rest of his life. He never touched that woman; and, now, I'm quite sure he was not only innocent but ignorant. Oh, I know what you want to quote: "A fool is more wise in his own conceit than seven men that can render a reason." Don't mind my seniority!'

'Hang it,' said Flynn, 'I don't mean that; but – you – well, you are a bit obstinate, you know. By the way, here's a letter for you. I brought it in from the office. More abuse, I suppose!'

Simple Simon put the letter in his pocket, and they finished their game.

'I'll read the abuse,' said the mystic, taking a chair by the fire, 'it may be amusing. *Qui m' abuse m' amuse!* to alter one of Wilde's remarks a trifle.' But as he read his face did not lighten; and at the end he put the letter away carefully in his pocket. Flynn watched him in silence. For ten minutes Simon Iff remained as still as an Egyptian god. Then he rose.

'I want you to come to my house,' he said, 'I have something particular to discuss.' The other fell in with his mood; they walked in silence across the park to Carlton House Terrace. The footman must have been trained to expect his master, for the door opened as the old magician and his friend reached it. Simon Iff led the way up the old marble staircase, with its satyrs and fauns at every corner, until they came to a small door of brass, on which was a relief, a curious pattern of geometry, with Greek capitals. This door opened at the touch of a secret spring. The room within was draped in black; it was lighted by a plain lamp of silver, such as one sees in churches in Italy, with a red glass and a wick floating in olive oil. At one end was a great chair of carved ebony, above which was a single blue ostrich feather. Below the lamp stood a small square altar, painted white, on which were a golden cross and a rose of scarlet enamel. On a small desk before the chair was a great book, on one side of it a naked sword, on the other a pair of balances.

'I want you to sit in that chair,' said the magician to Flynn. 'This is my House of Judgment. But I want to ask you to judge in this case; I am not qualified to judge the matter that I am about to put before you; for I have already recorded my opinion.' Flynn, a little awed, obeyed with a certain diffidence.

Simon Iff stood before the altar, drew the letter from his pocket, and began to read:

> My dear Sir:
>
> This letter is due to you, for you understand the nature of Truth.
>
> In your article upon the recent murder, that of my wife Sybil, you had no knowledge of what happened, for you had no facts on which to base your judgment; nor indeed was the discovery of the murderer the object of your enquiry; you confined yourself to proving not what did happen, but what could not have happened. In this limited investigation you were extraordinarily accurate.
>
> I have adored my wife since the day I met her; more, I have revered her with a passionate devotion as of a

man to a goddess. For this exaggeration of proper feeling I am punished.

I have always believed in her purity and fidelity, despite numerous rumours which reached my ears. But in July last I allowed myself to be tempted by an old friend, who was importunate, and justifiably so, since the honour of his own wife was involved in a way to which I need not refer more precisely.

I therefore purchased a disguise and presented myself at the Costume Ball at Covent Garden on the 3rd of July last. I soon recognised my wife, and observed her conduct closely. She danced several times with Dr Haramzada Swamy, and they left the ball together. I followed them; I still hoped that no serious wrong was contemplated. They went up in the lift; I took the opportunity to slip upstairs, unobserved. I was just able to distinguish into which door they went. At this door I waited and listened. In ten minutes I had heard enough. The blow was crippling; I must have fainted; for the next thing I remember is that I was sitting on the floor, but alert and intent upon the dialogue. I heard first the whimpering voice of the Eurasian, punctuated with a nauseating giggle. 'It is a most unfortunate necessity, dear lady,' were his first words. She replied with a torrent of oaths and curses. She was apparently defying him, but I could not tell why. 'You see, I put the dainty little thing away,' he said, 'where you can't find it, dear lady; you surely wouldn't deprive your adorer of such an intimate souvenir. And you mustn't make a noise in the flat, must you, dear? We're so respectable here.' Again she cursed him, but in a lower voice. I had no idea she knew such words; some of them I did not know myself. 'Your husband will certainly kill you outright, or divorce you at the very least, if he finds you out; personally, I'm inclined to think he'll kill you, you know. He's such a severe type of man, not at all a ladies' man, dear, I'm afraid. So you'll give me all those pretty little toys, and you can make up a story about a robbery; I'm sure he'll believe you, you're so clever, rather like my wife in some ways.'

I cannot describe the impression made by his little whining voice, but it made me screw up my face like one who has bitten into a sour apple. I heard the noise of clattering; evidently Sybil had thrown her jewels on the floor. 'I'll take the rings, too,' he went on. 'It will be better for the story you'll tell him. I'm advising you in your own interests, you know.' Again the horrible little giggle. 'Such a sensible little lady!' he added, 'and now I'll get my hat and coat and leave you for an hour, so that you can dress and go home. I'm so sorry I haven't got a maid to help you.'

By instinct, I suppose, I withdrew from the door and concealed myself beyond the elevator. Let him go out, jewels and all; my business was with my wife.

He slipped hurriedly and stealthily out, as I could see through the gilded palings of the elevator shaft, ran up one flight of stairs and rang for the lift. The moment the machine started he began to run down the stairs again. At the same moment I strode across the landing and struck my fist upon the door. It yielded; he had left it unlatched.

You, Mr Iff, are probably the one person in England who can imagine – that is, in the proper sense of the word, make an image of – my state of mind. Coincident were, firstly, a blaze of wrath at her treachery of a lifetime; and, secondly, a habit of protection. She was an infamous woman who had destroyed the life of a good man; and she was also a helpless woman who had been blackmailed and robbed by a man more wretched and infamous than she.

I honestly believe that my brain had become dull to the former of these impressions; that my main conscious idea was to comfort. But I had not counted on the effect of the scene itself. Some people, as you know better than anybody, visualise everything; some don't. Tell one man to shut his eyes; then whisper 'church': he will see twenty familiar churches in a moment just as if they were in front of him. I am not one of these men. When my eyes are closed I see nothing. So, though I had the fact of adultery in my mind, I had nowise staged the act in the theatre of my mind. Therefore the opening of the door was a new shock. Sybil was standing, clad only in a light garment, and that torn across; her hair was dishevelled, her eyes bloodshot; the paint and powder on her face – that was itself a revelation of infamy to me.

The divan was in a state of disorder; everything testified with open mouth to the atrocity perpetrated against me. I believe that doctors would prove – I believe that you yourself would agree – that I became totally insane for the moment. This is probably then true; yet what I know of it is this, that I lost all sense of anger or distress. She said one word, a word of extreme filth, at seeing me. I simply stooped, picked up the poker, and struck her down. I had no idea that I was killing a woman; so far I will agree with you; my act was entirely reflex, like a knee-jerk, or as one brushes a fly from one's head without consciousness of its presence.

Still without true volition, I went out and closed the door. The interview was at an end. I walked down the stairs; Daniels, preoccupied with predatory ideas, apparently failed to see me at all.

Why did I not explain this a week or two ago? Sir, I was desirous that a certain half-breed cur should meet with his desert.

This done, I am at your service. I shall not kill myself; you may hand my letter to the Public Prosecutor; I hope at least to go to the gallows like a man.

REGINALD BROOKE-HUNTER

Jack Flynn broke the long silence which followed the reading of the letter. But his voice, in that dim hall, sounded like the echo of some god's voice – some god who was speaking elsewhere, a great way off.

'I take this letter as true.'

'I also.'

'What am I to say?'

'What I am to do?'

There was a long pause. Finally Flynn's voice boomed, fainter and hollower than before.

'Nothing.'

The mystic held the letter in the flame of the lamp. He blew the last ash lightly into the air, and led the way out of the House of Judgment.

In the study they found Lord Juventius Mellor, a young disciple of Simple Simon, who acted as his secretary. 'Little Brother,' said the magician, 'I want you to ring up Sir Reginald Brooke-Hunter and ask him to spare me an evening as soon as he can to dine at the Hemlock Club. I want to persuade him to stand for Parliament. I think we can promise him the Presidency of the Board of Education; Willett-Smith is resigning, you know. Tell him, of course, that the Prime Minister has asked me to see him about it.'

The young man went off, while Jack Flynn stared. 'So that's how you do things?' he said.

'Yes,' said the old man, 'we do things by the simple process of doing them. You remember the butcher in the *Tao Te Ching* – no! in the writings of Chuang-tzu! – who cut up oxen until he did it without knowing that he did it, so that his knife never needed sharpening, and his arm never tired? Which muscle of our body never tires? The heart, though it works all the time. Why? Because our silly muddled brains don't meddle with it. That is the art of government. So, having found the perfect man to educate our youth, we slip him in!'

'Good,' said Flynn, laughing. 'A double murderer! If I rob a bank will you make me Chancellor of the Exchequer?'

'Oh, no,' said the magician with a sigh. 'I must have a perfect robber. Our best thief is Lord Chief Justice, as you know; but for the Exchequer, we ought really to look on the other side of the Atlantic. Oh, dear! What a pity they threw that tea into Boston Harbour!'

'By the way,' said Flynn, 'to return. I still don't see why Haramzada confessed to a murder he knew he didn't do.'

'As I said before – and you had ears, and heard not – it was all of a piece with the rest of his life. He did not know the truth about the murder, though in one of his numerous confessions he probably told all he did know. He wasn't believed; he knew there was no chance to cheat the gallows; so he thought he would cheat God. Splendid idea! to die for a crime one has not committed. One goes to heaven with colours flying, one of the noble army of martyrs. It's a cowardly idea, a liar's idea—'

'A Eurasian's idea?'

'Yes; and that's the ghastly thing about it. His nature is not his own fault, any more than a toad's. But this I want you to understand, that as sex is the most sacred thing in life, so the sins of the fathers are visited on the children most of all in violations of eugenics.

'Whether it's tubercle, or alcoholism, or marriage between kin too close, or sub-race too distant, the penalty is fulminating and disastrous. Generation becomes degeneration.'

'What's the remedy?'

'Oh, we might restore the worship of Dionysus and Priapus and Mithras, perhaps, for a beginning. Then there's the question of polygamy, we shall have that; and harems; and groves, with sacred men and women. You can read it up in Frazer if you're rusty.'

But that was the worst of Simple Simon. He would constantly change the key of his discourse without warning; and unless you knew him as well as Jack Flynn, you could never be sure when he was joking.

INELIGIBLE

Simon Iff, the mystic, was the most delightfully unclubbable man in the Hemlock Club. But all was forgiven to a man of his powers – and of the extraordinary charm which he radiated, even when sitting silent in his favourite window. It was a genuine triumph for anyone to get him to talk. One Christmas evening after dinner, the editor of *The Emerald Tablet* informed him that the Committee had made a new rule to the effect that the eldest member of the club who happened to be present must tell a story under penalty.

It was a genial lie, and appealed to Simple Simon's sense of humour. 'What sort of a story?' he grunted.

'Tell us of the first occasion on which you used your powers of reading men.'

The mystic's face darkened. 'It's poetic justice. You shall be well paid out for your impudence in inventing new rules. The story is hideous and horrible; the gleams of heroism that shine in it only serve to make the darkness more detestable. But you shall hear it: for one reason, because the result of my interference was to save this club, and therefore the universe (which revolves about it) from irreparable disaster.

I

'His Majesty's sloop *Greyhound* was wrecked in the Bay of Biscay in the month of April, 1804, of the vulgar era. She was carrying despatches to Sir Arthur Wellesley. Captain Fortescue, who was in charge of them, escaped the wreck, in company with a sergeant of marines named Glass. They found themselves cast ashore on the north coast of Spain. Many days' journey lay between them and their destination. However, they fell in with friendly guerrillas, who aided them in every way. But the luck changed when they were within sight, almost, of their goal. A battle had taken place; and Masséna, retreating, had chosen a line which cut them off completely from Sir Arthur's positions. Becoming aware of these facts, they broke away at right angles towards some mountainous country, intending to traverse it, and, descending the opposite slopes, to fetch a compass round about the flank of the French army. Unluckily for them, they were perceived as they crossed the first range of hills, and a detachment of light infantry was sent in pursuit.

'Immediately on seeing this, their Spanish guide took to his heels. They were thus not only hunted but lost. They knew the general direction of the British lines; they had about two hours' start; otherwise they were hopeless.

'They gained the crest of the second range just as their pursuers, spread out in a long line, swarmed over the first; but in beginning their descent, which was excessively steep, with only a narrow mule-path among the enormous tangle of rocks, they came upon a cottage; and the path ended. Fortescue recognised the place, for the guide had spoken of it on the previous day; it was the home of a desperate brigand, a heavy price upon his head from French and English alike. They had no choice, however, but to go on. Chance favoured them; the brigand was away, leaving but one drowsy sentinel. Fortescue ran the man through with his sword before he had time to seize his gun.

'The two Englishmen found themselves alone in the cottage. Could it be defended? Possibly, but only for an hour or two; reinforcements would arrive in case of a prolonged resistance. The vital question was to find the way to the valley.

'The cottage was perched upon the edge of a cliff; they could see the path winding away below. But access to it seemed to be cut off. Glass it was who reasoned out the situation. There must be a way through some cellar. Quickly he searched the cottage. A trap-door was found. Glass descended the ladder. All was well. He found himself in a large room, half filled with barrels of gunpowder. A narrow door gave exit to the path below.

'"Come on!" cried Fortescue.

'"We shall be caught, sir," answered Glass. "Let me stay here; I can delay them long enough to let you get away." The officer saw the good sense of this; his first duty was to deliver the despatches. He wrung Glass by the hand, and ran out.

'The sergeant of marines knew that he had barely an hour; but he had a plan in his mind. His first action was to twist a long match from the gunpowder to that window of the cottage which looked over the cliff; his next to strip himself and the dead sentinel of uniform, and to dress the corpse in his own. He then found a piece of rope and hanged the body in the doorway.

'He dressed himself in the brigand's best clothes; but, not content with masculine adornment, he covered himself with the all-sufficing mantilla. He was a smooth-faced good-looking boy; with the shawl, he made a quite passable Spanish girl – to the waist.

'He then took up his position at the window by the door, so that the lower part of his body was hidden, and awaited the pursuers. It was near twilight when they arrived.

'Their leader grasped what he thought to be the situation. "Where is the other?" he cried.

'Glass smiled divinely. Unluckily for him, he knew only a few words of any tongue but English. But a finger to his lips, and the sign of beckoning, reassured the others; they filed down the path, and crowded into the cottage.

'"Where's the girl gone?" cried the leader, "are we in a trap? Look to your arms, men!"

'Before he had ended, Glass, who had run upstairs to the other room, had touched fire to the match. "Let Samson perish with the Philistines!" he roared, and at the same moment leaped from the window.

'The cottage sprang into the air, killing every man in it; Glass lay fifty feet below upon a thorn-bush, with one arm broken and many bruises, but good for many another day's adventure.

'A day later he had scrambled to the valley, where a shepherd showed him kindness, and led him by a circuitous route to the British lines.

'Here he found himself a hero; for Fortescue had seen the explosion, and given all due credit to his companion. But the sergeant's arm went ill; for default of treatment, it had begun to mortify; the same night the surgeon removed it at the shoulder.

'Sir Arthur Wellesley himself came to the hospital to salute the gallant lad. "Be glad it is the left arm"; he said brusquely: "Nelson lost his right. And for you, we'll salve you with a commission as lieutenant in the regular army."

'Glass was overjoyed; the loss of his arm seemed little, if he could have a sword at his side, epaulets on his shoulder, and the rank of an officer and a gentleman thenceforward.

2

'Lieutenant Glass, obtaining six months' leave, at the end of the campaign of 1805, returned to his ancestral croft on the northwest side of Loch Ness to find that both his father and mother were dead. A friend in Inverness had warned him as he passed through; but piety made him persist in his journey; he might as well spend his leave there as elsewhere.

'It was a stone cottage of two rooms, set high above the loch upon the moor. Away westward stretched the desolate slopes of

Mealfourvonie; below, the gloomy waters of the loch growled with the cold anger of the Highland winter.

'There was no other habitation for a couple of miles. Around the croft was a niggard space of cultivated land, yielding with bitter toil a few oats and a few potatoes; nothing more.

'The laird, Grant of Glenmoriston, had sent a man to take possession of the croft, pending instructions from Glass. He was a sturdy lad of sixteen years, self-reliant and secretive; he had kept the cottage in excellent order, and tilled the soil as well as a man might in that inhospitable country. Glass kept him on as permanent gardener and servant; but he was rather an accentuation than an alleviation of the loneliness. However, on the first Sunday, when the lieutenant walked down the Strath Errick to church, he found himself the apple of the congregational eye. Even Chisholm, the minister, a dour narrow Calvinist of the oldest school, was moved to make a complimentary reference in his sermon; and, after kirk was over, carried away the officer in triumph to the manse, there to share the miserable substitute for a meal which is all that any Scot dare eat on Sunday, in apprehension of the Divine displeasure.

'Chisholm was a widower. He had one daughter, skinny and frosty, with a straight back, thin lips, a peaked nose, bad teeth and greedy eyes. But her flat chest almost burst as the idea came to her, as it did in a flash, to become Mrs Lieutenant Glass. It was a way out of her horrible environment; despite the lost arm, he was a fine figure of a man; he was a hero, had been mentioned twice in despatches since he had gained his commission; he would get his company very soon. Promotion was quick in those days. Captain, major, colonel – possibly even General Glass! She saw Strath Errick left far north; instead, presentation at Court, social advancement of every kind; possibly a stately visit or so later on, and a snubbing of the local gentry who had always looked down upon the minister's

3

'That is not such a horrible story, so far, is it? And there seem few elements of tragedy. Well, we go on.

'After the banishment of Napoleon to Elba, Major Glass rejoined his wife. This time there was no trip to Bath. The cottage was furnished with just the extra things needed for Joshua; Glass himself helped to till his own land, and market the produce.

'Ada resented this bitterly; there was no open quarrel, but she hid poison in her heart. "I have six thousand pounds in bank," he had said, "but there's no hope of a regiment now the war's over; let us play safe a year or two until we have ten thousand; then we can live where we like, as gentlefolk, and make a greater career for the boy." She saw the prudence of the plan, and could not argue against it; but she really hungered for social pleasures, as only those do who are not born with the right to them.

'The boy himself gave no concern on the score of health; he was hardy as a Highland lad should be; but his disposition troubled his father. He was silent and morose, was very long in learning to speak, and he seemed lacking in affection. He would lie or sit, and watch his parents, in preference to playing. When he did play, he did not do so simply and aimlessly, as most children do. Even when he broke his toys, he neither cried nor laughed; he sat and watched them.

'Major Glass went back to his regiment at the end of 1814; his wife once again took shelter with her father. But a month later the minister fell ill; in March he died. Another minister occupied the manse; and there was nothing for Mrs Glass but to go back to the croft on the moor. The boy still worked on the little apology for a farm; and his sister came to help tend Joshua, and assist in the housework.

'In 1815 Major Glass was present at the decisive battles in Belgium. And here befell the fate that transformed this simple career into the tragedy of horror which you have insisted that I should relate to you. The major was in command of the last party that held the shot-swept walls of Hougomont; and he rallied his men for their successful stand against Napoleon's final and desperate effort to regain that critical point. The British were flooded at one spot; Glass, with a handful of reserves, led a rally, and broke the head of the French dagger-thrust. And then it was that a sabre-stroke beat down his guard; a second blow severed his sword-arm. He was carried hastily to the ruins of the farm, and his wound bandaged; but Napoleon, seeing his troops flung back, ordered another artillery attack; and a cannon-ball, breaking a rafter of the building, brought down the remains of the roof. A heavy beam fell across the major's legs, and crushed them.

'Such, however, was the prime soundness of his constitution that he did not die. It was a helpless, but perfectly healthy, torso which was carried some months later into the little croft above Loch Ness. His wife recoiled in horror – natural horror, no doubt. It was only when he told her that the surgeon said that he might live fifty years that she realised what infinite disaster had befallen her. All her schemes of life had gone to wreck; she was tied to that living corpse, in that wretched cottage, probably for the rest of her life. "Half-pay," she thought; "how long will it take now to make up the ten thousand pounds?"'

4

'If Ada Glass had been a woman of intelligence, either good or evil, she would have found some quick solution. But her thoughts were slow and dull; and she was blinded by the senseless hate in her heart. Her days had been infinitely dull, ever since her father's death; now, in that emptiness, a monster slowly grew. And her husband understood her before she did herself. One day he found it in his mind that she might murder him; she had dismissed the girl who had helped her, saying that now they must save money more carefully than ever. His quick wit devised a protection for himself. Calling the boy Andrew, now a stout fellow of twenty-six years old, he sent him into Inverness for a lawyer.

'With this man he had a long private interview, during which several papers and memoranda were selected by the lawyer from the major's portfolio, in accordance with his instructions.

'That evening the lawyer returned to the croft with the new minister of Strath Errick, thus disposing of the difficulty caused by the inability of the soldier to sign papers.

'Later that night, Mrs Glass having returned from Glenmoriston, where she had been sent so as to have her out of the way, the major told her what he had done.

'I have placed my money, he explained, in the hands of two excellent trustees. If I should die before Joshua comes of age, the whole will be left to accumulate at the bank, and you must live upon the pension you will receive as my widow. The capital will then be transferred to him at his majority, under certain restrictions. But if I live, I shall be able to bring the boy up under my own eye, and therefore as soon as the capital amounts to ten thousand pounds, we shall not only be able to educate him properly, but to bring him, while yet a child, into those social connections which seem desirable.

'Once again the wife could raise no protest; but once again her heart sank within her.

'Yet, as the days went by, the hate devoured her vitals, began to eat her up like some foul cancer. She began at last, deliberately, to pass from thought to action, to make her husband's life, hideous at the best, into a most exquisite hell.

'You are perhaps aware that our greatest misery is impotence to act freely. Deprivation of a sense or a limb is wretched principally because of the limit it sets to our activities. This, more than anything else, is at the root of our dread of blindness or paralysis. You remember Guy de Maupassant's story of the blind man on whom his family played malicious tricks? It seems peculiarly cruel to us because of the victim's helplessness. Now, of all the savages upon the earth, there are none more ferocious or more diabolical than the Highlanders of Scotland. Dr Frazer gives many instances of incredibly vile superstitions, in vogue even at this hour as we sit in the enlightened Hemlock Club. "Scratch the Russian and you find the Tatar?" The sex-instinct is especially powerful in the Celt; where it is nobly developed, we find genius, as among the Irish; but where it is thwarted by a religion like Calvinism, it nearly always turns to madness or to cruelty – which is a form of madness.

'To return to the point, Ada Glass set her wits to work. The hideous loneliness of the Highlands in the eye of all those who have not the true soul of the artist is a true antecedent condition to morbid imagination; and Ada Glass and her sexlessness the pendant to it.

'She began operations by neglect. She postponed attention when he called for her; and she became careless in the preparation of his meals. He saw the intention, and agonised mentally for weeks. Ultimately he resolved to kill himself in the only way possible, by refusing food. She retorted by the tortures of Tantalus, setting spiced and savoury foods under his nose, so that he was physically unable to resist – after a while. The fiendishness of this was heightened by its manner: the whole plan was carried out with inconceivable hypocrisy on both sides. She would use such words of love and tenderness as had never occurred to her on the honeymoon.

'Such courses are set upon a steepening slope of damnation. Soon ideas incredibly abominable came into her mind, perhaps suggested by the tortures of hunger and thirst to which she submitted him. For she varied her pleasure by offering him sweet-smelling foods that on tasting were found to be seasoned with salt and pepper, so that only extreme hunger would make a man eat of them. Then she would excite his thirst by such hot dishes, and put salt in the water which he demanded to assuage it. But always she would apologise and blame herself, and weep over him, and beg forgiveness. And he would pretend to be deceived, and grant his pardon. And then she would speak of love, and – but no! gentlemen, I must leave you to dot the i's and cross the t's in the story.

'Presently – after months of this miserable comedy – she took it into her head to excite his jealousy. (I want you to remember all the time, by the way, that these people were absolutely alone, with no distraction whatever save the rare and formal visits of the minister. And Glass was far too proud and brave to speak of what was going on.) She began to set her cap at the gardener. As I said, she had no more feeling than a saucepan; it was all bred out of her by Calvinism; but she knew how to act. She knew her husband's own stern view of marriage; she thought she would break his spirit by infraction of her vows. For that is what it had come to, though she probably did not realise it; she wanted to see the hero of a dozen campaigns snivel and whine and whimper like a cur. Many women indulge a similar ambition.

'So she set herself to snare the gardener. It was an easy task. He was a rough, rude labourer, a vigorous, healthy animal. And she wooed him as she had seen the fine ladies of Bath do with their cavaliers. Once his first shyness was overcome, he became her slave; and from that moment she began to play her next abominable comedy. Her husband must suspect for a long while before he knew for certain. And so she laid her plans. She watched the fleeting thoughts upon his face hour by hour. Soon she imbued her lover with hatred of his master; and she persuaded him one day to kiss her in the room where the major lay on his pallet of straw. She had long since deprived him of a bed, urging the trouble of making it up. The spasm of pain upon his face, the violent words that he addressed to her, these were her greatest triumph so far. She went on with her plan; she went to the utmost extremity of shamelessness; the gardener, with no sensibility, thought it merely a good joke, in the style of Boccaccio. For weeks this continued, always with increasing success; then Glass suddenly made up his mind to bear it – or something in his heart broke. At least it became evident that he was no longer suffering. Her refinement imagined a new device, a thing so abominable that it almost shames manhood even to speak of it. She resolved to corrupt the child. Joshua was now old enough to understand what was said to him; and she privately coached him in hate and loathing for his father. Also, she taught him the pleasures of physical cruelty. (I told you this was a hideous story.)

'Major Glass, deprived of all exercise, had become terribly obese. He was a frightful object to look upon; a vast dome of belly, a shrunken chest, a bloated and agonised face. Four stumps only accentuated the repulsion. It was only too easy to persuade the child to play infamous tricks. By this time she had thrown off the mask of her hypocrisy; she taunted him openly, and jeered; she spat out rivers of hate at him; and she let him know that she no longer wished the society of Bath, that she was glad that he might live half a century; for never until now had she known pleasure. And she incited the boy to stick long pins into the helpless log.

'"You're not even like a pig any more," she laughed one night, "you're like a pin-cushion!" And Joshua, with an evil laugh, walked up upon that word, and thrust three pins into the tense abdomen. He ran to his mother gleefully, and imitated the involuntary writhings of the sufferer.

'This game recommenced every night. The intervals were but anticipations of some further abomination. He had long prayed audibly for death; now he began to beg her for some means of it.

'She laughed at him contemptuously. "If you hadn't settled the money as you did, I might have thought of it. After all, I ought to marry again."

'He answered her in an unexpected vein.

'"I'll make it easy for you. One night, when snow threatens, take Joshua down to a neighbour's. Pretend you are ill, and stay the night. Leave the door open when you go; I think a chill would kill me. And I want to die so much!"

'She gloated over the weakness of his spirit.

'"If you'll swear on the Bible to do that," he went on, "I'll tell you the great secret." Instantly she became attentive: she divined something of importance.

'"When I was in Spain," continued Glass, "I was quartered in a certain castle belonging to one of the grandees. He was an old man, paralysed, as helpless as I am today. His lady, at the first of the invasion, had buried the family treasure in a secret place. There are diamonds there, and pieces of eight, and many golden ornaments. They told me this one night under the following strange circumstances –" He broke off. "Give me water! I'm faint, of a sudden."

'She brought it to him. Presently he continued in a firmer voice. "One day we were attacked by a body of French troops – a reconnaissance in force. The castle was surrounded. I and the few men with me, our retreat cut off, prepared to defend ourselves, and our host and hostess, to the last. We were driven from floor to floor. But one of my men, sore wounded, lying below, determined on a desperate resource. He managed to crawl to the cellar, where great quantities of wood were stored, and he set it on fire. The French, alarmed, beat a hasty retreat from the precincts; I and my few remaining men pursued them to the gates. The fight would doubtless have been renewed, but at that moment the plumes of our dragoons appeared in the distance. The French sprang to their horses and rode off. I returned hastily to the castle, and we succeeded in extinguishing the fire. I bore the lady in my own arms into the fresh air, through all the smoke; two of my men rescued the old count. That afternoon they had a long conference together, and in the evening said that they had decided to tell me of the treasure.

'"In case misfortune should happen to them both, I was to pledge myself to convey the paper, which they then intrusted to me, to their only son, who was fighting in our army. I readily agreed. A few nights later the devil tempted me; I opened the paper. It was a mass of meaningless figures, a cipher; but I had the key. I worked it out; I went to the place indicated; there lay the treasure. But my heart smote me; not mine be a fouler than the sin of Achan! I replaced the earth. I returned, and prayed all night for a clean heart.

'"Shortly afterwards I changed my quarters; we were retreating. On our next advance I returned to pay a visit to my kind hosts. Alas! They had been murdered by a band of guerillas. As duty bade, I sought the son; but again I was too late: he had fallen in battle on the third day of our advance.

'"I have kept the secret locked in my breast; I would not touch the treasure, though it was now as much mine as anybody's, because I had been tempted. But now I see necessity itself command me; I am no longer man enough to endure the torture which I suffer—" Here his voice broke. "I will give you the key if you will do as I say; and when I am dead you are free to go and find it."

'Ada Glass made her mind up in a moment. She was eager. After all, there were other pleasures in the world than – what she had been enjoying.

'"Take the Bible," said Glass, "and swear!"

'She did so without a tremor. It was an oath to commit murder; but the Scots mind does not halt in such a case.

'"Good," said the major. "Now look in the uniform case; you'll find the cipher sewn into my tunic; it's in the lining of the left sleeve."

'His wife obediently unpicked the stuff. A small map, with a row of hieroglyphic figures, was in her hand.

'"Now tell me the key!"

'Glass began to breathe with difficulty; he spoke in a faint voice. "Water!" he whispered. She brought him a full glass, and he drank it, and sighed happily.

'"The key's a word," he said.

'"What? I can't hear you." She came over close to him.

'"The key's a word. It's in the Bible. I'll remember it if you'll read the passage. I marked it in the book. It's somewhere in Judges."

'He was evidently speaking with the greatest possible effort; and even so, she could hardly hear him. She brought the Bible across to him, but it was too dark to read; so she fetched the lamp and set it upon the floor at his side.

'"About Chapter Eight: I can't remember."

'"Chapter which?"

'"I think it's eight."

'"Eight?"

'"Yes." It was the faintest murmur. He had been like that for some days; now it alarmed her; he might die without revealing the secret? She fetched some whisky, and gave it to him to drink.

'"Oh, is it this," she said, "about Samson in the mill? It's marked in red."

'"Yes," he said, still very faintly, "read from there."

'She sat down by his head, and began to read. After each verse she questioned him; he signed to her to go on. Presently she came to the verse "And Samson said 'Let me perish with the Philistines.'"

'"It's there," he said. "It's—" His voice died away to nothing.

'"You're not ill, are you?" she cried in alarm.

'"'m going to die," he gasped out, word by word.

'"Tell me the word!" she screamed, "For God's sake, man, don't die first!"

'"It's— " Again the voice died away.

'"Do, do try!" she said, putting her ear over his mouth. Instantly, with utter swiftness, his iron jaw closed like a vice upon her ear.

'She pulled away, screaming, but she might as well have tried to dislodge a bulldog. Indeed, she helped him to roll over toward the lamp. A jerk of one stump, and the oil flamed among the straw of the pallet.

'The dying shrieks of his mother woke Joshua. He jumped out of bed, came into the room, saw the two bodies writhing in the flames. He clapped his hands gleefully, and ran out into the snow.'

'I admit it's a pretty ghastly story,' cried Jack Flynn, who had evoked it; 'but I don't see what in heaven's name it has to with you, and saving the Hemlock Club!'

'Because, my young friend, as usual, you have not condescended to wait for the end of it. The events that I have been at the pains to recount occurred during the usurpation of George III, so-called.' (It was the club custom always to speak of the Georges as usurpers.)

'My part begins in the year 1850 of the vulgar era. In February of that year an anonymous book entitled *A Jealous God* was published through a well-known firm – I forget the name for the moment. The book made a great stir in religious circles. The author, evidently an authority on theology, had taken the teachings of Victorian Science as a commentary, and his work was principally intended to complete the ruin of Deism. The author insisted upon the cruelty and imbecility of nature; pointed out that all attempts to absolve the Creator from the responsibility must culminate in Manichaeism or some other form of Dualism; and proceeded to interpret the wisdom of the Deity as His ability to trick His creatures, His power as His capacity to break and torture them, and His glory as witnessed chiefly by the anguish and terror of His victims. I need hardly say that the author, although anonymous, professed himself a member of the Exclusive Plymouth Brethren.

He was proposed for this club, as a prominent and deserving heretic of great originality, and I was the youngest member of the committee appointed to enquire into the matter. I took an instinctive dislike to the unknown author; I opposed the election with all my ability. I proved that the book was perfectly orthodox, being but an expansion of John 111:16. I pointed out that Charles Haddon Spurgeon had endorsed the principal teachings of the book; that evangelical clergymen all over England were doing the same thing, with only negligible modifications; but I was over-ruled.

'We then proceeded to enquire into the authorship of the book; we discovered that his name was Joshua Glass.'

A thrill of terrible emotion passed through the old man's hearers.

'I refused to withdraw my opposition. I investigated, and I discovered the facts which tonight I have set forth before you.'

'But there's nothing in the rules against that sort of thing!' interrupted one of the men.

'You will not let me finish!'

'I beg your pardon.'

'I studied the facts with intense care; I tried to trace to their true source the phenomena displayed by all parties. Ultimately I came to a conclusion. I began to believe that in this case a physical correspondence with the mental and moral state exhibited might exist...'

'And so?' interrupted Jack Flynn, excitedly, a gleam in his eye.

'I insisted upon a physical examination. I found a malformation so curious and monstrous that, despite his human parentage, it was impossible to admit him any title to membership of our race.'

There was a long silence of complete astonishment. The old magician opened his case, drew out a long cigar, and lighted it. 'Anyone coming my way?' he asked, rising.

'I'm coming, if I may, sir,' said Flynn, sprightly. 'I want to talk mysticism for an hour, to get the taste out of my mouth.'

2

Simon Iff in America

WHAT'S IN A NAME?

Simon Iff was a magician. A magician is a superstitious idiot. Therefore, Simon Iff, travelling to America, carried nothing but a convenient hand-bag.

Why?

'To carry more,' said he, 'is to pretend that America is a long way away. This would be an insult to the ghost of Robert Stephenson; I do not mean Robert Louis Stevenson. It is not safe to insult ghosts.'

Now there were certain people who believed that the madness of 'Simple Simon' was as carefully calculated as a table of logarithms, and those of this creed who happened to be in New York, at the Cunard Pier, just as he crossed the gangway from the *Mauretania*, were rejoiced to observe that his absurd fear of ghosts had saved him from any similar emotion in the presence of the customs house officials!

'Through already?' cried his friend, Keynes Aloysius Wimble of *The Literary Chyle*, a native of Birmingham, England and sometime of Nairobi and a very minor college at Oxford, but esteemed by Simon on account of his astonishing talent for ecclesiasticism, his profound knowledge of foreign tongues, his atrocious insolence of manner, and his over-mastering determination to get to the bottom of everything that came his way.

'My dear man!' replied Simon heartily, 'I am "through" on one condition – that you do not ask me to spell it t-h-r-u.' This was his first and only criticism of the American continent. Like Hamlet – there cracked a noble spirit – the rest is silence.

'This way, then,' cried Wimble, 'this way for my tin Lizzie.' Thus unassumingly did he refer to his tremendous roadster. The journalist was a power in America. Without the *Chyle* no one would have known what not to read. As nobody would have read anything in any case, the value of the publication was universally agreed to be immense. Its circulation was beyond anything ever discovered by Harvey, and it paid its editors almost as well as if they were man-milliners or cooks.

'Thought I'd drive you to the cottage,' said Wimble. 'Lizzie's been eating her head off all the week. Besides, we have to pay a visit of condolence. Our local saint has lost his wife in the most distressing circumstances. It appears that she took bichloride of mercury in mistake for aspirin.'

'Ah! the chemist's boy in *Pickwick*!'

'Don't joke! The old boy's the best fellow alive, and he's utterly broken up over it.'

'I thought "local saint" was sarcastic, perhaps.'

'Not a scrap. He's not ostentatious about it; but he does good everywhere, and is beloved by everybody.'

'Religious?'

'Intensely so. Has a bluff frank way with him that you and I might think irreverent; but it's better than cant and hypocrisy. He's very highly thought of in the Presbyterian Church.'

'Ah! a Scot?'

'Name of Burns. Phineas Calvin Zebedee Burns.'

'No, no!' cried Simon Iff, 'I don't like that. The man certainly poisoned his wife!'

Wimble roared with laughter. 'Dear old England! I used to feel that way myself; but eight years here have put me hep to all the bug-house monikers. (You may as well begin to learn the language.) Where a member of the United States Senate, finding himself named Hogg, can call his daughters Ima and Ura respectively, there's nothing in a name!'

'I've heard that. It's a stupid joke, of course.'

'No; it actually happened. There's no background. Anything can happen; anything. Anything!'

The car crossed the great bridge, and gained new speed as the open country welcomed it. The day was frosty, and a black sky to northward held snow in its shroud. The two friends fell to silence; then Wimble broke out into a passionate attack on the Belgians – for this was in 1911, before the year of the Great Enlightenment. He was not content to blame isolated officials for the atrocities of which his paper published weekly photographs; he proved that the fault lay in the inherent cruelty of the Belgian nature. He even blamed Cléo de Mérode and Anna Robinson, thus casting a slur upon Charlemagne and George Washington.

Simon Iff did not appear particularly interested. 'When I was in the Congo,' was his only remark, 'I had boils. I ate standing for three weeks. Nobody sits down in the Congo!'

Presently the assailant of King Leopold desisted in favour of topographical information. 'That,' said he, pointing, 'is the house of P.C.Z. Burns. *Zee*, not *zed*, please! Inside and out, materially and spiritually, one of the best houses in the section.'

'It is really quite delightful,' said Iff, though he would probably at the moment have preferred a wattle hut in Annam.

'We shall lunch with Phineas, for it is two hours more to the cottage. He has a perfect cook. Pray for Squab Soup, and a Celery Cream Broil of Saddle Rocks!'

'I have too long omitted these items from the schedule of my daily supplications.'

The car passed through magnificent wrought brass gates swung upon marble pillars, and entered a long avenue of trees. It was evident that love had made a paradise, not money alone. Simple Simon expressed his pleasure.

'Yet Burns lives a life of Spartan simplicity. Here at least, wealth has not corrupted Republican manners.'

'Was that what I saw on the boat?' murmured the magician.

Wimble displayed the renegade's obstinacy.

'There's something fine and big about the frankness of these people; there are a few Anglophile snobs, but the real American is a man all through. And Burns is one of the best of them.'

The man himself was pacing the terrace of the house when the car drew up before the door. His whole attitude denoted dejection, even agony; yet one could see that he had braced himself to meet his sorrow. 'It is the Will of God' was written on the face that he lifted to see whose importunity disturbed his grief. By his side waddled a somewhat self-important little man, a chubby good-humoured parson dressed in rustic black cloth, his face rubicund and plump, his attitude rather like that of Monsieur Rostand's chanticleer, who believes that he has just caused the sun to rise. His fingers gripped an oblong of drab paper.

'My dear Wimble,' cried the little fellow, running forward as Iff and his host alighted, 'you have arrived at the psychological moment! Our friend's munificence has surpassed itself; we are to have a Memorial Hospital. He has given me a cheque for a million dollars!'

'It is very touching,' remarked Simon Iff. 'It reminds me of the Sultan who built the Taj Mahal.'

'I didn't know they had hospitals in Turkey,' said the little minister.

'No?' said Simon Iff, politely.

Phineas Burns walked up, greeted Wimble with subdued warmth, and extended a hearty hand to Simon. The conversation became general for a few moments; presently the Presbyterian went away, hugging his cheque, and Burns asked them to be seated in the library. 'I want you to stay over dinner,' he said; 'it is full two hours to our friend's cottage. And I should like you to meet my daughter. I am no physician for such grief as hers; I beg you to do all in your power to distract her thoughts from our bereavement.'

Simon Iff liked even the word 'dinner' as applied to the midday meal; it smacked of that Republican simplicity which his chance companions on the *Mauretania* had somehow missed.

The door opened, and a slight girl came in. Her father was repeated in her. His tallness, his leanness, his narrow brow, his thin lips, his pale complexion, his solemnity, his nervous tension; all these were already marked in the child of fifteen years old. But what most struck the old mystic was the extreme misery in her eyes. Burns himself had none of that; rather was his eye moist, genial and humorous. And Iff saw too that she moved as if under some most powerful constraint. So unpleasant was the impression that he was shocked into silence.

Burns left the room, making an excuse about 'ten minutes with my secretary'; Wimble started an animated conversation with the girl, whose name was Claudine, and Iff never stirred. But his face darkened and darkened as the conversation went on. Only after some minutes did he seem to pull himself together.

'I think we shall have snow soon. There is a heavy black sky to windward,' he said, addressing himself pointedly to Claudine. 'Don't you think so?'

The girl hesitated. 'I shouldn't be at all surprised,' she answered at last.

Simon Iff did not reply. He rose abruptly, clapping his hand to his forehead, and went out on to the terrace.

Wimble was cynically amused. Was his old friend in 'love at first sight'? He had always had the reputation of an ultra-English aplomb – and here he was, violently agitated about absolutely nothing. However, he went on talking to Claudine.

Iff, on the terrace, was literally kicking his way from nowhere to nowhere. A lank gentleman with a little black bag came up to him.

'Excuse me, Sir,' he said, 'can I do anything for you? I'm a doctor, and you look to me in pretty bad shape nervously.'

'Nerves still holding out,' replied Iff grimly. 'I only landed this morning. But you can help me – if you were in attendance on the late Mrs Burns. You were?'

'Surely.'

'She died of mercury bichloride poisoning?'

'Surely.'

'Where did it come from?'

The doctor was silent.

'I ask,' pursued Simon Iff, 'because, in England, don't you know, bichloride of mercury doesn't grow on bushes.' He had been warned that he would be expected to say 'don't you know' as often as possible, and was trying to behave.

'I never thought to enquire,' replied the doctor at last.

'Do you mind if I put that down in my note-book?' said Simon joyfully. 'It's a wonderful phrase. It explains the world as nothing else does. "I never thought to enquire." Columbus did, don't you know? Which shows that there are two sides to every question.'

The doctor thought that the old man was decidedly in need of his skill.

'You never prescribed mercury for anyone in the house?'

'Certainly not.'

'Ah!'

'What are you suggesting?'

'Nothing. I was waiting for you.'

'Well, good morning.'

'Good morning.'

Simon Iff drifted back to the library, and gazed blankly at the books. There was a wilderness of theology, a sobriety of 'classical' English and American novelists, nothing modern. At the end of the shelves was a strong room door, and the old man looked upon it with a wistful eye.

'Where is your father's place of business?' he asked Claudine.

'Wall and Vine,' she said, after a pause.

'He must be a very busy man to make so much money?'

Another pause. 'Oh yes!'

'I hope he never brings his business home?'

Still hesitation from Claudine. 'Oh yes! he has an office at the other end of the house, where he works at night, sometimes.'

'I think we shall have snow.'

Wimble was thoroughly irritated by Iff's imbecility, and might have said something but for the return of Burns, who took them to the dining-room.

The conversation took the subdued turn natural to a house of mourning. Once the bereaved husband spoke in low tones of his dead wife's goodness. He hardly touched his soup. The second course was a planked shad. Wimble in a few well chosen phrases introduced this remarkably excellent fish, and instanced its delicacy of flavour as an example of the effeteness of Europe. As it happened, however, the shad was abominably cooked. It was impossible to avoid remark. 'Mary was so beloved by all,' explained the host; 'nothing has gone right in the house since she passed over.'

Simon Iff hated people 'passing over' or 'being taken from us' when they had merely died, for he hated every kind of camouflage. He observed his host narrowly. It struck him that his words were entirely false. Unless his whole power of psychology were at fault, the man was boiling over with impotent anger. It was quite incommensurable emotion, out of all relation with any visible circumstance.

'I understand, Mr Burns,' he said slowly, 'that the servant problem is very acute in America.'

He kept the conversation to this subject throughout lunch, to the despair of Wimble, who tried again and again to change the topic. The victory was Iff's, and he crowned it by inducing their host to suggest a visit through the kitchens, to inspect the labour-saving devices in use in America.

Simon Iff thought that mechanical perfection might have been more fortunately attained had the cost in morale been less severe. The cook was a quadroon woman of thirty, muscular, high bosomed, with a strong, even a domineering face. Her sensual mouth and arrogant eyes told of selfish passions never restrained. She made her independence felt, even to the strangers. In Europe her manner would have been called self-assertive; Wimble whispered to Iff that the price of liberty was eternal vigilance.

'Yes,' said Iff, 'but "Halt, friend, and give the countersign" becomes a little wearing after a while. I think I'll consult that doctor, after all.'

'We can do that,' said Wimble laughingly, 'On our way to the cottage.'

Once in the automobile and well away from the house, Iff sat up and began to take notice. 'Do me a favour, Wimble,' he said. 'Let us dine in the city. I want to spend half an hour there first of all with a new and unexpected but I trust much-to-be-valued friend.'

'Why, what's the big idea?'

'I want a chat with the Commissioner of Police.'

'Wha-a-at?'

'About this murder, you know.'

'Murder?'

'Mrs Burns.'

'Goodnight!'

'Didn't you expect this? I had an idea that my fame had crossed the Atlantic.'

'Yes, but I thought you were the real thing, not a Sunday magazine detective!'

'Come! you've seen all the people, and you know all the facts. Can't you put two and two together?'

'They only make four.'

'Oh, this case has some very mysterious sides to it. For example, there are two things of unknown origin in it.'

'As?'

'One: bichloride of mercury. The doctor couldn't suggest how that got into the house.'

'It might have come in fifty ways; it doesn't implicate anybody.'

'Yes, but there's a thing that only came in one way, and implicates somebody very much.'

'That's?'

'Claudinc.'

'She's the child of her parents, isn't she?'

'The name, I mean.'

'Americans are always giving odd names to children. Why, we discussed that already.'

'We did. Didn't it mean anything to you? "Ima Hogg" and "Ura Hogg": does that tell you nothing about the father?'

'Peculiar sense of humour.'

'Precisely. Now then, what about Claudine? Any "free association" about Claudine?'

'Why, Willy, of course. *Claudine en ménage, Claudine s'en va* – that's all, though, I think.'

'Right. Willy, naughty French novels. Now then, that's a curious name for a stern Puritan father to give to his daughter, isn't it?'

'Possibly a relative of that name.'

'Possibly. But how does that connect with an unexplained supply of mercury? In your imagination, I mean.'

'All this is the most far-fetched, fantastic stuff. Better argue frankly that Funny Ass sounds fishy!'

Iff bore up under that foul blow.

'Consider Claudine herself. I say it's Wednesday, and she takes thought before admitting it. What does that mean?'

'Mannerism.'

'Suppression resulting from years of brutal tyranny.'

'Oh nonsense, she's a happy, care-free, charming child.'

'It's as much as her life's worth to be anything else. Look at her eyes!'

'Rats!'

'Next, that shad.'

'Well? Badly cooked – I suppose the cook – oh bunk!'

'On the contrary, bed, I hope, for me tonight. But did you observe that our philanthropic friend excused the cook on account of her desolation at "poor Mary's" death – and that he was inwardly boiling?'

'I did. He was sensitive, no doubt, about the quality of his hospitality; but his good heart forbade him to blame anyone.'

'Wimble, you are a very young and very innocent child. I like you. Here is a harsh tyrannical type, a terrible fellow both in his business and in his home; but he daren't blame his cook when he had every right to do so. I can only explain that attitude by guilt and fear. You, on the contrary, are mother's darling.'

'You are yourself a loveable character – especially if asleep.'

'That however rarely occurs.'

'Well, here's headquarters.'

The Commissioner was delighted to meet the famous Simon Iff. And what could he do for him?

Mr Iff would like a photograph of Phineas Burns shown to every doctor of high reputation in New York, Boston and

Philadelphia, with a query as to whether he had come for treatment; and if so, for what?

The Commissioner was amazed. 'I shall have to ask for something more than that,' he said slowly.

'Very good,' said Simon Iff. 'I prefer a charge of murder in the first degree.'

'On what grounds?' asked the Chief.

'Well, he called his daughter Claudine,' said Simple Simon.

'English law?' queried the Commissioner.

'There's more than that. He hides his feelings in the matter of planked shad, and Claudine hides her feelings in every matter, and the cook doesn't hide her feelings at all.'

'You can't tell that to the grand jury.'

'I know it. That's why I want the evidence of the doctor. Once I get that, I'll show you a little of our Thirty-Third Degree.'

'Damn it, I'll do it for the fun of the thing!'

'That's all I do it for, don't you know?' Simon Iff remembered his manners just in time, and clinched the Commissioner's opinion that he had to do with a crazy Englishman.

A week later Simon Iff received the information that Phineas Burns was undoubtedly the Godfrey Smith who had been under the treatment of Dr James Gregg Tardie of Philadelphia for ten years past. Dr Tardie had prescribed the bichloride of mercury in small doses for months at a time. And would Mr Iff favour the Commissioner with a visit?

Mr Iff conferred the favour requested.

'We found out some more while we were on the job,' said the big man. 'Burns has been leading Some Double Life all these years. "Black" seems to be the bug in his dome. You've given me confidence, I'll admit; but it's still a long way to that grand jury and the little arm-chair with the pep.'

'Oh, no!' said Simon. 'It's as easy as falling off a log. Leave it,' he added with an embarrassed blush, 'leave it to your Uncle

Dudley.' And then he added 'don't you know?' in a spasm of modest confusion.

'Surely'

Iff decided that he had passed the test.

'But what exactly do you propose to do?'

'Just put it to him nicely and simply, don't you know?'

'I do not. But, "don't you know," he's liable to throw you out.'

'Yes, I would like to have you come down with me. I think if you were there he'd listen quietly because he wouldn't quite know what your presence implied. My knowing the name of Tardie will be another little scare. But all I need is that he should listen; and he'll listen – if only just to call my bluff!'

'And you're only nine high!'

'The number nine, according to the Pythagoreans, is sacred, and attains the summits of philosophy'

'Very good. I certainly want to sit in to the game.'

They went down to Burns' house, and found him alone. He greeted the Commissioner with just the proper feeling. Iff asked for a special interview 'on important business,' and came straight to the point.

'I want to say my say,' he began, 'before my friend here says his. I have only one remark to make, which is this: The wages of sin is death.'

Burns smiled, and lighted a cigar. This fanatic amused him. But he restrained an early impulse to answer anything.

'Whatsoever a man soweth,' went on the mystic, 'that shall he also reap. He that soweth to the flesh, shall of the flesh reap corruption. Doctor Tardie tells me—'

Simon Iff broke off as he saw that Burns had let his cigar go out. He waited for him to relight it. The Commissioner noticed how great an effort it cost him.

Iff did not have to lie; he switched off from an indicative to an apodeictic proposition. 'A man of your nervous tension is particularly liable to end with locomotor ataxia, general paralysis of the insane, or softening of the brain.'

Burns took no second chance with his cigar, he puffed vigorously.

'It is hard for thee to kick against the pricks. You indulge in secret your desire toward an inferior race, as you deem it – and you end by finding yourself in the power of your own cook.'

Burns smoked more easily. A slight smile touched his lips. But Simon Iff was watching his eyes; there was no smile in them.

'He that, being often reproved, hardeneth his neck, shall suddenly be destroyed, and that without remedy.' Simon Iff shut his mouth like the snapping of a trap.

Burns, unmoved, smoked his cigar steadily to the end. Then he crushed the fire of the butt upon a silver ash-tray. Then he went to the door of the strong-room and opened it. From a drawer he took a heavy revolver, and deliberately blew away the top of his skull.

The Commissioner was on his feet, gasping. A second glance assured him that the man was dead. He turned upon Iff with a mixture of awe and horror.

The mystic, in his turn, had drawn a long black cigar from his case, and was lighting it with a hand that did not tremble in the least.

'My dear man!' was all the Commissioner could say.

'You want to know, of course? Come here!'

The magician stepped across the body, and opened one of the drawers in the strong-room at random. It was full of photographs.

'Pah!' cried Teake in disgust.

'Observe!' said Simon, returning to his easy-chair. 'When I came here I had no idea at all that the death of Mrs Burns was anything beyond the accident it appeared. But the moment Claudine stepped into the room I understood from her manner that she had been bullied secretly and subtly until she was afraid to express herself in the simplest matter without thought, earnest thought, as to whether it might not get her into trouble. Yet a mask was always put upon the truth; she and her mother were always obliged to exhibit a "happy home," an "ideal American family life." I began to understand the hard brutality of the man from that as well as from his success in business. I know also that he had expressed his own vices in the naming of his daughter after an immoral woman. Of course he would not have dared to use any name which the general public would have connected with lasciviousness, such as Cleopatra. He chose a name to which not one American in a million would attach any significance whatever. Returning to the mother, then, what must her life have been with such a man? I began to suspect suicide rather than accident. So I asked the family doctor whence the mercury had come. He could not tell me. "Claudine" gave me a clue.

'Before I could go further, lunch arrived. I found this hard brutal cynical sensual man, annoyed at his cook's blunders, making excuses for her. Fear, I thought! What else could explain the situation? So I contrived to see the cook, and found an ambitious and intriguing woman, a woman of almost a male quality of lust, grasping at power like Browning's John the Pannonian. Then I perceived what influence might have forced him, with the mercury ready to his hand, to murder. Oh, a safe murder! Who would suspect him of having such a drug? Who would guess, when he had been so careful as to go to Philadelphia to consult a physician under an assumed name? Even were the mercury traced to him, still an accident! "Poor woman, she took my tablets in mistake for hers!"'

'Yes, yes!' said the Commissioner, 'I follow. I understood your train of reason before we came here. But how in God's name' – he crossed himself – 'did you come to suppose that the hardest-headed man in America would fall for all that stuff from the Bible? Man, it isn't common sense!'

Simple Simon smiled with wide-open, childish eyes. 'But, my dear Commissioner, think of his name! Phineas Calvin Zebedee! Don't you know who Phineas was? He "stood for the Lord" when all Israel "went a-whoring after Moab" or something. And Zebedee, the father of James and John, the "Sons of Thunder." There's your religious atmosphere! And Calvin! Why, the boy sucked in Calvin with his mother's milk. He was born and bred to that one great idea of inexorable fate. Though the mills of God grind slowly, yet they grind exceeding small, and all that, don't you know? On the top of that, too, what do we know of the father who named him? A narrow bigot, who repressed his son's normal instincts, and named him after a tyrant like himself, but with a passionate revolt against enforced chastity seeping at the very base of his nervous system! Well, the lust side of him was the art side too; he naturally dramatised the fate that his other side assured him must one day fall upon him, and he saw that fate in my person when I quietly reminded him of what penalties he had incurred.'

The Commissioner sat a while in silence. Suddenly he shook himself like a dog. 'I suppose I'd better get after that cook,' he said, mechanically.

'Spare yourself the pains and the humiliation,' said Simon. 'He will have left her every penny – you don't have one chance in a million.'

'True; but can't we do something for Claudine?'

'We can get back to New York, and dine at the club. Claudine will be either a courtesan or a nun, and we can't help in either case.'

'We can get back to New York; in fact I must; but somehow I don't feel like dinner.'

And so it came about that Simon Iff dined that night with Wimble; but the only explanation that he would give was most unsatisfactory.

'It's my idiotic vanity, child!' he said, with his eighth creme de cacao; 'I said to you jokingly that a man with a name like that was bound to have poisoned his wife, and so of course I had to prove it. I think I will have another Corona Corona.'

Wimble, who always pretended to be excessively mean, pretended to writhe; but the waiter brought the cigar.

A SENSE OF INCONGRUITY

I

'This is the sort of puzzle we get every day,' said Commissioner Teake to Simon Iff. The head of the New York Police was doing the honours of the organisation to the distinguished stranger. 'Here's a shabby individual – speaks Hungarian, not a word of anything else – can't give any account of himself. Has lost his memory absolutely.'

'Oh!' said Simon Iff. 'And where did you pick him up?'

'In a raid last night on a dive on Tenth Avenue. Possibly the shock of arrest – there was a little shooting practice, too – has destroyed his memory. He's a pretty tough guy, as you see; but I feel – well, traces of intelligence and refinement. We're holding him for observation, and to try to get in touch with some relatives.'

They passed on. In the next room Simon Iff stopped the Commissioner. He put a hand on his shoulder, and said slowly, 'If you get a puzzle of that sort every day, you must be a fairly busy man.'

Teake was struck by the extreme significance of the mystic's tone. 'Some funny business, eh?'

'Well,' said Simon, 'I perceive a certain incongruity. Will you do me the favour to answer me just one question? What well-known man of high position in a foreign government did you find in that – dive, I think you called it?'

Teake was taken entirely aback. His eyes blazed. 'What do you know?' he cried. 'Is this a sample of this black magic of yours?'

'So the cap fits?'

'Why, Captain Nikko, naval attaché to the Cerisian Embassy, was there.'

'In a dive on Tenth Avenue. Strike you as strange?'

'Not very. He was showing the sights of this little old burg to a compatriot, a Dr Nagasaki, who has just come over from Cerisia. But how did you know?'

'I didn't know. I was only trying to find a reason for the presence of a member of one of the great imperial families of Europe. It might have been just curiosity or just vice, but the disguise was so very thorough.'

'Say!'

'Didn't you notice his hands? Of course you did. But you didn't go on one step, as I did. Under that ten days' beard was a lip that only grows on one family face on the planet.'

'And he's lost his memory?'

'If he remembers nothing else, he remembers me! I can't place him; but he knew me in a second.'

'This is the most extraordinary dope!'

'So much so that I want you to tell the sergeant not to let him go; charge him straitly "by his affection for the Archangel Michael," I think it is. Don't let him wash, or monkey with his clothes, or destroy anything. And come over with me to the Secret Service, and we'll talk.'

'Well, there is a little thunder in the air, now you mention it, about the attitude of Cerisia.'

'Especially in connection with that country – not Hungary – where that – tough guy, I think you said – has his nails manicured every morning by a duchess!'

'Aren't we taking a chance if we put any indignity on him? I've my job to think of. I don't want to catch a Tatar.'

'My friend, you've caught a Tatar. And your one best bet is not to let go.'

Teake gave some rather elaborate orders, and drove with Iff directly to the Headquarters of the Secret Service.

Colonel Blagden listened in silence to Iff's story. 'It wouldn't do for England any more than it would for you,' the magician concluded. 'So I came round.'

'Nikko – Nagasaki – man with a Brzoloff lip – Tenth Avenue. Hum. Washington. Excuse me.' Blagden took the telephone. Ten minutes later his face was as white as his collar. 'I'm coming round,' he said, and called for his coat and hat.

Teake took the sergeant into a private room, but Blagden did the questioning.

'Pockets?' he snapped.

'Two hundred and three dollars, sir, four fifties and three ones; two quarters, a dime, six nickels and three pennies. An old envelope, addressed to Stefan Boluski, Hotel Tart, Cincinnati. Postmark, Boston, December twelve, noon. Hotel has no record of any such name. Pencilled accounts, in Hungarian, scribbled on back of envelope. Nothing else but a cheap pocket-knife.'

'Linings?'

'Not a thing, sir.'

'Wait outside.'

Blagden turned to Simon Iff. 'I feel we owe you a great deal; I should like to increase the debt. What do you make of it?'

'Are those accounts written in indelible pencil?'

Blagden called the sergeant, and sent him for the envelope.

'No,' said he, 'faint pencillings, almost rubbed out.'

'May I see?' Blagden passed it over. 'Done with a devilish hard pencil, about 8H, at a guess. I could rub the marks clean, and still read by the impression. He valued those accounts. An 8H pencil on a prince or a tramp strikes me as an incongruity. Let's see. Room 25 – Car 7. Where does one pay seven cents for a car-fare?'

'Nowhere – yet.'

'Aha! Cigar II. There's another funny figure. These aren't accounts; it's the key to a cipher.'

Blagden grunted angrily. 'Mr Iff,' he said, 'I must take you into the confidence of the government of the United States. We have been expecting something serious in this direction for a month or more. I can't say exactly what, or how serious. But I think our man's Prince Theodor Brzoloff, who is supposed to be big game hunting in Central Asia, well out of touch with telegraphs.'

'Yes, that's the man. I remember him perfectly now. I met him in the rest-house at Burzil, on the Gilgit Road, ten years ago. A great traveller and a fine shot.'

'A damned mischief-maker,' growled Blagden. 'Now there's only one reason why he should be here – to bring some kind of a paper to Nikko, a secret treaty of sorts. I see now why he's shamming amnesia. If by some impossible chance – just what's happened – he were recognised, he might be traced to his rooms, and the paper discovered.'

'He's not going to take a second chance of being seen with Nikko if he can help it. He had that paper on him at the dive.'

'What sort of a paper?'

'It would be a fairly long document, I imagine. Five thousand words or so, perhaps.'

'It's on him. It must be on him. Suppose we have a look at those clothes ourselves?'

Blagden recalled the sergeant. 'Bring that Hungarian's clothes here. Tell him it's the regulation to have them disinfected.'

The clothes arrived. Blagden began to turn them over.

'Please!' interjected Simon Iff. 'The police have done all that can be done by touching them. Let us content ourselves with looking at them.'

Blagden put his hands in his pockets with a smile. 'Well, what do we see?'

'I see an incongruity.'

'Good. Reminds one of the personal disguise. Same trick.'

'These clothes are very old, very worn, very ragged in places. They were originally cheap but respectable. Nice dark blue. Where's the princely touch?'

'Simple Simon' tapped the lining of the coat. 'The lining's new. Very high quality linen. Dark blue. Suggests litmus to me. Writing on litmus would be quite invisible. Suppose we brush it over with acid?'

'And read it in red?'

'In red – very likely' Simon Iff did not care to conceal his view of the menace implied by such extraordinary precautions.

Teake summoned an expert, who began to brush the blue lining with a pencil of soft camel's hair dipped in vinegar.

A faint rusty red appeared upon the indigo of the linen. Blagden bent over.

'Good God! It's the Imperial holograph. His majesty's rescript! They've photo-lithographed the original and printed it in litmus. What perfectly beautiful work!'

Iff seemed lost in thought. 'It's not in cipher, then?'

'Perfectly plain French, to begin, at least. It wouldn't be a cipher. They needed the holograph. This is an Authority; it has to be legible as his Majesty's own handwriting.'

Iff lapsed.

'This needs careful restoration,' said the expert. 'May I take it for half an hour?'

'Right,' agreed Blagden. 'Teake, could we have something to eat here? It may be my last chance for some time.'

The Commissioner ordered a meal.

'I don't know how to thank you,' said Blagden to Simon Iff, raising his cocktail, 'for your miraculous solution of this mystery. My God! To think of getting on to a thing this size from – from – from literally nothing.'

'You irritate me,' replied Simon, in a burst of furious ill-temper, 'you humiliate me. You rub it in. Oh go on! It will do me good. It will cure me of the sin of pride. Also,' he added in a more reflective tone, 'perhaps it may buck me up.'

'I don't get you,' returned Blagden, rather annoyed.

'Why, don't you see, it's all come out WRONG.'

The last word was a shout. 'It's too easy. There's an incongruity – the worst kind of all the kinds – an apparent simplicity in what one knows to be most highly complex. Here, do you play chess?'

Blagden admitted it; Teake was silent.

'Well, take a chess problem by a good composer. I see – at a glance – what looks like a solution. Carefully concealed key – elegant line of play – neat mating position. But what's that rook doing in the corner? It is not essential to our solution. Then why did the composer put it on the board? It's bad economy, and a good composer doesn't do that. Our supposed solution must be a mere "try" – a false alarm.'

'Yes,' said Blagden, curiously disturbed. 'Meaning what?'

'What's Nagasaki doing? He doesn't come into it at all. A man of his importance doesn't come over here to be a make-weight. Then, here's a key to a cipher which turns out not to be a cipher at all.'

'I don't follow. There are plenty of explanations. An imperial rescript sent in this extraordinary form outweighs all the facts. The sun blots out the stars.'

'Yes, but some of those stars are bigger than the sun.'

The door opened, and the expert came back.

In his hands was the lining of the tough guy's jacket, pinned neatly to a board. The red writing showed out brilliantly. But the amazement was his face. It was one web of twinkling wrinkles; decorum was hard put to it to keep him from relapsing into the fits of laughter into which the perusal of the document had thrown him.

'I'm afraid it's a hoax, sir,' was all he could trust himself to say.

'What do you mean?' snapped Blagden, furious.

'It's a joke, sir. This is the production of a lunatic. I should say, sir, it's some stunt for advertising a sensational story.'

His amusement overcame him for a moment; then he repressed himself with infinite embarrassment. Blagden took the board. He read with dropped jaw and eyes that seemed as if they would burst from their sockets.

The rescript began by expressing the Imperial sympathy for 'the catastrophe which has recently overwhelmed the government of the United States.' It went on to say that in view of the state of anarchy prevailing in consequence of this catastrophe, of the collapse of the financial system of the country, of the revolt of the negroes in the South, and of certain lawless and disorderly elements of the population describing themselves as socialists, anarchists, working men's reform associations and what not, his Majesty and his government 'would view without alarm any steps which might be advisably taken by the Dewan of Cerisia to restore the blessings of peace and order to the people of the United States of America.'

'This,' said Blagden, 'is an authorisation to Cerisia to invade this country – which is absurd – on the grounds of various events which haven't happened, and are not in the least likely'

'True,' said Simple Simon. 'Today's the twentieth of May. We have some sixty days to stop it.'

'What do you mean?'

'Nagasaki had slipped that envelope to the Prince. The figures give the date which he was to fill in when he signed it as witness to his Imperial nephew's signature. Room 25 Car 7 Cigar 11. That's July twenty-fifth. On that date those events would have occurred; but the Dewan had to have the rescript in his possession before he touched the button.'

'That sounds reasonable – if you can use the word in the presence of such an atrocious plan. But, as to stopping it, it's stopped already. Wait till I pass this little document around the embassies!'

Simon Iff shook his head. 'I'm afraid that would only mean war.'

'It would be pretty bad,' agreed Blagden. 'One can't say how Cerisia would act, but the regular allies – not Hungary – would stick to her. It would be hell.'

'Hell's coming,' replied Simon, 'but we're not quite ready. And you are less so. Better hush this up, don't you think?'

'I must take it to the Secretary of State, in any case. He's in town; I have an appointment at three o'clock, as it happens. Well, sir, I must say that we are very grateful indeed to you. You have certainly done wonders.'

'I never saw a puzzle solved so neatly and completely,' put in Teake.

'Solved!' cried Simon Iff. 'Why, the problem aroused by this incident hasn't even been stated!'

The two men stared. Blagden's taciturnity thawed into quick-firing speech.

'I don't understand! Surely, the whole thing is cleared up – the mystery explained, the villains baffled. What more do you want? Of course we shall indicate that Nikko is no more *persona grata*, and find a convenient reason for Nagasaki's return to his flowers. Prince Theodor will get a quiet warning. Why, the whole bubble is burst.'

'Ah, gentlemen,' said Simple Simon, rather sadly, 'I think I had better put in a little work on this matter. It is not quite in shape to put before you; I will let you know when it is.'

He took a cordial farewell; but when the others left the building, they found him standing on the steps, gazing blankly into the Realm of Nowhere.

Teake thought that, as a stranger to New York, he did not know his way. 'Can I help you?' he said. 'What are you looking for?'

'Two men from the south in the north, and two men from the east in the west. I'm afraid you can't help me! What I really need is just brains. Do you think a fish diet would be any good?'

'What about whale?' Teake made the laughing retort, and passed on.

2

If our mystical friend Simple Simon, luckier than the great Sam Weller, had possessed a 'pair of double million magnifying gas microscopes' instead of normal eyes, he might have been distracted – even he – from his concentration upon the problem by what was taking place at that moment directly in front of them, but shielded from their observation by the wall of a famous skyscraper. For in Room 3715 of that building a perfectly senseless procedure was in course.

It was a very ordinary office, rented by the Society for the Relief of Indigent Immigrants. A portly and benevolent gentleman was leaning back in his chair, smoking an expensive cigar. His secretary, a Miss Wakefield, a tall woman of forty, plain and severe, was seated at her typewriter, taking the dictation of a little dried-up monkey of a man, obviously of Mongol type. He was bending towards the woman, intently. After a few minutes he rose, took his hat and coat, and left the room with a few casual words of farewell.

The fat man pulled out his watch and noted the time. He then told the woman to take some letters. Twenty minutes later her hands dropped suddenly to her lap; she turned a curious questioning gaze upon her employer. She gave a cough; then, with a sudden spasm, torrents of blood gushed from her lungs. She rose, then collapsed upon the floor. The fat man telephoned excitedly for a doctor. As he did so he consulted his watch once more, and put it back in his pocket with a satisfied snap.

Nobody heard anything of this matter as it transpired, and Simon Iff would not have learnt even the published facts if he had not been exceedingly bored during his journey to Atlanta, Georgia. As it was, the paragraph caught his eye. It was entitled 'A New Disease?'

At the autopsy of Miss Wakefield, one of the physicians had stated that he had never seen so complete and sudden a destruction of the tissues of the lungs. There was no trace of tuberculosis or any other known destructive agent, and the woman's health had always been perfect. On the other hand, no other possibility suggested itself. She had been in the service of the Society since its formation two years previously; she had no relatives or other enemies, and no love-affairs. She enjoyed the full confidence of her employers in their very simple and very noble work, which, the writer continued, for he was hard put to it to fill his allotted space, was a perfume peculiarly grateful in the nostrils of the Great American Ideal. Its directing body was a living proof of the assimilation of diverse elements, and of their harmonious cooperation in helping to realise the Great Thought of America, the Home of the Homeless. Rakowsky, the famous banker, was its president, a man who had landed penniless in New York twenty years before, and was now reported to be worth his two hundred millions; Broglio, the labour leader, who by tact and insight had done so much to foster friendly relations between employer and employed, and enjoyed the confidence of the working-men more than any of his colleagues; and, perhaps above all, the Reverend Joshua Henderson, the eminent revivalist who stood in his own person as the symbol of the solution of the Problem of the South.

'Incongruous,' mused Simon Iff; 'but America is the land of incongruities.'

He found further evidence to this effect on arrival at Atlanta. The friend whom he proposed to visit, a Colonel Boughey, greeted him with a stately courtesy equal to Iff's own. But his idea of after-dinner entertainment was of a kind rarely visible in those European circles where similar manners obtain.

'You've run right into it,' he said to his guest. 'One of those damned buck niggers has been at it again, and they caught him this afternoon. Tonight we'll show you how we fix things south of Mason and Dixon's line.'

It was a starry night, cloudless, with a warm breeze from the southwest. Boughey, who drove his own car, pulled up on the outskirts of a village some twenty miles from Atlanta.

The scene will never fade from Simple Simon's mind. By the roadside stood a live oak, under which a bonfire was blazing. Children were gathering sticks and throwing them into the blaze. Several women were standing around, and the noise of their chatter was deafening. Masked men on horseback guarded every approach; they welcomed Boughey with sighs of delight manifest in every hearty boyish greeting.

'Just in time, Colonel,' cried one; 'we were just getting down to business.'

Simon Iff noticed of a sudden that from a bough of the great oak a naked negro was swinging by his thumbs, his feet a bare yard from the ground.

'Southern justice, I gather?' he queried politely.

'Yes, sir, the real thing,' replied Boughey.

'I am fortunate,' smiled Iff; 'we see none of this in Europe – or even in India.'

'No, sir. I reckon this scene may be kind of painful to you,' he added with strangely harmonious intuition, 'but we've got to do it. I was a little squeamish myself when I first came south, forty years ago.'

At this moment Iff perceived that the bonfire was full of iron bars, heated to whiteness.

'Stand back!' said a cool determined voice. 'The man's my prisoner.'

The speaker was a sturdy man, armed with two revolvers. With his left hand he turned back his coat, and a sheriff's badge gleamed in the light of the fire.

One of the masked men approached him. 'You're not sheriff in this county, are you?' he said, with equal formality.

'I protest,' said the sheriff.

'Over-ruled,' replied the other. 'Seize him, boys!'

Two other men came into the light, and laid hands on the sheriff, who drew his revolvers and emptied them into the air.

'Just a little necessary formality,' explained Colonel Boughey. 'He resisted desperately, see, but missed his assailants owing to the darkness, and he don't know 'em from Adam.'

'Get busy!' ordered a stern voice, from somewhere in the dark. 'Now, Mrs Grant!'

A hag of fifty, bowed and wrinkled to seem eighty, leapt toward the fire. Her face was a picture of all the passions of the damned.

'The wronged woman,' explained Boughey.

'Thank you,' murmured Iff.

'See her avenge the honour of the Southern Woman!'

'Ah, yes. I've read about it, don't you know?'

Mrs Grant deliberately plucked an iron bar from the furnace, and came dancing up to the tree. From her wried mouth poured a torrent of the filthiest abuse. The negro never moved or moaned. But for the light in his eyes one might have thought him already dead.

Mrs Grant went up to him and spat upon him; then with her blazing bar she performed an unutterable mutilation.

The negro writhed. A shriek utterly ghastly and horrible burst from his throat.

Mrs Grant, foaming at the mouth, fell upon the ground in a fit suggesting epilepsy.

'Poor woman!' said Boughey. 'What she must have suffered!'

Several men ran to her aid, and carried her, now screaming and kicking, from the tree.

'Now, boys!' said the same voice as before. 'First come, first serve!'

It was a scene wholly demoniacal. Even the children aped their elders, striking the negro with their fiery bars. In the lulls of the shouting one could hear the sizzling flesh. The breeze bore its reek into the nostrils of Simon Iff. For an hour the revel raged.

Suddenly a shrill whistle pierced the night.

'Beat it, boys!' cried the leader, and, emptying his Colt into the bowels of the negro, jumped into his car, and led the flight.

Boughey and his guest were a mile away from the scene when they encountered the posse sent, at a carefully calculated time, to prevent any violation of the law.

'If Josh Henderson had his way, all this would be stopped,' said Boughey.

'Strange, indeed! Is the man right in his mind?'

'Well, he's a queer guy. Son of old Doc Henderson, of Memphis, Tennessee. Mother was a durned good-looking yellow girl; clever and educated and all that. Gosh! She had some pull with the doc! We had to rescue him; he was plumb crazy about her. And when Josh was born, he talked of going to Canada, and tying up to her. So, by Gosh, there was only one way out. We got her and the kid one night, and ran them over to a brothel in New Orleans. The old man went right off the handle; but when he tracked her, six months later, to a shack with "Fanny. Come in boys" on the door, he came sane again.'

'This is the Joshua Henderson who is so anxious to reconcile the negroes with their masters?'

'No masters here in America!' Boughey rebuked his guest with democratic earnestness. 'The negro is a free man, sir, in these States.'

'I understand,' said Simon Iff, thoughtfully.

The next morning he was 'Obliged to go on to St. Louis to see another friend, on his way to San Francisco'; but at the first station he changed trains, and went back to New York. He had wired Commissioner Teake to make a certain enquiry, and to meet him at the Chiliad Club for dinner, without fail, on the night of his arrival.

Commissioner Teake drank his cocktail. He then drew a slip of paper from his pocket, and pushed it over to Simon Iff. It read

B. 3,500,000.00 H. 2,500,000.00

'This morning,' said Teake.

Iff burnt the paper in the ash-tray by his chair.

'I'm utterly at a loss,' remarked the Commissioner. 'What do you know of these men, and why should you suspect any such transaction?'

'I have arranged for a special train to Washington,' returned Iff. 'We have not a moment to lose. Shall we drive down to the Pennsylvania Station? We can talk on the train.'

Teake agreed; he had become an automaton. He had no idea what was going on, but he trusted Iff that it was something gigantic.

Dinner was served in the car, and Simon talked only of indifferent matters; but the waiter having withdrawn, he changed his whole manner. He became earnest, eloquent, electric; and as he proceeded, the Commissioner grew pale as death.

'I want to tell you the whole course of my investigation,' said Iff. 'Let me begin with my views on prophecy!' A touch of his normal lightness infected his tone for a moment.

'When a man prophesies, it is either a guess or a calculation of probabilities. Yes? Now the rulers of the world don't act on guesses. And calculations of probabilities have their limits of accuracy. Take the weather! "It will be cold in December" is all right; nothing in that; but "There will be a blizzard on December first which will destroy the Woolworth Building" is a specific prediction which, as it happens, nobody is in a position to make.

'Now the rescript was in the nature of such a prediction; and the question is how its author came to make it. He must have had what he thought to be absolute foreknowledge of events. Now, if I say to you, "I shall have dinner with so-and-so next week," you rightly judge that the matter is already arranged. The person in power has declared his will, and the event will come to pass. Now the author of the rescript has no power to cause the events which he prophesies; he must therefore have been assured that they would take place by people who have that power. Who, then, are they?

'You will remember that the rescript declares that four things have taken place.

'An anarchist outbreak. Who could arrange for that? Some leader of labour.

'A revolt among the negroes? Who has power over them as a class?

'A collapse of the financial system. Here we must look for some great banker.

'A man who could cause a "catastrophe" to the government of the United States. Note the word "catastrophe." It implies more than a mere political upheaval. I thought that it meant death. Now who is a master of death?

'I answered the fourth question easily. There was already such a man within the field of our vision. Dr Nagasaki is the first chemist and bacteriologist in Cerisia. But the others? Evidently people already in power, in their various lines, over here.

'I had no clue. I took the hardest case first – the question of the negroes. I went south to make enquiries.

'As it happened, I was reading that murder of Miss Wakefield in the paper—'

'Murder?' gasped Teake.

'Murder. Wait a moment. I noticed – or rather, I did not notice – the name of Joshua Henderson. I went to a lynching bee on the night of my arrival in Atlanta, and – who should come up in talk but this same Joshua? My mind flew back to the Wakefield case. My friend from Georgia told me Henderson's story. He and his mother had been most foully treated by the Southern Gentlemen. Who then was this revivalist, "the man who had awakened a million hearts," as the paper called him? Who but a man whose whole soul must naturally be eaten up by hatred of the white man?

'And with whom is he associated in this Indigent Relief Show? With the banker and the labour leader, the very men who could fill the blanks in my equation!

'Instantly my mind began to reconstruct the situation. Prince Brzoloff is let out – without the lining of his jacket, which would tell him that the game was up. He will immediately communicate with Nikko and Nagasaki. They will have but two courses – either to throw up the sponge or advance the date of their action. I see them – in my mind's eye – desperate men in hasty conference. Nagasaki has made good on his "mastery of death." Miss Wakefield was merely the *corpus vile* on whom they tried the experiment. They decide to trust Brzoloff's verbal account of the rescript, or he has a copy. They decide to act. This is certain, for Rakowsky distributes the funds according to the prearranged plan, and probably sets in motion the machinery that he had prepared for causing a financial panic'

Simon Iff paused.

'But all that will take time,' said Teake, with confidence. 'We can arrest these men, and stop the whole business.'

'Certainly,' said Iff. 'But our hurry is in the other matter. The efforts of these men would be in vain, and they would not take the final step unless the government were first put out of the way. Nagasaki is probably in Washington at this moment. He had evidently some plan for wholesale murder in his mind. The date appointed proves that. Possibly the President and cabinet dine together on July 4 or some such date. But if he can't get them together, he'll try to do it piecemeal. Remember, it's a "new disease" – no suspicion attached to the murderer.'

'Good God!'

'I know Nagasaki's work fairly well. He did some wonderful research on leprosy. And on helium—' He suddenly rose and clapped his hand to his brow. 'By Jupiter,' he shouted, 'I wonder if *that* could be it!'

He paced the car for five minutes; then returned, and sat down abruptly.

'I believe I have it,' he said shortly. 'We must get Nagasaki without a moment's delay. But oh! if we could only catch him in the act! Can you think of an excuse to see him at once – without alarming him, you know, in case the shot misses?'

'Oh, I guess so,' replied Teake after a moment's thought. 'I can tell any third party that my wife's dying of beri-beri – she was in Japan, as a matter of fact, last year – and in view of his great reputation, and all that—will that do?'

'I should think so,' said Iff. 'But we'll hope for the best of the luck. Heaven knows it's been with us so far! Better touch wood, I suppose.'

In fact, Teake did not have to resort to any subterfuge. The servant at Captain Nikko's house, where they enquired first of all, informed them quite simply that his master had gone out with Dr Nagasaki, only an hour before, to Mrs Blebeney Bland's ball.

They hurried thither. A word from Teake to the hostess, whom he knew well, was enough. She led him and Iff to a curtained alcove, where, at a small occasional table, sat Nikko and Nagasaki with three ladies and the Secretary of the Navy.

Simon Iff motioned his friends back. Unperceived, he peeped through the screen.

'I am sure you do not take snuff, my Dear Mr Secretary,' Nagasaki was saying, as he held out a small jewelled box tentatively, 'but no doubt you and these charming ladies will permit an old fossil his indulgence.' He leaned back in his chair, and inhaled a pinch of light brown powder from between delicate finger and thumb.

'But what I should like to ask you confidentially,' he went on, 'is this.' He leaned forward, and the Secretary unconsciously followed his example.

But Nagasaki did not speak. Simon Iff leaped on him like a terrier, wrenching his head by the hair.

'Quick, Teake!' he said, in a low intense voice.

The Commissioner appeared. The Secretary had risen, intending to attack Simple Simon, whom he took for a madman. Nikko sat absolutely impassive.

'Get the ladies away, sir,' said Teake. 'And have a few men whom you can trust to keep away intruders. Don't disturb the guests!'

'What's all this about?' said the Secretary angrily.

The Commissioner was taken aback. 'My God, sir, I don't know!' he stammered at last. 'But it's all right. It's a long story.'

'Allow me!' said Simon. 'Ah – yes! I think I can do it with a penknife.' He took one from his pocket and opened it. The point of the thin blade moved gently and tentatively within the lobe of the doctor's nostril. Then Iff, with a smile, and light leverage, produced a small platinum tube.

'Let us try a little experiment,' he said pleasantly. 'A little of that powder, Mr Teake, if you please, in the orifice. We then reinsert it, gentlemen, but with the valve opening in the other direction.' Neither Nikko nor Nagasaki moved or spoke. 'We shall now close the mouth firmly, and the free nostril.'

A couple of minutes passed. When Iff perceived that the old man had drawn in his breath he released him entirely.

Nikko spoke calmly. 'If this abominable farce is ended, we shall go home.'

Simon Iff bowed, and stood aside.

'No,' said Nagasaki, still more calmly than his compatriot, 'the curtain falls in fifteen minutes more. With your permission, gentlemen, let us wait in peace.'

Again Simon Iff bowed. The Secretary of the Navy had been standing in annoyed and puzzled silence; now he resumed his chair.

'I have a weakness,' said the doctor after a moment. 'I have always wanted to know. (Very soon – perhaps – I shall know – many things.) How did you come to know, sir?'

'I did not know much,' said Simon humbly and rather deferentially. 'But I understood that Miss Wakefield had been murdered, probably as a mere experiment, to convince Rakowsky that you could do what you claimed. I felt that you were in that circle – owing to my analysis of a certain Imperial rescript. I looked for a means of death worthy of your genius. I needed some device sure, subtle, undetectable. I looked for some substance capable of destroying lung tissue in a swift, even a fulminating, manner. Then – I am a little ashamed – I began to imagine things. I imagined an odourless gas, intensely radioactive. Then I looked for a means of administration. That, too, must be without suspicion. Several suggestions came to me. But when I saw you take snuff, I knew the truth. You had a little muzzle-loading gun in your nostril. The warmth of the nose would volatilise the powder; all you had to do was to lean forward and breathe quietly on your victim. I interfered in the interest of Mr Secretary here; in the interest of science, I made your experiment on yourself.'

'You need not be ashamed, sir,' said Nagasaki very quietly indeed; 'yours is the scientific imagination.'

He rose and bowed; then, turning to Captain Nikko, he made a gesture of dignified farewell. 'You will know,' he said, 'what must be done, and what report made in what quarter.'

He turned to the Secretary. 'This gentleman,' he said with a smile, 'has explained to you the causes; it is for me to demonstrate the effects.'

With that he gave a slight cough. Torrents of blood gushed from his mouth; he collapsed upon the carpet.

The Secretary had risen to his feet, his face drawn and white.

'It seems, sir,' he said to Simon Iff, 'that I owe you my life.'

'Not exactly to me, but to my very strong sense of incongruity.'

Teake protested. 'Mr Iff is an incorrigible joker, sir, and this is no time for such matters. Mr Iff has disclosed a plot of gigantic, of incredible proportions. The whole country would have been in flames, and in the hands of a remorseless invader, but for him. But excuse me – I have my duty to do, Captain Nikko. International law or no international law, you are my prisoner.'

Nikko bowed slightly, and followed the Commissioner.

'How – how – how – can we reward you, sir?' stammered the Secretary.

'By not connecting my name with the affair,' answered Simon Iff. 'I have saved your life – do you want me pilloried as a Meddlesome Matty in the next number of *Life*?'

THE OX AND THE WHEEL

All that we are from mind results, on mind is
founded, built of mind;
Who acts or speaks with evil thought, him doth
pain follow sure and blind;
So the ox plants his foot, and so the cart-wheel
follows hard behind.

– *The Dhammapada*

1

A Persian philosopher once remarked, on being questioned about the climate of Bushir, that if he had one house in Bushir and another in hell, he'd rent the one in Bushir. Anglebosk, New Jersey would have been congenial, one may suppose, to that philosopher, on the night when Simon Iff's car broke down in the main street, for the thermometer stood at seven degrees below zero, and a blizzard was blowing at a rate of over seventy-five miles an hour.

The car had been forcing its way gallantly into the teeth of the gale, possibly encouraged by a feeling that it was only a few miles more to its warm garage in New York; but the short steep hill of Main Street, sheeted in ice, broke its brave heart. Less poetically, there is no doubt that something broke, and broke with a grinding shriek that for one second 'outchid the North Wind.'

The car immediately yielded to the fury of the blast, and slid down the hill. It was too fantastic to assume a homing instinct in its machinery, but it certainly brought up with a bang against the door of Anglebosk's solitary hotel, kept by one Silas Hooper.

'Very thoughtful,' said Simon, stepping out, and entering the hotel. 'Come in!' he cried aloud to his chauffeur with an imperative gesture, 'leave her right there! We can do nothing till the day breaks.'

The two men were hungry, and Iff ordered the very scanty meal that proved to be available. As was his custom, he chatted genially to the inn-keeper, a jolly-faced, burly individual with a humorous smile and twinkling eyes; but it did not escape his observation that mine host's merriment was singularly forced. He sent the chauffeur to bed, and asked the man to sit and drink.

'Indeed I will, sir!' he replied, heartily. But Iff suddenly dropped his end of the conversation. The inn-keeper's embarrassment and preoccupation became immediately obvious.

'My friend,' said Iff, with his third glass of brandy, 'I'm not Buttinsky (isn't it?) but I'm a bit of a doctor of souls, and I know your symptoms. Like to tell me?'

'Why, sir, it's nothing,' said Hooper, 'but it's hell.'

'Naturally, naturally,' returned the sympathetic magician.

'The fact is – I may be arrested any minute.'

'So may anyone, in America.'

'Oh no, sir, that's only in New York State. This is New Jersey,' said Hooper, with more enthusiasm than he had yet shown. 'But this is murder.'

'Oh well, you didn't do it. Why worry?'

The man was immensely reassured by the confidence of Iff's tone. He did not even trouble to confirm the denial. 'I was probably the last person – but one – who saw Mrs Craddock alive.'

'Tell me the whole story. I haven't heard about it. To me Mrs Craddock is a name possessing all the fascination of the unknown.'

'It's in all the evening papers. It happened last night.'

'I never read the papers; I value my mind, such as it is. Go on.'

'It's hard to say one thing, though the reporters – blast their impudence, I hope every mother's son of 'em's out in the blizzard! – get it all down in six inch lettering. My father was a decent man, sir, and he told me when to keep my mouth shut. Well, better tell you myself than show you what they said about the poor girl. She was what we call a good sport, sir. Plenty of money, fond of cards and a drink, may be, and perhaps a kiss on the sly. Anyhow, I went around there a heap. I've no wife, if that's any excuse.'

'I see no need for any excuse,' said Simon simply. 'I'm an old-fashioned philosopher. I think cows were made to give us milk and beef – and women for kisses.' He could always adapt his thought and expression to his audience – and this man was a coarse type.

Hooper brightened up considerably. 'Last night I was there from nine till about half-past eleven, perhaps later. Then I came back home. We were both pretty drunk, I guess. Of course the kid had been in bed for hours.'

'The kid?'

'She has a little boy of ten, sir, Jack, the dead spit of his poor mother. See here!' He pulled out his pocket-book and extracted a photograph, a modern Isis and Horus. It showed a charming woman of a well-built, voluptuous type, a little loose and coarse about the mouth and jaw, and with eyes full of glad excitement.

As Hooper had said, the boy was her image. No one but would be struck instantly by the astonishing resemblance!

Tears gathered in the eyes of the good inn-keeper. He kissed the picture reverently before he returned it to its resting-place.

'Go on with your story,' said Iff, very gently.

'You don't know what a woman of that sort means to a man, in a place where there's no other amusement.'

'Oh yes, I do!'

'This morning poor Grace was found dead in bed, her throat cut, with a razor, they say. God help me, I shave with a straight-razor!'

'There's something else the matter – not plain scare,' said Simon.

'Yes,' replied Hooper, frankly. 'According to the papers, I wasn't the only lover. Curse them, they've run down half the village! They say there were three other men with her last night.'

'Do you blame her very much?' asked Simon. 'You keep a hotel, don't you? Shouldn't God's blessings be free to all? And shouldn't we honour most those who are most generous with them?'

'I never heard anyone talk like that before. Everyone knows it's wrong.'

'In 1850 everyone knew it was wrong to protest against negro slavery. In Germany it's wrong to question the divine right of kings. In Turkey it's wrong to eat pork. In Hindustan it's wrong to eat beef. In 1500 it was wrong to say that the earth moved. In 1900 it was wrong to say it didn't. Time and space, my friend, time and space, the illusions, breeders of all other illusions! Right and wrong are fashions, like women's hats.'

Hooper, dumbfounded, could only scratch his head.

'Who lives in the house besides the boy?'

'Her old nurse, Maddie. And a coon girl comes in every day to do the chores and the cooking.'

'What time was the murder done?'

'I don't know, sir. They say about two in the morning.'

'And haven't you an alibi?'

'No one saw me leave, or on the way home. And I slipped up to bed without waking the others.'

'A little awkward. They're so stupid, at times, about psychology. Tell you what: I'll send Dobson into the city in the morning for spare parts to that motor of mine, and we'll walk up to the house together, and see what happens to be visible. I'm Simon Iff, a bit of a crank, perhaps; but I'm in good – isn't it? – with the bulls (I think) just now. New theories about crime, don't you know, and lately they've been panning out rather well.'

'That's awfully good of you,' said Hooper.

'Tush!' replied Simple Simon. 'Let me rather behold a bed!'

He was particularly pleased with himself in the morning when he learnt that Hooper had slept like a child.

2

The day had broken windless and cloudless. It was in a brisk and joyous air that Hooper walked over to Mrs Craddock's with the old mystic.

They found one Jonas Black, a detective-inspector, in charge of the house. Jack Craddock was on his knee, learning a new form of 'Patience.'

'Run away, Jacky boy' said he, on learning Simon Iff's name. 'I've some business with these gentlemen.'

The boy, however, insisted on a proper presentation. He took to Simple Simon with utter cordiality of glee, and made him promise to stay and play for a while after the interview was over. Black signed to Hooper to take the boy off.

'We've heard of you, Mr Iff,' said Black, with a chuckle, 'and I've got you beat right here!'

'A hard case, eh?'

The inspector roared with laughter. 'Caught!' he cried. 'Psychology at fault at last! You didn't get me at all; no, not one little bit!' He leant across the table and whispered mysteriously. 'What was I doing with these cards?'

'Canfield, isn't it?'

'Ha! Ha! Ha! No, sir, I was investigating the murder upstairs!' Simon Iff was interested at once.

'Yes, sir, believe me! Simple as a Supreme Court ruling, and clear as Mississippi mud! Fifty-two cards – fifty-two men, all equally likely to have done it. I think four of them have medium good alibis, though. Shall we play some more? Ha! Ha! Ha! I caught you fairly, sir, admit it!'

Iff laughed heartily at the other's wit.

'You've certainly got the dramatic way of putting things,' he said; 'and that's a long way towards their solution, since all the world's a stage. Seriously, though, is it as wide open as all that?'

'Sure,' said Black, suddenly surly, as his sense of humour gave way to a realisation of the fact that there was not much glory coming his way. 'Say, would you come up, and talk it over? I'd be real glad, honest I would.'

'Right you are!' agreed Iff. 'Everything as it was?'

'Yep. I'm waiting for Briscoe, from headquarters. A born sucker, by gum!'

They went up one flight of stairs. The dead woman's bedroom stood open. A police officer was lounging in a chair, chewing a cigar. He sprang to attention as Black entered. The body of Mrs Craddock lay on the bed, dressed in a flaming yellow kimono with black embroidery. Her dyed yellow hair was loose, but the blood from her throat had clotted it.

Simon Iff bent over her closely.

'Mr Black,' said he, after a moment, 'do you see anything peculiar here?'

'Well, the guy that did this job was no barber.'

'Good!' smiled Simon. 'Carry on the thought!'

'He was drunk, I guess.'

'Go on!'

'Nothing doing!' said Black, after a long pause. 'This is the last stop.'

'Elaborate your thought!' said Iff. 'This – er – guy – was new to the job, as you said. Also, he was not drunk. He was very particularly sober. He was trying in a very pain-staking way to make a good showing, and he was extremely conscious of his entire incompetence. Reminds one of a newly-married man trying to carve a chicken for the first time.'

Black burst into a barrage of laughter. Simon Iff did not know what 'chicken' meant. The inspector explained.

'Very apt,' agreed Simon. 'This chance serves the patient seeker after the *mot juste*.'

Mot juste was his little revenge.

'But look!' said Simon. 'One more thing about this bungler. He had not the slightest fear that she would wake during the process. What does that suggest?'

Black was silent.

'Again, do you see something else – something very astonishing – something very peculiar indeed – something quite in contradiction to every fact in the case?'

'Not a thing.' He shook his head strongly.

'Look at the eyes!'

'Rather nice eyes. A bit wild!'

'The whole of the upper part of the face contradicts the lower.' Iff covered the eyes with his sleeve. 'There's Mrs Craddock as everybody knew her. Now there!' He lowered his sleeve, six inches. 'There's another woman. Did you ever see such intensity of sadness?'

'Jehosaphat! That's so!'

'It's accentuated, in my mind, to the point almost of insanity.'

'Suicide, by the Great Horn Spoon!' Then he checked himself. 'Steady, Jonas Black, my lad; this ain't no jumping competition. Where's the razor?'

'Somebody might have come in, seen the body, lost his nerve, and run away, taking the razor with him. But – as we're asking questions about razors, how did Mrs Craddock come to have a razor about the house? Women often shave the arm-pits, but they use safety-razors.'

'As it happens, Mrs Craddock had a horror of razors. Her husband killed himself with one, six years ago.'

'Come, that's really interesting. Any record of the case?'

'Right here.' Black pulled out a portfolio, and extracted a memorandum, which he unfolded.

'Quite a straightforward case. Business losses – something about a missing debenture – heavy insurance with no suicide clause – every legitimate inducement!'

'Pathetic note to the coroner?'

'No; did it right in front of his wife's eyes. She was in her bath, early morning—'

'Oh, was she?' said Simon Iff, in a very nimble tone.

The inspector laughed heavily.

'I'm afraid that it is you who fail to interpret me, this time, Mr Inspector!' said the mystic with a certain asperity. 'I may add that you make a very serious mistake – I've given you a clue to the mystery.'

'Oh come!' said Black. 'You can't kid me, you know. I'm from Missouri.'

'Go on then.'

'He walked into the bathroom, took his razor out, and cut his throat with a single sweep.'

'Exact time? And date?'

'November twelve. Between seven and half-past.'

'He was a commuter?'

'Nope. Money of his own.'

'That settles it.'

'Settles what?'

'The case.'

'Chase me!'

'I am prepared to lecture to the entire population of Missouri. Come, let us go downstairs, and clear up this matter. It is both better and worse than you can imagine.'

They returned to the main floor. In a little room dedicated to his pleasure, Jack Craddock was sitting on the floor with Hooper, engrossed in the construction of a mechanical monument from a number of metal parts. Maddie, the nurse, in cap and spectacles, placidly knitted.

'Hooper,' said Simon, 'do me a good turn. I'm out of cigars. Something strong and black from the village, if you don't mind.'

Hooper sprang to his feet, and obeyed with alacrity. No sooner had he left the house than Simon Iff took a large crocodile-skin case from his pocket, and offered a big Upmann to the inspector.

'I must have overlooked these,' he said whimsically. Maddie pursed her thin lips.

'We'll leave you to play for a bit,' smiled Simon, patting the boy's shoulder. 'We have to persuade Maddie to make us a cup of tea in the kitchen.'

The old nurse seemed to hesitate before complying.

'You'll take pity on a chilly old man, won't you?' went on the mystic.

The tone of his voice decided her. 'Sure you haven't a thermos flask in your pocket?' she snapped, with a thin smile.

'A fair hit!' laughed Iff. They followed her to the kitchen.

'No harm shall come,' said Simon very gravely, 'if you are sensible. You are a clever woman; you ought to understand that I am a friend.'

'What do you want of me?'

'Just silence and a cup of tea, for the moment.'

She was amazed; she had expected a very different request.

Simon motioned Black out of the kitchen. 'Take your boots off,' he whispered, 'and follow me.'

Tiptoe in their socks, Iff led the inspector back to the play-room.

Jack Craddock had ceased to build up his machine. He was sitting praeternaturally still, his head drooping, his eyes fixed on vacancy. The men went softly back to the kitchen.

'Come!' cried Simon gaily, 'let me carry in the tea-tray! I must do my share, mustn't I?'

Maddie refused indignantly. She stalked majestically back to the play-room, and set down the tray with what came very near to being a bang.

'Two lumps, Mr Iff?' she enquired with some acidity.

'Hardly,' he replied. 'But I will take both milk and lemon.'

Her eyes were gimlets.

'I want to tell Inspector Black my secret method of disclosing mysteries. It is quite a new idea. I go to the people who happen to know, and I ask them.'

The inspector seemed to be enjoying the cigar. 'I would like my tea strong,' he said to Maddie. 'I want to wake up!'

'Indeed you do!' cried Simon.

'One to you.'

'Now Maddie, tell us the whole story, and you'll feel better. Come, Jack, let's build a Great Wheel!'

The old man squatted on the floor like a Buddha, and began with incredible swiftness to construct his model. Jack was entranced. Black smoked intently. Maddie sipped her tea.

'I know nothing,' she said at last.

'Ah! the formula of recognition of a secret society, wasn't it?' said Iff. 'I'm in good standing. I know nothing too, and I know I know it. However, we're all attention!'

'You don't seem to have any doubt,' said Maddie, 'and I own, you appeal to me somehow. But you must be crazy to think I'd say a word before Master Jack.'

On the contrary; send me and Black out of the room if you like. But you've got to tell him, if you never tell anybody else.'

'Crazy,' she murmured.

'You're a good woman, and I'm a bit of a doctor of souls, in a small way.'

'I've committed a crime.'

Black pulled out a note-book, and warned her formally in the usual terms. Maddie laughed rather bitterly.

'You're rocking the boat,' said Iff to Jonas. 'Put away the note-book. Your memory is going to receive some very indelible impressions, or I'm wrong again!'

'Duty,' grunted Black.

'Well, go on, Maddie. He doesn't count, does he?'

'Nothing counts, now.'

'Oh yes, Jack's a boy, isn't he?' and he began to sing:

> 'Jack's the boy for work! Jack's the boy for play!
> Jack's the lad
> when girls are sad
> to kiss the tears away!'

Maddie took up her knitting. 'Least said, soonest mended,' and she shut her mouth like a springe.

'Then I must tell my story – first.'

'I'll leave you with Mr Inspector.'

'No, no. He desires your charming company, I feel sure.'

Maddie understood that the detective was itching to arrest her. She did three plain and three purl. Then Simon Iff began to speak.

'You remember the points I called to your attention upstairs, Black?'

He nodded his assent.

'Take the first in point of time. Here is a debauched woman – excuse me, I must speak out – who takes a bath at seven o'clock on a November morning. Why? It suggests a "white night."

Her husband, with no reason in the world for rising early, does so also.'

'Well, he had to cut his throat, didn't he? Early morning's the favourite time o' day.'

'Yes, yes, the bath's the point. Water isn't hot at that hour as a rule, is it?'

'Nope. Get busy.'

'If you ever want to cut a man's throat, Black, do it when you're naked, and plenty of water handy.'

Iff never stopped building his Great Wheel; but Jack had ceased to cooperate. He sat with ears cocked.

'But she had no reason in the world to do it!'

'Oh yes! ask any woman who knows what husbands are!'

'Say, am I riding the goat in this lodge?'

'I know; I'm deducing everything from nothing. But that's just what creation is, eh?'

'You can't create that sort of dope in New Jersey!'

'Well, I'm just sort of knitting. Three plain and three purl, isn't it? Two and two don't make four until you have two and two! Listen to point number two! Here is a woman who is all jollity and drunkenness and free love, till the lower part of her face might be a model for a female Silenus. And all the time her forehead is tightening with agony, and her eyes growing wider and wilder. Just suppose for one instant that my crazy suggestion about the bath is correct. Then it's natural. She tries to forget with cards and lovers and drink. When she's alone she's half crazy – probably that means dope. Cocaine, for guess No. 2. I didn't mention it upstairs, because I hadn't made up my mind what to do, but there was a speck of shining white caught on a hair in one nostril.'

Maddie put down her knitting. Simon Iff waited for her to speak. But in a few moments she picked up her needles and went on.

'Go on? Good idea. Point number three. Imagine one and one make two. Then we have a woman – a half or three parts crazy woman – who probably has something very like melancholia whenever she is alone for a little, whenever the friends leave her, or the drink wears off, or the dope fails. With this melancholia she probably has hallucinations. Very likely she acts as did Lady Macbeth.'

'This is a whole lot of "very likely," marked down from "perhaps" for the spring stock-taking sales,' laughed the inspector.

'Wait for point four. Who murders her? Somebody absolutely incompetent, but very much in earnest. Somebody who knows for certain that she will not wake while he is at work. Somebody who quite fails to adjust thought and deed; for throat-cutting is a swift, passionate business. One gets the idea of a sleep-walker, perhaps?'

Maddie smiled grimly. 'I own up,' she said swiftly.

'My dear good woman,' protested Iff, 'you're the most efficient person I've seen in ten years. You never bungled or fumbled in your life.'

'But sleep-walking alters that.'

'True. How do you know you did it?'

'Blood on my night-gown.'

'Show us!'

'I got scared, and burnt it.'

'Good for you! Consider me as having risen and bowed. We can then continue with common sense.'

Maddie took up her knitting. 'With all due deference,' she said, 'damn you, Mr Iff!'

'Well,' laughed Simon, 'I was rather damned when I saw what I saw. To proceed. Here is a crime exactly like her own in every point but what might appear the essentials. Hers was deliberate and skilful malice, the other a mere childish imitation.'

'Damn you, Mr Iff.'

'Only one person could have done it – a person with a mind exactly like her own. We must rule out all men; a man would have made one sweep. We must rule out all women; a woman would have fled when the first half-hearted cut drew blood. That leaves us with children – and there's only one child in the picture.' Iff ended with a sort of amiably triumphant snap of the fingers.

'I'm sorry to bother you about a trifle,' said Maddie; 'but there isn't a razor in the house.'

'Oh yes, there is – or was. It's the razor that she killed her husband with; and it is – or was – in the hiding-place where the cocaine is. I can trust Mr Black to find that place.'

'You can,' said Black, 'if there is one. But this yarn's still a bit of a pipe dream.'

'You saw for yourself how Jack behaves when he's alone. With us, the jolly laughing boy; this talk has only made him half serious. Alone, he becomes a brooding solitary soul, the vulture of misery, misery without cause in environment but wholly in heredity, gnawing his vitals. Can't you see his mother's eyes and forehead again? And her mouth as it was before it was corrupted? We must work upon that mouth and jaw; we must teach them to transfigure the eyes!'

'Excuse me,' said Maddie, quietly. 'I have been wrong. I have very little to say, but I will say it. I nursed Grace Chalmers – as she then was – at my breast. Her mother died when she was born; she was just such a child as Jack is now; her very melancholy fits made her more loveable because more pitiable; only, she was always as deceitful as the devil. At seventeen she married Craddock. From him she suffered the most intolerable wrong, and I guess it went to her brain. She couldn't sleep any more. A friend of hers – some friend! – taught her to use drugs. Then she killed Craddock, killed him with utmost cunning. She told me; I helped to avert any suspicion. There's my crime, inspector, write it down! I stuck to her as, God helping me, I'll always stick to anyone I love. I lost my husband in a railroad wreck, and my boy died a month later. Well, that's neither here nor there. After Craddock's death her melancholy increased. She took to drink and men; when she was alone it was morphine, or ether, or cocaine. She got to seeing things. She couldn't bear to be alone; Jack slept in the next room. Her thoughts turned always to the one scene – the scene in the bathroom. She would take out the razor and act it again and again. One night her screams woke me; I went to quiet her. I found her rehearsing the murder with Jack. But she was too lazy to stand up. The cocaine hit her heart, I think. So she made Jack stand by the bed and play at cutting her throat. I was horrified: I stormed; I threatened; I cajoled. Of course she promised never to do anything of the sort again. Of course she broke the promise. But what was I to do? I could prove nothing; and if I did, I made it worse. I could only pray. God! how I have prayed—'

'This Great Wheel is an awful mess,' remarked Simon Iff to Jack; 'we must not think of ourselves as all-wise, all-powerful, all-benevolent, perhaps. The best way to judge a workman is by his work, eh?'

Jack nodded merrily. 'We'll build a new one, better.'

'Good boy!' and they pulled their experiment to pieces, and began again. Maddie took up her story once more.

'Two nights ago Jack came to me. His night-dress was covered with blood. He was very frightened, in a very calm way. Weren't you, Jacky, boy?'

'Course I wasn't. Mummy said to hold my tongue about it. Come on, Mr Iff.'

'I hid the traces as well as I could,' said Maddie.

'Where's the razor?'

'I don't know. I never knew her hiding-place. She was as cunning as the devil.'

'Hum.' Iff meditated a moment. 'Will you two go and make some waffles for us?'

'I trust you,' was all Maddie answered, as she rose to comply.

When Simon Iff was left alone with Jack, he very soon began to exhibit signs of weariness. Building wheels became a bore. The boy reflected his new friend's emotion; lassitude seized him. The conversation lagged. Iff lay at full length on the carpet. Jack fell into his mood of wretchedness.

Simple Simon, watching him keenly, said at last, in a soft voice, 'Let's play killing Poppa.'

'Mummy said to hold my tongue about it.'

'But Mummy isn't here, and I want to play.'

'I haven't got the razor.'

'Let's go and get it!'

They went upstairs, the boy giggling as if he were being tickled, and came to the room where the dead woman lay.

'Will he play Poppa?' asked Jack, pointing to the policeman.

'No, I'll play Poppa.'

Iff turned to the constable. 'Say, buddy, Mr Inspector wants to see you right away,' he said in his broken American. 'I'll see all's fair.'

The constable yawned, stretched himself, and departed. Simon knew that Black would understand, and keep him out of the way.

The boy spontaneously began to play.

'Oh darling, I haven't slept one wink,' he lisped, in an affected feminine voice. 'I do think I'll take a bath. I've such a headache.'

'I'll turn on the water,' replied Simple Simon.

'No, you say "Hell, it's half-past six. Do you think I'm a damned stenographer?"'

Iff, kicking himself mentally, repeated the phrase.

'Oh well, I guess I can do it myself.'

Warned, Simon growled out 'Oh, lemme sleep!'

Jack clapped his hands merrily.

'That's fine; but you say "Hell, lemme sleep. All women are the same."'

The mystic obeyed, though his nerves were chattering with horror.

The boy began to imitate the noise of running water. It was an extraordinary piece of mimicry; Simon Iff could hardly believe that someone had not in fact turned on the tap.

'You lie down,' said the boy. Iff obeyed. Jack took a chair, put it by the wall, and climbed upon it. A narrow wooden rail, intended for hanging pictures, ran round the room about a foot below the ceiling. He pulled off a loose portion of this rail. There was a recess, small indeed, but excellently calculated to hold a year's supply of dope and – a razor.

'Mummy said always to hide the razor before anything else.' Jack took it out. It was heavily crusted, ivory handle and all, with blood.

'Now you say "Damn that noise!"'

'Damn that noise!' said Simon Iff, with the appropriate gruff intonation.

'I'm supposed to be behind the door. Now I say "Oh darling, here's the debenture!" and you say "What?" very loud.'

Iff complied with the ritual of this ghastly game.

'Now I say, laughing, "Annette has used it to fix the mirror" and you say, "Christ, I hope you're not joking. Lemme see!"'

Simple Simon repeated the words.

'I can't get it, it's jammed. And you say "For Christ's sake, don't tear it! Here, wait!" Only, you're tired tonight; so I come to you instead.'

Was the spirit of the dead woman in the room to haunt and to obsess? The great magician felt himself a mere automaton.

'Then, as you come through the door, I jump, and do it!'

But Simon pulled himself together. He caught the boy's arm.

'The game's over, sonny. We'll find a nicer game for you. You know how frightened you are when you find blood all over you.'

'All right, Mr Iff!'

'Let's go downstairs! They'll wonder what we're doing, and that will never do.'

'But Mummy said always to put the razor away first of all.'

'Right you are.'

This done, they went down laughing, hand in hand.

'Take him!' said Simon Iff to Maddie, and beckoned Jonas Black.

Again the bedroom; Iff climbed the chair, and produced the razor. Black smiled grimly.

'Partial to cocaine?' queried the magician, throwing a packet to the detective. 'I am, rather,' and he pocketed one for himself. 'In strict moderation; only when already feeling jolly, and desirous of working all night without fatigue.'

'Hum!' said Black, 'isn't it taking a chance?'

'So is getting born. The man who takes no chances takes nothing.'

'A dangerous doctrine, Mr Iff.'

'So are mountaineering and big-game shooting dangerous sports. But they fit you for the big risks of life. Never be afraid of anything, least of all of yourself. Dope-fiends are born, not made.'

The mystic had replaced the section of railing, and climbed down from the chair. He handed the razor to Black, and stood looking at him, attentively.

'In her death-struggle,' said the inspector, without a quaver in his voice, 'the unhappy woman must have thrust the weapon beneath her body, perhaps with some unconscious idea of concealment. I blame myself severely for having failed to discover it on my first inspection. On the other hand, I deduced its position by pure logic. May promotion follow upon this example of the remarkable penetration of Inspector Black! Unless you want a write-up,' he added, rather nervously.

'No,' laughed the other. 'Thine be the kingdom and the power and the glory!'

'Very good of you,' Black stammered.

'Come along!'

As they descended the stairs the house-bell rang.

'Briscoe!' said Black.

Maddie was opening the door, and Black ran forward.

'I'm a fool! I've troubled you for nothing. It's a clear case of suicide; I've found the razor right under the body.'

'I'll beat it,' replied Briscoe. 'Let's go get a drink.'

'I'm on.' Black waved a farewell.

Simon turned to Maddie.

'I need a house-keeper,' he said. 'Not much of that insurance money left, perhaps. Between us we may be able to put Jack and Jack together, don't you think?'

The old woman could not contain herself. Her apron went to her eyes; then she ran pell-mell into the kitchen.

'And so,' remarked Simon Iff to himself as he left the house, 'in my old age I find myself obliged to shut the door. Yet – should not Dobson be back from Manhattan? Intuition crieth yea. I will test it. Anon.'

AN OLD HEAD ON YOUNG SHOULDERS

Mr Simon Iff.

My dear Sir,

It would give much pleasure to Mrs Barker and myself if you would dine with us tomorrow night, May sixth, at The Pleasance. Seven o'clock precisely.

Very truly,
ANDREW P. BARKER

This letter was written on the stationery of the Bank of Barker and Barker. Its president, who wrote it, was in fact the bank itself. He was one of the most formidable figures in American finance. He was not spectacular; the public never heard his name; he had never lent it to any movement of dubious or speculative character. In Wall Street his name was a synonym for extreme conservatism. He was a 'gold-bug' of the deepest dye. He made no attacks upon any market. But in defence he was impregnable; the few who had dared to test his resources came out of the brief struggle with their own knocked about severely.

His principle was a simple one indeed; it was to consider only real, as opposed to market, values. Once, in his early days, his copper holdings had dropped to derisory prices. At the conference of his scared colleagues he had sat silent, turning over the pages of a medical journal. Asked point-blank for his opinion, he had said: 'I see here that copper is an ingredient of

Fehling's solution, which is used in testing for sugar in diabetes. I think we should buy some copper. It will always be useful.' He was three millions to the good when the bear raid collapsed.

In his private life he was the same vigorous, sensible, dominant personality. He never had trouble in his household, because he never allowed it. People called him truculent, but it was their mistake. He merely watched for possible germs of trouble, and sterilised them before they multiplied and grew. His wife and his children and his servants were devoted to him. They understood that he never needed a harsh word or action because he had gone out to meet the first causes which lead to such events.

His physical appearance was in complete harmony with these characteristics. He was tall, robust and athletic, six feet and seven inches in his socks, with the chest development of the Farnese Hercules. A heavy shock of hair, jet black, was all untouched by time. He wore a full beard, square-cut. But, mostly striking feature of all, his complexion was of a strange pallor. This was due, no doubt, to a habit of life most singular in so physically gifted a man. He never took exercise. He ate most sparingly. He slept hardly at all. He hated the open air. He employed three confidential private secretaries, in shifts. They were his shadows. At any moment he might begin dictation.

His clothes were as remarkable as himself. Winter and summer, snow or shine, he wore always the same plain suit of grey. He had gone to his tailor, twenty years before Simon Iff's journey to America, chosen a cloth, and ordered the entire supply. Send me three suits every year, said he. He had arranged similarly for a supply of tall silk hats. For overcoat he wore always a vast Italian mantle. In this he would sleep, as often as not, lying in his long lounge basket-chair. He had a small Turkish bath in his house, and it was his rule to spend an hour daily in 'elimination,' as his phrase was. He had never known an hour's ill-health. His life was absorbed in his plans and his domestic affairs. All who were really familiar with him loved him as much as they respected him.

The result, curious enough even in this world of paradox, was that he had the name of a tyrant, a brute, a satyr and a brigand. He was one of those men about whom strange stories gather, without a vestige of foundation. Perhaps the principal reason for this was envy; but he certainly contributed to it by his detestation of words. No man, he held, had any right to intrude on the sacred solitude of another man's self-communing. Permission to speak once given, as by companionship at a meal, he was genial and even loquacious; but his wife would hardly have dared to telephone to the bank if the house had been on fire.

It was this man who was not in his house when Simon Iff came, invited to dinner. Mrs Barker apologised in the most charming style. 'A sudden and inexorable call to Washington, Mr Iff, at the last moment. Nobody less than the President, I am sure, could have made him break an appointment with you.'

Simon expressed his regrets.

'But the Signorina will be here, of course,' continued Mrs Barker, prattling. 'I don't know how much my husband has told you – and he doesn't know her well, you see. She's really the most wonderful woman alive. Do you know, three years ago every doctor in Europe and America had given me up. I had had eight operations. And then I met Signorina Visconti. In a month I was well, and though it has taken me a long time to regain my full strength, I have never had the slightest return of the trouble. Isn't that wonderful?'

Simon Iff had a prejudice against all spiritual healers and their kin. He thought that bodily ills should be treated by bodily means, mental ills by mental means, moral ills by moral means, and so on. '*Suum cuique!*' he would exclaim. 'Render to Caesar the things that are Caesar's, and to God the things that are God's!'

Moreover, his experience had taught him that most of such people were quacks – some ignorant, some devilish – and he could never make up his mind which of those two classes was the more dangerous.

But when the little Italian lady arrived, he was instantly disarmed. She had not a milligramme of charlatanism in her whole being. She was rather short and divinely plump, the most exquisite Botticelli type he had ever seen in the flesh; and she might have served Boccaccio in his merriest mood. She brimmed with beauty and brilliance. She was a lady to every tingling fingertip, yet she had initiative without a shadow of suppression. As Simon shook hands with her, he realised that one would have to be very ill indeed not to feel the radiance of her vitality. Her laughing eyes and her full lips seemed to promise the temperament of Venus, but the high, pure, cloudless brow made one think rather of Diana. She implored Simon not to think of her as the celebrated healer, but as the unknown sculptor. She had never exhibited, but it was known that she worked night and day. Iff marvelled at her thumbs, modelled by years of masterful contest with clay and wax. It was clear that she had sublimated her natural force into the creative energy of art. All through dinner she kindled the whole world in the lightnings of her imagination, she flashed from wit to wisdom, and from roguishness to pathos. Was it wonderful that the magician, responsive, stimulated infinitely by the mere contagion of her person, felt that he himself had never appeared to better advantage?

No sooner was dinner at an end than she excused herself; she had to work on the foundation of a 'Bacchus and the Tiger,' for which the model was to arrive at seven o'clock the next morning.

'The Bacchus or the Tiger?' asked Iff.

'Bacchus,' she said – '*Evoe ho! Evoe*! The most wonderful boy in the world – one of those wine-stained languid types, like a spoiled girl! *Evoe ho!*'

She went out. It was as if a flame had swept through the room. It left the others feeling as saints feel when they sink back to the realisation that they have enjoyed the Beatific Vision.

'Isn't she perfectly delightful?' cried Mrs Barker. 'Oh, do smoke!' and she took a cigarette to keep Simon's Larrañaga in countenance.

He waited till the butler had withdrawn before replying. Then he said slowly in a very serious voice: 'A friend in need is a friend indeed.'

'Oh, yes! Believe me, Mr Iff, I should have been in my grave these two years but for Fiamella!'

'I meant tonight.'

'Oh fisherman, oh fisherman! You were perfectly amazing. To hear the pair of you, what a pleasure! What a match! Oh, you ought to marry Fiamella!'

'Marriage has its grave anxieties.'

'Don't be depressing!'

'Need I?' A long pause followed the incisive question.

'Mr Iff, you are right. There is something most terribly wrong. I've been crazy to tell you about it, but I wouldn't spoil your evening if I could help it. But you've seen through me, so I'll talk.'

'You've been as plucky as women always are, in the big troubles. That's how I knew it was something ugly. And I could see you wanted to tell me, or I'd have held my peace.'

'I told you a lie about Washington. I don't know where my husband is.'

Iff nodded.

'I must explain some of his ways, to begin with. He's a very strange man – most strong, most loveable – but with ideas that in a lesser man would be fads. He said he had no time to learn the name of a new secretary, it was enough bother changing, anyhow, so they are always Mr Morning, Mr Noon and Mr Night, according to whether they are on the eight o'clock, twelve o'clock or four o'clock shift. Often I myself don't know their names. Well, early this morning Mr Noon rang up and asked Mr Morning to stay on till one o'clock, as he had a sick headache, and wanted a little extra time to get over it.'

'Forgive me!' interrupted Simon, 'but I want to say one word to give you confidence. You are a most wonderful woman. I won't guess whether Mr Barker was the cause or the effect of that fact!'

'I don't understand.'

'May I make a guess? What you have just told me has nothing whatever to do with the story.'

'True,' said the lady, in surprise. 'How did you guess?'

'You had trouble to remember that you ought to tell me.'

'Yes.'

'And you told me – here's another guess – because you have trained your mind. You thought – rightly, as I judge – that the most apparently irrelevant irregularity might be pertinent on a day during which a great irregularity has occurred?'

She thought a moment. 'I believe that was actually my reason. But it's subconscious.'

'Just so.'

'You have given me confidence, indeed, indeed!' she cried eagerly. 'I know you'll tell me what has happened.'

'I will try.'

'Mr Barker always takes lunch at midday precisely, thus avoiding the crush of a later hour. It is Mr Noon's duty to await him at the door of the private office from five minutes before the hour. They go together to lunch. Mr Noon orders the meal while my husband goes to wash his hands. As a rule the tavern is empty, save for a stray customer or so, until twelve-thirty. Today there was a rather hilarious party of a dozen salesmen. They have met there weekly at eleven-thirty for the last three months. It's a kind of informal club.'

'You are certainly a miracle for details. I suppose Mr Morning told you all this?'

'Yes, in a memorandum which he sent to me by Mr Noon. But I had a second account from Julius Barker. Well, Mr Morning, assuming his absent colleague's duty – this had happened at odd times before – began to extract the gist of the telegrams in the evening papers, which he would retail to my husband at lunch. He became absorbed in this work. The waiter would of course not bring the lunch until Mr Barker resumed his seat. Mr Morning quite forgot the flight of time for a while; then he awoke to it. His watch said twelve-thirty-five. Instantly he thought of an accident – an apoplexy, perhaps. He ran up to the "men's room." The attendant, who knew Mr Barker well, of course, said that he had left, taking his coat and hat, twenty minutes or so before. The secretary returned to his seat, absolutely nonplussed. But, in the absence of orders to go, he decided to stay. He would be off duty at one o'clock; so he would eat his lunch, and report at the bank at that hour. He did so. Mr Noon was waiting, as in order. Where was Mr Barker? The vice-president had seen him come into the bank. He remembered the minute, twelve-twenty, as he himself was hurrying out to lunch, uptown, a trifle pressed for time. The cashier had seen Mr Barker go into the vaults. He came out again a few minutes later, and went directly into the street, turning towards the tavern.

'This was all a little unusual, but perfectly satisfactory, so far. The alarm began at two-thirty, when Mr Berger, of Berger and Watts, called to complete the sale of an important block of real estate. The purchase price was two million, three hundred thousand dollars. At ten minutes past three Mr Barker was still absent. His cousin and partner, Julius Barker, held hasty conference with the vice-president and Mr Noon. Julius had full power to sign cheques; it would never do to put off Mr Berger. They decided to lie: "Mr Barker has just telephoned. He has been delayed in the traffic, but is on his way now." Three o'clock; it was impossible to postpone a decision. Julius apologised, signed Mr Berger's cheque, and got rid of him. He then gave the deed of sale to the cashier to place in the vaults. The man came back to Julius, and asked him to come down. The vaults had been robbed! Bills of various denominations, and negotiable securities, amounting to over six hundred thousand dollars in all, were missing. Julius simply told him to compile a list of what was gone, and to hold his tongue. He then went straight to Commissioner Teake, of the Police.

'It was not a simple matter. The men on guard had seen Andrew take the securities, as he had a perfect right to do. But it was utterly unreasonable and without motive. He went to Teake merely as to a man experienced in mysteries. Teake could only suggest an enquiry as to whether any of the securities had been negotiated.

'The whole street knew about it! A dozen different men, perfectly unknown, had thrown large blocks of stock into the market. The wildest rumours were afloat. The principal stock attacked had fallen four points. The whole thing was utterly unexpected, and everything fell in sympathy. It was a crazy hour. You know there's trouble brewing in Morocco? Everyone jumped to the solution – bad news from Paris!

'Teake dismissed the whole affair with a laugh. "Your cousin has a little coup in hand," he said. "Of course he's keeping out of the way; he doesn't want the reporters at him. And if the news of his disappearance leaks out, it will be another little point in his game." Julius was perfectly satisfied. He drove out here, and told me the whole story.'

'Has Julius any brains?'

'Oh, Mr Iff, I see you agree with me, and I'm crazy with anxiety. I know Andrew, indeed I do.'

'The whole story is utterly absurd. Your husband is the sanest and strongest financier in the city, and we are asked to believe that he's engaged in an absolutely melodramatic gamble.'

'I telephoned to Mr Teake. He said he would come out after dinner. Isn't that his car coming up now? Oh, if it were only Andrew!'

Simon Iff shook his head. 'Your husband would have telephoned.'

In fact, it was Commissioner Teake who was admitted. 'The very man I wanted!' he cried. 'You must help me to convince this dear lady that there's nothing amiss! Boys will be boys, ha! ha!'

'I'm sorry. I don't see it in that light at all.'

Teake became suddenly sober, like a drunkard in fresh air. 'Well, where is the light, then?'

'Mrs Barker, may I talk this over with Mr Teake? Take an hour's rest; we may come to some conclusion.'

'You'll find me in the parlour,' she acquiesced. 'Order anything you need.' She went away, paler than a foggy dawn.

'Now, young man,' said Iff at once, 'you've been making a very great fool of yourself. We must clear this thing up right away; it looks dreadfully bad to me.'

'Why shouldn't the old boy have a little flutter on his own?'

'Because he isn't an old boy; he's a middle-aged man. Now tell me, is there any bad news from Paris?'

'Washington says not. They're sure it will blow over.'

'Morning, Noon and Night are here, I hope. Oh yes, she would be sure to arrange that. Let's have them in – no, let's look in on them!'

The butler, summoned, directed them to the billiard-room. The three men were playing pool, listlessly, not talking.

Simon observed them intently. They reminded him, whimsically enough, of the Three Gardeners in *Alice in Wonderland*. They had the effect of paste-board; they were as unreal as their names. The personality of Barker had overshadowed them completely, had left them high and dry, jetsam of the ocean of humanity. They had no orders any more; there was therefore no reason why they should do anything whatever! So they played pool without even trying to play it. They all looked up simultaneously; but Night, being technically on duty, advanced first to greet the guests and effected the introductions very simply and suavely.

Physically, they differed a good deal. Morning, slight and dapper, was tall and dark. He was obviously suffering from lack of sleep, and strain on the nerves. Noon was short, remarkably short, but sturdy, with somewhat sparse red hair. He seemed a little elated at being well outside the case. A sick headache is usually its own reward, like virtue, which it resembles strongly in many other ways.

Night was taller even than Morning, a pale blonde type, very handsome, but full of sober energy.

'I want to ask you some questions,' began Teake, sitting on the big chesterfield and crossing his legs. 'I may inform you, as a starter, that I've looked up your records, and your movements, and you all seem to be candidates for stained glass windows. So let's get plenty of action in the film! Anything strange in Mr Barker's behaviour of late?'

Morning shook his head. Noon pursed his lips tightly. Night smiled.

'Come across!'

'Well,' volunteered Night, 'I think there may be a little *shershy lafamm.*'

'I don't think there's anything in that,' said Noon.

Shielding his employer, reflected Teake, and concentrated his energies on Night. This youth was however quite unable to contribute anything definite; he became more and more confused as he went on; in the end he amounted to an 'impression.'

Teake now went through the events of the day with each man in turn. Their accounts were most unsatisfactorily satisfactory.

The enquiry did not elicit a single new fact, or cast doubt upon a single old one.

Morning's movements were known at the bank; Noon was still in bed at twelve-thirty, according to his wife, the landlady who called for the rent, and the servant who cleaned the apartment, so that he must have gone straight to the bank in a taxi, as in fact he did, by the driver's story. Night had also slept till one o'clock, as was his custom, and then dined at his boarding-house.

Teake got up, disgruntled. 'May as well go and sample that port,' he growled. 'Ever see such a rotten case? Not a thing to take hold of.' He lurched off, with Simon Iff in his wake.

'I rather thought those young men were deliciously illuminating – very beacons in our darkness – but alas! they blaze above a dangerous lee shore.'

'Well, I'll drink the port, and you'll tell me the story.' The good Commissioner was for the first time a little piqued.

'You're angry with yourself, not with me,' said Iff, answering his tone rather than his words, 'just as Mr Night, being himself a woman-fancier, thought he saw just that trait in his hero.'

'O ho! So that's the way the cat jumps!'

'But Noon, who has some real brains, of a sort, tried to give, by denying it, the same impression as Night by affirming it.'

'That's so.'

'Had Barker any enemies?'

'I think not. Everyone who doesn't know him swears he hates him; but in his own circle he is popular.' Teake suddenly interrupted himself. 'Did you say "has" or "had"?' he added, with curious violence.

'It is possibly not the correct American usage, but I said "had"!'

'You mean he's dead?'

'I'd risk a dollar on it.'

'Why?'

'Because he's not the type of man to go insane.'

'Right.'

'He had no mental liabilities, so to speak; but he was bound to come to a bad end sooner or later, through his pitiful moral weakness.'

'Say, have you got any mental liabilities of your own? This chap is our shining example of Force of Character.'

'Well, in one way, of course. He did manage to put a suit of armour on the poor old woman!'

'I don't get you one little bit.'

'An athlete doesn't wear corsets. You don't put bars and struts to shore up a sound building.'

'Try again!'

'If you want steam to exert pressure you have to confine it; you don't have to put an iron jacket on a steel bar. If a piston had a will of its own, you wouldn't have to fix it in a cylinder.'

'How do you mean? You're using a soft drill yourself on this ivory dome!'

'Well, this is the way I see it. Andrew P. Barker was a man of routine. He had all the virtues. That's the mark of a man without virtue. Barker couldn't trust himself, so he made a machine to confine his energies to proper channels. He forced all that loose steam to work in only the one direction. A real man doesn't have to sign the pledge; it's the weak drunkard who is helped by that. A real nation doesn't need restrictive laws, prohibition, and God knows what other degenerate follies. A free people doesn't keep on shouting "Liberty"; a chaste people, howling over the Pewrity of Wimmen – or rather Wummon.'

'Good old England!'

'Well, don't you know, we do rather notice something wrong! This Barker, to resume, is so afraid of failing to use his time well that he even invents this ridiculous morning, noon and night business.'

'That's a funny idea.'

'Now it's easy to keep yourself from being run over by a railway train, because it runs on rails. Also, you can be sure to catch your railway train, because all you have to do is to wait by the line till it passes. If it runs on schedule, you can make all sorts of plans to do what you want to that train. An automobile isn't so easy to avoid or to attack. Its movements may not suit your ideas.

'And so it is with men. A creative artist is a strong man with a will of his own. You never know what he may do next. And so we find that the world has an instinctive fear of him. He's an incalculable force. But the man of habit is strong only in so far as his habits furnish him with armour. So all that one who wishes to attack him has to do is to find the weak place in the armour. This was why rapier displaced battle-axe and broadsword. The elastic, active, willed, invisible defence proved stronger than the immobile plate of mail. Here's a guess for you: in the next war these impregnable concrete and steel fortresses of Brialmont will crumple like egg-shells; the best defence will be the thin red line of 'eroes. It's always happening; the old stone castles were no good as soon as people invented a mobile artillery instead of the old catapult and battering-ram.'

'So you think somebody has been getting after Barker.'

'Sure of it! Barker would never have trusted himself to gamble. Suppose he had really had some secret tip from Paris; he would have refused to win on the "sure thing." He would have said, "I daren't break my principles. The first win will tempt me to a second flutter – until one day I plunge on a rotten tip and go under, as I've seen so many poor devils of gamblers do." Eh? Then, even if he had decided to take the dive, he would still have got the money in a regular way. He wouldn't have called attention to the game by breaking his routine. So I'm perfectly sure that the man who took the money was not Andrew P. Barker.'

'But, good God, who could possibly hope to personate him? The most familiarly conspicuous and eccentric figure in New York!'

'That Italian cloak would be an asset as far as the figure goes. And he always wore a suit of the same cloth, always the same singular pattern of top hat. Then the beard is a great help.'

'But his extraordinary stature! There aren't fifty men in the whole of the United States who could be mistaken for him, however well disguised, even in twilight.'

'Ah, by taking thought one may add a cubit to one's stature.'

'About an inch, perhaps, with special boots. More, and the walk would be thrown out.'

'Quite so. I'm not clear on this, mind, yet. But the personation is helped once more by his habits. An imposter, well-advised as to Barker's routine, would know that no one would dare speak to him. Every rigid defence has its weak spot. Conspirators could play up to him with absolute safety. He would never do anything unusual which would disturb them.'

'Well, on that hypothesis he's been murdered or at least kidnapped. They have to have his keys. It could have been done in the street, with a car. I think I'll get busy, and look out for a very tall man.' Teake rose, and rang for his coat and hat.

'No,' said Simon Iff, 'On my hypothesis, you should look for a very short man.'

'Well, he's not short any more!'

Teake laughed heartily at his play on words, and thought it safer to explain it. 'Six hundred thousand or so! *And* the squeeze of the bear raid! Some haul!' He went down the steps of the house.

'By the way, dine with me tomorrow night?' cried Iff.

'Right.'

'I'll 'phone you time and place.

'Single-track mind,' mused Iff, when he had gone. 'He never even waited to hear my theory of Morning, Noon and Night, and their very interesting revelations.'

He went upstairs, and told Mrs Barker that Commissioner Teake thought her husband had been kidnapped. Someone must have known that he would leave the bank that day with that money on him – perhaps the party to whom he intended to pay it.

This pious fraud accomplished, the mystic returned to his apartment, and spent the night in meditation upon the Four Formless States, ending with that which is "not Nothing, and yet neither *P* nor *p*′."

At ten o'clock, however, he was at the tavern where Barker always lunched. In his hand was a grip-sack. 'I want you to look after this,' he said to the attendant, 'and have you got a place where I could dress for dinner? I want a table for six-thirty.'

'Sure; there's a dressing-room in here.' He led the way through the 'men's room.' A little corridor gave access to four private rooms, small but comfortably furnished, and fitted with all toilet accessories.

'Keep this for me. Six o'clock,' said Simon Iff. 'And tell the head waiter to book me a table for four at six-thirty.' Then he went out to a telephone booth. Teake promised to be punctual.

He then called up Mr Noon. 'Mr Barker has been found,' he said; 'he had a lapse of memory, and is not quite recovered. But he has asked me to tell you to take up your duties at six-thirty tonight, at the usual table in the tavern. Please tell Mr Night and Mr Morning to report at The Pleasance at their regular hours.'

Simon Iff was looking at the second hand of his watch. Twenty seconds elapsed before the reply came. 'I'm very glad to hear your news, Mr Iff. I will be on hand at six-twenty-five.'

The mystic hung up the receiver. 'Yes,' he mused, 'the young man may well be astonished.'

Lastly he rang up Signorina Visconti, and asked her to join the little party – to celebrate the return of the banker. The girl was frankly and spontaneously overjoyed. Iff told her that he was motoring out to convey the glad intelligence to Mrs Barker. Indeed, he went to The Pleasance; but his errand was another. He broke it to the widow that she need have no hope.

The three guests were punctual to the moment. Iff ordered dinner to be served.

'Oughtn't we to wait for Mr Barker?' suggested Noon.

'He will not be here,' replied Simon; 'I will explain his absence.' He applied himself to his oysters with a will. The others followed his example, but it was a poor pretence. The nerves of all three were terribly on edge. Simon Iff ate and drank remorselessly, now and again speaking of the weather, or asking some question about American customs or politics. By the time he had lighted his cigar the social atmosphere was impossible.

'I will now keep my promise. I will explain the absence of Mr Barker. As I told you last night, Teake, he was a moral weakling. He had strong passions – even horrible vices, one might say, if one were conventional – and he was afraid of them, as he was afraid of everything else. So he pigeon-holed them. "I must be absolutely safe," he thought, I doubt not; "I will give ten minutes daily of my time to this indulgence. And I will choose a time and place where no one can possibly suspect me." So he took one of the dressing-rooms upstairs for his house of assignation. Hardly anybody comes here before twelve-thirty; the attendant, well bribed, could easily slip anyone through without suspicion being aroused. He chose his secretaries for their sympathy with his ideas, and made them his accomplices. So much you and Mr Night were good enough to tell me, don't you know, with that *shershy lafamm* talk. Besides, I knew it all before. The weak character was enough to inform anyone who happens to have read the works of Doctor Sigmund Freud. I was looking already for something of the sort when your appearance and manner brought the fullest confirmation.' He smiled pleasantly at Mr Noon.

'What has this to do with Mr Barker's absence?' said the Italian girl. 'Has he eloped?'

'I think he must have lost his head,' replied Simon, lightly. It was quite ten seconds before he obtained an echo to his laughter.

'Now, how should we attack this person, if we wished? We know exactly what he will do at any moment – and we have a matter of ten minutes or so daily when he is – in his way – off his guard. Ten minutes when he has contracted out of the regular protection which a policed society affords its members! Some genius conceives the idea of killing him and personating him, taking his keys, and robbing his bank. The only weak moment in the man's day is this fatal ten minutes. So the attack is timed accordingly. But the attendant must suspect nothing. Therefore the body has to be disposed of. Difficulty Number One. You can't carry the corpse of a giant out of a public restaurant without causing comment. Difficulty Number Two. You can't look like Andrew P. Barker. However, our genius put the two difficulties together, and made one ease of them. It's a case of an old head on young shoulders.' Again he laughed pleasantly, and again the others forced their courtesy to echo him.

'Now, to play the part of Barker, we need someone who knows the bank like the palm of his hand – for he may not be able to see very well.'

'Why?' said Teake.

'A technical difficulty, merely technical. I dare say there was a clever dodge to obviate it. To proceed, our friend must know Barker and his little ways very well. Possibly Morning, Noon or Night. Eh? All three have alibis, true. But a man in bed with a sick headache in a darkened room – couldn't we get away with a waxwork bust?'

'Are you accusing me?' asked Noon, with a face as black as a thunder-cloud.

'Of course not. I'm merely theorising. You forget altogether that you're a very short man – a full head shorter than Barker, I should judge.' Again he rippled audibly, and again his guests automatically copied him.

'Now suppose that we had a surgeon of exceptional skill waiting in the dressing-room with Mr Noon. Barker arrives, and is killed with a single blow. Our surgeon has a water-proof sheet, and all sorts of paraphernalia, ready in the dressing-room next door. They take in the corpse. He cuts off the head, stops the bleeding with paraffin wax or some such simple device, and fits it into the framework which has been fitted to the head and shoulders of our young friend here. The difficulty of the stature and the likeness disappears at a stroke. The cloak completes the device, and off marches Mr Noon to do his work at the bank, while the surgeon divides the trunk and limbs, and packs them away into the sample-cases of our convenient salesmen. The surgeon, possibly enough, drives off in a closed car, picks up Noon, removes the disguise, goes home, and destroys the traces. Each salesman gets rid of his trophy easily enough – one-twelfth of a two-hundred pound man is only a little over thirty pounds – there are fifty ways of working it. Then Noon distributes the swag, and they are all separately offering the stock on the market before one o'clock.'

He had been addressing the ceiling, but now he turned his eyes on Commissioner Teake.

'Have I explained Mr Barker's absence to your satisfaction?'

'You sure have. I think I'll take Mr Noon along with me. There will be no trouble in getting evidence.'

Noon smiled. He knew that Iff's accusation had been merely guesswork. But Teake, once started, went on like a steam-roller.

'We happen to have had all this dope on Barker for ten years. If Mr Iff could guess that right, I'll take the rest of the guess on trust, and work it up. Come along, Mr Noon.'

The young man followed with a grin. Teake was plainly puzzled by his attitude.

The Italian girl smiled. 'A most charming surprise dinner, Mr Iff! It was really perfectly wonderful. But now I must get home to Bacchus – will you take me?'

'I had hoped you would allow me.'

She asked him up into her studio, and threw off her wraps. Simon was more fascinated than ever with her beauty and vivacity.

'I'm going to tease you,' she said.

'I hope so.'

'So you dare put me off, like that wooden Teake, with a half-finished story? And poor Mr Noon! Really, it's too bad to play such a joke on a creature like that!'

'Yes, I thought I should like to finish the story in less unimaginative surroundings.'

'I should really like to know how you deduced what you did.'

'You should be ashamed to be envious. Creation's far finer than analysis – and you are an artist!'

'I shall not quote *Intentions* against you.'

'Well, there was no difficulty at all in seeing what had occurred. Step one: Barker wasn't the man at the bank. Therefore someone else was. Step two: Time and place became extremely limited. Step three: Noon's manner in the billiard-room showed that he knew something. I saw at once that his alibi was shaky. A wax model. Then where was he? Personating Barker. To succeed he must have either a very large stature or – a very small one, and another wax model. Then I saw that no wax would deceive people in the street or in the bank for a second. Disguise is cut out, as soon as one cuts out the tall man. Then what could resemble Barker's living head? Obviously, his dead one!

'Step four: Limitation of time and space help us to cast the persons of the drama, and to pick the scenery. When I went down to the tavern this morning I took my grip, in the fullest confidence that I should find a locale suitable for a murder. Mr Morning's story of the Twelve Jolly Salesmen went very nicely with Teake's tale of the Twelve Jolly Stock-dumpers. The disposition of corpses and stocks is made easier by the Great Economical Principle of Division of Labour. Need I say more?'

'About the – *dramatis personae?*'

'Oh, the mask of Noon? Yes, somebody had to make that, and somebody had to do that brilliant bit of rough dissection against time. And somebody had to devise the whole scheme – a lovely mixture of the ghastly and the grotesque – the finest gargoyle on the Black Cathedral of Crime! Well, possibly one person might have done all three. Personally, I think so.'

Signorina Visconti rose slowly from her chair.

'I wonder if you'd care to see my work – my other work.'

She pulled the damp cloth from the clay bust. Simon Iff jumped from his chair: the figure was a head of Christ, the conventional Italian type in all externals. But the mouth wore a smile satanic in mad merriment, and the eyes glared with a cold ferocity which was only the more fearful for their sardonic triumph.

The girl's laughter rang brilliant through the room.

'I asked you here because I knew you knew, and I thought I had better appeal to your better feelings. Noon will hold his tongue until he hears from me; but you must tip off that ass Teake, or he'll blurt something out.'

'I imagine so.' Simple Simon was slightly inclined to asperity, whose source he did not seek to trace.

'But it won't do. Observe, I shall come out into the limelight.'

'I imagine so.'

'But, my dear master, you are not in Europe. This is the State of New York.'

'I believe so.'

'You have not been here long. So I suppose you want to read *The Story of the Bad Banker and the Wronged Woman: or the Martyred Maiden's Madness.*'

'Oh!' said Simon Iff.

'With all your penetration, you have missed one vital fact. I have a pituitary body.'

'So has everybody.'

'But mine is hypo-hypertrophied; that is, of normal size. Consequently, I can do anything without knowing it; but that can only happen once in my life. So I'm not only innocent, but I can never do it again. The greatest alienists in the country will swear to this nonsense, partly for the fee, but most of all for the advertisement.'

'I see,' said Simon Iff, very slowly and painfully.

'All you can do is to hush up the whole affair. Surely Noon's grin surprised you? Mrs Barker is the dearest old lady; why should she find out what her adored husband was?'

'Thank you. May I use your telephone? I'll tell Teake it was just a practical joke.'

'English humour?'

'That's it,' said Simon, and called the number. 'By the way, why did you do it?'

'For fun.'

'American humour?'

'I see no joke there. Look once again at my God!'

'Hullo! That you, Teake? Simon Iff speaking. Let that chap Noon go now; the joke's gone far enough. Yea, J.O.K.E., joke. English humour. Yes, too bad; but I'll explain when I see you. All right; twelve-thirty. Don't be too cross; I really wanted to show you something. You were a bit hasty; tomorrow I'll tell you what really happened. Goodnight!' He hung up.

'And now I must leave you, most fascinating of assassins!'

'Yes; I fear you have a long night before you, thinking out an alternative theory for poor old Teake! But drop in whenever you feel lonesome – I suppose you wouldn't come to pose? You have a miraculous head. A little sad – three months now, isn't it? *Pan in Baeotia*, perhaps?'

'It appears that the *esprit de corps* of Olympus prevents even hostile deities from quarrelling when they meet on their travels in the remoter and less hospitable planets.'

'Gods that pass in the night, and bump each other in passing, should say "Please excuse it"! So?'

'The phraseology is perfect.' He took his hat.

'I want you to come and see me. Really, really, really, there's nothing, nothing, nothing to enjoy here. So what could the poor girl do?'

'I think I understand. But I should continue my travels, if I were you.'

Suddenly she threw her arms round his neck and kissed him passionately. Then she sat down and began to cry.

Simon Iff stroked her hair gently; then he let himself out.

'What a lot of stars!' he murmured to himself. 'Probably all different, and certainly all necessary. *Ne sutor ultra crepidam* – who am I to judge a genius? Satan finds some mischief still for idle hands to do; I'd better think out that story for Teake, or I shall find myself planning something atrocious.

> A deed of blood, or fire, or flames,
> Was meat and drink to Simple James:

Be wary, Simple Simon!'

And, lest he should fall into temptation, he decided to wind up the evening at Jack's.

THE PASQUANEY PUZZLE

Sir Humphry Davy, after his first experiment with the inhalation of ether, exclaimed, 'The Universe is composed solely of ideas.' Simon Iff had obtained that, and many another experience, without the aid of drugs. But although he was perfectly convinced that 'everything is illusion,' like the most advanced transcendental philosophers, he was equally sure that all illusion was interwoven in a causal nexus. There was no place in his universe for accident; there was no force so small that the cosmos failed to vibrate in due degree with it; and there was (further) no means of erasure applicable to any action. Nothing could be destroyed; so it was there if you could only find it; and the task of finding it was nothing but the removal of the masks and veils. He was only interested in crime because its detection sharpened the wits which he needed in the solution of philosophical problems. He used to say that the fundamental laws of thought were the true obstacles to thinking. 'My conviction that two and two make four is the limitation that hinders me from realising that they make five, as they must, or how could the universe itself have come from nothing? It is the difference between the human mind and the Divine!'

That was the conclusion of a little interview that he gave to a particularly enterprising lady reporter. He had succeeded for three months in keeping everybody away; but Miss Mollie Madison had been one too many for him. She had found a way to induce his Japanese servant to let her wait in his apartment, and, once installed, had caught his interest by asking him point-blank for his solution of the Pasquaney Puzzle.

'In me,' she exclaimed dramatically, 'you behold the unhappy Dolores Cass!'

'Excuse me, I do not,' he answered; 'I never heard of the Pasquaney Puzzle, and I know nothing of Dolores Cass. But you are certainly not an unhappy anybody.'

'Indeed, indeed, do not mock my misery!' she cried, tears standing in her big blue eyes.

'Delightful infant! Old birds are not to be caught with chaff. You're functioning – functioning in absolute harmony – which is the medical equivalent, in bad English, of being happy. At this particular moment, I perceive, you are unusually happy, even for you; and as you are an American, I assume that you are, somehow or other, putting one over on me. You're getting what you came for – be frank, now! It won't hurt you with me!'

She dropped her masquerade and laughed at him like the beautiful doll she was.

'Surely, Mr Iff! I'm getting the most adorable interview.'

'All right: what can I do for you?'

'Do tell me your views on everything!'

This was walking into the enemy's country, had she known it. Simple Simon took his revenge by doing as she asked. When he got to the 'two and two make five' peroration, she was sitting with note-book and pencil fallen despairingly in her lap.

'It's a shame, truly it is, Mr Iff! You know I can't write up all that high-brow stuff. It's absorbing to me, but the public won't stand for it.'

'Oh Democracy! Why is it that everybody I meet in this country is so eager to explain that everybody else is a fool? If you really respected and trusted the people, you wouldn't treat them as mental and moral imbeciles. I refer to your literature and your laws.'

Miss Mollie Madison was not quite sure of the answer.

Observe me, now!' said the mystic. 'I go on the opposite tack. The unknown fascinates me. So I implore you humbly to put me wise to the dope on the Pasquaney Puzzle.'

His sudden slang put her tremendously at her ease. She took a packet of yellow paper from her vanity-bag. 'I've got it all pat. I've read nothing else for a week. It was my one hope of getting you interested. You can rely on the facts; most of this was written up by one of the best men in the office.'

'We'll hope your bait of falsehood may catch a carp of truth. Put in your clutch!'

'Lake Pasquaney lies among the mountains of New Hampshire. It is about seventeen miles in circumference. Bristol, the nearest railway station, a town of twelve hundred inhabitants, is some three miles from the lower end. The lake contains several islands, and its shores are dotted with summer villas, mostly of the log-hut type, though here and there is a more pretentious structure, or a cluster of boarding-houses. Bristol is about three hours from Boston, so the lake is a favourite summer resort, even for week-enders. Automobile parties pass frequently, but keep mostly to the road on the east shore, that on the west being very rough. The scenery is said by Europeans who know both to compare with Scotland or Switzerland without too serious disadvantage.'

She looked merrily at him, and he smiled in grim appreciation of her subtle attack.

'Mrs Cass is a woman of fifty-three years old, the widow of a wealthy Bostonian of good family known all over the world for his attainments in pure mathematics.'

'Oh, *the* Cass! Indeed, this becomes very enthralling! I was exceedingly intrigued by his monograph on hyperbolic geometry, and his criticism of Sir William Thomson's theory of a labile ether.'

'Mrs Cass has four children: Newton Gauss, thirty, a prominent engineer; Hope Ada, twenty-five; Dolores, twenty-two; and Emily, nineteen. Last summer she rented a cottage which occupies one of the islands from July first to September thirtieth. Hope Ada is married to a surgeon named Smith. He and Newton used to come up from Boston whenever they could leave their work, and with them Geoffrey Travis, a ship-owner, twenty-six years old, who was engaged to marry Dolores. Emily was also engaged; but her fiancé, Arthur Green, was away in Los Angeles on some business connected with moving pictures.

'Mrs Cass did a good deal of entertaining; every evening the cottage would be filled with a merry party of friends from other cottages on the lake. The day was filled with boating, fishing, bathing, walking, motoring, every conceivable form of amusement. There was not a disagreement or a dull moment, week after week. The servants were all old and tried friends of the family'

The girl paused. 'Do you know, Mr Iff, there is really no object in my telling you all these details? The problem which arose on August the eighth is utterly insoluble. It is entirely remote from the situation. It means absolutely nothing.'

'All the better. But describe Dolores a little.'

'She is a college girl, taking after her father in looks and in mathematics. She was a pupil, also, of Professor Hugo Münsterberg, and had made a profound study of the evidence for spirit return. The year before, she had gone to Europe especially to sit with Eusapia Palladino and other famous mediums. Her mind is always at work on these lines. After a swim she would dry off on the beach with a note-book. But she is not a blue-stocking. She is pretty, blonde, plump, lively—'

'You called her unhappy.'

'I'm describing her as she was up to August the seventh.'

'I see.'

'She had not a care in the world. She was the life of the whole family. The others were more serious, but without her distinction. She lived in extremes; one minute she would be romping like a mad creature, the next immersed in conic sections.'

'Nobody envious?'

'Not a scrap. Not enough imagination, I should say. Besides, she was the most unselfish, sweet-tempered woman that God ever made.'

'Enter August the eighth.'

'With all the calm and brilliance of heaven itself! On that morning, the three girls got up early for a swim. They paddled up to a neighbouring islet in a canoe. This islet contains a particularly secluded cove. There is no cottage on it; only a few trees; there is no place to hide a rabbit. It stands well out in the lake. Dolores, though a brilliant athlete otherwise, was a poor swimmer; if she had been left alone on the islet she would have had to stay there till rescued.

'The three girls proceeded to bathe. (Of course they had gone out in their bathing suits.) Suddenly Hope missed Dolores, took alarm, and called her. No answer. She and Emily searched the islet; no sign of Dolores. They became hysterical. Just then they saw the other canoe; the men, Newton, Smith and Travis, were paddling out to find them. Hearing the girls scream, they redoubled their speed. A further search was made; it was as futile as the former. The whole party, except Smith, seem to have gone crazy with horror. Smith had hard work to get them back to the cottage. But, as they approached the island, what was their amazement to see Dolores walking up to the front door? With shouts of relief and joy they paddled gaily onwards, not considering at that moment that an impossibility had occurred; that she literally couldn't have got there, and had therefore no sort of right to be there!

'They entered the cottage. Mrs Cass was at the breakfast table, Dolores was just sitting down, and saying "What's the big idea, moms?"

'And then they all realised, as Mrs Cass had just done, that it was not Dolores at all!

'Her lover and her sisters had run forward to embrace her; they recoiled in sudden terror. Mrs Cass was shocked almost senseless; yet it was she who first cried, "Then where is Dolores?"

'Smith told his story; then Hope told hers. Everyone was aghast.

'Then Smith, whose scientific training seems to have served him well, grasped how bizarre the problem was. He turned to the girl in the chair: "Who are you, and how did you get here?"

'She stood up, pale as death. "Is it a charade?" she cried. "I'm Dolores; don't you know me?"

'"How did you get here?" insisted Smith.

'She could not or would not say.

'"That settles it," said he, and went to the telephone to call up the police, and Maddingley, a detective-inspector from Boston in whose powers he had great confidence. Meanwhile a storm raged in the dining-room.

'"Don't I know my own daughter?" cried Mrs Cass.

'"Where is the ring I gave you, if you are Dolores?" said her lover.

'The argument raged all morning. Smith rang up a general alarm; the whole lakeside population turned out to scour the woods, to dredge the lake about the fatal islet. Nothing was found. Maddingley had caught the early train from Boston and arrived a little before noon. He entered what he thought was an insane asylum! He and Smith obtained silence, and a rational examination began. There was absolute agreement between all the witnesses. The stranger looked like Dolores, talked like her, acted like her; there wasn't a thing missing of the tangible kind, except the ring; but it was not Dolores. She, on her side, underwent the most critical tests. She knew the family history, every detail correct; she described the position of the furniture in her bedroom, the contents of every drawer, even the secrets of a cash-box with a Yale lock, which she asked them to open, after telling them where she had hidden the key. The servants were examined also; they agreed with the family. It was the story of the Tichborne Claimant reversed. The only flaws in her case were her failure to explain her arrival from the islet, and the absence of her engagement ring; the only flaw in theirs was the appalling question "Then where is Dolores?"

'Maddingley was of course at a complete standstill. He could only form one conclusion, that the whole family, including the girl, had entered into a conspiracy to lie. He washed his hands of the matter, and returned to Boston, where he angrily and rather foolishly opened his mind to the Press.

'Unfortunately, most of the friends of Dolores in Boston were entirely on the side of the family. Everyone admitted the astonishing physical resemblance; everyone admitted the force of the fact that she knew every conceivable thing that Dolores had known; everyone agreed that the disappearance of one girl to nowhere, coincident with the arrival of an exactly similar girl from nowhere, was an unparalleled and incredible improbability. But they clung to their "interior certainty" based on unavowable, impalpable, unconscious impression – for all the world like so many mystics! Mrs Cass turned the imposter out of the cottage, after fitting her with an old dress; for the stranger was unquestionably wearing Dolores' bathing suit. And then she put up the shutters of the cottage, and went back to Boston. The family went into mourning, and refused to see any but the most intimate friends for the rest of the summer.

'The stranger found asylum with the proprietor of a sensational newspaper, who saw his way to exploit her. He had her psychoanalysed, and tested in fifty different ways; her handwriting was photographed and enlarged – I may say that her bank cashed her first cheque without a word, and then went back on itself, refused to pay any more, but on the other hand refused to prosecute for forgery. She sued them; they put up a half-hearted fight, and she won handsomely. They hunted through the effects of the missing girl for finger-prints – there was no end to it.

'Jenkins, of the *Turkey-Buzzard*, most certainly knew his business. He got experts from all over the country at loggerheads; he kept the whole of the United States in a turmoil for six months on end. It's still going on, fairly strong; safe for an argument in any gathering in the United States. The stranger's doing well, too; they say she stuck out for a thousand a week. And she's certainly earned it! That looks, by the way, as if she were not Dolores; for Dolores had all the money she needed. And Dolores wouldn't have given her family all that sorrow. No, if it's she, she must have one whale of a motive!'

'And what do you think?'

'I can't. I can't see what happened to the Dolores of the islet, unless they're all lying. And people don't turn out the best beloved for a joke; not people like the Cass family.'

'Have you photographs?'

Miss Molly Madison promptly produced a docket.

'Nothing to go by, as I expected,' grunted Simon Iff. 'Yet – this is last week's – was it taken last week?'

'Surely. New dress; new pose. The Press has to keep up to date in this country!'

'Well, I suppose the best of us has a failing. This girl doesn't seem to be suffering as much as one would expect. She's got the anguished look, all right; but she hasn't lost much flesh since the fatal eighth of August.'

'Oh, some people get fat on worry.'

'Then you think it is Dolores, after all?'

Miss Mollie Madison was caught. She gave up. 'Yes, I do; I think everybody does; only that makes the mystery more insoluble than ever.'

'Then you think psychological difficulties are more serious than physical ones?'

'How you do pick one up! Yes, I suppose that's what I do think.'

'My own course is simple. I will publish my solution. Or – wait – that's hardly fair. Was Dolores in love with Travis?'

'Very much. Friends and playmates from childhood; not another man in her life. We went through that with a tooth-comb.'

'Mr Geoffrey Travis is not so faithful. He is engaged to be married to another girl.'

'Impossible! He's heartbroken!'

'Ah, it's the double standard, I'm afraid!'

'I won't believe it of Geoffrey Travis.'

'Well, you watch the papers. If there isn't an announcement to that effect in three days, you may come up here and get the box of gloves I'm betting you about it.'

'Is it a joke?'

'Well, it is rather. Don't put it in your interview, though, or you'll spoil everything. But you may say that – er – I think I'll write it down for you; I want verbal accuracy in this one thing please.

> 'Mr Iff said that the case showed clear evidence of certain influences connected with what is commonly and erroneously called the supernatural; and that he would publish a full analysis of the case in these columns, and in the journals devoted to psychical research, in one month from date.

'I think that will do. Only – don't put it in unless I'm wrong about Travis. So come up at four o'clock on Friday, and have tea, and we'll have another chat.'

'You're as mysterious as the case itself.'

'Just so,' smiled Simon. 'Quite plain sailing, if you think it out!'

Miss Mollie Madison sailed queenly out of the apartment, blessed above women in the possession of a number one 'scoop.'

Simon Iff called to his Jap to pack a bag. 'I'll be back Thursday evening, at the latest,' said he.

And on Thursday morning, Miss Mollie Madison, waking late after a hard night covering somebody's début, opened her paper at the society column to read the formal announcement of the engagement of Mr Geoffrey Travis to Miss Alberta Crosman of Philadelphia.

'How could he possibly know?' she wailed. 'He is a magician; it is all supernatural! But oh! what a scoop! What a scoop!'

She made the world's record for a lady's toilet look like a basket of eggs dropped from the Woolworth Building, and reached the office to write up the prophecy just about the time when Simon Iff, sitting with Geoffrey Travis in his office in Boston, saw the door flung open and an impetuous young lady, with a really remarkable diamond on her business finger, burst in with the cry: 'Don't you dare, Geoffrey, don't you dare!'

By the men's faces she saw that she had been tricked; but she didn't mind much.

Simon Iff slipped out with a wave of the fingertips. 'Won't disturb you now; see you at the wedding.'

'Don't forget you're the best man!' shouted Geoffrey, through the waves of loosened gold that flowed about his head.

It was with reverence and godly fear that Miss Mollie Madison knocked at the door of 'that uncanny old man' on Thursday afternoon. She had just heard on long distance of the reappearance of the real Dolores, and Simon Iff's reference to the supernatural, which she had of course completely misunderstood, had set her imagination awhirl.

She was decidedly reassured to find him making the tea in a very fantastic and elaborate but very practical manner with one hand, and toasting muffins over a silver spirit lamp with the other.

'Welcome, my child!' he cried. 'It may be you can lift the burden from my soul!'

She offered her utmost: what was the trouble?

'I despair of humanity,' cried he. 'I can trust no living creature either to make tea or to toast muffins, save myself. Yet they must be accomplished simultaneously, or all is lost!' He comically resigned the task to her. 'You finish it! I must lament alone. I am getting old. The appalling catastrophe in the Pasquaney Puzzle has ruined my last hope for Man!'

'Why, haven't you heard?' she said, aglow. 'The real Dolores has come back this morning.'

'I was there,' said Simon. 'Pour out the tea, and I will declare to you this mystery. But I will declare it decently and in order; the catastrophe whereof I speak will therefore come last.'

'I love being teased.'

'It was evident from the first that the family was not lying. A joke might have been well enough for a day or a week, though a high-bred Baaston clan is the last place on earth – if Baaston can be said to be on earth – to look for it. It is unthinkable that they should keep it up for six months and more. One might have explained the mere disappearance of Dolores by supposing that the two girls were lying for some strong motive, but that would involve a Second Girl, with all the difficulties attached to that theory. It was pretty clear to me that the Casses were absolutely honest, and absolutely bewildered.

'It followed that Dolores herself was the mainspring of the mechanism. She could not have been drowned in the shallow water of a calm lake within a few yards of her sisters; she could not have been kidnapped. No: she was the creator of the plot.

'Now then, we have to find a motive for her action. Here is a high-minded and noble girl, without a care in the world, loved and loving. We must exclude any idea of scandal or even of escapade. She was a jolly happy girl. But she had more in her than that; and that was not any secret passion or vice. It was an intense ambition to follow her father to an equal fame. She put in every spare moment on the higher mathematics or on the problems of psychical research.

'I said to myself that a very strong motive must be attached to this – er – I believe the Baaston for it is *urge*.

'And then I saw instantly a quite inexplicable coincidence. You told me of her "profound study of spirit return." The crux of that problem is proof of identity. And the Pasquaney Puzzle is just such a problem. It was impossible to doubt that Dolores had deliberately invented a test case, and challenged all the wise men of the world to solve it. She knew well enough that the notoriety would attract every intelligence on the planet, if she only gave them time enough. It would not do to give the game away in a week or a month.

'No scandal would be attached to the family, once her motive was made clear by the publication of a thesis analysing the evidence in the case.

'Her action would cause extreme pain to those she loved; but science first! She would atone by the distinction of her achievement. At twenty-two one has such ideas.

'So far, so good; but how did such an idea arise in her mind? Possibly long ago, as an A. B. case; but if so, she must have seen immediately that it was perfectly impracticable. In what conceivable set of circumstances could she get her mother and sisters and brother and lover and friends to disown her? By some change of manner? Some assumed forgetfulness of her identity? They would merely have supposed her ill or insane; no public controversy could ever have arisen. No: the only plan would be to have a Second Girl; and my idea is that she found the Second Girl first, and that the likeness put the scheme into her head.

'Just then a flash of memory came to assist me. I met Professor Cass several times in Europe. He was just such a man as I imagine Dolores to be a woman. He would go to any lengths in the interest of his work. He once nearly killed himself in an experiment with digitalis and hyoscine – he wanted to map out the conflicting curves in the record of his heart action produced by those drugs. And as for some reason or other he couldn't bring Mrs Cass on his travels, and as he "couldn't work without her inspiration," he simply contracted a liaison with a woman as much like her as possible! It occurred to me that some such union had been fruitful, and that Dolores, by accident or design, had met a half-sister on the trip to Europe, two years ago, of which you told me.

'Now suppose that this half-sister, or some other girl equally well qualified, agrees to the suggestion of Dolores. They must first put in a great deal of work, prompting the Second Girl in family knowledge, teaching her to imitate Dolores' handwriting, and so on; and they must then invent a dramatic quick-change scene, if possible one so extraordinary as to exclude all trickery – except The Trick. Dolores had made a special study of this with her "mediums." She thought of the summer cottage, and an excellent idea came to her. She would learn to swim like a fish, and keep up the pretence of being a duffer. I suspected something of that sort from the first minute – the statement of her incompetence was as weak as negatives usually are, especially in spiritualistic circles. When a man begins to argue that a medium couldn't know this or couldn't do that, he's either an expert or an ignoramus; and he's rarely an expert.

'She would need one further essential, the cooperation of somebody powerful, somebody who could hide the Second Girl until the right moment, and arrange for her own getaway and concealment while the play was playing. Probably she knew already of some people of wealth, deeply interested in the spirit problem, who would join the merry throng.

'I could not see any other solution that was not barred either by the psychology or by the physics of the known facts.'

Miss Mollie Madison had got it all down in her note-book. As Simon Iff was now politely offering her a cigarette, she decided to ask what she wanted to know. Analysis and deduction were nothing in her young life; but how did "that uncanny old man" prophesy the engagement of Geoffrey Travis, whose name he had just heard for the first time?

'I'm a vain old person, my dear; I ought to have let well alone. But I'm still young enough to be annoyed that a chit of a girl should think to puzzle me, even if she merely includes me in Carlyle's "mostly fools." So I determined to twist my knuckles in the golden locks of Miss Dolores and drag her to my wigwam. Therefore I arranged with you – as a last resort – to publish that I would deal with the matter from the point of view of psychical research. She would see the point at once, of course. Her press-cutting people must be keeping her supplied with all possible material for her book. She would know my name, I hoped, and know from that notice that I knew the whole story, and meant to take the wind out of her sails by publishing my own analysis of the identity problem before she had got hers ready. In which case, goodbye to her fame, to the whole purpose of her plot.

'But alas for humanity! I bethought me also of a simple plan, a plan which would humiliate her even more before me. I would tell Travis my conclusions, and end: "If you want her back, you've only got to advertise that you've got a new girl now." So, as I said before – and Shakespeare even earlier! – that bait of falsehood took that carp of truth. She came round in a rage the next morning, and delivered the goods. To think that one whose aspiration soared so high should fall so low! 'Tis "vaulting ambition, which o'erleaps itself and falls on t' other"! To aim at mathematics and to hit mere man!'

'Oh how wonderful you are, Mr Iff! How you know the Heart of a Pure Woman!'

'Oh no, my dear, it's not original at all; it's just a modern adaptation of Solomon and the Baby. And now I have to run away and dress for dinner; you may publish all I've said, except the bit about the half-sister. Just invent a marvellous coincidence, won't you? It's the crucial difficulty of the whole business, but nobody will know that. So run away, little girl, run away and play with your nice toy, the Public!'

THE MONKEY AND THE BUZZ-SAW

1

'Desperate Bear Raid on Coal, sir,' announced Simon Iff's Japanese servant, cheerfully, as he brought in the morning chocolate, and pulled back the curtains to let in the lovely sunlight. The mystic had instructed him carefully in this manner of announcing the weather; for he had observed that Americans, informed of any event, from a railroad accident or a strike or a war to a change in the fashion of hair-cutting, would invariably consult an internal monitor, asking '*Cui profuerit*' – Americanice: 'Who's the grafter?' – accompanied by a rapid calculation of 'Where do I come in?' Thus they would attribute an epidemic to financial distress in medical circles, the ravages of the boll weevil to a conspiracy to put up the price of cotton, or a shortage of sugar to a plan to discredit some particular set of politicians.

Simon Iff had merely extended this theory to cover natural events; rain, according to him, was caused by the united praying-power of the umbrella manufacturers combined with such farmers as needed it for their crops. The San Francisco Earthquake had been engineered as an advertisement by those builders whose edifices had been found to stand the strain.

'Bring me a cigarette and the newspaper!' he called. The servant appeared immediately with an enamelled box, and a Chinese manuscript in vermilion and gold upon palm leaves, dating from the sixteenth century, of the *Tao Te Ching*. Simple

Simon would perhaps have explained to a questioner that he had read it every morning for forty years without once failing to find something new in it, while the exact contrary had proved true of *The Times or The Telegraph.*

He was still engaged in this occupation when the telephone rang. 'Mr Philipps speaking,' said the voice. 'I hope you remember meeting me at dinner at Fleming's last month. I hope I haven't awakened you too early. The fact is I've had a most mysterious and threatening communication this morning, and I want to trespass on your kindness by consulting you.'

'Come right round!' said Simon genially. 'You won't mind a dressing-gown, will you?' Philipps replied that he would be at the house in ten minutes, and Simon, laying down the 'newspaper,' rushed through his bath, and was found sitting, clothed, and in his right mind, by his visitor.

Philip P. Philipps junior had just succeeded to an important wholesale jewellery business on the death of his father, which had taken place a fortnight before his visit to Simple Simon. He was a prosperous citizen of forty-five years of age, with a wife and family; a typical burgess, but attractive to Simon Iff on account of his extraordinary knowledge of the history of famous gems. On this he had expatiated eloquently at the dinner referred to in his telephone conversation, and Iff, delighted, had expressed the hope that one day he might be of some service.

This opportunity had now come. Philipps drew a letter from his pocket, and handed it silently to the old man.

Iff contemplated it at length. The message was short and simple.

Don't monky with the buz-saw.

'No idea of origin or purport?' asked Simon.

'None.'

'Then let me think.'

The mystic examined the letter with fresh care. He even smelt it carefully, and tested it in one or two spots with the tip of his tongue. Then he wrapped himself anew in the voluminous folds of his grey silk robe with its dull gold embroidery. Even his head disappeared. It was five minutes before he emerged.

'This,' said he slowly, 'appears to be from Jonathan Spratt.'

Philipps sat staggered for a few moments. Then the one possible conclusion forced itself into his mind, and thence through his speech. 'You're in with this gang!' he exclaimed.

'Oh no!' said Simon, laughing. 'I'm only telling you what the letter tells me.'

'I beg your pardon. But it's perfectly impossible that you should get the name of the writer.'

'Not a bit. Please follow the thought. A common paper – common man. Letters formed clumsily – learnt to write late in life.

'Shaky lettering – elderly man, or a sick one.

'Hasty lettering – not a sick man, therefore elderly.

'Postmark Hoboken – suggests a sailor.

'Paper smells of fo'c'sle – unmistakable – letter written on ship, or soon after landing.

'Characters printed – man wants to conceal identity.

'Letters perfectly aligned – what uneducated man would do that, but a carpenter?

'It is sealed with shellac – just what a carpenter would have handy, and it's written with what looks to me like a carpenter's pencil. Letter bears special delivery stamp – evidence of urgent haste. Why not telegram, telephone or special messenger? Easier to trace sender. Why haste? Result of previous delay. Afraid he'll be too late. Otherwise, he has only just got the information on which his letter is based. Or both.

'These conditions will all be fulfilled if we suppose an elderly ship's carpenter to have landed at Hoboken this morning from some distant port. Does the letter tell us anything about the ship?

'There is a smear of oil – a kind of oil that is only used for big engines. And I think there is only one big ship that docked in Hoboken this morning – the *Hyrcania*, and she was three days late.

'Now just before I left for America I travelled on the *Hyrcania* from Naples to Marseilles, and I got to know the carpenter, whose name was Jonathan Spratt. Is that clear?'

'It all corresponds, of course,' said Philipps rather doubtfully.

'Obviously, my friend the carpenter may have been superseded. But, as it happens, I have reasons for thinking that it is the same man – I'll tell you in a minute.

'Rather unworthy to spring the name on you as I did, of course: but I never resist temptation when miracles are on the carpet—'

'A most strikingly fortunate coincidence, at least,' replied the jeweller, seriously.

'Not very. We have the man and his job, and could find his name, did we lack it, in an hour. After all, the name matters little—'

Simon Iff pulled himself up short with a snarl. The blood flooded his cheeks. He ground his teeth. His eyes were suddenly misty with a film of tears, as, casting out the shame of his precipitate judgment, there came the vision of a pale sad frightened girl—

'Claudine,' he muttered. 'Too extraordinary – if a name should be of virtue here as well—'

He sank into deep thought. 'Jonathan,' he murmured. 'David—? A little honey on a rod—? Bah! I'm an old fool. The name is common enough, and the man no such unusual type. I mustn't lose my grip, and look for light and leading in every Will o' the Wisp.'

Philipps had picked up the letter and examined it carefully. 'Yes, I dare say you're right. But—.' He did not know how to conclude his sentence. Iff's identification had merely replaced a superficial puzzle by a genuine problem.

The magician looked up gleefully at the thought he read in the other man's mind.

'But, as you are about to say, it doesn't in the least explain why a perfect stranger should send you a threatening message in such a deuce of a hurry. You weren't intending to monkey with a buzz-saw, were you?'

'My relations with the whole world are absolutely peaceful.'

'No big business pending?'

'The season's over; nothing doing for three months to come.'

'I remember Jonathan Spratt as a singularly shrewd, sane, cautious man. The precautions in this letter agree there too. Whence the excitement, and the perfectly pointless threat or warning?'

'It's inexplicable.'

'I think not. The man has been abroad for some time. He may not know of your bereavement.'

'It might be intended for my father?' cried Philipps.

Iff nodded. But the jeweller's face fell again.

'The poor old gentleman had taken no active part in the business for five years. He had practically no communication with the outside world. He would sit in the house all day and play with his collection of gems. He hardly ever went out. Sometimes he would play chess with a crony. He was the one man in the world unlikely to monkey with a buzz-saw!'

'Yes, I'll tell you one other thing. Jonathan Spratt, though a self-educated man, was a very thoroughly educated man, within his limits. The nature of the letter confirms that. A man must have read widely, and thought deeply, to invent so cryptic a plan. He would certainly not have spelt monkey without an "e," or buzz with only one "z," unless he had a particular reason for it. In short, I think it's some kind of a cipher. Spratt knew a little about the subject, by the way. The occasion of my employing him was the making of some fret-work stencils which I designed to offer to the government for a particular object which we had in view. So we got to chatting over the subject; he knew several capital methods. Your father would probably have understood the purport of this paper.'

'I can't imagine what my father would be doing with this Spratt!'

'Used him to catch whales, perhaps! The old man was a very keen collector, wasn't he? Suppose he employed Spratt to smuggle precious stones? A clever tool: trustworthy, prudent, ingenious, silent; all one could desire! Then suppose the letter was meant to convey exactly what it did *not* say: the letters omitted instead of those expressed; in plain American, E.Z. "Easy" would have told your father that he had had no trouble with the Custom House people, and perhaps advised him to take certain prearranged steps for the transference of the smuggled stuff. The haste is now fully accounted for; he must have feared that your father would be anxious, as the ship was so late. Or, possibly, he had promised to make good on a definite day.'

'It's all in the air, of course.'

'I've caught many a ten-pound trout on single gut. We can test it by having Jonathan arrested. He wouldn't risk the Bhopur Emerald anywhere but on his person.'

'The Bhopur Emerald?'

'That is the only recently stolen stone which I can think of as likely to interest your father. The thieves were traced to Alexandria, you know. So likely enough Jonathan got his little job through at Naples while the *Hyrcania* was in harbour.'

'But why have him arrested?'

'He's broken the law, hasn't he? Or do you want the stone?'

'I suppose my father paid for it. I don't mind paying the duty.'

'A stolen stone?'

'Oh, the Rajah of Bhopur's a nigger.'

'In India, my dear sir, the people enjoy the advantages of religion, morals, art, literature and good manners. When I notice these, my second glance will embrace telephones and tall buildings. Incidentally, his complexion is considerably fairer than either yours or mine.'

Philipps winced. 'Right's right,' he said rather angrily.

'True,' said Iff. 'But allow me to pass you a copy of the Jewish and Christian scriptures. You will there find many texts of a character to buttress your case. Thou shalt not steal and Thou shalt not kill are followed by many illustrations of the wrath of Jehovah against various people who didn't steal and kill – when the victims were "heathen." Does that help you?'

'It does,' said Philipps. 'We cannot go against the Word of God.'

'Speak for yourself,' said Simon Iff. 'I am now going to call up the Custom House people and the police. Here is your letter. It's for you after all; don't monkey with a buzz-saw!'

Philipps went away in a black fury. He saw – not red, but green! A passion to acquire the famous Bhopur Emerald swept through his whole being. He had not a moment to lose! He must find Jonathan Spratt. What arrangements could his father possibly have made? The only hope was to go home and rummage among the dead man's papers.

Simon Iff, having done his duty by Law and Order on the telephone, returned to the perusal of the 'newspaper.'

2

Mr Philip P. Philipps was disturbed in his search among his father's papers by the arrival of the midday mail.

One letter stood out from the rest like the sun among the stars – it was the printed pencil of Jonathan Spratt. Philipps tore it open with crazy anxiety. But the contents was nothing but a chess diagram.

It was a perfectly conventional chess problem, motto, author and description complete; but Philipps had no difficulty in understanding that here was another ingenious cipher.

And the only man – probably – capable of solving it had just turned him out of the house for a thief!

But Philip P. Philipps had inherited some of his father's slyness and resourcefulness. He thought of a friend named Bloom who – so he was wont to boast – knew Simon Iff very well. He would copy the paper, and take it to him, asking him to show it to Iff and ask for a solution. In case the old magician played him false (for he could not imagine anybody being straight) and went personally to the assignation – he was certain the 'problem' was a cipher time and place – he would have him followed by two sure men whom he had often employed to guard packets of jewels. He himself would wait at home, on the chance of Jonathan Spratt turning up in person.

Having made these arrangements, he went on with his search through the papers but discovered nothing connected with the matter, unless the dozens of odd chess diagrams were also part of it.

Bloom rang up Simon Iff at his friend's request and arranged, quite casually, for a meeting at the club that afternoon. The sleuths were on the mystic's trail before he left the house, determined to follow to the death.

Bloom talked of many casual things; it was only by apparent chance that, in pulling out his cigar-case, the chess problem came with it.

'By the way, you're a chess-fiend, aren't you? This seems in your line.'

Simon Iff picked up the paper and studied it carefully. 'These seven-movers are a bit out of date,' he said at last, 'and I'm a bit out of practice at them in consequence; they were all the rage when I was a boy. You don't play, I think?'

'No,' replied the innocent Bloom.

'How did you get this?'

'Found it the other day as I was turning over some old papers.'

'And made a copy of it this morning, all for my benefit?'

Bloom began to stammer. 'I – er – that is – you see – ah – just so. The original was very nearly worn out.'

'Don't you know me well enough to tell me the true story?'

'Well – er – a friend bet me you could solve it, and I wouldn't believe it.'

That was true, so far as it went.

'I suppose this was in strict confidence?'

'Yes,' gasped Bloom, grasping at the sorry straw.

'Very peculiar,' remarked Simon. 'Only this morning a friend of yours showed me a cipher, of a nature that made me expect a second cipher to follow. And here we are; only, instead of a cipher, we have a chess problem. And between you and me, it's a pretty poor problem, if it's solvable at all, which I doubt. Suppose it were the cipher after all?'

'Suppose it were?' echoed Bloom helplessly.

'Well, if it's a cipher, it's as plain as print.'

'And what does it mean, then?'

'I think your friend Mr Philip P. Philipps is more of a fool than a knave. With your permission, I will show this little problem to Commissioner Teake, whom I perceive in yonder window. If he chooses to tell you, I have no objection.'

'I say, you can't do that, you know! That's my paper!'

'Your loyalty is honourable, but its source is in your ignorance. Your Mr Philipps is making you accessory to a felony. Ask him to show you the first cipher: don't monkey with the buzz-saw. Here, don't be an ass, come across with me, and tell Teake all you know!'

Bloom surrendered. But his information was meagre enough; Philipps, with an imbecile's false cunning, had told him nothing, not even prompted a plausible explanation.

'I don't know whether I ought not to hold you,' said Teake, 'if only as a material witness.'

'Let him go!' urged Iff; 'he's the most immaterial witness I ever saw in my life.'

So they stood him a drink, to show there was no ill-feeling; and off he went with his tail between his legs.

'I can make nothing of this, Mr Iff,' said Teake.

'Oh, surely you can. The only difficulty is that it doesn't look like a cipher. Once suspect it, and it blossoms into flower.'

'Well, the Bloom's off the peach,' grinned the Commissioner, to the horror and agony of the magician.

'It might of course be a dictionary cipher,' explained he; 'you've only got to number the squares from 1 to 64, and your pieces from 1 to 12 – six white and six black pieces diverse – and mark up words in a dictionary accordingly. But the number of words is very limited, and you would need an extra code to account for the order; the whole scheme would be inefficient and clumsy, though it might serve some special object.

'However, that's barred, because it would need an incredible coincidence to have the code message appear as even you, who don't play chess at all, see it appear – or will, in a minute or so. Come now, doesn't the arrangement of the pieces strike you as peculiar?'

'So would any arrangement. The pieces mean nothing whatever to me.'

'Oh yes, they do. Forget about their being chessmen; think of them simply as a child would.'

'Oh!' cried Teake. 'What an ass I am!'

'Every article marked in plain figures!'

'4315. But what's that?'

'Safe bind, safe find! Otherwise, memorandum about a safe where something is put away'

'I see. And it has something to do with this Philipps-Spratt business – um! But where's the safe?'

'Possibly "by R. W. Waterton"? Either a third party – which I doubt, these people not needing assistance, so far as I can see – or an address. R might stand for 18 and W for 23. Is there a Waterton Street in these parts? Or a West Waterton Street?'

'Probably – I'll find out.' He took a table telephone and called up headquarters. Yes, there was a Waterton Street in Hoboken. 'Get the officer, and have him call me here – Chiliad Club.'

Two minutes later the officer on the Waterton Street beat rang through. Among the tenants of No. 1823 was a watchmaker, Aminadab Spratt, a bachelor – steady, decent, sober, reputed to have saved much money.

'A hot trail,' said the Commissioner to Iff, as he replaced the receiver. 'What do we do now? Raid 'em?'

'I think that "seven moves" may mean "call at seven o'clock." Otherwise, it's part of the combination. I expect Aminadab is a brother of Jonathan – pious kind of a family, eh? – and lets him keep a safe in the place to store things while he's away at sea.'

'I think I see the idea now. Jonathan daren't meet Philipps, so he tells him to call at this house. Very likely, as you say, at seven o'clock, to make sure Aminadab is at home. He would describe old Philipps, and the latter's knowledge of the combination would make all secure.'

'Exactly my idea.'

'But why risk sending the figures? Why not leave word with his brother?'

'As man to man, Teake, would you trust a plugged nickel to anyone named Aminadab Spratt?'

Teake laughed. 'I guess you're right. So we'll time the raid for seven. I'll call up.'

Two detective-inspectors were waiting for the Commissioner and his friend as they came out of the club after a hasty dinner, saluted, and got into the car with them.

The sleuths of Mr Philipps looked at each other. They were not exactly out to follow the Commissioner of Police; they might thank their stars he wasn't following them. So they went over to Philipps' house and reported their discomfiture.

'That cipher was right the first time,' he said comically. 'E.Z.'s all wrong, but he certainly got the right dope about the buzz-saw!'

Precisely at seven o'clock the police car drew up before No. 1823 Waterton Street. They had enlisted the aid of the Chief of the Hoboken Police. The little party entered, and a number of constables quietly moved into position.

But no such precautions were necessary. Aminadab Spratt rose and received the Chief and the Commissioner with perfect calm and respect.

'You are Aminadab Spratt?'

'Yep, your honour.'

'I am the Chief of Police. I have a warrant to search this house.'

'Yep, your honour.'

'You have a brother named Jonathan?'

There was a moment's pause. 'Cousin, your honour.'

'Does he rent a safe with you?'

'Yep, your honour. It's behind that rubbish in the corner.'

The two detective-inspectors went forward, and cleared the spot indicated. Let into the wall was a safe of recent pattern, excellently made.

Teake himself operated the combination. In the meantime Simon Iff had fraternised with the watchmaker. The mystic carried a 'perpetual motion' watch, wound by a steel weight which rises and falls as the wearer moves in walking.

'I have to walk five miles a day,' he explained to Aminadab; 'so I keep my watch wound and my waist slender by the same healthful procedure. Have you ever seen Ozanam's mercurial water-clock, or a copy?'

Aminadab admitted cheerfully that he had.

'If you had had one here,' said Simon, 'you would have been able to tell me exactly at what time your brother – I mean cousin – looked in today. The second time, I mean.'

'So that's what you're getting at, mister.'

'Yes; I noticed your quiet amusement at the futile proceedings of our friends in the corner.'

Teake was just in the act of stooping to open the safe, with an electric torch held to the dial by one of the inspectors. He looked up over his shoulder with a quick startled face.

'What's that?' he snapped.

'Go on, go on. Try all things; hold fast that which is good!' This was in Simon Iff's most ironical tones.

Aminadab laughed outright. Teake went at the safe like a whirlwind.

The door swung open. The safe was furnished as a correct and chaste imitation of Old Mother Hubbard's celebrated cupboard.

'Damn it!' said Teake in a rage, 'you led me into this, Iff. This is as bad as that damned foolishness with Mr Noon.'

'Oh no!' said Simon. 'Iff's only for short. The whole of it is "Iff at first you don't succeed, try, try, try again!"'

He seized Aminadab Spratt by the waist, and executed a blithe polka. It went very much against the grain of so sober and respectable a watchmaker; but he supposed Iff to be drunk.

The Commissioner was not to be pacified. His colleague from Hoboken was smirking too broadly.

'We'll hold this Spratt, I guess, on suspicion.'

'Suspicion of smiling to himself? We come here on the evidence of an alleged chess problem sent by some unknown person to a man named Philipps who

Has nothing to do with the place;
And we've got to take under our wing

Tra-la,
A most unattractive old thing,
Tra-la,
With a caricature of a – case!

We find nothing where no sane person would have expected to find anything; and yet we must arrest the unhappy Aminadab. For shame!'

'Damn it, which side are you on? The whole thing has hung together miraculously till now.'

'My dear friend, it hangs still better. Aminadab's smile – a very sweet smile, mark you, and passing subtle – told me that the Bhopur Emerald had been here today. Then why isn't it here now? Jonathan learnt somehow that old Philipps was dead. There was his cipher out in the cold world. It might fall into the wrong hands – as in fact it did. The only course open to him was to hurry back and remove the stone.'

Aminadab's expression had altered. It had not struck him until then how strange it was that the hour of the assignation should be known, and the combination of the safe.

'Your brother – cousin, I mean – boasted of the safety of his ciphers, I imagine? Be a sensible man, now; can't you see what you're up against? Don't monkey with the buzz-saw! I've tried to save you from arrest; now, what time did your brother – er – cousin take the emerald away?'

'About an hour ago,' grumbled Aminadab.

'Which way did he go?'

'I don't know.'

'But he was an emerald thief – and an impertinent one, surely?'

'What do you mean?'

'I was joking. Of course you couldn't know. But you must know what you did with the body'

Aminadab Spratt collapsed into the arms of the detective who stood by him.

'Brandy,' said Iff. 'Put him in a chair.'

'Sure we will,' observed Teake playfully, 'unless this is another of your "purely theoretical" arrests "for the instruction of rising police commissioners," I think you said.' He was still a little sore, and Iff's lightning developments were on his nerves.

'Better now?' asked Simon.

Aminadab's face had some colour in it from the stiff dose of brandy which the Chief had poured between his teeth. He held hysterically to the arms of the chair in which they had seated him. Then he saw Iff's sardonic grin as the mystic's eyes fell on those tightened muscles, and he sprang up with a shriek of horror.

'Sit down!' said Iff, sternly.

'No, no!' he yelled, 'you shan't kill me; you've no right to kill me.'

'Is that remark original with you?'

Spratt clenched his teeth, and said no word.

'I should arrest him, sir, and warn him in the usual way'

"This is absolutely serious?' said the Chief of Police. 'You understand what this means? I can't even see a ground of suspicion. Incidentally, we haven't found a dead body yet.'

'Oh technicality! What a blessed word is Mesopotamia! Keep him till I find the emerald! He, Aminadab, your eyes are wandering again just where they shouldn't. Near the kitchenette. Ah! the galled jade winces; this is perhaps our young friend's first serious crime. Now, Teake, use your brains! Where would a watchmaker hide an emerald in a kitchenette?'

Simon threw open the doors. 'Bread? No; you can't join up bread neady. A watchmaker, remember! What be these? Eggs. And have we not invisible cements, we watchmakers? I'll take a chance on an egg.'

He banged the box upon the table. The eggs broke, flowed every way. And in the midst, behold! – the Bhopur Emerald.

'Now can't you arrest him under the Sullivan Law for carrying concealed eggs – which are notoriously weapons, in politics? Or for being in possession of narcotic eggs? I often go to sleep after a debauch on Omelette Espagnole—'

But they had already arrested him.

'Good!' continued Simon, turning to observe, at the click of the hand-cuffs, 'let me now continue my prolix yet informative discourse. Seventeenthly, I noticed that Aminadab – lovely name! – while very much amused at our preoccupation with the safe, became quite serious when I spoke of his brother's – I mean his cousin's – movements. Forty-fifthly, he changed his position in the room rather furtively, immediately afterwards. He strongly resented my whirling him away to the strains of The *Blue Danube*; possibly because he doesn't like Austrians, possibly not. Why this fuss about his position? Did it remind me of that chess problem? (Position is everything in chess, don't you know?) No, gentlemen, it did not. Still, I wondered. It had occurred to me that Jonathan's refusal to trust his brother – er, cousin – with the combination of the safe was unflattering – and I knew Jonathan for a most prudent man. And then I thought that Jonathan was not so scared because old Philipps' death sent his ciphers astray – he probably believed in his ciphers – but because old Phillips was the man behind the gun. Not a fool like his fat son, oh no! He had built up that business from nothing – it's one of America's standard examples – and he was carrying on all this funny business on the sly under his son's nose, though he was in his dotage. A big man in his way, old Philipps! The Spratts didn't dare to go against him. But, Philipps dead, nobody knew of this emerald but Jonathan and Aminadab. I have told you how prudent Jonathan was; he must have realised instantly that if his cousin – or was it brother, Mr Spratt?'

The man in the chair drew his breath heavily.

'My first suspicion was your tone when you said cousin. You could not bear to think of him as brother – why? Does "cousin" lighten your burden, does "cousin" efface the brand of Cain, oh you whose father brought you up upon the Bible?'

Simon Iff was tense and inflamed, a modern Isaiah. He dropped, as suddenly as he had risen, to a bantering tone.

'Well, as I was saying, dearly beloved brethren, umpteenthly, if Aminadab knew that Philipps was no longer there to avenge bad faith, he would force the safe and be off with the emerald. There is no time to lose; the non-arrival of Philipps at seven o'clock might put some such thought in Cain's mind. So Abel hurries back. But his action arouses Cain's suspicions. Perhaps Abel tells him that the plan is changed, or that there is danger. Yet surely the danger was for Abel to be near the stone. Cain smells a rat; he will strike a blow for the great prize.'

He stopped, out of breath.

'This is all the merest surmise, Mr Iff,' said the Chief of Police, a little annoyed again.

'Be patient. I produced the emerald. Faith is the substance of things hoped for, the evidence of things not seen. This surmise ambling amiably about my vacant cranium, my thought wandered still further, right back to the question of Cain's position on the floor—'

Aminadab Spratt uttered an inarticulate cry.

'You are a tidy man, Son of Adam!' said Simon Iff. 'Your hands are washed, your hair is trimmed, your chin is smooth, your collar is white, your dress is neat, your tools betray every evidence of loving care. But the room itself, apart from your person and your trade, is singularly unkempt. I have often remarked this trait in persons devoted to some skilled profession. Yet, sometimes, such persons notice quite suddenly how badly their surroundings need cleanliness and order. They transform themselves into veritable demons of spring cleaning. Of course it is as bad as ever in a week. Amusing to observe, eh? Well, gentlemen, kindly direct your eyes to the position so carefully taken up by Cain. Do you see that small patch of floor, recently scrubbed, an hour or so ago, still damp, dust from other parts of the room brushed over it? You scrubbed well, Cain, I doubt not; you scrubbed for dear life; but will cleansing a floor cleanse your hands?'

Again he shot prophetic thunderbolts of tone upon the prisoner.

'I expect a microscope would show blood still – in the cracks anyhow.'

Again he towered over Aminadab Spratt.

'The voice of thy brother's blood crieth unto me from the ground. Where is thy brother Abel?'

'I put the body in the water-tank on the roof,' said the murderer. 'The hammer is there too. I meant to have got it away tonight in my Ford. He wouldn't have been missed; he'd been paid off from the ship; old Philipps was to have paid him twenty thousand for the emerald, and he had money saved besides.

'Oh, don't look at me, don't look at me!' he cried piteously to Iff. 'All this time your eyes have tortured me, and your voice saying "Cain!" and a voice inside me beating, beating, beating with my heart "Thou God seest me!"'

Simon Iff turned away his eyes. The Chief of Police and the two inspectors led away the murderer to his doom.

Teake saw with wonder that Simple Simon's eyes had shifted from the mood of Sinai to that of Bethlehem.

'Why, man, you're crying!' he said in amazement. 'I don't see anything to cry about.'

'I know you don't,' replied the mystic, 'and that is one more reason why I'm crying. You can't see the agony of humanity. We're all monkeys, with fate as the buzz-saw! Oh frail ladder that leads up from the beast to the God, how slippery are thy rungs! That man fell in one moment from a hard-working, worthy life to a most shameful death. Humanity itself might so fall from the summit of civilisation to a primaeval barbarism. Sometimes I think I see it coming. This Count Zeppelin, you know, and the people who are working on the submarine. Ever think what that may lead to? No, Teake, let us go out under the stars with pure hearts, gazing with agony on him who has gone to his death. I caught him and I killed him, my brother, even as he killed his brother, like a lion springing upon a deer. So, as Charles Baxter or somebody once said, "There, but for the grace of God, goes Simon Iff." Come!'

Teake followed in silence, shaken by an awe whose nature he hardly understood.

'Don't forget the emerald!' chirped Simple Simon over his shoulder; 'it belongs to the Rajah of Bhopur, a very dear friend of mine, a very dear man. One of the best!'

A DANGEROUS SAFE TRICK

1

'Ladies and gentlemen! I have a confession to make to you. I am leading a double life!'

Laughter.

'To tell you the truth, I got tired of being as ugly as you see me now.'

Laughter – 'Opopo' was a singularly handsome man.

'Fortunately one day as I was walking down Broadway, I met a benevolent fairy—'

Laughter.

'—who offered, as a reward for my well-known nobility of character, to give me a wish. I asked to be allowed to become a beautiful girl for at least part of every day. We fixed it for 10.15; dear me, it's nearly 10.15 now. I thought you would like to see the change – and so you shall. But fairies are very particular about their work; the actual operation must be done in darkness. Very thick darkness, ladies and gentlemen, for such powerful psychic force as this! So permit me to retire to the very complete seclusion of this excellent safe, which I perceive tasks the strength even of these four successors of Hercules.'

The audience in fact beheld a safe, just large enough to hold a man's body, borne from the wings by the staggering porters.

'Let me now introduce Mr Nash, of the Manganese Safety Corporation.'

Mr Nash stepped forward with a bow.

'Ladies and gentlemen,' said he, 'I represent the Manganese Safety Corporation. This is one of our latest pattern safes, of the regular type. It is not a trick safe. I have inspected it tonight. It has not in any way been tampered with. I have here a thousand-dollar bill' – he waved it – 'which I shall be pleased to present to anyone who can prove the contrary, or to any yeggman in the theatre who without knowing the combination can open it in less than twenty-four hours, by drills, blow-pipes or high explosives.'

Mr Nash retired, with another little bow. 'Opopo' continued his address.

'Now, ladies and gentlemen, it is of course quite obvious that anyone can get out of a safe – sealed as this will be by a committee from the audience with their own private seals, and covered with a tarpaulin, corded, and seals again placed upon the cords – and disappear by means of a trap-door. To obviate this, a large sheet of tin-foil will be placed beneath the safe. Hey, tin-foil, where are you? You're keeping the stage waiting. You'll hear of this on Friday!'

Two men entered with a square of quivering steel, three yards by three.

'Now, may I request half a dozen ladies and gentlemen to come upon the stage? I should like the audience to feel assured that there is no trickery about this plate. No sliding panels, secret doors, springs, hinges or places of concealment!'

After the usual momentary hesitation, the required committee stepped sheepishly upon the stage, and took the chairs provided for them by the 'supers.'

'Welcome!' cried Opopo. 'Roam freely where you will. Examine everything you see! Yes, sir.' He addressed a man who was looking at the plate with what he possibly supposed to be a knowing air. 'Yes, sir, you are right again. That is how the trick is done!'

The men turned the edge of the steel sheet every way to the audience. It was obviously what it appeared to be. It was barely thicker than a sheet of paper.

The men laid it down carefully. Opopo picked up a roll of green baize, brought in with the safe, and tossed it with apparent carelessness on to the plate, which it was large enough to cover completely. 'Put the safe on the middle!'

'Excuse me!' said one of the committee. 'I should like to examine that cloth!'

Opopo protested. 'We don't want to draw out this examination; we're tied for time. Miss Frolic was furious last night because we kept her waiting.'

'I apologise to the lady,' said the committeeman sturdily, feeling like the Elder Cato, 'but I must insist.'

It was a perfectly ordinary piece of green baize in every respect, and the committeeman retired, with the Elder Cato feeling gone '*avay in der Ewigkeit.*' Opopo replaced it. The tarpaulin was next produced and examined. It was shaped to the safe, and could be fastened by a cord running in and out through a series of rings. This cord, tied and sealed from without, appeared a singularly simple and secure protection. Two men put this loosely about the safe, which they then placed in the centre of the steel plate. Opopo threw back the tarpaulin and opened it.

'You will now please rope and hand-cuff me as much as you like, and shut me in. I will ask one member of the committee, and one alone, to reset the combination, so that neither I, nor any possible confederate, can open the safe from without until it is done in full view of the audience. You will kindly seal the door with your own private seals. You will then be good enough to fasten the tarpaulin, and seal that. In order to make sure that I do not escape north, east, south, west or above, as you have already arranged in the matter of the floor, you will please adjust the tent, which as you see is made of ordinary linen sheets supported on a light bamboo framework.'

The committee verified this statement. Opopo then removed his evening clothes, appearing in tights, and they affixed ropes and chains to their hearts' content. He then got into the safe.

'Goodnight, ladies and gentlemen! When you next see me, I shall be a beautiful young girl. You will know when the change has been operated by my beginning to sing in a mezzo-soprano which has been highly praised. You will then kindly release me from my imprisonment.'

He closed the door. The committee went through the dreary formalities to the foregone conclusion: having removed the tent, and investigated the seals, which were intact, the safe was opened and a charming young lady stepped out upon the stage.

'I am sorry to bid you goodnight,' she said. 'Just one snatch of song while our friends here regain their seats; and then I will be off to dance at Yvette's.'

She sang a pretty Italian air, and down came the curtain behind her. As she turned, Opopo advanced from the wings, and took her hand for the final applause. It was a very finished performance; fourteen minutes and seven seconds by Simon Iff's watch.

'Neatly presented,' he remarked to Signorina Visconti, 'but the method is a little too obvious.'

'I don't see how it's done at all. But I rather suspect that steel plate.'

'Delightful child! That's true imagination. The trickery is likely to lie in the simplest and surest precaution against it. Like a problem by Sam Loyd. You're probably right.'

'Is that it, then? But how?'

'Oh, about a dozen ways of doing it suggest themselves.'

'I think it is pure psychism,' remarked a very fat lady on the other side of the magician, in a very loud harsh voice, meant to be languishing.

Iff's lips curled rather bitterly.

'None of my dozen explanations involve hypnotism, double personality, brain-storms, undeveloped thyroid or the fourth dimension. What a pity! But I really cannot rise to those ethereal heights.'

The Visconti appreciated the remark.

'Some people are all soul,' she murmured, with an eye on the fat lady's corset, which reminded her of the Last Stand of the Old Guard.

'Yes; we should have insisted on confining him in one of those,' laughed Iff gently, in her much-too-highly-convoluted ear.

Miss Frolic was 'chronic'; Iff and his companion wandered out into Broadway, and sought supper.

2

It was a sweltering day in August. The air was utterly stagnant. The thermometer stood at 102°; but 102° in Manhattan can be worse than 120° elsewhere. The moisture was insufferable. The air was heavy with electricity. Those who had enough strength left to pray prayed for a thunderstorm.

Simon Iff was at work on a mathematical-philosophical treatise. He wished to follow in the footsteps of Pythagoras, Raymond Lully and the founders of Freemasonry; to do for the modern scientific conception of the universe what they had done for their own conceptions, the expression of all known relations synthetically in an arithmetical or geometrical notation.

There were not many people at work in New York that day. Men and horses were dying like flies. Enormous crowds lay gasping on the beaches, like fish taken from the water. The Mayor of the city was in the Adirondacks, fishing in the vicinity of cottages 'with a double coach-house' whose owners called him by his Christian name, and would do so as long as he was mayor, and could deliver the goods.

But Simon Iff stayed grimly with his folios. Nor did he spare his servants. He had three cars delivering ice on the East Side, careless of their upholstery. Nor did his men complain that he asked them to put in twelve hours of that fearful day; they made it sixteen, of their own accord. They had it all to themselves; no jealous millionaires jostled them in their errand.

It was a Monday, and far away in Chicago the bills of Helmuth's Sublime Vaudeville had Opopo for a top-liner.

The newspapers of Tuesday morning had the sensation. The trick had failed; Opopo had been found dead when the safe was finally opened. There were no details; Opopo's wife, who had been present, forbade any of the assistants to say anything that might disclose the secret of the trick, which was her late husband's principal asset, unless and until official enquiry demanded it. The cause of death was beyond question, even before an examination of the body. As the door of the safe was opened the committeeman was sent staggering back, shocked almost out of life by a gust of prussic acid.

Suicide! His last supreme achievement in advertisement. For to the first impression of the public any alternative appeared physically impossible. But *The Chicago Pigeon* had telegraphed to New York for Wake Morningside, the famous expert in all manner of conjuring tricks and illusions, and exposer of many a fraudulent medium, to investigate the case. An hour after the despatch of the telegram, Morningside walked into the office of the paper!

'Say, some stunt!' was the editorial greeting. 'How 'n '11 you get here? I wired an hour back, and nine hours after the story. Speak, mystic stranger!'

'Oh, I happened to be lecturing in St. Louis, and I stopped off here to see the show. I was one of the committee.'

'Gee, some luck!'

'I made an extremely careful examination of the apparatus. I got the facts exactly as they occurred. I examined the apparatus again after the safe was opened. And I have a story for you, complete from A to Z.'

'Gee-whiz, we've got the world beat!'

'I put the whole thing down from my notes. I worked all night on it – finished twenty minutes before your wire came, forwarded on from New York.'

3

At the same moment as this interview, Miss Mollie Madison rang with timid desperation at the door of Simon Iff's apartment. She would have braved a Rockefeller in his lair with greater courage, so far as awe went; but she felt, as did everyone who knew him, the intensity of the mystic's loving kindness, so that with her shyness went an inexpressible confidence.

'I am unfeignedly glad to see you, my dear,' he cried, coming forward with both hands outstretched; 'you are an exquisite excuse for me to abandon my work. On a day like this too! It is a favour I shall not readily forget.'

'You are the kindest, dearest man!'

'Well, tell me your sad story.'

'It's the Safe Mystery, of course.'

'What safe?'

'Haven't you seen the newspaper?'

'There isn't a word about it in the *Tao Te Ching*.'

'Oh, silly! I mean the New York papers.'

'Better tell me!'

'Opopo is dead.'

'All must die!'

'But not of prussic acid in a safe!'

'True, very true. Now I perceive a less altruistic object in your most timely visit than that of luring me from the blistering crags of transcendental philosophy to those primrose paths that lead to the everlasting bonfire of Titianesque Mollie Madison!'

She blushed delightfully.

'The minute I saw it I called up the office and asked if I might cover the story, and mentioned you. They said there were no facts come through yet; I told them it was all the better – you didn't need anything so crude.'

'Again I am betrayed!'

'I've told you practically the whole story already. Of course it's suicide, because it couldn't possibly be anything else; but there's no reason why he should have done it, except the stunt itself, and that's going a little far. His wife talks crazily, from grief.'

'It isn't really a mystery, then; it's merely an eccentric action.'

'Yes, I suppose so.'

'But Opopo was not at all an eccentric man. He was prosperous, I imagine; his wife was apparently devoted to him; he must have been a steady, sober person to hold down his job; he was always inventing new tricks; he has written three books on illusions. Let us consider if his wife's talk is as crazy as it sounds. What is it?'

'She claims Miss Max – the girl he pretends to turn into, you know – did it.'

'Let us consider this hypothesis. How is the trick done, anyhow?'

'Nobody knows.'

'Oh yes, I know. I saw the show when it was at the Gloria. Let me show you at least how it could be done, on what I saw that night.

'First. A very thin elastic steel plate is put on the floor. Over this a green baize cloth is thrown, very carelessly. This action raised a protest, as the cloth had not been examined; time was occupied in the argument about it. Something important was certainly being done with that time. When ultimately replaced on the plate, it was not thrown loosely, but spread out carefully, leaving a yard of plate visible in front, and overlapping the bare stage behind. The safe was then placed on the centre of the plate, after being put in its tarpaulin.

'We can stop there, for the moment. We have a complete picture of the apparatus which is subsequently hidden by the tent for a few moments. We need not worry about the cords and hand-cuffs; Opopo would have had them off before the echoes of the clanging door had died away. The safe is of a pattern which opens from within at a touch.

'It is sealed; but as he enters it, he affixes a strip of oiled paper to the jamb, so that the seal comes away whole. He can then remove the paper, heat the back of the wax with a special instrument, and reseal the safe so as to defy detection.

'Opopo, then, hearing the tarpaulin pulled into position, puts out a hand and offers a "false end," as it is called, to the man who is tying the cord. This cord is then not fastened at all till Opopo fastens it, later on. This he must do, lest the fraud be discovered during the opening.

'While the baize is lying on the plate, a second plate, containing an orifice large enough for a man to pass, is pushed, under cover of the baize, through a slit in the stage, beneath the first plate. While the baize is being spread – after the little controversy; he would always find a new way every night, no doubt, to distract attention – the first plate is pulled back through the slit.

'We thus have a simple means of exit. It is merely necessary to open a trap beneath the hole in the plate. The moment that the tent is in place, Miss Max comes up from beneath and helps, if necessary, to adjust affairs plausibly. Possibly she is really needed to assist in the unfastening, though I doubt it. Opopo shuts her in the safe, attends to the resealing, and vanishes through the hole. The trick is turned.

'On the night I was there, the time between the rise and fall of the curtain was fourteen minutes and seven seconds; between the veiling and unveiling of the safe, thirty-eight seconds and three-fifths. That is, the safe was actually hidden from my sight for that period. It is a splendidly smart performance. Of course, I cannot be sure that they do it in the way I have indicated; but it is not far out. The escape is certainly through the stage, not in any other direction.

'It follows that every action must be done with incomparable verve and snap. They have to drill for weeks. Of course there's a little leeway, but that's in case of a hitch. The brilliant effect depends entirely on the shortness of the time of veiling. Take sixty seconds, and people would begin to be bored.

'Now then – whom have we here? Opopo himself, Miss Max and a man to work the exchange of the plates, unless she did it herself, as is possible. These people hate to multiply assistants; each one means a chance to let their secrets get out. The porters are mere supers, of course.

'However, it doesn't matter if there were twenty assistants. One person, and one only, had access to Opopo during that forty seconds more or less when the safe was veiled. At any other time, no one had access. Of course, Opopo was alone after he had shut her into the safe, but a third person could hardly have killed him and put him back and taken her out, without her noticing something unusual! We must therefore take our choice between suicide and murder by Miss Max.

'We know nothing about Miss Max; but would any human being choose to commit murder in such a way? Her only chance of escape is the suicide theory, which she must have known to be unlikely – else why murder the man, for one thing? It would be sure to strike someone to suspect her, as the one person with access to Opopo; the prussic acid would soon be traced to her; and so – "Goodnight, goodbye," as Swinburne says. She must have had a dozen better opportunities daily. Bring me motives by the wagon-load, circumstantial evidence by the rod, pole or perch, and I shall still say that she didn't do it, unless she is an epileptic maniac'

'I may print that?'

'Yes; but add that I think it is a case of murder.'

'You just proved it wasn't!' cried Miss Mollie Madison in comic despair.

'Never in the world! Read over your notes! Also add this. My opinion is provisional, but it is the best that I can do without having any facts at all to guide me.'

And so it came about that Wake Morningside's article and the interview with Simon Iff were printed in parallel columns under the heading:

OPPOSITE OPINIONS:

THE MAN WHO SAW AND HEARD EVERYTHING,
AND THE MAN WHO SAW AND HEARD NOTHING

4

Wake Morningside's article was a feather in Simon Iff's cap in one respect. He agreed entirely as to the method of the trick. The second plate of steel, which was of course exposed by the authorities as being part of the apparatus, made that clear.

But what was new was actually the record of the events of the fatal night. Morningside had been on the committee.

The trick had passed off normally up to the moment of the veiling. The 'green baize argument' had been started by a voice from the gallery, an accomplice stationed for the purpose in case the committee failed to challenge Opopo on the subject.

Morningside took out his watch to time the period of veiling. Ninety-two seconds elapsed; he thought 'What a badly worked trick!' Then the curtain came down suddenly, cutting off the committee from the audience. He heard the stage manager apologising, and a singer coming on in front of the curtain as the orchestra struck up. At the same time as the manager began his little speech, Miss Max ran in from the wings. 'There's something wrong!' she said; 'Open the safe, quick!'

Of course she had not the combination; only the committeeman knew that. The man fumbled; Mr Nash ran up, got the word from him, and spun round the wheel. Both he and the committeeman were overpowered by the fumes of the acid, and had to be treated medically.

Morningside kept his head and examined the safe, discovering the trick by which the seals were affixed to a 'camouflage' strip of paper instead of to the steel jamb. He also discovered the 'false end' of the tarpaulin cord. Nothing had been touched from within; it was certain that Opopo had died almost immediately on entering the safe. In fact, he was still partially bound: his legs were tied firmly; his left arm still wore a hand-cuff. Only the right forearm was wholly free.

An inspector of police now appeared on the scene. The manager wanted the stage cleared; the inspector insisted that the audience be informed of the nature of the accident – so far as that it was not fire – and the house closed for the night so that the coroner might view the body. The inspector took the names and addresses of the committee, that he might call them as witnesses.

Morningside dismissed the suicide theory as incredible. The evidence of Opopo's wife was extremely sane and strong. He had bought a house only a month before; he was spending every day with her in delighted purchase of old furniture and pictures, in which he had always revelled. That very morning he had received a telegram informing him that the Supreme Court had confirmed a judgment in his favour relative to certain breaches of his copyright in the 'act,' and he had ordered a supper after the performance to celebrate it. He was not entangled with any woman; his marriage was only six months old, a baby was on the way, and his great wish had always been for a son to carry on the Opopo tradition, he himself being the third of that dynasty. Friends and colleagues confirmed this statement on many points.

Morningside then proceeded to prove that in the ninety-two seconds at her disposal Miss Max could easily have accomplished the murder. She had almost certainly some quick method of learning the combination of the safe. There were fifty ways of informing her. It was probably necessary, since now and again Opopo might fail to free himself from the cords, and she would then have to help him. Therefore, she had but to open the safe, administer the poison, readjust it and the seals, do the same with the tarpaulin, and give the alarm. The closed safe was her alibi.

As to the motive, that was not the affair of Mr Wake Morningside, and he was always the servant of the public.

The Chicago Pigeon had not been content with one angle of the case. Another reporter had got after Miss Max, and Morningside's article was followed by her biography.

> She was of poor parents of doubtful character, both dead or disappeared. Her mind was amazingly precocious; she had gained a scholarship at Bryn Mawr and specialised in chemistry. (Chemistry, pray observe.) She had led a wild life there, and been expelled for an outrageous escapade. For two years, it seems, she had walked the streets, and on three occasions narrowly escaped conviction as a thief. She then fascinated a photographer – in whose studio, remarked the reporter, potassium cyanide abounds, and only needs distillation with sulphuric acid to produce the poison that killed Opopo. This photographer had died under suspicious circumstances. Miss Max disappeared

for a while; she was next heard of in connection with a gang of coiners, but the police could get no evidence against her. She began to have plenty of money, however, and with the help of an 'angel,' appeared in a cabaret as a dancer. She next tried vaudeville in a Japanese juggling act, but failed lamentably. Here, however, she met Opopo. This was a year before his marriage. He engaged her as his assistant. She set her cap at him, but in vain. Shortly after his engagement to the lady whom he married, somebody threw vitriol at them, which luckily missed. She was suspected, but proved an alibi by three wealthy men, probably all of them under her spell. Recently she had renewed her advances to Opopo. Her extraordinary cleverness in the 'act,' which was making big money, prevented him from discharging her. But ten days before his death he had interviewed another girl, it is said, and engaged her from the end of the following month. Miss Max might or might not have been cognisant of this fact, but it was natural to suppose that he had given her notice to quit.

An hour after the publication of this issue an 'extra' was being cried on the streets. The coroner's jury had brought in a verdict of murder against Miss Max, and she had been arrested.

'This,' said Simon Iff, 'is where I become the darling of the Great American People. Rise, Sir Simon Iff! My arms, thou gallant squire! My battle-charger, Eustace! Hie thee to King Arthur, Clarence, and bow thee low, and say Sir Simon is afield. Beauty and Innocence in danger! By'r Lady, the varlets shall rue it!'

This singular outburst was entirely unintelligible to Iff's Japanese servant, but he judged from his master's tone that brandy would fit the case; so he placed on the table a bottle of date eighteen hundred and eleven.

'Pack!' commanded Iff, 'and telephone for berths to Chicago on the first good train we can conveniently catch.'

It is to be regretted that Simple Simon now becomes a character more infamous than Benedict Arnold. He telephoned Miss Mollie Madison, and told her his intentions. She was not going to miss that chance, and she followed him to Chicago on the very next train. Thus simply and without effort do we incur fifteen years' imprisonment in the Land of the Free.

The wretched woman, now completely in the toils of the vilest of mankind, had breakfast with him at the Hotel Obsidian. He drank neat brandy like a fish, and became more sober and more angry every moment.

'We are up against it, little one,' said he, lighting a Florida cigar in order to become still angrier; 'we have Idiocy and Malice to contend with in the persons of Wake Morningside and this dog Walter Gale – whose name I should prefer to pronounce in the French fashion.

'There isn't a hint of any investigation, or evidence of any desire to discover the truth. It's the most blasted balderdash from one, the foulest libel from the other. Let's run through it! Here!

'Evidence of the wife. Very anxious to prove how much her husband loved her, isn't she? Methinks the lady doth protest too much. Well, never mind her – she's nobody; wives often are.

'Evidence of Mr Expert Wake Morningside. Wake is either *lucus a non lucendo* or short for Quack. Hear him!

'"She had *almost certainly* a way to get the word of the safe." Almost. "There were fifty ways of informing her." Why not say one way, and mention it?

'"It was *probably* necessary. Opopo *might* fail." He hasn't failed in thirty years on the stage, with the whole world, and his enemies in the profession, out to make a fool of him.

'"She *had but to*" perform a most complicated trick, which would certainly convict her. The wife, at least, would know how easy it would be for her, and her alone, to do it. And she is to do this, if you please, when Opopo is already out of his bonds, and free on the stage. She is to kill him and pack him up again, is she? The safe would certainly be open before she ever reached the stage. Thirty-eight seconds and three-fifths, for the whole transfer, the night I was present. Opopo didn't read any novels to pass away the time!

'So much for Mr Morningside and his conjugation with may, might, could, should and would. Now for the unspeakable Gale!

'"She was of poor parents" – pah! Poor! How disgusting! "of doubtful character" – of course, no money. "Dead or disappeared" – disgraceful of them! Then comes a fact, a fact in her favour. She gained a scholarship. That fact can be tested. "She was expelled for an escapade." Was she judged fairly by those arbitrary dons? A poor girl, with no pull? And what's an "escapade"? An innocent freak, or an assassination? Mr Gale doesn't trouble to find out.

'She then walks the streets – "*it seems*." Where else would anybody walk?

'She "narrowly escapes conviction as a thief." In English, she was acquitted. Pretty good for a *poor* girl, I think.

'"She then fascinated a photographer" – English, she got a job.

'"In the studio potassium cyanide abounds" – there's no English, thank God, for this filthy type of innuendo.

'He died "under suspicious circumstances." Who suspected what?

'She is "*heard of in connection with* a gang of coiners." What's the connection? "The police could get no evidence against her"! Those miserable police – we reporters could teach them something! Then she dances in a cabaret – dreadful. Then she goes into vaudeville – more dreadful still.

'"She set her cap at him, but in vain." Who says so? The jealous wife, again? "*Somebody*" throws vitriol – and misses. Who was it? Miss Max, of course, a girl who has been in a Japanese juggling act. Yet she misses two people completely, not with a rifle at a thousand yards, but with vitriol!

'"She was suspected," and her alibi is so good that it must be false. The three men were "*probably* all of them under her spell" – when the theory is that she is crazily in love with Opopo, and would have to explain the object of the alibi to the false witnesses. "Wealthy men" have to be under all kinds of a spell to take a long chance of prison for the sake of a girl in love with another man!

'Then she "renews her advances" to Opopo after his marriage. The wife again? And then he engages another girl, "*it is said*"? Green-room gossip.

'And it all ends up "it is natural to suppose." I suppose it *is* natural to suppose, to some people! The long and the short of it is that this whole article is a most damnable tissue of malicious lying and guessing. There's not one single proved fact to her discredit. And is it "natural to suppose" that this debauched harlot keeps herself clean and keen, every muscle taut, every nerve alert, as she must do to go through that act? I saw her. She's as swift and slender as Artemis, her eyes aglitter, her lips firm, not an ounce of waste flesh; as you would perhaps say in an outburst of frankness, "Gee, what a peach!" I may be an old dotard, but I thought her a perfect type of woman. She may be "immoral" in your vile Puritanical sense, but she's mistress of herself, if I ever saw one. Why, it's Love that gives strength and courage and vitality to those that serve Him wisely and gaily and with passion!'

'I'm feeling ever so much better, Mr Iff!'

'If you're through breakfast, suppose we go and hunt up some real evidence!'

Simple Simon had bethought him to ask Teake to telephone the Chicago Police to help him, and the Commissioner had gladly complied. In fact, he was cursing fate that his duties would not let him leave New York. He would have dearly loved to hunt with Simon Iff.

He found Rogers, the 'Whip of Chicago' as they called him, in consultation with the District Attorney. They greeted him warmly, but were not particularly pleased when he announced his belief in the innocence of Miss Max.

'You're butting into an impossibility,' said Rogers. The truth was that both men were extremely sore over a wrongful arrest, which had let the city in for heavy damages, and a fiasco in the matter of a raid, which had made the administration ridiculous. Their political existence was at stake; they could afford no more blunders.

Iff, with matchless tact – the wrong way round – tackled them directly. 'Go slow!' he said, 'the longest way round is sometimes the shortest way home, and kind hearts are more than coronets, and all that. Give that poor girl every courtesy and comfort that you can; with a little luck, I'll have the right man for you in four-and-twenty hours, and you'll be glad you did it.'

'That's a bet,' said Rogers, heartily, clasping Iff by the hand; 'she shall have champagne and caviar till tomorrow morning.'

'Done!' cried Iff, 'and now may I have an hour with the exhibits?'

Rogers conducted Iff to a vast room where the apparatus was stored. It had been set up in position; the corpse of Opopo was replaced by a wax model, the cords and hand-cuffs replaced exactly as they were when he was found.

'Beautiful!' cried Simon, 'you really merit your success. This is true imagination. Beautiful, beautiful!'

Rogers was much gratified.

'But where,' asked the mystic, 'is the phial containing the poison?'

'She destroyed it, obviously.'

'You looked for it?'

'Everywhere.'

'Beneath the stage?'

'Especially there.'

'Good.'

'She wasn't arrested till yesterday; she had plenty of opportunity to get rid of it.'

'But she didn't know that; she might have been arrested at once – with Mrs Opopo in the house. She would have got rid of it before giving the alarm.'

'An accomplice under the stage?'

'Possibly, possibly. But do you mind if I look for it myself?'

'Sure. But where?'

'Here – and now.'

Simple Simon inspected the inside of the safe with extreme care. He had the model removed, and renewed his effort. His delicate fingers seemed to caress the steel. Presently he withdrew, and began to examine the bonds that held the model. He seemed less interested than before; he was languid and distracted.

'What's the use,' he said slowly after a few minutes, 'when one knows?'

Rogers was not at all impressed.

'Let's get down to business,' suddenly snapped Simon, an entirely different person. 'I want to see that committee. I may get some sense out of them.'

'Wake Morningside's here now, as it happens; he wants leave to go on to New York.'

'Lucky; let's see him! Here, for choice!'

'I'll send for him.'

Morningside arrived in a few moments. After the usual phrases of commonplace, Simon Iff began his attack.

'Forgive the impertinence of an old man to a young one, won't you? But you should always stick to the indicative mood. The subjunctive's poison to you. I think I may say that I've never known you wrong in a fact, or right in a theory. You've got observation skinned to a whisper (isn't it?) but your imagination is absolutely on the blink.'

He looked mildly to Rogers for encouragement in his efforts to talk the vernacular, but that deity was wholly occupied in chewing a cigar. Simon Iff thought of the priests of Baal, and wondered if he would do any good by crying and cutting himself with stones. Morningside was making his defence, and it would have been impolite to interrupt. Consequently, his mind was absolutely free to roam.

The moment Morningside concluded, he began: 'This, Morningside, is why I rely absolutely upon your memory to solve this mystery. Which of the numerous fools on the committee brought those hard cords to tie a man up with?'

'They came from the theatre. Opopo provided them himself. Most people don't know how easy it is to slip the knot up with such stuff as that.'

'I thought so. You, of course, are the wily old bird who supplied that soft cotton cord, and tied it properly?'

Morningside, pleased, nodded assent.

'There's one cord, thicker than yours and nearly as soft, with a curious knot behind the man's back that has pulled very tight.'

'Yes.' Morningside began to take interest. Rogers chewed his cigar like a cow with its cud.

'A cord which is neither quite right, nor quite wrong, for its purpose. A knot which implies considerable knowledge of knots, and quite wrong for its purpose.'

'Now you mention it, that's so.'

'Remember who brought that cord?'

'Yes, a tall thin man of about thirty.'

'Because, when we pull that knot open in court, at the critical moment, we shall find a film of paraffin wax, or some very similar substance.'

Rogers chewed his cigar with unabated determination; he spoke through his teeth.

'Very pretty work, Mr Iff. I'll go get Professor William Henry Stubbs, born in Cincinnati, Ohio, May twenty-nine, eighteen hundred and eighty-two, educated at public schools and at the University of Cornell, travelled in Europe from June nineteen hundred and one to October nineteen hundred and five, took degree of doctor of science at Heidelberg nineteen hundred and five, inherited four thousand three hundred and sixty dollars in August nineteen hundred and six through the death of his mother, his father having died in infancy; lectured in Middle West and around the Coast during nineteen hundred and seven and nineteen hundred and eight; November of that year met Emma Susan Cooper, aged thirty-one and married her – January third, nineteen hundred and nine; obtained post of Professor of Physics in the Hazelrigg Simons University, Botts, Colorado, in March of the same year; separated from his wife May nineteen hundred and ten, she visiting the east under the name of Miss Madeline Adams, and exchanging constantly letters of affection with him; met her in Denver, Colorado, and spent a week with her at Christmas of that year; ceased to correspond with her in February of this year, but left Botts, Colorado, for this city on Tuesday of last week on receipt of an unsigned telegram, giving the Dyer's Convention as an excuse for his absence, which convention he has punctually attended; was present at Helmuth's Sublime Vaudeville on Monday night of this week, and joined the committee on the stage at the presentation of the act of the late Opopo, alias John Drew Westcott, which was the true name of that performer.'

He recommenced a more active mastication of his cigar. During his whole speech he had never faltered, or changed his tone or his expression.

'Beautiful, beautiful!' cried Simon, as delighted as he had been with the reconstruction of the stage scene. 'And I take it that you will also get Emma Susan Cooper, or Stubbs, alias Madeline Adams, or Westcott.'

'I shall,' said the Sphinx, stolidly. 'She put him up to it. Plenty of property, all settled on her; and twelve thousand plunks from the insurance people.'

'Why didn't you act?' put in Morningside.

'Couldn't see the possibility, same as you couldn't,' retorted Rogers, rather cruelly. 'Simple, ain't it, when you get on to it? Paraffin capsule in a knot. His first jerk for freedom, and the knot pulls tight, and the capsule crushes, and it's up the golden stairs singing Glory Hallelujah! Say, Mr Iff, that was bully work, though, when you didn't know. Gee! I was sore on you this morning; thought you'd stall me off by proving that girl didn't do it, and scare the game!'

'We've both gone wrong,' murmured Iff, 'through taking each other for quite unpardonable fools!'

'How'd you get wise?'

'Easy,' said Simple Simon. 'Miss Max couldn't have done it. The man was dead before she reached the stage. Then somebody else did it. One of the committee, for certain. Morningside had examined everything, and found no prussic acid. I just ran over the walls of the safe, on the chance of some attachment there which he might have overlooked. Nothing. Then who could have introduced what into that safe? Only a committeeman; only a cord. It was then merely a question of which cord. One couldn't easily fix a delicate capsule – a mere film of wax, in order to escape detection – in a hard cord, or a thin one. I knew the kind of cord Morningside would bring, and it wasn't he that did it. He hasn't got the imagination. Only one cord remains. Morningside's admirable faculties at once enabled us to discover who brought it. And then you opened with all that heavy artillery. Great work!'

'It's rather shocking,' said Morningside, 'Mrs Westcott, or rather Stubbs, being *enceinte*.

'Now, they all try that. Ovariotomy, following disease, in September, nineteen hundred and nine.'

'And it's been a terrible experience for Miss Max,' was Morningside's final broadside.

'Wish I had a cent for every dollar she gets out of the *Pigeon*. Gee, but she'll pluck that bird! Guess I'll fix Old Man Stubbs and Missus Emma Susan now. You can hike right on down east, Mr Morningside. We'll want you for the trial; you'll get a wire, all right! Might I have the pleasure of your company at dinner, Mr Iff; I'd like you to meet my wife. She keeps my records.'

'Thanks, I'd like to. And may I bring Miss Mollie Madison? She keeps mine.'

THE BITTER BIT

1

Evidence of Identity, by Dolores Cass, was the book of the season. It was as dry as a treatise on trigonometry, but people read it and discussed it as if it were a novel. The Washington Square group all tried to look like each other so as to deceive the very elect, and succeeded perfectly, as there was not one with an ounce of individuality in the whole gang.

But what annoyed everybody was that the mystery was nowhere disclosed. How Dolores had managed the affair was still perfectly obscure – if she *had* managed it. All that she revealed was that a Second Girl existed. Simon Iff had contributed a powerful preface, in which he explained nothing at all but his theories on love. "*Amor omnia vincit*,' he concluded furiously, 'Love is *inimicus humani generis* – the enemy of the human race.'

For before Miss Mollie Madison had reached her office after her interview with him, Simon had been rung up from Boston. It was Dolores, and she begged him, in the interests of science, to suppress the story. There was nothing for him to do but to follow the beacon of Miss Mollie Madison's little red head, and put an extinguisher upon it.

They compensated her by making her chief bridesmaid at the wedding of Dolores to Geoffrey Travis, which was the most fashionable affair that even Boston had known in a long while.

The presents were wonderful. Simon Iff had given the bridegroom an alabaster image of Ganes'sa, very glorious with gold and vermilion; but he had apologised to Dolores with empty hands, saying that he hadn't been able to think of anything suitable so far; he hoped to repair the omission a little later.

She was snowed under with jewellery; also she had a pair of piebald ponies, and a hydroplane, and a twelve-inch reflector telescope in case she wanted to study astronomy. Publicity has its points, even in Beacon Street.

People thought it all rather remarkable; but if Mrs Cass and Mr Travis had nothing to say, why, nobody else had. One couldn't attach any importance to newspaper reports, could one, or where would one be?

So everything went off splendidly. Travis took the usual month from his business, and it was decided to cruise down the coast in his steam yacht, the *Opossum*, a magnificent turbine-boat of two thousand tons.

Simon Iff, having done his duty as best man, returned to New York. Miss Mollie Madison was in the chair-car, and, the train being due in New York at seven o'clock, he asked her to come and have dinner with him.

'Do take me to Chinatown!' she begged. 'It will be so wonderful, as you can speak and read Chinese so marvellously. You spent years there, didn't you?'

'Young woman,' replied Iff, sternly, 'consider yourself suspected. You wish to find yourself in a labyrinth of secret passages, with gambling halls, opium joints and Even Worse Things in full blast. You want tong wars and unspeakable tortures. You have been reading cheap fiction.'

She tried to make her face match her hair, and nearly succeeded.

'It's all rubbish,' pursued the mystic inexorably. 'The Chinese is an exceptionally simple, quiet, honest, kind-hearted individual. You should try to imitate him, even if from afar.'

'To me he seems absolutely mysterious.'

'When I last left China – for my sins – I travelled on the same steamer as Sir Robert Hart, who had just completed his fifty years in the country. He told me that he had got to the stage where he could tell pretty well what a Chinese would do in any given set of circumstances, but that he hadn't the faintest notion of why he would do it.'

'But there is a common basis of motive throughout human nature.'

'I don't believe it. I think the Chinese has a peripheral consciousness, instead of an egocentric one, as the Aryan has. Hence his attitude towards death, for example. To him the universe is a continual flux, individuals being but transitory accretions. Why should he expect permanence in the impermanent? It is idiotic, to his mind, to quarrel with the Law of the Universe. For he is the supreme realist. He never shirks facts. That is why he has to use opium if he wants to dream. Europeans can fool themselves much more easily.'

'I thought it was just the opposite.'

'Man made God in his own image; but it has been reserved for Anglo-Saxon conceit to make everybody in *its* own image. Could you oblige me with the loan of an illegitimate child?'

Mollie jumped out of her chair, really aflame this time. 'Mr Iff! Do you know what you are saying?'

'Sit down, my dear!' laughed the mystic. 'You're Aryan, all right. A Chinese would have been simple about it, said "no," and gone on with his business. You, instead of answering a plain question, minding your own affairs and leaving me to mind mine, made a fuss, incidentally exhibiting another quite Aryan quality, a guilty conscience.'

'I have not!'

'Oh yes, you have! You don't worry about matters unless you are potentially or actually capable of them. Tell me that my house in Pittsburgh is burnt down, and I do not fret, because

I have not a house in Pittsburgh, and please God, I never will have!'

'I seem to have given myself away!'

'You have. Now try something unheard of on Tze-wei, who shall be our host tonight. Try to surprise or to upset him. You get a jade bracelet if you succeed.'

Miss Mollie Madison revolved the matter in her head a while, and at the conclusion of the Chow Mein dinner of no particular importance, asked the proprietor for the head of his father. She had some vague idea that ancestor-worship would make this a peculiarly horrible request. Tze-wei however replied quite calmly that it was impossible, he having been beheaded by the German troops when they entered Peking, and the head having been used for pistol practice thereafter. Miss Mollie Madison was smitten with great agony of remorse; but Simple Simon reassured her, and drew her attention by showing her how Chinese writing was done. He covered the whole menu with the queer characters before he tired. Then he paid the bill, and took her to her apartment.

'We shall meet,' was his gay farewell, 'at Philippi.' And she lay awake half the night wondering what he could possibly mean by that.

2

A heavy sea-fog hung over a windless Boston one Friday night, nigh a month later. Mrs Cass was reading a wireless message from Dolores. The *Opossum* was hung up under the banks in the fog, but the captain hoped to be able to make Boston in another forty-eight hours.

As a matter of fact, the *Opossum* – at that moment – was not at all a good place for a nervous person. The fog hung like a wet sheet upon the sea; everything in the boat was clammily warm, like a freshly killed corpse. The air was horrible to breathe; its stagnation was oppressive beyond all words. The blare of the half-minute horn was torture to any sensitive ear, and the solo became a concert whenever other ships came within earshot. It was an inferno of discomfort, boredom, and that apprehension which impotence or constraint always begets in a man whose one true passion is his supposed Free Will. It was impossible to forge ahead, even dead slow; the captain was caught between shoal waters and the North Atlantic sea lanes. He was safest where he was.

Geoffrey Travis and his wife – who had decided to call each other Mutt and Jeff – were fearfully bored, and horribly ashamed to confess it. It seemed to them the Doom of Love, the Dawn of Divorce; so they said nothing, and made brave pretence to be amused. Dolores had a brain that simply would not work on such lines; her forced cheerfulness gave her a genuine number one headache, and she went off to bed, though it was just after tiffin. Night was the same as day in a fog such as this! Travis himself tried to sleep, failed, started piquet with the mate, tired in an hour, finally drifted on to the bridge, where the captain was doing his trick.

'There's a crazy skipper loose,' growled he as Travis approached. 'Remember that queer boat that picked us up just out of Halifax?'

'That four-funnelled sea-serpent? Some new destroyer on her trials, we thought.'

Yes, that's the chap. *Flying Dutchman*, I guess. Come past us just now, within three cables, doing his forty knots! It's not believable. For the land's sake! There he goes again!'

Travis peered through the fog. A slight breeze had sprung up, and lifted it in patches here and there. In one comparatively thin streak, where waifs of vapour drifted slowly upon the dead waters, he could perceive the hull of the devilish warship, if it were one; it looked like a shark or a seal on a gigantic scale. She bored her nose constantly into the seas, which broke clean over her, so great was her speed. It was a brief glimpse; a few seconds took her again into the unchallengeable greyness of the sea without bound.

Both Travis and the captain were most peculiarly impressed, and not very pleasantly. An apparently new type of craft, of astonishing power, behaving like a dangerous lunatic! The captain smelt something sinister.

An hour later, the breeze began to freshen seriously. The *Opossum's* engines began to revolve. But hardly had she gathered way when the look-out cried from the forecastle.

'Raft ahoy! Raft on the st'b'd bow, sir!'

Twilight, and swirling fog; yet Travis, leaning on the rail, could see the vague outline. There was a man, plainly enough visible. He ran to the bridge; but the captain had already rung off his engines, and ordered out a boat. He then bethought him: 'By Jove, an adventure after Mutt's own heart!' And he ran down to her cabin.

The headache left her in an instant; she snatched her sou'wester, and was first into the boat. A few minutes carried her to the side of the raft. They grappled it with boat-hooks and she sprang aboard.

It was a small rough raft, some eight feet by ten. A short thick mast stood up, and to it was nailed the Union Jack reversed as a signal of distress. Below this, something else was nailed. A marlin-spike was thrust through the hands of a dead man; another through his feet. He had been horribly mutilated; his ears and lips cut off, his nose split, his eyes gouged, his scalp removed.

A sailor's clasp-knife was forced between his ribs; it pinned a paper to his side, and this paper was the cover of a Chinese missionary magazine. The man himself had, Dolores felt sure, been of the yellow race; the skull, the nose, the cheekbones, were conclusive. He wore a torn flannelette shirt, a cheap suit of coat and trousers. In the pockets were stuffed twelve silver salt-cellars of no great value, some still half full of the condiment. His chest was bare; on it was tattooed a design of a blue snake twined about an anchor. The body showed signs of extreme emaciation.

'This,' pronounced Dolores with ineffable unction, 'is no ordinary crime.'

Detective fever set in with extreme virulence. She insisted on tackle being rigged to hoist the raft, intact, upon the deck of the yacht. Every cable of the way to Boston Harbour she sat and studied it.

On arrival, the police immediately took charge of the exhibit, and proceeded with the usual formalities. The Press adopted a peculiar attitude. Some papers reported the incident briefly and without comment; others, less sophisticated or more intent on circulation than on reputation, gave the story straightforwardly and at length; but the *Turkey-Buzzard*, the paper that had backed the Second Girl, was excessively peeved, and, under the headline

TOUT LASSE, TOUT PASSE, TOUT CASS – E

accused Dolores point-blank of having created a new stunt of some kind, and warned her that this article was the last piece of publicity she would get in those columns, unless through legitimate channels such as the divorce court.

Dolores was furious; she set her teeth to show the world that this was no fake.

It was clear to her from the start that the murdered man was the victim of revenge, probably the result of treachery. The executioners had mutilated him partly for the sake of the punishment, partly to prevent identification. The snake and anchor were left, because few would recognise him by these marks, except, possibly, some people whom it was wished to warn. The silver salt-cellars were possibly the price of his treason, actually or symbolically. The missionary magazine cover perhaps indicated that he was a 'native Christian,' the Union Jack that he was from Canada, or originally from a British possession. For Dolores could not get it out of her head that the raft had been deliberately set adrift. It was entirely bare: no food or water, or any receptacle; no trace of the presence of any other person. The object of the whole performance was paramountly clear: 'Don't let it happen to you!' was the English for it.

The police had failed to identify the man; there had been no missing Chinaman within a month, as it happened, except a few whose bodies had already been claimed. Dolores, on the Christianity clue, had made enquiries at the various missions, but her only fresh fact was that the snake-and-anchor was a common device among sailors from Canton.

She formulated her quest under two heads: Who is the man, and who killed him? The spectacular nature of his punishment led her to think that her best plan might be to find out who needed the warning.

And then she began to revolve about the point: Why a raft? Why take this risky method of advertisement? The coast is patrolled. Unless the man had been killed at sea, which could hardly happen unless in a Chinese-owned and Chinese-manned ship, it would have been much more sensible to leave the body in the streets. There must be some very cogent reason for the raft.

This business began to eat into her life. Social duties went by the board. 'Jeff' was happy enough that 'Mutt' should be so intensely occupied; he did not even mind her talking in her sleep. He fell naturally into lunching downtown at Louis', or the club; usually Mutt would drop in, and distractedly toy with a chop. She was really in despair; if only she could have appealed to Simon Iff! But her pride prevented her.

She tried to trace the salt-cellars; but they were of a common pattern, sold by the thousand. There might be more in the idea that the number twelve had some significance. Possibly, again, the Chinese had some peculiar superstition about salt.

3

She now spent most of her time in the Chinese quarter. Her charm earned her plenty of friends, but of course nobody knew anything about the raft incident. There was, however, one old man who gave her some excellent advice.

'A child!' he said; 'see its body, which is like the bough of a rotten tree, and its mind is like slaked lime. Be at peace; this is Heaven's appointment, and the way of perfection.'

Dolores, every nerve high-strung, reacted instantly against the philosopher. His words were kindly and sensible, but she was certain that a threat was intended: 'Keep your nose out of what doesn't concern you!' Somehow or other she must be on the right track.

She took to watching the old fellow closely. She learnt that he had kept a drug-store of the Chinese variety for thirty years; he was of good character, so far as the police knew.

A Japanese went to his shop, at nearly the same time, nearly every night; the man was a tattooer, and bought inks. But why should he not lay in a stock of inks to last a month or a year? The purchase was an excuse; they really conferred about other things.

The next day she called on the Japanese. She was certain that he had lied to the police in saying that he had never executed the snake-and-anchor design. She ordered him to do a dragon on her shoulder, and gained leisure to observe. There was only one object visible which was at variance with the obvious characteristics of the tattooer. This was a letter-file. She determined to get a chance to examine it. So, on her second visit, she pretended to faint with the pain of the needle, and sent him out for brandy. She opened the file; almost at once she came on a miniature of the snake-and-anchor design, with a page of writing beneath it; a list, perhaps. She secreted it. The brandy failed to restore her courage; she left, promising to come back in the afternoon. She had the paper photographed, and restored the original on her next visit. She had the list translated, and looked up the owners of the names.

Wu Lee, the last but one on the list, was the only name not in Boston. His address was given as Mott Street, New York. It might be worth a trial. She took the afternoon train.

Wu Lee was a washerman. He had never been to Boston, he said. He willingly exposed his chest to his fair visitor. There was no snake-and-anchor to be seen.

For all that, she felt that she was on the trail. Here, at least, was one thing pertinent. Wu Lee was a 'Kilistian,' and a copy of the same missionary magazine as was on the raft lay on the table of his little sitting-room.

As she went out, a certainty gripped her that Wu Lee knew something. She would watch for a few moments. It was 'a good bet if she lost.' She concealed herself in a doorway. Ten minutes passed, and then she was rewarded by seeing her 'old philosopher' go quietly down the street and into the washerman's shop. He had hardly time to say two sentences, she judged, when Wu Lee staggered from the shop, a scared man if ever there was one in this world. The old man followed him out, stopped and took snuff; he grinned terribly as he watched Wu Lee reel into Chatham Square. Then he turned and came across the road, directly to Dolores. He opened his mouth, and showed his toothless gums.

'You think?' he said, and made a grimace so sinister and menacing that Dolores shrank back appalled. 'You go home; nice house, nice man; this side, bad weather.'

She brushed past him, and went back to her hotel to think. It was certain that Wu Lee was threatened; she would offer him protection; he would have to tell her the whole story. But had he fled? What a fool she had been not to follow him!

However, the next morning she found Wu Lee at his work. But he was going about it with the air of one resigned to die. She told him frankly who she was, and promised all the might of Uncle Sam to save him. He was impassive as fate itself. She began to apply a little 'third degree' of her own, described the finding of the body. It moved him – but not normally. 'Oh not the raft – not the raft!' was all he would say, and he said it over and over.

Again she retired in disorder. To fill in the time, she called on a missionary who worked in Chinatown, and asked about the snake and anchor. Was it a secret society?

'Not very secret, poor fellows!' said the missionary. 'It's a Cantonese mutual help society, and its qualifications are two: Christianity and tuberculosis. The snake stands for healing, and the anchor for hope.'

'Then you can't imagine its members getting into trouble as such?'

'Oh, you're thinking of that raft business? No; that's a most mysterious affair. I'm afraid I can't suggest anything. You ought to go to Mr Simon Iff; a godless man, I fear, but with a wonderful knowledge of all things Chinese.'

'Ah!' smiled Dolores sadly, 'he's the one man I mustn't ask,' and took her leave.

At her hotel she found Miss Mollie Madison waiting to see her. She was overjoyed; the puzzle was on her nerves, and she longed to pour out her soul. But she refrained gallantly from asking Mollie if she had discussed the matter with the mystic, and even shut her up when she began to volunteer some data on the subject.

4

They went in to the luncheon-room. Dolores stopped at the desk on the way, and enquired for her mail. There was a letter from 'Jeff,' enquiring pleasantly when she meant to return. And there was a long envelope without name or address. The clerk said that it had been handed in 'by a man'; he hadn't noticed what he was like; it had been a particularly busy morning.

Dolores had a presentiment. She wouldn't open the letter until she had ordered lunch for herself and Mollie. When she did so, two documents fell out. Their meaning could not be mistaken. One was a railway folder with the service from New York to Boston; the other a Chinese drawing of herself. The clothes left no doubt of that; it was the dress she was wearing, and she was pictured on a raft, nailed as the dead man had been nailed, and mutilated as he had been. The world swam for a moment before her eyes.

Mollie seized the drawing. 'You must absolutely come right away to Mr Iff,' she cried. 'It's too horrible; it's too horrible!'

Dolores swallowed a Colony Club cocktail. 'Mollie dear,' she said very gently and sweetly, 'please ring up Mr Iff after lunch – and tell him I'll see him damned first!'

'Oh Dolores!' Mollie was genuinely shocked at such expressions from the Hub.

'I mean it,' said her friend firmly, and attacked a Seatag oyster with baresark fury.

'I'm sure Simon won't stand for it,' said the red mouth, with a pout. 'It's my duty to tell him, and he'll get right on to the case, and solve it, and leave you flat. But if you go to him he'll help you out, and leave you the glory.'

'Get thee behind me, Satan!' retorted Dolores, with energy.

It developed into a quarrel; if Mollie uttered one syllable about this picture, which was a sacred secret – further, should she write, mark, engrave or otherwise it delineate upon any object moveable or immoveable under the canopy of heaven – she, Dolores, would never speak to her again; no, not if Mollie were dying in Sing Sing, for which she was a certain candidate!

The Amazonian fury of her friend ultimately cowed Miss Mollie Madison. They went to Dolores' bedroom, wept in each other's arms, and discussed underwear for three hours. Then Dolores drifted back to Chinatown; she would wring the truth out of that toothless old scoundrel, or die for it.

But on the way she paused. This was all wrong. She was working like a detective; she had left the starlight heights of pure analysis for the mire of shadowing and following clues like a common 'bull.' Simon Iff would work out the whole problem from the data without uncrossing his legs. She retraced her steps slowly, and had dinner in her room. She ate a hearty meal, and then settled down to think furiously.

She went over the facts, one by one. She tried to reconstruct the drama.

Here is a Christian Chinaman, dying of tuberculosis – she now remembered the extraordinary emaciation of the body – who yet accomplishes some treachery so abominable as to deserve the most fearful death that can be devised. It is connected, evidently, with his change of faith. Several men are concerned to punish him; one alone could not have done the labour required.

Wu Lee, also a Christian, is in danger of similar vengeance. 'Toothless' is the spokesman of the gang. Yet he is said to be of excellent character. Can even Chinese duplicity account for it?

But Wu Lee is himself a puzzle. He is listed by the tattooer, yet he had not the marks. He is certainly not consumptive.

'I am a perfect fool,' she exclaimed; 'I begin to believe with Simon Iff that marriage is a failure!'

She mused a while. 'Let me look at this new evidence!' She took up the folder. It was not marked in any way. 'But what kind of man sends that sort of hint?' She stopped short, and bit her lips. Then she seized the drawing and examined it with eager attention. 'This was done this morning by someone who saw me in this dress. It's the first time I've worn it. He is an amazing genius, with an imagination, and an appreciation of cruelty, and of beauty in cruelty. I don't think it's "Toothless"; he hasn't got the eyesight, or the type of hand. That envelope, too; that was bought uptown. No mark, but a smart American-made paper. I bet the artist, whoever he is, is a rich man, and devised the whole affair. Who can be threatening him? And about what?'

She took up the drawing once more. It fascinated her despite herself. The treatment of the fog was peculiarly clever. More and more she riveted her attention on the background. There was an almost shapeless smudge of darker cloud between wind and water.

She sat back, lost in reverie. A telegram disturbed her. It contained the words

GIVE IT UP. SIMON IFF.

'No answer!.' she cried to the boy, and crushed the paper in her hand. She dismissed Mollie's betrayal with one word, 'Cat!' And then she returned to her thought.

Deeper and deeper she sank into the pure abyss of mind, until the facts of the case became etherealised and vitalised in symbols of force rather than of matter. Hour after hour she sat. Then she rang for her maid.

'Pack!' she cried, 'I'm going to Boston on the midnight train.'

The maid began her work, while Dolores sat at her desk with a quill pen between her teeth. At last she scribbled a note.

Dear Mr Iff,

I am going back to Boston after all. I wish you would spend the week-end with us.

Yours ever,
DOLORES CASS

She smiled very curiously as she signed her maiden name.

5

Simon Iff sat in Mrs Travis' boudoir in the immense arm-chair usually consecrated to 'Jeff.' Dolores, ravishing in a golden tea-gown, was pouring him champagne.

'And so?' said he, very doubtfully. 'I may not be able to drink this wine, don't you know? I thought that signature very suspicious.'

Dolores laughed gleefully, like a child.

'This is very serious. Please talk!'

'You see, I asked you up here, because I wanted to thank you in person for your magnificent wedding present. It was worth all the rest.'

'I surrender,' he said. 'Excuse me, but – You – Little – Beast! I love you. Excuse me again!'

'May I go over it with you?'

'I should be delighted.'

'I did make an ass of myself! Even now, I'm a little doubtful about one or two things.'

'Yes, you blundered badly at first. Problem No. 1, if I may put it so, was the raft. You had two pictures, one Chinese, and the other not Chinese, in one frame. The mutilation and torture indicated one type of mind; the marlin-spikes, the clasp-knife, the Union Jack, the missionary magazine, quite another type. It's not conclusive, but it should have made you think.

'And what about the salt-cellars? You never did anything with them. Yet, as the most fantastic and incongruous items, they should have received most attention. The other things were more horrible, and you allowed that fascination to overlay the purely mental deduction. Had you considered the point, you would have noticed that the salt was still dry, and therefore deduced that the raft had not been floating about in that fog for many minutes.

'Then you evidently missed the point of the mysterious ship that seemed to be always hovering round you, though she had a speed of forty knots to your fifteen. A strange coincidence, to say the least of it, on a day when you run into so weird a derelict as your raft.

'Again, you altogether omitted the crucial point of autopsy. You would have learnt that the wounds were all inflicted after death. That was a dreadful omission.

'Now then, problem No. 2, the snake-and-anchor business. Not so bad, most of your work, but oh! what a fall was there! Dolores Travis had quite destroyed Dolores Cass, the brilliant author of *Evidence of Identity*. You assumed that the man in Wu Lee's shop must be Wu Lee, despite the absence of the tattoo-marks. You could easily have found out that the man was Wu Lee's brother, he himself having died of consumption a few days before you met him on the raft.

'Again, you never became in the least aware of the real incongruity in your experience, a matter which needed no enquiry whatever. You should have seen that your Chinese were acting totally out of character. They were Dr Nikola Chinese, all melodrama; not real Chinese at all. It ought to have been evident that they were going through a clumsily constructed play.

'Problem No. 3. The letter of warning. As you solved that, you had better tell me how.'

'I saw something wrong. The Chinese artist used inappropriate stationery, and I thought the railway folder hint was not quite in tone, either. The truth is that I began to see the light as soon as I started on your lines of looking at minds instead of at facts. There seemed to be two people at work. Then that same incongruity on the raft occurred to me. That made three people, perhaps four. And "Toothless," too, didn't fit in at all well. There was something radically wrong.

'Then I looked again at the drawing. And I began to realise that the smudge was not quite an accident. I recognised the *Flying Dutchman*, as we called her. Who, then, would know that we had seen her that day? Why connect her with the raft? And, above all, why the raft in any case? The thought came that the raft might have been lowered from the *Dutchman*. More mysterious than ever – the *Dutchman* had been flitting about us ever since we left Halifax. Then came the answer to that horrible first question: "Why the raft?" – it must have been so that the *Opossum*, and no other ship but the *Opossum*, should pick it up. And who was on the *Opossum* but a chit of a girl who rather fancied herself at analysis, and put up problems for the world to solve? A dose of my own medicine? But who could have had such an object in view?

'I could only think of one object, and one mind capable of conceiving it.

'Then I thought of your telegram. "Give it up" might have been a polite interrogative.

'And I became quite sure that you had been at the pains to send me a present, as you said at my wedding, as soon as you were "able to think of anything suitable.'"

'Very pretty!' replied Simple Simon; 'no trouble at all, I assure you. I merely enlisted the services of a friend in Chinatown, Tze-wei, for the gruesome horror part of it. The *Flying Dutchman* is a toy boat we are trying out – I'm in the Admiralty, you should have remembered – in connection with your government. Pray observe, I have decided to drink your champagne – a symbol of triumph – and you may refill my glass. For my triumph is not in beating you, but in convincing you, as I have done, that the proper method of attacking problems is transcendental analysis.'

'Especially when I thought I knew it,' sighed Dolores, in mock sorrow. 'Oh, but I know what you are gloating over in reality! You've convinced me that I ought to go on with my life's work instead of being merely Mrs Travis. I suppose part of the "suitability" of that wonderful wedding present was to wean me from the honeymoon!'

'My dear child, it would be ungracious to criticise so admirably argued a thesis.'

'I believe there's a planet outside Neptune; and I'll start to look for it tomorrow.'

'With the new telescope?' was Simon's last arrow.

'With a table of logarithms, and all I can muster of brains and imagination.'

'And a little touch of spite!'

'Merely the malic acid in the apple of love!'

Geoffrey Travis, coming into the room, heard the last three words.

'Apple of love,' he cried; 'always the same old theme. Oh, you women, you women!'

NEBUCHADNEZZAR

'I am always bothering you,' murmured Miss Mollie Madison, apologetically.

'You are,' admitted Simon Iff; 'but I suppose I am old enough to like it.'

It is possible that he might have tolerated her even had he been young. There was never hair so plentiful, so irrepressible or so golden red as hers; and it framed a face warm, creamy flushed, round and innocent and laughing as a Greuze, with an impudent nose, and a mouth, perpetually pouting, which was redder even than the hair. Her body was slim and snake-like, every gesture sinuous and seductive. And she had no trace of self-consciousness or vanity. She never put a price upon herself, but gave freely as a queen should do.

'You frequently impress me as being a human being,' continued the mystic; 'and real human beings never really bother me. What is it this time?'

'It's a very small matter, Cephas,' which was her pet name for Simon. 'I had a dear friend at Vassar, Agnes Mills, and her mother's in trouble, and I thought you would advise her.'

'All right,' said Simon, resignedly, 'but I shall be very insulted if it isn't the eye of an Indian idol, at the very least.'

'I'm afraid it's a perfectly ordinary business matter; only she says she can't trust anyone but a—'

'A stranger,' suggested Simon, half playfully. But Mollie looked daggers at him. She never forgot the President in her ancestry.

'Another breach of the Monroe Doctrine?' he smiled, almost impudently.

She decided to ignore him. She had frequently found it safer.

'Mrs Mills is waiting downstairs,' she said, as stiffly as so little and luscious a little lady could be expected to do.

He rang down to tell the janitor to ask her to come up.

'Why on earth didn't you bring her up with you? You know, or you ought to know by now, that I never say no to a Distressed Widow.'

'How did you know she was a widow?'

'Why wouldn't she be going to her husband for advice?'

'Oh, they might be separated or divorced.'

'Dear me, no! If there had been any scandal about it, you would have told me, first thing!'

It was perhaps lucky for Simon Iff that the curriculum at Vassar had included a special course in training young ladies not to throw anything at anybody.

Mrs Mills entered the room. She was the kind of individual who doesn't matter to anybody. She had everything in a mild form. Simon Iff was reminded of Mrs Nickleby, but one without enough imagination to be flustered over The Gentleman Next Door. He had to use all his tact and acumen to disinter her story from the graveyard of General Reminiscences.

Rather than inflict this excellent lady upon others, Simon decided to champion her cause. The circumstances were thus inscribed by Mollie from dictation (aside) whenever he extricated what appeared to be a relevant fact.

She had lost her poor husband in 1895. His sole important asset had been the Ruddigore Copper Mine near Glanders, Montana, of the stock of which he had held 51 per cent. The mine was a paying proposition, though never a bonanza. The average yearly dividend – as Iff found on reference to Mollie – had been 1¼ per cent. This was good income for Mrs Mills and Agnes, the face value of the stock being over four hundred thousand dollars.

Her trustee, Mr Samuel Grass, had no interest in the mine. The active managers were Mr Kuhn and Mr Arnheim; they held nearly the whole balance of the stock between them. Both men were enormously wealthy, and extremely competent in business.

Kuhn, in particular, was noted for his sly secretive methods. He was called 'Pussy' on the Street. Arnheim was of a more obvious type; he was associated with Kuhn in many great enterprises. Next to Paul Powys, there was no financier in New York City so dreaded as Theophilus Kuhn; and there had been great enmity between them. With Arnheim's assistance Kuhn stood a fair chance of pulling down the great little Welshman; indeed, he had always held his own, and come out of many a battle with not too unfavourable a draw. But Powys was master of a power not his own; he represented the conservative element, and could always rally the forces of sanity to his banner.

The manager of the mine was a Scotsman named Craig, a dear friend and protégé of the late Mills. Agnes was informally engaged to be married to him. He was a man of thirty-five, exceptionally shrewd and competent, his character simple, honest and affectionate.

Neither Arnheim nor Kuhn had taken any very active interest in the mine; it was a very small matter compared with their gigantic interests elsewhere. Kuhn's nephew Caspar had the position of chief engineer, but it was admittedly a probation to train him for more important work. Mills, on his deathbed, had implored his wife never to part with her control of the mine, and never to allow the supersession of Craig.

Such were the disjointed avowals of the discursive lady, and this last was the point of her visit. For she was sorely tempted to sell her interest.

The last annual report, conceived in a more concise style than that of Mrs Mills, threw considerable light upon this point.

No dividend had been declared. Misfortune after misfortune had fallen upon the mine.

Miss Mollie Madison, knowing Simon Iff's little ways, had supplemented this with a report obtained from Craig, through Agnes, of the events at Glanders.

The first incident had been a fall of rock in Gallery 13 – the deepest level – which had in consequence become flooded. Mr Caspar Kuhn had attacked the problem with characteristic skill and energy, but his pumps had failed again and again. The machinery had jammed and broken. Kuhn had suspected malicious interference on the part of one of his men, and discharged him. His mates had taken offence at this action, and declared a strike.

Mr Kuhn, senior, had travelled from New York to investigate conditions, and his tact had succeeded in composing the quarrel; but work had hardly recommenced when a gang of irreconcilables had waylaid the engineer, and beaten him so seriously that he was confined to his bed for ten days.

Three days after his return to work, the mine had been deliberately dynamited, wrecking the main shaft. Experts reported that three months at least would be required before another ounce of ore could be extracted. The police were entirely at a loss to explain the conditions.

Craig had shared in the hatred aroused by young Kuhn's first action, for he had heartily supported his engineer. On two occasions he had been shot at. Both he and Caspar offered their resignations; but Mrs Mills, faithful to her husband's dying wish, had refused to accept Craig's suggestion, and of course included Kuhn in this reply. He, however, had insisted, and left for another position procured for him by his uncle. He told Craig frankly that he valued his skin.

His ill luck had not ended there, however. Before he had been a week in his new job he had been set upon in the dark near his house, as he returned from dinner with the manager, by a dozen men. But this time Mr Caspar Kuhn was armed; he put a bullet through the brain of one of his assailants. This affair was wrapped in absolute mystery; not a trace of motive could be discovered, and practically the whole camp produced alibis which were at least plausible. Kuhn, however, developed a severe attack of cold feet, and decided to take a holiday in Europe.

The annual report dated from the time of the first assault on Casper Kuhn. It therefore made no mention of the amazing developments of the following month.

A perfectly unknown individual named Ransome had appeared with what purported to be a first mortgage on the property. He alleged fraud, duress and various other illegalities against Mills. If his claim were well founded, the mine was his.

Mrs Mills had been advised by her trustee that the man was an ignorant crook, probably in the hands of some clever shyster. No court would consider the case for ten minutes. Grass had taken the title-deeds and other necessary papers from his safe-deposit vault, intending to hand them to his attorney. That night his house was burgled, and the papers, among other things, stolen.

When Ransome appeared in court, the company's attorney asked for an adjournment, hoping that time would permit him to recover the papers.

Ransome asked for an interim injunction to prevent the operation of the mine pending decision of the ownership. Having shown a *prima facie* case, this was granted. In fact, the company preferred not to oppose it, lest something should transpire which might disclose the serious nature of their loss. He might, for all they knew, coolly challenge their *locus standi*.

Three days later, Ransome's rooms, which were in an old-fashioned house in the Tenderloin, were entered, and his papers destroyed in the fire which he had left burning while he went out for dinner. Experts had however been able to recover a great deal from the burnt sheets, and Ransome's lawyer had prudently caused certified copies to be made.

Mrs Mills had been very much distressed by the harsh attitude of Mr Arnheim, who declared furiously that he had no time to be mixed up in so petty an affair, with its eternal conferences. He washed his hands of the matter, and proceeded to throw his stock on the market. It had stood at 20 or thereabouts for a long while; it now fell to 3¼ with no buyers.

Mr Kuhn had however acted with loyalty and magnanimity. He secretly purchased Arnheim's stock, and made it over to Mrs Mills as a Christmas present. He had taken an entirely unexpected attitude with regard to Ransome, proclaiming that he would spend his last dollar to fight the case. It was not the value of his share in the mine, he declared wrathfully; but it was worth twenty millions to him to prevent any person of undesirable ancestry thinking that he could put one over on Theophilus Kuhn.

Arnheim was furious. He openly stated his belief that Kuhn had some 'inside dope,' and had bought his stock for the rise. Kuhn calmly displayed the transfer to Mrs Mills. Arnheim left Kuhn's office in a rage. The friendly collaboration of twenty years was broken.

Nor did he stop there. He withdrew from an important deal in which he had been associated with Kuhn, and created a temporary panic in that market. He was next heard of as engineering a colossal combine in copper, in the course of which he bought up a dozen mines in the immediate neighbourhood of the Ruddigore. Kuhn remained perfectly impassive, hardly troubling himself to laugh at his former friend. The general opinion on the Street was that Arnheim was more than a little crazy.

Meanwhile Ransome seemed to be in a fair way to prove his claim to the mine. Nothing could save Kuhn and Mrs Mills but the recovery of the stolen papers. The company had been obliged to declare the loss, and Kuhn, his back to the wall, had offered a reward not much less than the full value.

Mrs Mills was distressed beyond measure by all this commotion. She had always accepted the mine as a fact in nature, and supposed that the periodic receipt of a cheque for dividends was a phenomenon comparable to the recurrence of spring. It might be a little more or a little less, just as spring might be genial or severe; but it was bound to come. She had practically no income except that from the mine, and she had saved no money. She began to feel anxious, for the mine was closed up under the injunction, and her bank balance sank weekly. Arnheim offered to buy her interest at the 3¼ which Kuhn had paid for his. She was tempted.

Kuhn came to the rescue with a cheque for a year's income reckoned at 2 per cent. 'Hold on,' said he; 'this luck can't last forever. The mine's good; once we're rid of Ransome, I'll put in more capital and new machinery, and we'll have her paying ten per cent before we're five years older.' And he dictated a sarcastic telegram in reply to Arnheim's offer.

Another year had nearly elapsed. Despite Kuhn's generous kindness, she was horribly worried. There was a constant stream of legal papers, which she did not in the least comprehend, to be signed with formalities as to witnesses and notaries public, which irritated her almost to madness. Her whole life was disturbed; she lost her sleep; at last she began to try to escape, and sounded Kuhn as to the possibility of selling her interest. Kuhn told her that the stock was waste-paper, so far as the market was concerned; she had to hold on, whether she liked it or not.

Arnheim probably had news of her state of mind; he telegraphed a new offer. He would pay 5.

Mrs Mills took the wire up to Kuhn's office. 'Do let me accept,' she said pitifully. 'I'm so tired of all this. I could get a government annuity, couldn't I?'

'If you give way,' said Kuhn, 'I'll never speak to you again. Think of Agnes! You would only get two thousand dollars a year at the most, and it would cease with your life. Agnes would have to marry a rich man instead of Craig. You hold on! I'll see you through! May I wire for you? Just take this telegram, Jenks. Arnheim, Astor House, Butte, Montana. I have just offered to take over Mrs Mills' interests in the Ruddigore Mine at par. Theophilus Kuhn. How's that, Mrs Mills?'

'What does it mean exactly?'

'It means that I'm offering you four hundred thousand-odd dollars instead of Arnheim's twenty thousand odd.'

'You don't really mean that?'

'I never say anything unless I mean it. But don't you do it! That stock's worth more than par with M. E., me, Theophilus Kuhn, behind it.'

The poor lady had departed in absolute distraction, and laid the matter before Agnes. To her amazement, the girl had flown into a rage and delivered an oration, rivalling Mark Antony's, on her father's dying wishes. But the trustee, who was present, urged her to sell. 'It's a marvellous offer,' he cried, 'Utterly quixotic. Why, the mine may not belong to you at all!'

'And what *I* think,' concluded Mrs Mills, very impressively, in a stage-whisper, having explained that the above interview represented the situation to date, 'is that Mr Kuhn wants Agnes!'

Simon Iff roused himself from his exhaustion-torpor.

'Very shrewd, very shrewd of you, my dear lady. I am sure that if Agnes inherits one-tenth of your charm, every sensible man must want her. To what a very curious line of speculation this may lead! Love is a form of attraction, is it not, dear lady? And so is gravitation. Observe, the last incident in your story is the attraction of Theophilus to Agnes, just as the first incident in far-away Montana is the attraction of the Earth's mass to the roof of Gallery 13. To the philosophical mind this coincidence is infinitely significant! To you it does not seem so? Nor does it seem so to me. Our minds are therefore not philosophical, dear lady, and we may thank Fortune for that, philosophy being a very wearisome subject.'

Mrs Mills was completely bewildered by the characteristic imbecility of these remarks.

Iff joined his fingers, and gazed earnestly heavenwards. 'I think that the most pragmatic school of philosophy is Scottish, is it not? Then in such practical matters we should enlist the services of Mr Craig. I think you said he was a Scotsman.'

'Of Scottish family, Mr Iff, but born in Canada, as I understand.'

'Good; born in Canada, he should be canny. Exactly the man for our purpose.'

'I really don't understand all this. I'm afraid you are taking Agnes' part.'

'I am taking nobody's part until I have found out what happened at the mine before the fall of rock in Gallery 13.'

'But what has that got to do with it?'

'Well, you won't admit the fall itself as accounting for the love of the most excellent Theophilus. And as nothing has happened since the fall, something must have happened before. That something will probably explain everything.'

'I don't understand at all. But I promised Agnes that I would abide by your decision.'

'My decision is that you do nothing until I have seen Mr Craig.'

'He is at Glanders, of course.'

'I am naturally of a curious disposition, and, having once heard of it, I could in no case rest until I had beheld with my own eyes the place so favoured in the matter of nomenclature.'

'It is a perfectly horrid place.'

'No place where you have ever been could be horrid. By the way, please let no one, not even Mr Kuhn, know that you have seen me. That is highly important.'

Mrs Mills took her leave.

'Get Agnes,' said Simon as the door closed, 'get her here just as quick as you can.'

But even as he spoke the telephone bell rang. It was a voice unknown to the magician. It appeared that Mrs A had been telling Mrs B at Mrs C's dinner-party that Mrs D had heard from Mrs E that Mrs F had had a letter from Mrs G saying that Mrs H had met Mrs I at Mrs J's, the subject of discussion being Mrs K's divorce. Mrs L had then... it went on to the climax, where Mrs Y had advised Mrs Z to consult Mr Iff; and might she call to see him?

Mr Iff regretted that he was sailing, that afternoon, to take up his residence in a monastery on Mount Athos, and replaced the receiver.

'It won't do, Mollie, it won't do!' he lamented. 'I have changed my mind. I am not going to Glanders. And I will write to Mrs Mills while you get Agnes.'

He wrote:

> Dear Mrs Mills,
>
> Do what thou wilt shall be the whole of the Law.
>
> In the little matter which you honoured me by mentioning this afternoon, I have now made up my mind. Mr Kuhn's offer seems to me most liberal, and I should accept it without hesitation. Even should he lose his money, he can well afford it. And I recommend you to invest the proceeds of the sale of your share of the mine in sound government securities.
>
> Love is the law, love under will.
>
> Yours truly,
>
> SIMON IFF

'There!' he cried to Mollie, tossing the letter across, 'I wash my hands of any matter in which women are concerned!'

She read it, surprised. 'Then why do you want to see Aggie?'

'To advise her to marry Mr Kuhn.'

He called the servant, and told him to take the letter. Then he proceeded to teach Mollie how to play piquet, and had just piqued and capotted her for the third time in ten minutes when Agnes Mills appeared.

'It is you, I gather,' said Simon, sternly, after introduction, 'that suggested my meddling in your love-affairs!'

'I haven't the slightest idea what you mean!'

'My advice to you is to marry Mr Kuhn.'

'But—'

'But me no buts!'

'Mr Kuhn has never hinted at such a thing.'

'Observe the artfulness of modern wooing! Your mother – a shrewd mind – has told me the facts!'

'It's perfect nonsense. Anyhow, I'm going to marry Mr Craig.'

'That fickle Scot! Maiden! I despise myself that I should have to wound your noble heart, to bring the pearly dew to those gazelle-like eyes, but the stern truth must out. He loves you not!'

'I told you he was a little funny in his talk. You mustn't mind him, dear!' put in Mollie.

'Be silent, wench!' thundered Iff.

But he had no need. Aggie was on her feet, aflame with indignation. 'Mr Iff! I don't know by what right you speak to me like this; but let me tell you that not one day has passed in these three years that I haven't had an eight-page letter from him!'

'That hard-headed Scotsman writes you a daily bucket of slush? Faugh!'

'How dare you say such things? He writes me nice sensible letters, telling me everything that happens at the mine.'

'In that case, you can tell me exactly what was going on just before the fall of the roof in Gallery 13.'

Mollie burst into a ripple of laughter that swelled to full diapason as Aggie joined rather hysterically in.

'I told you what a funny man he is!'

But Agnes became very serious. She saw that Simon had had some reason for playing on her emotions, for keying her up to a high pitch before revealing his true purpose. She hesitated.

Mollie understood the gesture. She went over to Simon, and patted him on the head. 'He's the best and dearest and biggest baby in the world,' she said, 'and I'd trust him with my life.'

'Is this a proposal?' cried the alarmed magician.

'I wouldn't dare till 1912; that's Leap Year.'

'I'll be in Mount Athos before then. However, to business, Miss Mills! There's no time to lose. You haven't the letters here, of course? How's your memory?'

'I remember all that month as I do the multiplication table. I read and re-read all the letters of that period, because I wanted to discover why anyone should want to shoot poor Bob.'

'Of course. What an ass I am! It's entirely your fault, Mollie, for making me play piquet when I should have been thinking. Well, Miss Mills?'

'There was absolutely nothing but routine for months before the rockfall—'

'Until one day before?'

'Yes,' said Agnes, surprised and encouraged. 'How did you guess that?'

'I had a feeling that somebody or other had been reading *Macbeth*. "If it were done when 'Tis done, then 'twere well it were done quickly." Or, scorning the Thane's hesitation, turning the page to "There is a tide in the affairs of men" – something of that sort, don't you know?'

Agnes wetted her lips thoughtfully with her tongue. 'I seem to sense something. I've puzzled over this for ages.'

'Well, who was working in Gallery 13?'

Agnes cocked her head, and nodded. 'You're on the trail, and I can't see how, or why. Gallery 13 was the lowest level. It was a pure experiment; it didn't follow the geological indications. It was a pet idea of Mr Craig's.'

'Ah! I might have known that too, but for Mollie.'

'Johansen, a highly educated man, and a real friend of Bob's, was in charge of the drill. He was assisted by a Russian Jew named Lipsky, a steady clever worker, but full of socialistic ideas, and liable to fits of drinking. These were the only two men at work. It was a tiny gallery, you understand?'

'But sometimes inspected?'

'The engineer would go his rounds, of course.'

'Mr Kuhn?'

'Yes, I imagine so.'

'Clever man, Mr Kuhn?'

'Yes, splendid. He always got on first-rate with Bob. They used to study mineralogy and geology together nearly every night.'

'But he was harsh with the men?'

'Never, till this incident of the pumps fouling.'

'Go on about poor Johansen!'

Agnes started again at the adjective, and controlled herself. 'That afternoon Johansen was killed as he came out of the gallery.'

'A commonplace accident, for a driller!'

'Quite. He was near the junction of Gallery 12 and the main shaft when a trolley, running down the incline, knocked him down and killed him outright. The wheels crushed his head in.'

'Lipsky saw this?'

'Yes. He shouted a warning, but too late.'

'Thank you. I am interested in the remorse of Mr Lipsky. Was his temper upset at all?'

'Yes, he became virulent against mine-owners. He was one of the ringleaders in the attacks on Mr Kuhn. Mr Kuhn, senior, arrived from New York, and adopted a policy of all-round conciliation. He carpeted the ringleaders, one by one, and dealt with them in various ways. Lipsky was impertinent, and Mr Kuhn gave him his ticket to Mexico and a hundred dollars; anything to get such a firebrand out of the country.'

'And did he go?'

'He wanted to stay. But his friends meant to go back to work and have no more trouble; so they packed him off. In fact, they rode him out of town, as they say'

'Only one other question. Why do you object so strongly to your mother's selling out? The price is a splendid one. Don't trouble to tell me about your father's dying wishes! You're not that sort of girl.'

'No, that's only what I tell mother. It's Bob. He implores me in every letter to get her to hold on, no matter at what cost.'

'Why?'

'He won't say. He says I must trust him.'

'Well, I've advised your mother to sell. She had promised to abide by my decision. So if you want to stop her, get busy'

Agnes blanched. Then she saw something in the mystic's eyes that gave her second counsel. 'I'll stop her.'

'She has my note by now. I feel sure that she has telephoned to Mr Kuhn; also that she has mentioned my name.'

'You must tell me some more.'

'If you developed a very bad cough, would your mother hurry you to Palm Beach?'

'She might if I made a point of it.'

'These tablets will assist you in the production of a helpful cough. Depart in peace, and rely on me to put an entirely new face on things before Mrs Mills gets ready to sign any papers.'

'Goodbye, and thank you. But I expect a whole lot – from what I've seen.'

'Oh! I'm not to be bribed by flattery.'

She went out, exalted; and Simon Iff remarked that he must lose no time in settling this small matter.

'Mollie! *Mollior cuniculo cinaede!* We must have Paul Powys at our unostentatious board. Invoke him by the Qabalistic number which constraineth him; it is Fulton 11,000.'

She got the number.

'Ah, Mr Iff, so glad you called me; I was thinking of you only this morning,' said the magnate genially, not having thought of Simon for a month. 'Dinner? My dear man, I only wish I could; but I'm tied up with Sharp and McGregor. A business dinner, or I'd ask you to come along— Yes, I want to see you too; but I'm absolutely tied up all day. Haven't a minute; had no lunch yet, confound it, and I'm hungry. Won't you ring me up again soon?'

Iff smiled quietly. 'Will you answer me one question, only one very little one? Have you by any odd chance anything very big on just now? Something so big that it would break you if you lost out – say to a combination of—'

Powys broke in. 'Absolutely nothing at all like that. Dear me, no! (What's that?) Oh, how fortunate! Does that invitation hold, Mr Iff? My secretary tells me Mr Sharp has just rung through to call off the dinner.'

'Of course,' said Iff. 'Delighted! Shall we say half-past six?'

'Well, there's absolutely nothing doing today in the bank; dull as ditch-water. If you're not busy, might I run up now and play that game of chess you promised me?'

'Certainly. Come right round. I'll get the pieces out.'

Twenty minutes later Paul Powys stepped from his limousine. He was a small man, well-knit, well-groomed, with a great white mustache and imperial. His hair was still plentiful, of pale ashen grey, and it was smoothed carefully upon his head. His eyes were set very deeply in his head, and were intensely vital. He reminded one a little of Henri de Rochefort, a miniature of that great Frenchman. The mouth was thin and very red;

the nose unusually thin and long, with a decided angle, like Wellington's. His hat, gloves and cane proclaimed the dandy. His step was light, soft and elastic, and he possessed the quality of personality in the highest degree, magnetising the attention without doing anything whatever towards the attainment of that most desirable end.

He found Simon finishing the last sentence of a memorandum. Mollie was typing furiously; her hair, loose and tousled about her head, was like a comet of fiery serpents in the red glow of the afternoon sun as it streamed through the open casement, and cast her shadow upon the rich blue and amber of the Chinese carpet.

She pulled the paper from the machine. Simple Simon handed the sheets to his visitor.

'Your move!'

He enjoyed one of the treats of his life. Paul Powys spread the sheets, and closed them again, like a lady flirting her fan. Then he folded them in three, and handed them to Simon. The whole action did not occupy thirty seconds.

As he passed the paper to the magician, he said: Of course, they have found gold. But that won't queer my deal, however much it may be.'

'It isn't that at all,' said Simon Iff. 'They aren't thinking about that.'

'You had better give me your theory – in detail, please.'

Simon Iff knew that Powys could have quoted his memorandum textually from end to end, so he did not trouble to remind him of the facts. 'I saw two objectives in these operations from the first.'

'Somebody was trying to prevent access to Gallery 13, and trying to buy the mine. That meant they had found gold there in some unheard-of richness.'

'Quite. I think young Kuhn must have come on the men just as they struck it, and made up his mind in a few minutes what to do. Johansen was certain to tell Craig of the strike; he had to be killed right there. Lipsky was a good tool. But he drank; old Kuhn saw at once when he arrived that he must be got out of the country and pensioned off. Caspar and Lipsky proceed to wreck the gallery and then the mine. The strikes and assaults are all intended to prevent the mine from reopening, and to divert any suspicion from Kuhn. Note that he is careful to be assaulted even in his new job; argument, the ill-feeling against him has nothing to do with what happened in the mine.'

'This is very probable, and very interesting,' interrupted Powys.

'But, you are about to say, how does it concern me? Do you think I would waste a moment of your time?'

'I beg your pardon, Mr Iff.'

'I want to prove to you that the entire device, from the moment of Theophilus Kuhn's arrival at Glanders, was directed against you.'

But Simon Iff had wasted several moments of Powys' time; he need not have said that at all, and he pulled himself up with a frown. 'They invent this Ransome idiocy not merely to keep the mine unworked until they can force Mrs Mills into selling it – I agree with you that the mine is a trifle to such minds as yours and, indeed, Kuhn's – but to give a pretext for the pretended quarrel between Kuhn and Arnheim.'

'I may tell you that their quarrel has cost them over fifty million, to my certain knowledge.'

'I was sure Kuhn would do things well, on the grand scale. You have beaten him too often before.'

'How are you sure of this?'

'Miss Madison here told me that Kuhn was called "Pussy" on Wall Street. I saw him taking endless trouble and risk and loss; he would only do that for some great object: what object so great as you? His preoccupation with trifles proved a giant aim to be concealed; his advertised quarrel with Arnheim proved a closer alliance.'

'I agree with you. I thank you very much. I will attend to the matter.'

'Just one word more, if I may. I came into this in the interest of Mrs Mills.'

'Don't worry. He won't show anxiety to close the deal. The transfer would hardly be ready in less than three days. And – in three days – where would Theophilus Kuhn find four hundred thousand dollars?'

Simple Simon was taken aback for once in his life. The question was as if he were asked where a man on the sea-shore would find a pebble. He shook hands quietly with Powys at the door.

'Mollie, put your things on. I am going to buy you a new hat. I have had one of the most delightful experiences of my life. So much for my good temper, which bestows hats on blessed damozels. My bad temper, which makes mean me pay for them, is due to remorse for my egregious blunders in this very simple affair.'

She fixed her passionate blue eyes adoringly upon his face.

'No!' cried the mystic, in prophetic frenzy, 'you only betray your ignorance and your stupidity. Sit down, and let me lecture you upon my own base folly!'

She curled her snaky body into a cunning crook of the sofa, and, with her head thrown back, began to puff a cigarette.

'I sit upon the stool of penitence,' he continued, doing so, with the music stool, *faute de mieux*.

'You noticed, of course, that I changed what in moments of paranoiac megalomania I insult Nature by calling my mind. I did not allow to Mrs Mills her full measure of imbecility. I did not fully realise that she would instantly do the wrong and dangerous thing. So I let her see what was actually in my mind, or, to be more accurate, I made it possible for Theophilus to divine what was in my mind from her words or her manner.

'That telephone call from that female glossorhoeic reminded me that I was known all over New York, and that Theophilus probably knew already that Mrs Mills had come to consult me. My more tragic error, indeed, is a fatal underestimation of the calibre and range of Theophilus. For, trying to correct my first mistake, I made a worse one. I tried to deceive him. I wrote a letter which I thought he might accept as indicative of my contempt for Mrs Mills, and my lack of interest in her affairs. I gave him credit for less intelligence than a limpet's, a – a – a Simon Iff's! Put yourself in his place! "So Mr Simon Iff found nothing to interest him in that story? Really! Too bad!" He would then judge that I was lying to somebody. Who would that be? Who worth my while? Who but the quarry, himself? He would then – I mean, he will now – proceed to get after me. As he has the brains of the devil himself, and doesn't stick at murder – even his young hopeful Caspar shoots a man he never saw before merely to conceal his part in a game where no one had ever suspected him to be a player – the inference is that we are liable to be blown up by dynamite at any moment. My only hope is that he will think that letter of mine indicates permanent instead of temporary dementia.'

Miss Mollie Madison absolutely declined to take alarm. She crossed her feet over the arm of the sofa, so that 'Cephas' might take note of the fact that she had the right divine to wear white boots – unpinched feet no larger than new-born kittens. And she lighted a third cigarette, not even deigning to reply.

'You are right. I will buy you six pairs of white kid boots.'

She passed a hand negligently through her hair.

'Of course,' he added hastily, 'as you imply, the tops must be of green crushed morocco.'

'Think, Cephas!'

From her eyes he understood that she did not wish him to make light of the expected duel.

'Our friend, as we should expect from a disciple of the evangelist Luke, will be full of human sympathy; the Christian touch will be his long suit; his middle name will be Eleemosynaria. Then he will know that I am on to his little game; and I will bet you an emerald necklace to match your perfectly intoxicating Poiret – where, oh where are the Prohibitionists? – that he knows that Powys has been here, and what I said to him. But he will not know what Powys said to me, because Powys has always been a bit above his class. But he will be devilish well scared; he will imagine Powys as laying a trap for him, perhaps the more so as he may think Powys ignorant or careless of his own knowledge of the situation. We must hope that he has committed himself too far in this deal to withdraw. In fact, we may say that it is certain that he has done so, for Powys spoke of his ruin with entire assurance. Powys never guesses, or expects, or hopes. Indicative and imperative are the only moods in his defective verbs. Mr Theophilus Kuhn will therefore know himself bankrupt; there will be nothing left for him but revenge. The question is: Will he try to kill Powys, or will he try to kill me? We are to remember the necessity of this man's mind; his nature compels him to perpetual concealment of his purposes. Will he then try to gain access to Powys on some such pretext of conference, or offer to compromise, or some such obvious blind? He would know that he would stand not a chance in a million. With me the case is different. He knows that I am vowed to the service of humanity, and that, were he three hundred and thirty-three times the liar, thief and murderer that he is, I would see him if he came to me on the pretext that he needed my advice or aid in any spiritual distress or aspiration. Most people interested in occult subjects being potential or actual murderers, I therefore arrange for their reception in the following ingenious manner. Just look out of the window for a minute!'

Mollie obeyed. He drew the curtains behind her, and switched on three electric lamps, which shed a soft and cheerful glow in the apartment. He then made certain rearrangements in the room.

'Come and sit down by me, now, and we will play piquet until Mr Kuhn favours us with a visit.'

Mollie turned and came through the curtains. She walked, as she supposed, straight to him, and banged into a sheet of plate glass in a totally different part of the room.

'Theophilus will have to be a very bad shot in order to hit me.' He laughed, came swiftly towards her, and led her gently to the sofa where he had been sitting.

The bell rang. 'Ah! but here is our friend the enemy!'

The Japanese boy entered with a visiting card. 'Sir,' it read,

> I am in extreme spiritual affliction, and I implore you to receive me, and to give me your counsel.
>
> T. K.

'Ask Mr Kuhn to enter, and place a chair for him!' The boy obeyed. 'See!' he whispered in the girl's small round ear, 'so far we have read his mind aright.'

Theophilus Kuhn came in, walking heavily. He was an extreme contrast to Powys. His large frame was clad in loose, untidy clothes, and supported an enormous head, slightly asymmetric like Verlaine's, with an immense domed forehead crowned with a thick mat of curly black hair. He was clean-shaven; the mouth was large and prominent, the jaw aggressive, the nose fleshy, curved and spatulate, the eyes glaucous and cold, with an indefinable expression of cunning and malice that inspired Miss Madison with horror and Simon Iff with sorrow. Even in the dim light, they showed a curious inequality which was somehow uncanny. His hands were large and strong, heavy with fat as the face itself.

Simon Iff waited for him to speak. He fumbled long and clumsily with his black gloves before he got them off. Then he slowly drew a fountain-pen and cheque-book from his pocket.

'I understand, Mr Iff, that you are in need – temporary need, of course, purely temporary – of a little money. I am very happy to be able to accommodate you. I will make out the cheque for eight million dollars. I have had an excellent day on Wall Street. I have beaten Paul Powys. Yes, sir, we have had many battles, but he has come to his Waterloo. You can hardly imagine what this means to me. It gives me control of the whole wealth of this great country. I have America in my pocket. In five years Europe will be mine. Asia, Africa, the whole world shall bow before Theophilus Kuhn. Understand, Mr Powys, you are in the presence of no ordinary man. I have wished many a time to kill you; now I let you go, because I have beaten you, beaten you to hell, you dog. I despise you for the toy you are! Aha! you thought to make yourself equal to me. And I let you think it – do you know why? I have waited for this day of your humiliation to tell you the great secret. You puppet! You marionette! I made you. I am God! Now let me write you your cheque, Mr Iff.'

Mollie had crouched closer to Simple Simon in abject terror; she put her red mouth to his ear, and whispered: 'He's shamming mad. He thinks it will help him with the jury.'

But the magician patted her softly on the head, and went quietly over to the table where Kuhn was laboriously writing out the cheque, with many a hesitation. He could not make the upstrokes properly.

'Thank you very much for the kindly thought, Mr Kuhn. The money will indeed be my salvation.'

As he spoke, he touched a tiny hand-bell, and the Japanese appeared. 'Bring a doctor,' said Simon softly, in the man's own language. 'Mr Kuhn has been suddenly taken ill.'

Kuhn rose and handed the cheque to Iff with a flourish, and then began once more to babble of his fame and his success, his wealth, his empire and his godhead. He went away with the doctor like a child; he had forgotten Iff's presence; the new face took his attention, and he began all over again to boast of his money, and to offer millions to the servant and to the physician.

The door closed behind him. Simon Iff went over to the girl and put his hand upon her shoulder.

'We will not play piquet today, child, and we will not buy ourselves hats and boots. We have need to humble ourselves.'

He led her to a recess in the wall, where beneath a lamp of silver, with its red glass, and wick afloat in olive oil, stood the bronze figure of Thoth, the Egyptian God of Wisdom.

'I do not bend the knee in supplication to the Gods; but I bend the head in veneration of their infinite wisdom and of their awful justice. I have been proud of the powers of this poor mind, matching it against the greatest intelligences incarnate on this planet. And in this I did well. But this day have I erred thrice, and the third time is the greatest folly in all my life. For I knew not, nor understood, the infinite wisdom and the awful justice of the Gods. I did not comprehend that a mind so false, so cunning, and so malignant must be a mind insane. Of course the shock of knowing that he was outwitted and irrevocably ruined would topple the unsound structure. I did not understand that. Therefore I feared, and hid myself with a coward's device; and all the virtue is departed from me.'

He led her back into the room, and switched on the full light.

'Even in my confession pride thrust up its head,' he said very wearily and sadly. 'I had to explain to you just where I had gone wrong, and how clever I was to see it. And it's my pride that is urging me now to explain that to you; I wanted to prove how genuine my penitence really was. And now – when I am going to ask you not to come to see me for a week unless you really need me – it is still pride. I want to boast how great a sin it is that demands so fierce a penance for its purgation. It's in the marrow of our bones!

'However,' he resumed in his grimly humorous tone, 'I am going to do the week of meditation, for all that. It's my Vow. And the object of Vows is to prevent the devil getting at us by the road of Introspection.'

'I need you always,' answered Mollie, touching the vital spot that concerned her. 'But I shall not come to see you. I have a slight touch of pride myself.'

"*Retro, Satanas!*' cried the mystic cheerfully, 'you are flattering me where a true man feels it most. But, my sweet child, that is a lawful pride, and man would be indeed a worm without it. So, *Satanissa*, you miss the target.'

'I think I ought to go down to Palm Beach, and tell the good news to Agnes. You had better come too; that pride of yours comes from sitting cooped up in the city, when you need fresh air and exercise. And those errors of judgment are just plain indigestion. You can do your week of meditation down there.'

'I will meditate upon the Sun and Moon, upon Fire, Earth, Air and Water; and I will also write a short treatise upon how Eve got Adam to eat apples when he ought to have been naming pterodactyls. Oh woman, your fascination is in the intuition which serves you so well instead of knowledge. What a wonder of Nature to make such a compensation for you!'

'The compensation is for you.'

'There you go again! *Humanum est errare* – then thank the Lord I err. Now tell the *mikado* to serve dinner.'

She ran off merrily.

'Don't mind me!' was her laugh, 'I've always been *loco*, you know.'

'Well,' flashed back Simon, '*dulce est desipere in loco*.' Latin not being her long suit, she did not answer, and he became serious once more.

'It's the Wonder of Wonders! Not a self-respecting convolution in her whole cerebral cortex, and here she is telling me, the high and mighty Simon Iff, all sorts of things I don't know. I shall have a busy week with that meditation; I think I had better make it a fortnight.'

He did not even know that Miss Mollie Madison had made up her mind to make it a month.

SUFFER THE LITTLE CHILDREN

If Miss Mollie Madison supposed for one moment that Simon Iff meant to take his two weeks' penance lightly, she was very much enlightened on arrival at Ormond, where, and not to Palm Beach, Mrs Mills had taken the malingering Agnes.

He had bought a tremendous black stallion, seventeen hands high, and every other morning went for a fifty-mile gallop along the broad smooth sands. Alternate mornings he would swim from dawn to noon. His lunch invariably consisted of grapefruit and a big rare beefsteak, washed down with a bottle of plain spring-water. He did not smoke any more. From one o'clock till sunset he might have been found in a palm-grove, deep-hidden, sitting absolutely motionless with his legs tucked away under him.

At seven he joined the party for dinner, when he ate fish and drank a quart of milk. Immediately after the meal he walked swiftly to the beach and back, usually with Mollie or Agnes or both, and then retired to sleep. At midnight he awoke, and continued his meditation until dawn.

Reproached by Mrs Mills, who urged him to rest, he said: 'I am like the conqueror of Warsaw or wherever it was: I make a solitude, and call it peace.'

The good lady was exceedingly perturbed, after about a week, by the character of his conversation, which consisted in contradicting every statement made in his presence. If she said it was a fine day, he would reply, 'Pardon me, madam, if I cannot admit that it is fine. At the same time, it is not wet, cold, windy or anything else unpleasant.' His explanation was that nothing that could be thought was true, in the highest philosophical sense; similarly, nothing that could be thought was not true, so that his only chance of telling the truth was to deny everything, and its contradiction also, whenever opportunity arose.

Mrs Mills was very grateful to him for saving her fortune, and she thought that the least she could do to repay him was to have a doctor to look at him. She knew that he would never consent to a consultation, so she quietly asked a famous nerve specialist from New York, who spent his winters in Florida, making a fortune out of patching up the idle rich, to come to dinner and have an unofficial look at him.

Dr Buzzard was a very clever man, and knew enough never to tell a patient that there was nothing the matter with him; so he reported to Mrs Mills that he couldn't quite say that it was paranoia, that to call it neursthenia might be premature, that dementia praecox, while worthy of our earnest consideration, was not actually to be considered as definitively established at present, and that while there were or might be or seem to be decided symptoms of a medenologicolalic type, it could hardly be maintained diagnostically that psycho-pathological cachexia, in any of its commoner forms, at least, was inhibiting the *nous*, almost as noncommittally as Iff himself could have wished.

However, a second dinner-party might enable him to endeavour to draw out Mr Iff. If he could be got to take interest once more in the common things of life, the mind might take on a healthier tone.

The wind was somewhat taken out of his sails by the appearance of Simon Iff at dinner in full evening dress. He had ordered the meal, moreover: oysters, clear green turtle, pompano en papillote, mallard duck au sang with coeur de palmier salad, bavaroise au chocolat, and a savoury invented by himself consisting of Toast Melba spread with mushrooms, anchovies, olives and pimento made into a paste. This was covered with bay-leaves, on which was spread a mixture of caviar, raw onions, ginseng and Bombay Duck, sprinkled lightly with powdered hashish.

The wine list was equally elaborate. Cocktails consisting of two tea-spoonfuls of liqueur brandy, one of Curacao and one of laudanum, preceded the repast. With the oysters he caused Chablis to be served, with the soup Tokay, with the fish Chateau Yquem. The duck was accompanied by Mumm Cordon Rouge 1904. The sweet was enriched by a marvellous sauce with a basis of crème de cacao, and the savoury fortified with an astonishingly fine Burgundy of incomparable body and bouquet. The coffee was Turkish, prepared by Simon himself at the table, and perfected by the addition of an aromatic consisting of essential oil of cedarwood and ambergris.

The liqueurs were green Chartreuse of the original shipping, a particular absinthe from a private still belonging to a friend of Simon Iff living in Switzerland among the crags of Jura, and an *introuvable* Metternich brandy. With the nuts came Château Margaux, port and a Madeira dating from William IV. An unopened bottle of rye whisky was also placed prominently on the table.

'There must be a skeleton,' said Simon Iff, 'at every banquet.' For he had begun to do the honours by announcing that this was His Night Off.

'Am I,' he asked indignantly, 'of no more value than many housemaids?'

'A lucid interval,' thought Dr Buzzard, acutely. 'Let me improve the occasion!'

Towards the finale of the duck *rondo*, therefore, he expressed a wish that Mr Iff could be induced to apply his truly marvellous powers to the discovery of the Crime of Titusville.

'Useless,' rejoined Simon, 'I have already discovered it.'

'Why, what is the Crime of Titusville?' mooed Mrs Mills.

'Titusville,' replied Iff, with finality.

'He's off again,' thought the doctor to himself, having no sense of humour.

'I rode over there the other day,' explained the mystic; 'it is the worst of crimes – a crime against Nature.' And he began to sing softly.

> 'What though the spicy breezes
>   Blow soft o'er Titusville,
> Though every prospect pleases,
>   The people make me ill.'

'Do they "Bow down to wood and stone?"' laughed Miss Mollie Madison, who had up to that moment attended strictly to the business of dinner. She had been copying the master's asceticism with feminine fidelity, and now meant to make up for it.

'They do,' said Iff.

'But surely they are Christians?' tittered Mrs Mills, with surprise.

'They are,' crashed the magician. 'They worship wood in the head, and stone in the heart.'

'Oh dear!' faded away the good matron, wondering whether she had not perhaps drunk a little too much.

Dr Buzzard determined to put forth a great effort to prevent his prospective patient from slipping back.

'Yesterday morning,' he said thickly but firmly, 'the little daughter of Mr and Mrs Thorpe, who live some fifteen miles out of Titusville, on the St. John's River, disappeared. And she has not been found.'

'Tell me the facts,' said the magician, suddenly serious.

'Thorpe's grove is ten miles from the next inhabited dwelling. He employs several men to work for him, but they were all with him in the grove during the period of which we are to speak. Thorpe is a bluff bearded fellow of fifty or so; his wife Birdie is not yet thirty. They are intensely religious, devoted to I don't know quite which of the warring sects of Baptist. The grove is a large and flourishing concern; Thorpe has plenty of money in the bank, and owns real estate in Titusville to a considerable value. A rich man for these parts, you may say.

'Mamie, the only child, is not yet five years old.

'The house stands on the east bank of the river; access from the west is almost impossible – the stream is shallow, a mere trickle over thick banks of soft mud; it flows through many and changing channels; the swamp extends for many miles.

'A rough track leads through thick jungle to the grove; thence it becomes a little wider and smoother as it winds towards Titusville. The point to notice is that it would be difficult for any person to reach the house without being seen by the men at work in the grove. It would be easy for him, however, to hide in the jungle all night, and get away the following day after sundown when the men returned from labour.

'I must tell you that Mrs Thorpe was previously married to a man named Spring. There was a daughter, but the Thorpes are reticent on the subject. After Spring's death Birdie was courted by several men, notably by one James Harper, a man of twenty-five, of good prospects and religious character.'

'But Thorpe had better prospects and was more religious?'

'I think that was the case. Anyhow, she married Thorpe. Harper vowed vengeance; in particular he threatened that if she ever had a child he would kidnap it. He then went away and started a ranch in Texas. Here his character degenerated; he openly denied religion and took to drinking.'

'Dreadful,' said Simon, motioning the wine steward to refill the doctor's glass.

'However, he seems to have made himself universally liked as a good fellow. But he never would look at a woman. His heartiness appears to have been assumed for the benefit of his friends; when alone, he was morose. He was often found in his cottage with his head sunk upon the table, and the caller, greeted with a shout and a laugh, would yet perceive that he had been crying bitterly.

'Yesterday morning Mrs Thorpe was hanging out the washing. Mamie was playing in front of the house. She was last seen by her mother trying to climb a kumquat tree of unusual size to reach the fruit upon the upper branches.

'A few minutes later – naturally the poor woman cannot be sure of the exact period – the child had disappeared. She called out, and then went on with her work. Then, again she noticed that Mamie had not answered the call. She became anxious and went after her.

'The child's footsteps were plain to follow. They led along the track for a little way, and then turned off into the jungle. A strip of torn cotton was found at this point.

'The footsteps vanished. Mrs Thorpe, now thoroughly alarmed, ran back to the house and fired the shotgun which was the signal for the men to come in to dinner. She searched around the house – the swamp, the river banks – while waiting, and found no trace. Thorpe ran in from the grove, surprised at the untimely summons. She told her story. Thorpe fired again to call in the men. Together, they verified the evidence of the trail. There was nothing for it but to beat the jungle. Thorpe sent a man on horseback to Titusville to get assistance. The whole town turned out, and arrived on the spot by noon. The disappearance had taken place, roughly, at seven in the morning.

'The sheriff of Titusville is a fine fellow, and a very hot man on a trail. He verified the evidence once more, and entirely agreed with the previous indications. As luck would have it, I was passing through Titusville in my car, noticed the commotion, and offered him a lift. We arrived well ahead of the rest of the town. So, you see, I have my knowledge at first hand.'

'Excellent. Well, what did you discover?'

'A man's footprints, wide apart and softly impressed, leading from another part of the jungle, a quite different part, to the clearing about the house. They led to a knoll which overlooks the whole of the open space from the river to the jungle. He had stopped there, and shifted his feet about. Then he must have turned, and run like the wind. It was a series of wild leaps back to the jungle. He seems to have plunged head foremost into the thickest part of it. He did not choose an opening, but charged like a bull. Torn cloth and blood bore evident witness to the event.

'Sheriff Higgs and I followed with about a dozen men. The others were busy on the other side, hunting systematically from the place where the child's tracks ended. Ours was a terrible trail. Broken twigs and trampled grass made it easy to follow, save where the man in his fury had leapt across the ever-recurring pools – long snaky shiny stinking stagnations which the sheriff, although a great athlete, did not dare to attempt.

'But the longest trail ends at last. About three o'clock we came upon Harper. He was lying half-in, half-out of a pool. He was stone dead. I examined him; the cause of death was evident, the rupture of a bloodvessel on the brain.

'There was nothing suggestive in his pockets except an old worn photograph of Mrs Thorpe, with "Ever thine Birdie" scrawled across it in a slow uneducated hand. There was not a shred of evidence to prove that he had ever had possession of the child, though of course he must have done so. And she has not been found anywhere else, either. Not a trace!'

'"Not a button, or feather, or mark!"' quoted Simon, and they stared at his levity. 'I don't think I will explain just now. By the way, doctor, just one question. Do Mrs Thorpe's tracks anywhere cross Harper's?'

'Not within fifty yards.'

'I will take a look round. My holiday ends at midnight, but I might as well ride that way as another, and I hereby, in the superior interests of humanity, absolve myself from my Vow of Negation during my little pilgrimage.'

Punctually at twelve o'clock he broke up the party, and went to his room. Five minutes later he was in his riding-breeches with a blue poncho, striped with white and purplish brown. The moon, rising at one o'clock, fell on his pale face as he cantered on the great black stallion towards Titusville.

Following the directions given him, he turned off the main road a little before dawn into a narrow track that wound between the groves. Presently he came to a bifurcation; a few minutes later to another, more doubtful as to direction. In half an hour it petered out completely. He had lost his way.

He looked about him for signs of habitation. There were none. He decided to take the safest course, and return to a house some miles back, where he could refresh his orientation.

Just then, in the solemnity of dawn's silence, he heard a voice. Someone – someone within a few hundred yards of him – was singing.

The voice was untutored, but its range and its richness astounded him. There did not seem to be any words, and yet it was articulate. Higher it soared and higher, in trills and arpeggios, then fell as a cascade falls in luxurious cadences, then shrilled again. It was the wildest maddest music.

Some instinct prompted Simon Iff to play the spy. Perhaps it was that he did not want to disturb the singer, possibly to frighten her. So he slipped off his horse and tied the bridle to a tree, then crept warily through the undergrowth. He had been a successful *shikari* in the Hambantota province of Ceylon, and cared nothing for any shooting but the stalk. Five or six minutes later he was in full view of the quarry.

He judged her to be of sixteen years of age. Her body was sinewy and agile, though rather short and sturdy. Her face had something of the satyr in it, with a double curve to strong voluptuous lips. The face was oval, with deep-set violet eyes and dark lines under them, the complexion otherwise absolutely pallid, a dead ivory. Her hair was long and loose, deep violet like her eyes, hanging in heavy masses that curled Medusa-wise about her head. She was clad only in a cotton shift, but her dress, a coarse brown merino, lay with her shoes and stockings a little distance behind her.

Hardly had he taken notice of these matters when her song stopped, and she began to dance. It was a savage romp, reminding him of certain Spanish girls at Granada. But this was a true witch-dance, done with the deliberate purpose of invocation.

She stopped suddenly, with curious naïveté, sat down, and began to put on her dress.

The magician read her soul easily, for it was close kin to his own. He knew that there was but one way to approach her. He began in a very low deep voice, like the muttering of distant thunder, to chant the Hymn to Pan from the *Ajax* of Sophocles.

At first the girl did not hear; but as the magician grew louder and bolder and more dynamic, she rose and looked about her. Simple Simon was far too well hidden for such crude search. His voice soared and sank, roared and rolled in passionate ecstasy, like the beating of African drums.

Suddenly the girl fell upon her knees. She tore off her clothes – even the shift itself – closed her eyes, threw her head back and extended her arms.

The magician ceased his song. He came forward quietly toward her, and caught her in his arms. A terrible shudder passed through her frame as he put his mouth on hers; she went limp, and he laid her upon the ground unconscious. Then he covered her with her own dress, and stood with folded arms, waiting. In a few minutes she came out of her swoon. As she saw Iff she trembled, and put her forearm over her eyes. The word 'Pan' came in a whisper from her lips.

'Yes, child,' said the magician very gently. 'It is well, Syrinx, that you never "ran into the forest from Arcadian Pan." But I am not Pan only; I am one Simon Iff, "a desperate magician concealed within the circle of this forest." In that capacity, I am quite quiet and harmless, and I have lost my way. I will turn my back while you dress, and then you will come with me to my horse and put me on my way. Also, I will put you on yours.'

'My name is Alma,' she said very coolly. 'I am a witch.'

'Glad to meet you,' said Simon, 'and glad to hear it. But don't tryto bewitch me when I'm not looking. It's easier, anyhow, when I am!'

He turned his back. In two minutes he felt her arm slip through his. They went dancing together out of the hummocks.

'Oh, there's the Devil's black horse!'

'And me the Devil!'

'Of course you are. I belong to you, you know.'

'Certainly, certainly.'

'I sold my soul for an hour's happiness, and your voice told me that I should have it, and you would come to take me away in a year and a day. Oh how splendid of you to keep your word! The year and a day are up today!'

'But where am I to take you?'

'To hell, of course.'

The magician regarded her with growing surprise.

'I've had my happiness,' she said, 'when you put your arms round me and kissed me. Don't you dare think I want to get out of the bargain!'

'So you are really willing to go to hell?'

'Of course I am.'

Simon Iff considered her keenly for a few moments. '"The Prince of Darkness is a gentleman,"' he quoted at last; '"Modo he's called, and Mahu." As a gentleman, I don't want to take unfair advantage. So would you mind telling me exactly what you mean by hell?'

'Why, the bottomless pit, of course. The lake of fire and brimstone that burneth for ever and ever, whose worm dieth not and whose fire is not quenched, where there is weeping and wailing and gnashing of teeth, and they gnaw their tongues for pain.'

'I understand,' said Simon Iff. "*That* place!'

'Don't you realise how much better that is than Titusville I could be happy there, I think. There's a great gulf fixed, isn't there? No one could get across from heaven to torture me.'

'So that was why you sold your soul?'

'I just had to be eternally lost. I was in horrible danger. They had baptised me in my infancy, by total immersion, not the other kinds that don't count; at any moment I might have died and gone heaven to where mother is.'

'I am afraid I shall have to talk seriously to you about theology. Did it never occur to you that some of your pastors and teachers might be liable to some slight inaccuracy at times?'

'Do you mean – it might not be all true?'

'I fear I do.'

'But it is true, for I've sold my soul to you, and you've come to take me on the very day you said you would!'

'But I didn't promise to take you to hell, did I?'

'Not exactly. But where else could you take me?'

'Well, I rather thought I would send you over to Paris to some friends of mine who teach little girls to sing when they have voices like yours – only, they haven't. Yours happens to be the finest natural voice I've heard in forty years. And you've got the personality, and the temperament, and the religious feeling, and the dramatic power. When you are twenty-two you will be the greatest singer in the world.'

'But I haven't a cent. Oh if only I could have got to Jacksonville, like Selma Spring! She went on the streets, you know, and now she's a dancer in a cabaret in New York. Tom Biddle told me.'

'Spring! Spring! I know that name. Is that the girl whose mother married Thorpe?'

Alma nodded.

'So the plot thickens? Aha! I smell battle,' he murmured to himself. 'Well, let me extend my holiday a while, and save the living before I go to take vengeance for the dead.

'And you can't get away?' he added aloud. 'Ah, but you can when the Devil takes you.'

'My father would catch me and drag me back.'

'The only safe place is hell, you think? I'll show you that the Devil is Prince of this world. I'm sorry if you miss the brimstone, but I'll do all I can. Now up we get on the Demon Horse, and away!'

He lifted her lightly to the saddle.

'I have a friend at Ormond, a very charming girl named Mollie Madison. Let us get to some place where I can telephone – and this Young Lochinvar act will go great at the first house. Direct me, Alma child; we mustn't run into people just now.'

She knew the country perfectly. They never saw a soul until, near a cross-road, they came upon a hamlet which boasted a post office. Iff left her with the horse in a little grove, well out of sight, and went forward to send his message. His excellent French was too much, he hoped, for any eavesdropping clerks.

An hour later Miss Mollie Madison arrived at the edge of the grove in Simon's big limousine. She had one of her own dresses ready for the girl, who was sitting at the feet of the magician, acquiring elementary instruction in the Art of Geomancy. The change was quickly made, toilet and all, for Mollie would have made a first-class lady's maid had all else failed. Alma still looked a little like a satyr – but oh! a satyr in the very best society.

'Take her to Jacksonville in the car,' commanded Simon. 'There you can get the limited. Fix her up in New York with money and clothes and a story, and introduce her to plenty of nice people. Then leave her in charge of the apartment, and come back to finish the rest-cure.'

'But I thought you were going to take me away yourself,' pouted Alma.

'The fact is, dear child, I've a date to take somebody else away. And this time there's going to be the smell of brimstone, and a little over.'

'You'll come for me soon, though?'

'If you're good – I mean bad – and stick to your singing!'

'Kiss me goodbye!'

Simon Iff took the child in his arms for a moment, and touched her lips.

'The Devil gives good measure,' he said. 'You bargained for an hour's happiness; you shall have a lifetime of it. And your soul's all your own forever!'

He kissed her again, and put her into the car. Mollie put down the lever. They were off.

'Exit the Chorus,' observed Simon, a trifle surly. 'Now let us get to business!'

He made no mistake about his road on the second time of asking, and came to the house of the Thorpes a little before sundown.

Mrs Thorpe was at the door, sweeping. He looked fully upon her. Not yet thirty-five! Her eyes seemed enormous because of the emaciation of her cheeks, sunken upon her toothless jaws. Her hair was scanty and turning grey over the temples. Her lean breasts sagged in her thin dress. She stooped as if with age. Her hands were coarse, dirty, like claws. Her thin long straight mouth was colourless, the lips pinched inwards.

She turned from her mechanical sweep, sweep of the worn broom, and looked up. The sun was setting angrily over the swamps, whose miasma turned his rays to a dull red. In that light Simon on his giant steed towered terrific and menacing. The foul crone fixed her eyes upon his face. It was convulsed by a satanic sneer.

'Who are you?' she gasped, in a thin squeak.

His voice was hoarse and rasping and malignant. 'I am the Devil, come to take his own.'

'But I'm saved, I do assure you, I'm saved. I've been baptised, adult baptism by sprinkling, not the ways that aren't any good. I always go to chapel to Brother Teague's. I – I –'

Simon's frown had become more frightful than at first.

'Oh, you can't take me, you can't take me!' she screamed. 'I read the Bible every day.'

The magician gave a sardonic laugh, grating and hideous. 'Is that all? Come!'

'No, no, I'm not ready,' wailed the hag and, falling on her knees, began to call upon 'Jesus.'

It was an incoherent flood of blasphemies, had she known it.

Simon sat silent. Presently the prayer gave her some sort of courage, and became intelligible.

'Did I do wrong, Lord?' she screamed. 'Oh, don't tell me I did wrong to throw Mamie to the alligators – dear, dear Lord Jesus, don't say that! Didn't you say, Lord, "Suffer the little children to come unto me"? I couldn't, I couldn't let her grow up like Selma to disgrace me!'

She began to babble again; when she looked up, the horseman had gone as silently as he had come. She had a great story to tell her husband of a miraculous answer to her prayer.

Simon Iff rode all through the night. He was chilled to the marrow; he rode like a dead man. Dawn found him near Ormond; the rising sun awoke him from his trance. The stallion gave a weak sigh.

'Damnation!' cried Simon, 'I've been a brute to my horse!' He dismounted, and led him to the stable.

He stumbled wearily up the steps to the verandah of the hotel.

As it chanced, Dr Buzzard had been out early, and saw him. 'Lord, that man wants a doctor!' he thought, and ran forward to assist him.

Simon sank wearily into a chair. All the virtue seemed to have gone out of him. Buzzard called the waiter to bring some brandy.

Simon waved it aside. 'I only drink brandy,' he faltered, 'when I'm feeling fiery and martial.' He tried to smile.

'Damnation!' he roared suddenly, like a lion, 'and I ought to be feeling fiery and martial, not moping like a dumb beast in agony. That's better. A damned good suggestion of yours, doctor, here's thanks – and jolly good luck to you and to all brave men that are out to fight ignorance!' He drained the liquor at a gulp.

'I'm good at finding excuses for a drink, you see,' he laughed defiantly. There was a false note in his voice. To Buzzard it suggested the strained artificiality of a man in dreadful pain, striving with all his pride or courage to conceal the fact.

'But I *am* rather tired, now you don't mention it, and I think I'll go up and have a nap. Meet me at lunch, will you? I can "a tale unfold whose lightest word would harrow up thy soul, freeze thy young blood" – oh, you finish the quotation, it's all too ghastly apt!'

He left the doctor a little confirmed in the less optimistic aspects of his original diagnosis.

But at lunch he was his own jovial self once more, though he had gone back to grapefruit and beefsteak and mineral water.

'Dr Buzzard, you are a famous alienist. It is perhaps impertinent of me to offer you a clinical picture of what is called sanity in the back-blocks of America. But I have my object.

'Imagine yourself a woman born into a universe containing three sections. The first is a colourless place, described as joyful by people who have had no joy to colour their imaginations. The second is a place of dreadful, senseless agony, readily enough realised by those whose whole lives are full of pain. It is very much more real than the first, because both places are merely shadowy expansions to infinity of what they actually know. Eternal fire is much more suggestive than eternal – I won't call it music.

'The third place is a place of continual torment. Childhood is one long round of scoldings and punishments varied by threats of unknown terrors. Youth is an apprenticeship to slavery. Marriage means an increased dose of drudgery, with an annual agony of childbearing, more joyless and sordid than a sow's. All pleasures without exception are sins, and incur the penalty of going after death to the place which has been defined as the eternal and infinite exaggeration of all the known miseries of life. Oh strait is the gate and narrow is the way, when of the seventy-seven methods of baptism only one is efficacious, and the neighbours are as sure that their way is right as you are about yours! Life is a trackless abyss of pain and fear – above all, fear.

'Then remove all human society, even those naughty neighbours! Remove books! Remove music! Remove art! Remove even interest in politics, and the wide world! Leave such a woman for a while in an isolated house in a swamp, sick with malaria, acrid with mosquitoes, a year-long stench of putrefying weeds. Add a hot climate, with a summer of steaming rains. Can you, with all your educated imagination, picture a more abominable hell, physical, mental, moral, spiritual – can you?'

Dr Buzzard shook his head, and began to speak.

'Don't spoil my scenario! The scene changes. Could you not read the plain story of the footprints? I do not know why

Harper came so stealthily to the house, but he was evidently crazy about Birdie Thorpe. He reaches the knoll. He sees her – the desirable woman of six or seven years before – become the ghastly crone you saw two days ago. Not yet thirty-five!

'And what is she doing? She does not see him at all, for she is standing by a pool in the swamp, throwing her little child to the alligators!'

'Good God!' cried Buzzard, leaping from his chair. 'Who told you so?'

'She said so in my presence. She did not want her to grow up like Selma to disgrace her!'

'Good God! Good God!'

'I am sometimes tempted to doubt it,' remarked Simon Iff with acidity.

'I suppose that's right,' said Buzzard, chewing the cud of his memory of the trail. 'She could have taken the child, walking, to the jungle, and led it in, leaving that torn rag. Then she could have picked her up, and gone to the swamp. She had a good story to cover her tracks over there. Probably Harper saw just the end of it, the brute's snout snapping at the screaming baby, and the mother crying out to Jesus Christ! They do that in India too, don't they, by the way?'

'No,' snapped Simon. 'Only another missionary lie.'

'Well, no wonder Harper went clean crazy and ran from that accursed house until his brain burst!'

'That's how I read it.'

'Say, but I've got to put Higgs wise to this.' He got up to telephone.

'Oh, I wouldn't,' said Simon, very wearily. 'If you're peeved with her, why not just leave her in Florida?'

'I guess hell is too good for her.'

'No fear o' that. She had the only right kind of baptism.'

Mrs Mills swept into the room, radiant, with Agnes in tow.

'Oh, my dear Mr Iff, I'm so glad to see you back. I hope you have had a perfectly lovely time. There's more work for you, haven't you heard? Mysterious disappearance of a girl named Alma Something. I suppose it's only the White Slave Traffic, but probably you'd like to detect it, wouldn't you? It must be deliciously exciting.'

'I am afraid I must really go back to my meditation. But I'll tell you what, if you're fond of your joke, why not wire Dolores Travis – the famous Cass girl, you know? – to come and spend a week or so with you. Just indicate the facts of the mystery, and say I'm here, but too busy to take the case.'

Mrs Mills bustled out to send a telegram while Simple Simon lay back in his chair, chuckling.

'A little touched, too, for all his cleverness, just a little touched!' murmured Buzzard under his breath.

'The plans of mice and men gang aft agley'; and so, now and then, do those of Mrs Mills.

Dinner brought her a telegram. Dolores Travis regretted that social engagements in Boston prevented her, etc.

The 'Travis' and the 'social engagements' were two good hard slaps for Simon Iff.

He opened his own telegram with apprehension. It read:

ONCE BIT, TWICE SHY. DOLORES CASS.

Two more!

WHO GETS THE DIAMONDS?

1

Simon Iff was considered a crank by many people; they based their opinion on those of his acts which were in reality severely rational.

But he had a little temperament of his own, for all that; and it showed itself from time to time in sudden and acute attacks of discontentment with his environment. For instance, he would come in one evening and sit down to work, only to find himself conscious of a staleness in his surroundings. He would perhaps try to fight it off, discover that it was too strong for him, and put in an hour dragging the furniture all over the room into new positions.

At other times his routine of diet would become suddenly oppressive; on such occasions it was his practice to go out alone and find a restaurant where he had never eaten before. There he would search the bill of fare for some new kind of food, the wine list for some unfamiliar tipple. Disappointed, as a rule, in the quest – for the tendency to standardisation is an eternal menace to evolution – he would invent a meal for himself.

About a week after his return from Florida this mood took him. He went out on foot, and plunged into the tense and vital centres of crude life which make Seventh and Eighth Avenues between 23rd and 42nd Streets one of the most interesting districts in New York. It is, however, not a peculiarly happy hunting-ground for the disgruntled gourmet. But Simon, walking fast through the icy air, began to get an honest appetite; and he might have fallen into very bad hands had not his Fortune steered him to a fantastic inn called the Bas Bastion. Something in the manner of the exterior attracted him, and he entered to find a vast low-roofed room, where the tables were shut off from each other by wooden fences. The tables were innocent of napery, but each one was adorned with a dish of potato salad, which Simon, with true instinct, divined to be the supreme achievement of man's genius in that particular direction.

He sat down and a waiter approached him. Alas! nothing on the bill of fare appealed to his mood. The Bas Bastion has the best steaks in New York, grilled over fires of hickory; but he cared not for steak.

The potato salad, however, entering by his nostrils with olfactory gust into every gate and alley of his body, thence flooded the brain with etherealised blood to such good purpose that he ordered slices of chicken, beef, ham, lobster and liver sausage to be tightly rolled in thin cylinders of dough and baked. For drink, he concluded, let there be a great stein of the old musty ale laced with a wine-glassful of gin and another of rum; flavour the mixture with a tablespoonful of crème de noyaux.

The magician secured the execution of this remarkable order by slipping a ten-dollar bill into the waiter's hand. It convinced the man that his weird guest was sane, instead of, as had been properer, confirming him in the impression that 'the guy's bug-house.'

So absorbed was the mystic in the sublunary sustenance of his novel banquet that it was only when he began to fill an old black meerschaum pipe of the 'Boer' pattern, modelled on a giant scale with heavy amber mouthpiece, that he perceived that one of the party of four at the next table was an acquaintance, one John Caudle, a very famous lawyer.

His genial nod was intercepted by the waiter, who informed Iff, trembling, that pipes were not allowed.

Simple Simon knocked out the tobacco, and rolled it in a piece of cigarette-paper before replacing it in his pipe.

'This, my friend, is a cigarette-holder. Decision of the Supreme Court of New York, January 30, 1910. *Cyril Grey v The Waldorf-Astoria Hotel.*'

The waiter immediately visualised himself and his proprietor as mulcted of half-a-million dollars apiece, and went off to inform the boss that Iff was a 'fly cop.'

The boss rang up the leading politicians in his district, appealing for protection, as he had voted the straight Republican ticket (both early and often) ever since 1886.

Simon completed his nod with added geniality. Caudle's gesture invited him over, and he lifted his third stein of 'Simon Pure' – the name under which he had decided to market his new drink – and took the chair provided for him.

'Meet Mr Gatt, Mr Iff,' said the lawyer. 'Mr Robinson, Mr Carver.' The two latter individuals were lawyers of great eminence, though not equal (in the House of Local Fame) to Caudle; Gatt was President of the Obelisk Publishing Company, which owned a number of rather vulgar magazines such as *Thin Ice, The Knuckle, The Freudian, Camembert and Smutty Stories.*

'We were in the midst of a rather interesting discussion,' said Caudle; 'it might amuse you to hear it, though it is a purely legal problem.'

'I should like very much to hear it,' said Iff. 'And may I order a round of drinks? I to pay if I fail to solve the problem.'

'It's a bet,' said Caudle heartily. 'Go to it, Bob!'

Mr Robinson cleared his throat. 'My client, Mr Iff, is a Mrs Owen, a charming lady of Scandinavian blood. Her husband met her six years ago in Charleston, South Carolina, and married her in that city. I may tell you that South Carolina does not recognise the legality of divorce.'

'My client,' said Carver, after blowing his nose very vigorously, 'is a Mrs Owen, a charming lady of the purest African descent. Mr Owen, having obtained a divorce from our friend Robinson's client in Reno, Nevada, came to New York City and married my client.'

Caudle, sipping his claret, took up the tale. 'My client,' he echoed, 'is a Mrs Owen, a charming lady of French extraction. Mr Owen, having occasion to travel to Atlanta, Georgia, found that his New York marriage was not recognised in that state. He has an almost equal horror of immorality and of the bachelor's estate, so he took the only possible course, and married my client.'

'You must understand, Mr Iff,' put in Gatt, 'these three women are all unquestionably Owen's legal wives.'

'That is so,' admitted Caudle. 'But to continue. Business called Owen to Europe last year. For some reason unexplained – it does not concern us – he converted the whole of his holdings into cash and bought diamonds with it, to the value of some six and a half million dollars. The ship on which he was returning to America was rammed and sunk in a fog about fifty miles off Nantucket. Owen, who had the diamonds in a belt, escaped in one of the boats, which was almost immediately picked up by the *Mazuma*, one of our latest battle-cruisers. Owen died an hour later from shock and exposure.

'He was intestate. I beg of you to note that his property is in Federal hands, and the problem is one concerning the conflicting claims of his three wives. South Carolina recognises only No. 1, New York only No. 2, Georgia only No. 3. Who, in a word, gets the diamonds?' He concluded with an air of mild pride in the complexities of his profession.

Iff scribbled two words on a slip of paper, and handed it to him. Caudle, after one glance, put it away immediately in his waistcoat pocket.

'Gentlemen,' he said somewhat hastily, 'the drinks are on me. In fact, I will buy the next round also.' And he called the waiter.

Robinson and Carver were mightily intrigued by this performance. They divined that the decision was against Caudle, and had rather frightened him. But which of them was the victor? They began to renew their arguments when Gatt, scenting danger of a quarrel, broke in.

'Mr Iff's perspicacity seems so eminently convincing to Caudle that I should like to consult him about a very mysterious robbery which has just taken place in my office.'

'Do,' said Simon. 'I shall be delighted.'

'My firm occupies the whole of the eighth floor of the Isadora Duncan Building. There are on one side the private offices of the principals, on the other a single very large room occupied by the staff of stenographers, book-keepers, etc. The idea of the big room is to have them all superintended by a single overseer; it makes for efficiency.

'We close at five o'clock, but often have to keep some of the staff overtime. This however was not the case yesterday; by ten minutes past five everyone had left.

'The offices are not locked; as soon as the staff vanish, the cleaners appear. The building officials and detectives make themselves responsible for the safety of property. There is in any case nothing much worth stealing; the cash is banked daily before closing hours.

'Well, sir, one of the girl stenographers, a Miss Vickers, came to me this morning in singular distress. One of the cashiers, leaving early, had given her a box of cigarettes to hand to one of our travelling-men, who was expected to call. He did not do so, and she locked up the box in the drawer of her desk. This morning the drummer was on hand at nine o'clock sharp, and she called him over to deliver her package. The drawer was still locked. But the cigarettes were gone.

'I came over to inspect the desk. Other girls, hearing the news, crowded round; several told similar tales of petty pilfering.

'There was nothing much in this. Any one of the cleaning staff – or some dishonest official of the building, for the matter of that – could easily work the trick with a set of skeleton keys. But here's the queer thing – a trifle, Mr Iff, but devilish annoying, because it's such a stupid mystification! Miss Vickers, while I stood talking, took the cover off her typewriter. Immediately she exclaimed. The machine had been smashed. It was a new model Wemyss, a machine constructed for hard wear and perfect work. It is consequently built of unusual strength, the cast steel frame being much more solid than is usual.

'This frame had been hammered with great violence – there were a dozen marks on it – and at last it had been smashed clean across. There is no sense in the business at all; it is the act of a madman.'

'But when was it done? Such operations are noisy.'

'That's what beats us. There was somebody on the floor the whole time. A sly thief might have come in and out at almost any time, even manipulating locks without attracting attention; but this blacksmith business! It's unthinkable.'

'Very curious indeed,' said Simon Iff without enthusiasm. 'I should like to look into it.'

'Of course we shall afford you every facility.'

'Thanks,' replied the magician with a queer little grin, 'but I don't believe I shall have to trouble you at all. A couple of telephone messages and a morning call ought to do it; suppose you lunch with me and hear the story.'

'That beats cock-fighting! But the lunch is on me if you make good on that. By Jiminy; say, may I bring along the editor of Jags'? He'll simply eat it up.'

'I hope so, indeed,' said Simon earnestly. 'An editor with a poor appetite or a deranged liver is a public menace.'

2

The party broke up soon after, and Simon Iff walked home to bed. His eccentric evening had been a great success. In the morning he woke deliciously normal, and after breakfast made the two telephone calls he had promised, and proceeded in his car to the Isadora Duncan Building. But he did not go to the eighth floor; he went to the ninth, and entered the tiny office of Hodge, Peet and Co., publishers, of Indianapolis; New York Office, Mr Greil.

There was a small antechamber almost filled by a big raw country girl with hair dyed yellow and lips and cheeks stained red. She was pounding away upon her machine, and did not stop as she looked up to enquire the visitor's business, which she did with the words 'What's doin'?'

'I understand that Mr Greil is rarely here before eleven.'

'Thasso.'

'Therefore, as I do not in the least wish to see him, I made a point of calling a little before ten.'

The girl was up on her feet, her eyes ablaze. 'What's the game?' she shouted defiantly.

Simple Simon raised himself to his full height. Till then he had kept a hand upon her table, as he bent over toward her.

'Suppose I were to tell you that the bulls have got Ned again?'

'Oh don't! Oh don't!' she sobbed wildly. 'It's a shame; it's a damned shame, indeed it is. He's the dearest boy in the world.'

She paused and stared.

'Why, who are you? What d'ye know? Come across.'

'I will, my dear young lady. I'm Simon Iff; middle name, A Friend in Need. Now sit down: The bulls have not got Ned – at least, they hadn't at nine o'clock this morning. But why am

I a friend? To be frank, I came as an enemy. The truth is this: when I saw you, I was sure you were straight. Also, that you were not the sort of girl to make a fool of herself over a man. I began to think that Ned might have been hardly used.'

The girl had become calm. 'Sit down, Mr Simonev,' she said, familiar with few but Ghetto names in business circles, 'pleased to meet you. My name's Sadie White. Please tell me how you come to know Ned.'

'I don't know Ned, or anything about him except that his other name is Grattan, and that he escaped from the custody of a detective about three blocks from here, two days ago at a little after five o'clock in the afternoon.'

'Why, that's right, too.'

'Well, tell me the whole story.'

'I guess I will. I'm all hot over it. See here, mister, Ned's the straightest boy in this dirty grafting burg. He hasn't got a cent, but he loves me, and I'm gonna wait like till he gets clear through college and puts up his shingle. 'Tis like this. All winter he studies up at Youghal, and lives by doing tailor work for some o' the rich guys in college. He's the fastest boy in the football team, too, so all summer when they ain't no work, he comes t' New York t' be near me, and grinds out the mazuma doin' the African Ball Dodger stunt in a show down at Coney, which just suits him, too, for he keeps up his swimming and sculling in his spare time. Now they just passed a law against that, y'know—'

'Excuse me,' said Iff, with a little cough, and a wry smile, 'I don't quite know what an African Ball Dodger is.'

'Why, he blacks his face and shoves his head through a hole in a canvas and the boys throw wooden balls at it for coconuts. He was so quick they never hit him, not half a dozen times a day; he wuz just coinin' money for that show.'

'So they passed a law?'

'Up in Albany. But the show went on; nobody ever knows here what the law will be from one day to the next, not even the judges. So one day the bulls drops in, and pinches the whole crowd, and Ned gets six months.

'Well, 'bout a week after one o' th' warders comes an' whispers to Ned. "Beat it, kid!" he ses. So Ned lit out, and got clean off, into New Jersey where the law don't run. But o' course he could never come back in this state.'

'There seem compensations even in so harsh a fate,' murmured Simon Iff. 'But is Ned really any good at his work? Strange – to an English ear – to hear of a student earning his living in such ways.'

'Oh, it's the reg'lar thing here,' said Sadie. 'But clever, my! he's got three scholarships. But o' course he can't live on that.'

'I see.'

'However, he got safe to Youghal, and played football and took his examination fine. Now and then he got a day off and would come down the Hudson to see me.

'Well, one night I went over to Hoboken to meet him and we went to the movies. Comin' back, Ned goes in a saloon for a drink or su'thin', an' the nex' thing is three men throwing him into a motor-wagon.

'Four days after that he 'phones me to come out to Hoboken; they'd run him over to New York and dumped him in Central Park at two that morning. Sure 'nuff, the bulls was on him. When he gets to the station, the captain he says: "Throw him in the cooler; he's a desprit character." An' two hours after that the captain comes an' unlocks him, an' ses: "Go up ter my house, leg it, now," an' gives him the address. So off goes Ned, an' they treat him fine for two days, an' then the captain comes in one night late, an' ses: "All right, kid, come along in th' old gas buggy." Then he runs him over to Hoboken. "Goodnight," ses he, "and take care of yourself." Which he does till last week, when he thinks it's all forgotten, and he wasn't two hours in the city before they pinch him again. This time it's another frame-up – charge o' forgery – and he gets real scared. So he breaks away from the bull, an'—'

'I know the rest,' said Simon Iff. 'Ned seems a much more important person – to somebody – than appears at first sight. Has he got any enemies that he knows of?'

'Nary one. Everybody likes Ned.'

'It's very strange to me. The law appears equally anxious to arrest him and to let him go.'

'Thasso. I never thought of that.'

'By the way, here is a hundred dollars. You will know what to do with it.'

'Oh, I couldn't take it. I can save it out of my salary.'

'Nonsense. Besides, I want the matter settled this morning, for reasons of my own.'

'All right. Thank you ever so much.'

'I think I will run off now. Bc at casc, my dear; I can promise you that Ned will come to no harm.'

'Oh do do your best! You don't know how I love him!'

'Oh yes, I do. I've taken medals for it.'

'Ned has medals, too,' said the girl quite seriously. 'He won the Elijah Blossom Sculls two years running.'

'Ah,' said Iff, 'I thought I knew the name.'

3

Simon Iff walked down one flight of stairs and looked in on Mr Gatt.

'I want to bring a friend to that little lunch, if I may.'

Gatt was quite charmed. 'Shall we say the Holland House at one?'

'It will suit admirably.'

The magician went off in search of the friend at his club. He was rather in a hurry, for the friend kept very regular hours. At the stroke of eleven he invariably laid down his cue, whether the game was finished or not, and retired to sleep until dinner-time. Iff was well aware that, once in bed, he was less accessible than the Dalai Lama.

He found him, one Captain Lascelles, whose pet name was 'Cheero,' yawning his way through what proved to be a break of 121 18-inch baulk line. Despite this, he was in bitter humour, for the blizzards had prevented him from enjoying his one passion, yachting, for over ten days.

'Hello, Cheero!' cried Simon, 'and how's yourself?'

'Top hole, dear boy, but it's a dog's life. The bottom's dropped out of the damned barometer.'

'Well, buck up. Can't last forever. What d'ye say to a devilled kidney at the Holland House by way of a late supper?'

'Imposs! You know my rules. You've told me yourself a hundred times that a regular life is the key to good health – though I never saw you do it yourself!

'I've a story for you – something you value more than health is at stake.'

'Oho! a breeze from the nor'rard! Good. Simon Iff, you interest me strangely. Proceed with your esteemed narration. Nay, I must first castigate this presumptuous amateur.'

His opponent had just failed at an easy one-cushion shot through trying too much for position.

'Let me introduce Major Bimis, of the United States Army. Mr Iff.'

'Glad to know you, sir!' said Bimis. 'A cueist, sir?'

'Used to make 'em talk Chinese,' said Lascelles, gathering the balls with a superb three-cushion shot. 'I once saw him run off thirty-one, on an English table, at Empstone Manor, blindfold. Allowed to feel where the balls were before playing – wonderful, by Jove! That's my string, Bimis. So long – Mr Iff wants to ask my advice; he's got to see a man about a dog. Oh Simon Iff, beware, if she's a blonde!'

Bimis, with a slight list to starboard, headed for the open sea.

Lascelles sank upon a chesterfield, while Simon Iff, one thigh upon a corner of the table, made caroms with a ball spun between finger and thumb. Lascelles made circles with his eyes and mouth as the old mystic snapped out his story; but he said nothing beyond the occasional ejaculation: 'These are indeed deep waters, Watson!'

At the end he cried, 'A walk across the park, Iff, to chase away the clouds of sleep, to furnish me an appetite, and – above all – to get my monocle. We must not go among these criminals unarmed!'

Captain Lascelles R.N. was the youngest captain in the British Navy. He was generally admitted to be the Grand Panjandrum in matters of gunnery, and he was Iff's right-hand man in the secret mission which had brought him to the United States. But the British and American publics only knew of him as the yachtsman and patron of all forms of sport. He was particularly famous for madcap pranks, but nobody doubted his seriousness and integrity when need arose for its display. He was a steward of the Jockey Club, and had once won a match – impromptu – against Lord Abinghame over the Derby course by moonlight, thereby disposing of the theory that a sailor cannot sit a horse.

Luncheon at the Holland House was for five instead of four, as Gatt, inviting the editor of *Jags*, a humble person with galoshes, umbrella, no chest, a perpetual snuffle, a taste for ice-cream soda and a wife who beat him, found himself obliged to include the editor of *Smutty Stories* in the party. This was a long lean Yankee with a Nonconformist (or New England) conscience, sallow, wrinkled, spectacled with huge disks of horn, sharp-nosed, long-toothed, with a thin mouth that had never been seen to smile.

This lugubrious pair were inseparable companions; they had dined at each other's houses on 177th Street alternate nights, without a break, for nearly twenty years. After dinner, each would produce a bundle of manuscripts and peruse them conscientiously with many a groan.

They kept humbly behind the great Gatt, and could hardly be persuaded to sit at the table with so obviously distinguished an individual as a captain in the British Navy, complete with a monocle more dreadful than a Nordenfeldt.

Gatt, however, was in his glory. Here was a first-class detective story in real life, and he was to be present at the Ceremony of Unveiling.

He introduced the subject by recounting the dinner at the Bas Bastion, and telling the Story of the Man with the Three Wives. 'And Mr Iff,' he concluded, 'just scribbled on a piece of paper, and passed it to Caudle. I never saw anyone so crushed. The great Caudle! It was a treat, believe me! Mr Iff, I'd give a hundred dollars to know what you wrote on that paper. Who gets the diamonds?'

'The lawyers,' said Iff, laconically.

Gatt was delighted. 'And now, do tell us, have you solved our little mystery of the Broken Typewriter?'

'I have.'

'Splendid, splendid!'

'Just one question, Mr Gatt. You are a member of the Pi Omicron Xi frat, are you not?'

'I am. I am on several of the committees.'

'The frat is restricted to old Kingsbridge graduates, I think?'

'It is, Mr Iff.'

'Good.'

'But what has that to do with our mystery?'

'Much, Mr Gatt. I shall have a request to prefer, a little later. Allow me to explain.

'The outrages in your office fall naturally into two parts, as you yourself saw. There was some pilfering, which almost anybody might have done. The means would be simple, the motive obvious. But the thief would be a sly sneaky person, I imagine, one liable to take instant alarm.'

'Quite so.'

'The man – the person – who broke your – the – machine, would on the contrary, be perfectly fearless, ready for violence, careless of consequence.'

'Yes, I suppose so.'

'Two people, not one, then?'

'I quite follow you.'

'But – how did this person do it? And when? And why? Answer those questions, and "Who did it?" soon answers itself.'

'Quite so, Mr Iff.'

'The how and when are very awkward, though. At the only possible times there were people actually at work in the office. Why did nobody hear the clang of those repeated blows upon that exceptionally solid steel? As to the why, it is a regular stumper!'

'I see the difficulties very clearly, Mr Iff.'

'Who is benefited by the smashing-up of the machine? Nobody. Who is injured? Your two-million dollar corporation. A hayseed on an elephant's back! I therefore concluded that the breaking was an accident, an incident in some purposeful act. Now, how could that be? Any idea?'

Mr Gatt considered. 'If someone had thrown the machine at somebody?'

'Not bad,' smiled Iff. 'Really a very creditable conjecture. Apart from the fact of the repeated blows, quite satisfactory. But when? – and how? – and—' He broke off, and leaned over impressively to Gatt. His voice took on a grave and majestic intonation. But all he said was: 'And – where?'

Mr Gatt looked genuinely puzzled.

'It could not have been done in your office. Therefore it must have been done somewhere else. But who would take away a typewriter, break it, and put it back? It is absurd. I decided, Mr Gatt, that the broken machine is not your machine at all.'

Gatt gasped his amazement. The editors nudged each other with a kind of surly pleasure. Lascelles continued to contemplate his chop with distant contempt, as if it had been a hostile cruiser on the horizon.

'Then whose machine was it? It belonged, I thought, to someone in the building, since nobody could have entered or left after the regular closing hours, carrying such a bulky object, without arousing comment. So I rang up the Wemyss Typewriter Company. Yes, they had supplied a new machine, six weeks before, to a Mr Greil. But was Mr Greil a lunatic? I hoped not. Now think, Mr Gatt! To what use could one put that very solid frame? Why hammer it? There is no conceivable reason. But – might not somebody use its power of resistance? To hammer it is silly – but to use it as an anvil? – to crack some hard substance upon it? – that sounds more like sense.

'Now think again – what can Mr Greil wish to crack? Mr Greil, though? Would he, for the sake of a hundred dollars, take such a long chance as to bring the broken machine down to your room, and take yours up to his? Unlikely. It must be a subordinate of Greil's, someone who would fear the result of the discovery of what had happened.

'So much for the who, for it turns out that Greil has only one subordinate. Now turn to the why, shall we?

'What, in heaven's name, can a clerk – a girl in an office – want to crack in such a hurry, with so awkward an anvil, in a place where discovery meant trouble? Why not take it home and smash what had to be smashed?

'I could only think of one thing – a chain. I call up my friend Teake, of the police. The only escaped prisoner in the offing is one Ned Grattan, arrested that same afternoon for forgery. So I trotted up to Greil's office and got the girl to tell me the whole story. You may be glad to learn, Mr Gatt, that she has sent a hundred dollars to your cashier in payment for the borrowed machine.'

Gatt somehow felt uncomfortable, though he could hardly have told why. Possibly it was some side-consciousness of the monocle of Captain Lascelles, which appeared to be aimed at a piece of cheese, hull down, of low visibility.

'I say, Mr Gatt,' drawled the owner of this formidable engine of offence in a thin, dry, far-away voice, 'the fact is, Mr Iff and I have come about a little matter of sport. You see, this fellow Grattan is the only man that can beat our first string, Bruce of Balliol, for the Diamond Sculls at Henley this summer, and you can imagine that naturally we don't want him to compete. We just thought we might do something, see? And I remembered that you were prominent as a Kingsbridge man, aren't you? And you certainly don't want to see a Youghal man pull off anything, do you? Eh?'

'We don't want him to stroke Youghal this spring, surely,' said Gatt. 'If wc lick 'cm, our eight goes to Henley.'

'That will be A. 1., then, if he's in quod over this forgery, what?'

'I'm concerned deeply,' put in Simon Iff; 'you get him all right, but he keeps on escaping.'

'Lookee here,' exclaimed Gatt, in a burst of confidence, feeling himself a person of international importance. 'There's a pot of money behind this, bets and all that. So we put that little law through up at Albany to frame him. Only they've got Youghal fans in the police, and they always manage to let him go. There's a hell of a leak somewhere. So we thought we'd fix him proper with a forgery charge. More serious, you understand. We get a hand-picked judge or two, and we'll have it dead to rights. If he did escape, they couldn't let a convicted forger row for them. Besides, the federal government would be on to it. You can sleep easy, gentlemen. Grattan won't row.'

'Thank you very much,' said Simon Iff. 'Captain Lascelles will now fire his monocle.'

The naval officer turned on Mr Gatt, as who should sight a periscope among a welter of drowned women and children.

'Sir,' he said, and his voice sounded at least three thousand miles away, 'would you kindly inform the Pi Omicron Xi frat – I do not think you need inform the Kingsbridge Boat Club; I hope not – that unless Ned Grattan rows for Youghal against you, and unless he competes in the Diamonds, we in England shall not race against any Kingsbridge crew. And we shall publish the reasons for our decision.'

'Good gracious, you don't mean it,' stammered Gatt. 'This is a joke, Captain, of course.'

'Judging from the expression of Captain Lascelles, Mr Gatt, my opinion is that he was never quite so serious in his life.' Simon smiled cheerfully.

'Damn it! I don't understand it. I thought you were a sportsman.'

'From that,' said Lascelles stiffly, 'I beg to be excused.'

'But you can't want your own man beaten!' wailed Gatt.

'No,' said Iff. 'We want him to win. Now I put it to your very strong common sense, how can he win without an opponent? He must have an opponent, in his own interest, you see that? Then we must not be stingy about it; we must get him the best opponent available.'

'Iff,' said Lascelles, 'forgive me, but your humour is ill-timed. Personally, I can't stick this. Come and dine at the club tonight. Right-o!

'Here, waiter, take this. It's my cheque.'

He gave the man a twenty-dollar bill, and walked out without another glance at Gatt.

'Mr Iff,' said that unhappy man, 'what in hell am I to do?'

'Read your Bible,' replied the magician. 'Eleventh Commandment, as you know: Thou shalt not be found out.

Twelfth: When you are, play the game. I don't want this filthy business published. Kingsbridge is as fine as Youghal. It's only you and a low gang of blackguards, with your crooked politicians and your hand-picked judges – you don't stand even for the main body of your frat. I shall go round to your committee, by the way, and advise them to look into this business, for their own sakes.'

'How did you get on to it?' Gatt was twitching his fingers nervously.

'Oh, it was as plain as a headline. Why should anyone trouble to frame up this poor hard-working devil? (He has a damned fine girl, by the way.) He was a nobody. Personal jealousies wouldn't explain it. Half the police seemed to know all about it. Ned Grattan, somehow or other, was a public character. Of course: Sport. That told me at once: Kingsbridge was the only rival worth considering. I had no idea you were in it, of course; Lascelles meant to deliver his ultimatum to you merely as a convenient ambassador. That was why he put things – er – the wrong way round; and you very kindly gave yourself away.

'And now I must confess that his attitude has somewhat hypnotised me; I am feeling exceedingly unwell, and I will stroll up to your frat house while you explain to your false witnesses and hand-picked judges that it won't do this time.'

He got up and walked away.

That summer the Youghal eight only lost to First Trinity in the final, and Ned Grattan made a dead heat with Bruce of Balliol in the Diamond Sculls.

THE NATURAL THING TO DO

1

The Boston Turkey-Buzzard, having promised Dolores Travis only such publicity as might come through 'legitimate channels, such as the Divorce Court,' was genuinely delighted to offer her the hospitality of its columns five months after her marriage, on the occasion of her filing her petition.

'Father was right!' she wrote to Simon Iff.

> There was nothing there to keep me from the Cult of the Chortoid. Geoffrey, like most American men, if not all, is a neuter. They're lovely to look at – but oh! when you try them out! Thank you so much for sending me dear Alma; she has been more to me than any mere male thing, husband or not, could ever be; and I'm perfectly miserable at having to let her go to France. Of course I shall come down with her and see her safely on the boat.
>
> Yours – but my own first of all – truly,
>
> DOLORES CASS
>
> (*for ever and ever, Amen*)

Simon Iff chuckled hugely over this letter. 'I knew that girl would find herself,' said he. 'It was the natural thing to do.'

And the same afternoon Dolores got another dose of legitimate publicity by being a yard away from a man who was shot dead in Washington Street by three men in an automobile. The bullet only missed her head by inches.

A week later Simon Iff gave the God-speed dinner to Alma, whom he had finally adopted as his daughter. She had taken to civilisation as a swan takes to water, but she still kept that haunting woodland wildness that stamped her as Overwoman, Kin to the Gods.

At three in the morning she did a dance in a leopard-skin which brought the swirl of the Sahara sand about the guests.

Dolores Cass, drugged with excitement, beat time on a devil-dancer's drum from Ceylon.

Miss Mollie Madison, with her demure cat's smile, watched the face of the magician. He alone remained aloof; his eyes were inscrutable. But before the party broke up, he retired for a few minutes to his bedroom. He came back wearing a heavy tweed suit and a pair of rubber shoes.

'Sympathetic magick!' he gave as his excuse; 'our nightingale flits on to greener woods. I must create in myself the atmosphere of travel, that I may play the Good Samaritan to our fair pilgrim.'

Presently the guests were gone; only Dolores and Simon went to the wharf with Alma.

After the last waved handkerchief, Dolores turned to her master. 'Do you know what I have in my pocket?'

'Pocket? What will be the end of this Feminist agitation?'

'Silly! I've put my pride in it.'

'High time!'

'I've been doing some rather curious work in statistics, and I can't get beyond a certain point. So I'm going to talk it over with you.'

'I am glad of it,' retorted Simon rather grimly. 'You will understand why when I show you what I, for my part, have in *my* pockets.'

'Do you know what I'm talking about?'

'No, I don't. Nor do you.'

'What do you mean?'

'Why do I take this quite absurd way home? Why did I dismiss the car?'

Dolores suddenly realised that they were passing through unfrequented and disreputable streets.

'In pocket No. 1, observe, a pair of spectacles.' He adjusted them.

'But why is the left eye blocked up?'

'It enables me to see—'

His intonation told Dolores that he was deliberately leaving the sentence unfinished, and it threw her into a brown study which lasted several blocks.

'—what is behind me,' concluded Simon Iff. At the same moment he threw her bodily into a doorway, and completed the gesture by dropping to the ground, and opening fire with a pair of automatics upon the two ruffians whose bullets whistled past them.

The old man's eye was true, and his hand firm. The men dropped in their tracks before firing a second shot.

'Now,' remarked Simon coolly to the astounded girl, 'we can go across to the trolley.'

'You have really surprised me at last,' she said rather faintly. 'I never thought you would condescend to use the weapons of the flesh.'

'I do so,' replied he, 'only when escorting rash young ladies who put their heads into hornets' nests.'

'I give up!'

'I took a chance on this walk in order to prove the nature of your recent work.'

'But you don't know what that is.'

'True, but I suspected that you (and not that harmless working tailor) were intended for the victim of those men in the auto, and I thought I would try it out. It was the natural thing to do. Here's Tenth Avenue. Jump on!'

2

When they got to a wealthier district they changed into a taxi, and called at her hotel for her portfolio of papers before returning to the magician's apartment.

She spread them on the table.

'Exhibit A is a humorous article on the crime wave of the last few months. It teased me, and I thought I'd look it up. The statistics are quite peculiar in half a dozen ways.

'Firstly, the increase in crime is confined entirely to murder, manslaughter and homicide. There is a parallel increase in fatal accidents, some of them described as suspicious.

'Secondly, the curve of increase springs with a single bound to its maximum, and remains there with only small fluctuations. This jump took place last October.

'Thirdly, the increase is confined to Boston, New York, Philadelphia, Baltimore, Norfolk, Charleston, Savannah, New Orleans, Key West and Galveston, though there is a similar increase of about half the amount in Newport News, San Francisco and Seattle, and a third in Jacksonville, Tampa, Los Angeles and Washington, D.C.

'All this struck me as very strange. I constructed tables of the occupations of the victims, and found the increase to lie almost entirely with the educated classes. Professions seem fairly well distributed, however, even the clergy being proportionally represented.

'I next read up the reports of all violent deaths, hoping to find some common factor for certain groups. Here again I was disappointed.

'I then chose six of the most mysterious cases at random, and made personal investigations on the spot. It was now that the most surprising circumstance of all disclosed itself. In four of my six cases I found it quite difficult to establish the details of the environment, for the reason that the friends of the dead man were themselves nearly all in some sort of trouble. Some had just died, others were in prison, others had left the state or the country quite suddenly, others were involved in lawsuits, others again in bankruptcy; some were being assailed by scandal, others were sick. It was as if the murderer were some very powerful demon whose malice struck not only the victim but his friends!

'I then took a seventh case and struck oil at once. My investigation was shaping like a man's nervous system: ganglia here and there in the shape of murders, and fans of lesser misfortunes branching out from each, while a cord of graver troubles marked the direct links between the ganglia. But still I could find no common factor beyond the general obvious grounds of association between the parties concerned.'

'So you decided to ask Papa. Very wise. But why didn't you mind what Papa told you about thinking it all out at home? You have gone hunting up these cases, and our "very powerful demon" has put you on his list as a ganglion, for he tries twice to get you potted. And what do you suppose he will do when he finds you are in with Simon Iff?'

'He will know that it will not take you long to find out the how and the why and the who, as you say. So he will be beforehand with you, if he can.'

'Just so. Let's make haste – here are a few obvious points. One: the increase is confined to seaports, and varies (roughly speaking) with their importance. Exception: the District of Columbia, and there the victims seem to be people politically prominent, and for the most part connected with seaports at that, to judge by the few names I happen to know. Luckily, I'm here on a special mission for the British Admiralty, so this is just my ground. Now most of these people are educated – that is, take active interest in politics – and, as residents of seaports, foreign politics concern them particularly. Then again, this campaign of murder – with lesser campaigns corresponding –

begins quite suddenly and vigorously in October, as if it had been long prepared and only awaited the signal. What happened in October? Nothing; on the contrary, things had just settled down after the fuss over Morocco.

'But here are all these educated people being put out of action by death, imprisonment, financial disaster, ill-health or social discredit, just at that moment. Could the link between them be hostility to a certain personage who, baffled in one quarter, turns immediately to another? But there is no hostility to that personage, true – but suppose these people are banded together (informally perhaps) to do something apparently quite innocent which will hamper the plans of that personage, if we only knew them. Suppose, for example, he didn't want America to have any ships? I don't mean warships only, I mean merchant ships. Suppose he wanted to cut off England from American supplies?'

'But how could he, with the British Navy as it is?'

'He may be thinking ten years ahead. But this is only a plausible guess. Come, look through our names; take the most prominent people, skipping the small fry.' Iff picked up one of the lists.

'Abbot, died suddenly. Banker in Baltimore. A noted financier of new shipping concerns.

'Abel, bankrupt. Congressman bitterly opposed to La Follette's Seamen's Bill.

'Abercrombie, died of typhoid. I don't remember anything of him.

'Albright, Senator, killed in automobile accident. Was always advocating universal military service.

'Alford, naval engineer. Shot by injured husband, one Stenzel.

'Anthony, torpedo instructor to U.S. Navy. Sank with FN-131. Cause of accident mysterious.

'Baffin, the "fighting Parson." Convicted of arson. Your demon's a poet, Dolores!

'Barlow, Congressman. Implicated in Hulton frauds and crash. Personal friend of the Secretary of the Navy, and stumped the country constantly in the interests of more ships.

'Bowditch, cotton-merchant. Free trade advocate. Shot down in street.

'Brooks, never heard of him. Natural death, I dare say.

'Butler, naval constructor. Caught in the act of adultery and disgraced. The partner of his crime was a Gretel von Bulow, or I'm mistaken. So much for two letters out of twenty-six!'

'But you are picking out the names!'

'Because I can't place the parasites. Most of these people are barnacles on the big ships, or, more politely, destroyer convoys. Their names mean nothing to me.'

'I can agree, in any case, on practical grounds. There is certainly somebody at work – let me think!'

'Don't trouble. I know the culprit. It is the ghost of the late lamented James Monroe!'

'Whatever do you mean?'

'Dear child, when James Watts noticed the expulsive force of the steam of a kettle, the Monroe Doctrine got T.B. Your "demon" is trying to keep it alive by the artificial prevention of ship-building. Just look at this one name, Carstairs, shot in his office by a man named Schmidt (perhaps!) who claimed to be his natural son. An evident plagiarism from the murder of William Whiteley in London. What did the death of Carstairs mean to ship-building? You would have done less harm by torpedoing half the ships in New York Harbor.

'Let me add one fact that you don't know: there have been five attempts on the life of Paul Powys in the last three weeks. It is you that I must thank for showing that the campaign is of such immense scope and ramification. We thought of a financial or political group; I am now certain that we are up against an organisation with hundreds of millions of money, and thousands – perhaps tens of thousands – of men in its web.

Dolores Cass, these statistics of yours will wake up even the White House!'

'This is very exciting. Let's go down right away in the car!'

'We shouldn't get far. I'm going to put the Secret Service on to this. We must get busy. I shall feel easier when it's through.'

But no incident ruffled the day. The papers were duly delivered, with an explanation which did not particularly impress. The plot, it appeared, was 'politically unthinkable.' The official's car did have an accident at 42nd Street, where an elderly lady drove into him, luckily without upsetting him, but that was 'conclusively' proved to be the fault of the policeman in charge of the traffic.

Iff heard this story on the telephone with amiable pity. People – most people – could never imagine other people acting differently from themselves. America had an army of fifty thousand men, used mostly for parades; therefore a nation which drilled fifteen million men must be exactly three hundred times as fond of parades as America. Also, just at that moment the U.S. was looking in quite a different direction – as if that were not precisely the reason for an unsuspected enemy to attack her.

Dolores Cass snorted in unison.

'What's to be done?' she said at last.

'What I'm afraid of is that our brother demon may have the sense to leave us alone – flat! Surely he will dare trust the political incapacity, the parochial vision, of Washington! But these plotters are easily scared. It's conscience that makes cowards of us all! Remember the effect of the announcement of Mr Travis' engagement?'

Dolores Cass boxed his ears, good and hard. It was the sorest point in her life's history.

'*Dios mio!* What a fool I was!'

'We all have to learn by experience. I only hope (to return to the true subject of our talk) that America's lesson may not cost too much, or come – too late! Oh, child, the secret of success in life is to learn from little things! There is not a grain of dust in the whole universe which does not bear witness to the infinite Wisdom of God, and proclaim aloud His Glory. And there is not one trifle in the most common life which should not make us partakers of that wisdom and glory, had we but the wit and the enthusiasm to comprehend it.'

'Then let me contribute a trifle to our problem. Your clock, which kept perfect time last night – more than we did! – has gained an hour and six minutes since this morning.'

Iff walked over to the clock, a man-high affair of carved oak, worked by weights. He threw open the door.

'Very ingenious!'

A needle was attached to one of the weights by a piece of soft wax. Below, on the floor of the clock, was a bomb. The touch of the needle would complete an electrical circuit.

Dolores Cass made a rapid mental calculation. 'That would have gone off at about half-past midnight, correct time.'

'A warning to all those who go home to bed early.' He removed the bomb and the needle, and adjusted the clock.

'This warms the cockles of my heart. He is after me!'

'Aren't you going to enquire how that got there?'

'For shame, Dolores Cass! Will nothing ever teach you the folly of interfering with other people's business? Don't you see even now that this "demon" of yours is an ass? He's trying to beat an economic law, which puts him in the class of intellect which plays systems at Monte Carlo. Upon that firm conviction let us base our campaign! And never let us forget what I read in the newspaper this morning. It is in Chapter 69, "The Use of the Mysterious":

'A MASTER OF THE ART OF WAR HAS SAID: "I DO NOT DARE TO BE THE HOST; I PREFER TO BE THE GUEST. I DO NOT DARE TO ADVANCE AN INCH; I PREFER TO RETIRE A FOOT."

'Let us further take comfort from that passage in Chapter 55, "The Mysterious Charm":

'Whatever is contrary to the *tao* soon ends.'

'I never could understand all that about accomplishing everything by doing nothing.'

'It is quite easy. He will expect me to be pursuing him; I won't – I'll let him pursue me. I will even let him catch me – and he shall think that I am as great an ass as he is. It will all work out to the Appointed End, and our only error can come from a violation of the law of our own natures. We will therefore lay the train by doing the natural thing – getting very drunk at Melonico's. Will you bring Mollie Madison? I should like both of you to meet my good friend Lascelles, of the Royal Navy.'

'All right!' She put on her furs. 'But how can I help?'

'Oh, do as you like about it!' said Simon Iff, as if huffed.

Dolores was amazed at the curt rudeness of his tone. She chilled instantly and moved toward the door.

He got up and held it for her with an ironical bow. 'Melonico's at seven, then.'

'I will be there,' she answered coldly. Outside the apartment she stopped suddenly. 'There's something behind that,' she murmured, and fell a-musing.

3

It was no idle word of Simon Iff that he meant to get very drunk; and therefore, let us hope, he will not have to give an account of it at the Day of Judgment. His behaviour scandalised most of the very high-class guests at that most select of all New York's restaurants. He took the most unpardonable liberties with Mollie Madison, and Lascelles was equally impudent with Dolores, making violent love to her, drinking her health in crazy toasts of doubtful taste, telling stories which would hardly have passed even Mr Gatt's editorial staff, and roaring with laughter at nothing at all.

Simon Iff supplied the climax by pulling off Mollie's slipper, filling it with champagne, and draining it at a gulp. It was then that the manager came forward and requested the observation of common decency.

The shock sobered them for a while, but then Simon broke into a drunken torrent of boasting. He told everybody what a wonderful man he was, and what a lot of mysteries he had solved, and what mountains he had climbed, and what animals he had shot, and what an important job he was holding down that very minute. Wouldn't everybody be surprised if they knew just what the British Government had sent him to do in America? If they knew what was in a certain paper at the bank, a *casus belli*, no less? But with whom? Aha – there was the secret! And wouldn't everybody be amazed if they knew just what he knew about a certain subject that he wouldn't mention – not he! The Silent Tomb was a chatter-box compared with him!

The manager came forward again, and remonstrated about the loudness of his voice. This time the old man was angry and rude. He treated the man as a mere servant, said something about 'dirty Dagoes,' threw down a hundred-dollar bill and told him to keep the change and buy a treatise on 'How to Treat English Gentlemen' with it.

With that he flung drunkenly out of the room, followed by the others, who, though drunk themselves, were sober enough to see that he needed attention.

'I'll see you home,' said Lascelles, 'when we've put the girls in a taxi.'

'Home be damned,' roared Simon, 'the club. I'll play you a thousand up for a million dollars.'

This sportsmanlike proposition was not fated to find immediate acceptance. Just outside the door of the dining-room was Mr Commissioner Teake.

'Hello, old boy!' cackled Iff. 'Come along to the club!' He put out an unsteady hand.

But Teake did not respond. He laid his hand on the magician's shoulder, and spoke low, in a very formal and yet very embarrassed voice. 'I'm sorry, Mr Iff, but I am charged with the duty of arresting you for the murder of two men unknown, this morning, in Hell's Kitchen. Mrs Travis, I must take you also as an accessory.'

Simon toppled into Teake's arms. 'Tha's ri', ol' top,' he said. 'Ish a fair cop. I did it. But don' you forget, they fired first. I shwear it.'

Teake warned him. Dolores broke into a storm of passionate protest.

'Better go quietly,' whispered Lascelles in her ear.

Mollie Madison had broken into a fit of wild sobbing, and clung to Simon as if she would tear him from his captors. Two other men stepped forward and detached her.

'We don't want a row here,' said Lascelles; 'the time to fight is when the case comes up. I'll get bail, if they'll allow it, anyhow.'

'Bail be damned,' said Simon Iff. 'I've got a head bigger than the planet Saturn, and oh! such a lot more rings round it! Lemme sleep it off, tha's all I ask. Come on, Teake, ol' sport, only for God's sake stop at the drug-store and ge' me a bromo-seltzer.'

They floundered off to the police wagon. A tall gentleman, who had dined at the next table and watched their antics with apparent disgust, threw off his lethargy and, entering a fast car which was waiting for him, made all haste to a small house on East 63rd Street, where he asked for Count von Weibheim.

This personage received him at once, without a word of greeting; sitting down at a desk, he opened a notebook by way of asking for news. The man from Melonico's, whose name was Berkeley, told the events of the evening. The contempt of von Weibheim had no effect on him. He was used to that sort of thing. Berkeley was an Englishman of excellent family, and had been intended for the bar. From Oxford he had been sent down following a disgraceful attempt to cheat in Smalls. His people had got him into the army via the militia, but trouble with money-lenders, and a card scandal, had ended his career. He became a stockbroker, and again lost status through a doubtful transaction, after which he touted for a bucket-shop. This time he overstepped the law and got himself into prison. When he came out, his father sent him to New York with a weekly remittance of twenty-five pounds, to be forfeited forever should he communicate with his family or get into prison. A hundred and twenty dollars a week was beggary to a gentleman with the tastes of Mr Berkeley, and he had eked it out in one shady way or another until von Weibheim, recognising in him a great aptness for his particular work, by reason of extreme social amiability and tact coupled with complete unscrupulousness, had given him permanent and highly-paid employment as a spy.

'All well,' said von Weibheim coldly as Berkeley finished his story. 'You and the gang can get back on the Powys business for the present.'

'Aren't we to finish off Iff if a chance comes? Rinsberg is in the Tombs, you know.'

'Do not you dare! I have my mind changed. I want Iff alive. Do not ask my orders, but obey them.'

Berkeley nodded, and went away nonchalantly. No sooner had he gone than the Count sent for his butler.

It was a man of some sixty winters who entered the room, bowing profoundly.

'Close the door!' ordered von Weibheim.

As the old man did so, the Count rose and stood at attention, saluting, with a click of the heels. The old man gravely returned the salute and then threw himself into an arm-chair and lighted a cigar.

'Well, what is it?' he asked. 'You may sit down.'

Von Weibheim complied. He repeated Berkeley's story verbatim.

'What is your opinion?' asked the other.

'I humbly think, Prince, that it may suit Mr Iff very well to be in prison for a while. He discovered the bomb in the clock, I hear. And this morning was a narrow escape. He is an old man and must love life dearly. He has found a woman, too.'

'You are a fool, Fritz. Yet it was wrong to attack his life; he had knowledge which we must have. *Ach!* is not knowledge always better than life? But in this you are right, although your reason is wrong – that he wished to be arrested. Since it was not I who accused him to the police, it was himself. Then we must free him quickly. You will therefore detail a man to make confession of that shooting, and two men to confirm him as eye-witnesses. It must be impossible for them to hold him. He will then come out, also; he would know that to persist would show us his hand too clearly.

'Now then, listen with care. We do not know what his true mission is, as he did in his drunkenness boast. We do not know what is that certain matter of which he is so proud – oh he is so clever that he will not speak of it, even though he is drunk. But there is he so weak – that drink! He takes drugs also. I have many reports of this; it was not pretence tonight, therefore. Good: we shall get him. But he is very clever, yes; therefore he will make haste to do his mission. I have found that he plans to go to England by the *Deutschland*; that is in ten days more. He took a suite three weeks ago; that is long before this Cass woman put her nose into my business. So we know that all is nearly ready, and we will pick the fruit when it is ripe.'

'I think, Highness, that he has discovered our plans, at least in part, from the woman.'

'I tell you you are a fool, Fritz. This woman, what is she? A hysteric, a degenerate, a sex-madwoman, desiring publicity, with good brains in analysis but no energy in action and no skill. Pah! I laugh at her. Nevertheless, I shall kill her, on general principles. But to our important man! Listen! He has learnt only our rough work; he thinks we are assassins. Therefore we will be not so unkind – not until it is right. So we shall offer him one so dear problem, and thus lead him to Mother Meakins – the "Murder Stable" our rough friends call it, do they not? – and there I shall give him belladonna – oh will not his eyes grow great and bright? – and nitrous oxide and ether to breathe, so that he talks – oh yes! he will talk! and I with my will-power and my skill in soul-science will pick every secret from him, and then, my friend, you will ask Mother Meakins to make everything quiet. For yes! he is a dangerous man, Mr Simon Iff – too dangerous. Only he has too much ego; he values himself too much; he does not know about me, aha!'

The Prince rubbed his hands softly together with satisfaction.

'So you will please arrange with Mr Berkeley to call here in the morning, and I will have my plan ready for him.'

The two men exchanged salutes as before; then the Prince once again became the butler, and retired to the servants' hall with a tray of liqueurs.

4

Dolores, sitting in a prison cell, became a very formidable person indeed. The absolute silence and solitude, the remoteness of humanity, the absence of any possible distraction, acted upon her brain as a most potent stimulus. She began to understand what Simon Iff had once told her about the advantages of a hermit's life, such as he himself adopted at such frequent intervals. She felt that a few months of it would enable her to solve the secret of the universe, just as he had done. But for the moment the possibilities of mysticism did not interest her. She concentrated, naturally enough, upon the immediate problem.

In the first place, why prison? She felt pretty sure that her master was not there against his will. Perhaps he wanted just such facility for profound and undisturbed thought as she herself was enjoying. She had often heard him complain of the difficulty of concentration in New York City. Prison was a simple and ingenious substitute for a cloister! Also, it seemed probable that he feared for her life after two, perhaps three, such narrow escapes.

Next: why the great change in his manner towards her? He was going to expose the conspiracy, and he did not want her help. She was sure that he was not actuated by any ungenerous feeling. All she had to go on was the snub 'Do as you like about it!'

But what was his plan? To let the enemy pursue him, catch him. He had said so. He had some device in his mind, no doubt, for dealing with that situation; but then, why did he not want her to help? There could be only one answer: he was not perfectly sure of the result. He was going into danger, terrible danger, and he knew it. He would not tell her to go back to Boston, and throw up the case; he would know that that would be the very word to make her insist upon continuing.

The more she thought over the situation the more she felt sure of the correctness of that conclusion. There was then only one course for her to take, and that was to watch over him. Whether his snub were due to scorn or to fatherly care, she would go on, either to show her mettle or to prove herself worthy of his loving thought, as the event might declare.

She next turned her thoughts to the enemy. Who was it? Somebody with immense resources, with a brain altogether Machiavellian, and a supreme talent for organisation. It must be someone highly placed in his own country, or he would not be trusted. Yet it could not be an accredited representative; the discovery of such a plot would mean war, and the events of the previous summer had proved conclusively that war was the one thing which that nation wished to avoid, even at the cost of humiliation in the face of the whole world. Who then would serve but a man who could be disowned? Was there no man of this sort available? Possibly there was someone who had been publicly disgraced, who was supposed even, it might be, to be dead. Her mind ran back over the years. Had not her father told her something once – something that suggested such a personality? Of course. The cap fitted a certain Prince Joachim von Arnberg, a mathematician of the highest rank, a physiologist of extraordinary distinction and original views, who had become a specialist in psycho-therapeutics. In 1901 he had been mixed up in an intrigue to manipulate the succession to a principality by driving the heir-apparent into insanity. The Emperor had interfered, the Prince was disgraced, and the report of his suicide in exile a year later had ended the scandal. She remembered, too, that her father had discredited the report at the time, saying that he was the last man in the world to kill himself, and a year or so afterwards had produced an anonymous monograph on the Binary Theorem of Fermat, published in Philadelphia, as evidence of his survival. 'It's as characteristic as a photograph or a thumb-print,' had been his comment. Dolores thought that her own identification was more than a little more than guess-work; it was not likely that two men should so accurately fill the conditions demanded by her problem.

But her satisfaction was dimmed by the reflection that she had no evidence of his presence in America beyond her mere deduction, and that, even so, she had not the slightest idea where to begin to look for him.

The next morning she was freed, with apologies, and her first thought was to communicate her idea to Simon Iff, who, they told her, had been released an hour before.

She telephoned his apartment; he had not returned. A second call an hour later met with equal ill luck. She began to be alarmed. Already he had plunged into the abyss. He was in danger, she was sure of that; and she had lost track of him completely.

She began once more to analyse. Simon had told her that he meant to be caught, and that he would make the enemy think that he was an ass. Somehow, then, he was sure that they would no longer aim at his life, that they would try in some way to fool him. Simon's whole speech implied that he foresaw a personal interview – the most probable method of direct communication – and he intended to make no difficulty about this; he courted it. He must then be gone away on this business. But Dolores felt certain that the enemy – she already thought of him as Joachim – would terminate the interview, whatever its results, by the murder of her master. Of course, he might have taken some secret precautions; he might have arranged for someone to follow him, for instance, or for certain explosions to occur in case of his non-reappearance. She remembered with what unexpected foresight and resource he had acted on the morning Alma sailed.

But where was he? The Lord only knew!

Oh no! came the swift antiphone. There are men who know, and they can be made to tell.

But who?

5

Simon Iff, returning with cheerful resignation to his apartment from the prison, had found Miss Mollie Madison waiting in the hall. There was also a gentleman, said the janitor, a Mr Berkeley, on important business. Mr Iff would be glad to speak with him.

Mr Berkeley approached hastily. His very elegant dress was slightly disordered, and he bore other marks of extreme impatience and agitation.

'Shall we go upstairs?' asked Simon.

'If you would only come direct? Every second is precious, unspeakably precious.'

'Certainly; I see your car is at the door. But what is the trouble?'

Berkeley handed a letter to the magician: at the same time he gave the Sign of Distress of the Royal Arch. The letter, moreover, was written in the secret cipher of that Companionship, with which Simon Iff was well acquainted. But even when rendered into English, it remained quite unintelligible.

> Three-one in Washington Square
> Station of Principal Sojourner.
> Where was the Saviour born?
> Fourth from the East.
> I must die unless Companions rescue me.

'This letter means nothing to you, Companion Berkeley?'

'Nothing.'

'It is quite plain to me. Imagine yourself in a great Chapter-Room, with the Arch of Washington Square to represent the East, where the Three-One sit. Then where would the station of the Principal Sojourner be? Just one street away, to one side of Fifth Avenue. Where was the Saviour born? In a stable. There are several stables in that street; it's the fourth, counting from the East. Let's be off and help him! Come along, Mollie!' They got into Berkeley's car and started on their journey.

'I was sure you would solve the puzzle,' said the remittance-man.

'I was sure you were sure, because you wanted me to hurry before I had even seen it.'

Berkeley looked a little confused.

'I won't ask you how you got the letter, or why our Excellent Companion did not appeal to the community at large in the terrible situation in which he finds himself. Quite otherwise. I will ask you which college you were at.'

'Magdalen,' answered Berkeley, with a sudden note of pain in his voice.

'Ah, Magdalen!' cried Iff, with enthusiasm. 'I am Cambridge, of course, Trinity, but I had rooms there once – Lord Gorham's old rooms, do you remember? I was reading the Dee manuscripts in the Bodder.'

Iff took no notice of the devious route by which the chauffeur chose to approach Washington Square, of his sudden changes of speed, or of the interest he took in any car which came up behind them. He talked of Magdalen Tower, the Thames, Iffley, the Broad, the High, the Radcliffe Camera, Tom Tower, the Torpids, Carfax – everything that means everything to Oxford men. He made history itself vital and lyric.

Berkeley's interjections, at first mechanical, became gradually natural and enthusiastic.

Iff noticed it, and suddenly changed the subject. 'This is Third Avenue, isn't it?'

Berkeley went white. 'Yes, Mr Iff, it is,' he said in a tone of lamentable sadness. There was a moment's pause.

'Mr Iff, it has just struck me that the letter is some foolish hoax. Let's forget it, and go to lunch somewhere.'

'A letter in Our Cipher?' cried Simon in assumed surprise. 'Impossible!'

'I'm sure of it,' answered Berkeley. 'Now I come to think, I believe it's in Cummings' writing, and he's a practical joker if ever there was one.'

'It is none the less our duty to investigate the matter. This is your car, of course, but we go to this stable, or Miss Madison and I get out and take a taxi.'

Berkeley acquiesced with a groan.

'It is my first rule,' continued the magician, 'never to let anything interfere with plans once agreed upon. Think what would happen to the Solar System if the planet Jupiter suddenly decided to lunch at Delmonico's! The Way of the Tao is to allow everything to happen. It all comes right in the end.'

Simon Iff, perceiving Washington Square in the distance, gave his directions through the speaking-tube.

There was no difficulty in finding the stable indicated in the letter. The party got out, and the magician rapped upon the door. It slowly opened.

The interior of the stable was very dark, but Mollie, who kept close to 'Cephas' while Berkeley shut the door, caught the glint of levelled pistols. She sprang impetuously in front of the mystic.

'Charming of you, child!' he said calmly. 'But the revolvers are only for effect.'

'For effect indeed!' boomed a sinister voice from the darkness.

'This is merely a pleasant talk between old friends. Is it not so, Prince Joachim?'

'You know me – so!'

'Who could forget that wonderful voice – the very incarnation of will-power? Didn't we meet at Munich in July of '84?'

'Very good, Mr Iff. We may have light then for our pleasant talk!'

'Please do,' said Simon. 'I dislike to smoke in the dark.' And as an electric bulb glowed overhead, he offered his case to the Prince. The latter took one thoughtfully, but did not light it.

'I do not quite understand your attitude, Mr Iff,' he said slowly.

'Exactly,' replied the magician, very cordially, as he lighted his cigar. 'That is why I have come here. Pray observe: our apparent antagonism is entirely on your side. We are both agents of the Great Purpose; but perhaps you do not understand so well as I do how this can be so.'

'Ha!' said the Prince. 'Do they keep something back from me in the Wilhelmstrasse?'

'Possibly,' said Iff, with cool insolence.

'I do not like this,' said Joachim heavily; 'I do not like this at all; no, it is sure that I do not like this.'

He looked at his companion, who wore a black mask. The reply was a shrug of the shoulders.

'Yes, there is something wrong,' said the Prince. 'I know it is so because you think it is not so.'

'Yes; von Weibheim always was a fool,' chirped Simple Simon. 'I recognise him by the shape of his chin and the very characteristic creases in his waistcoat.'

'Hell!' said Prince Joachim, solidly and emphatically. 'Hell!'

'True,' said Iff.

'Berkeley,' said the Prince, in swift incisive tones, 'Mr Iff made no attempt to communicate with anybody?'

'None. I can swear to it.'

'And you were not followed?'

'Bauerkeller is your own man. Can't you trust him?'

'I give you my word of honour as a gentleman that I took no precautions of any sort. If anybody knows where I am, it is you, not I, who have told. I was particularly careful – for a very special reason which you may learn later – to leave absolutely no clue to my movements.'

The Prince knew enough not to doubt for a second that Iff was speaking the truth.

'Well, then, well. Perhaps Mr Iff has learnt the bluff of these idiotic Yankees. It will not go with us. I have perhaps a little surprise for you, Mr Magician. A little atropine in your veins, and a little ether and nitrous oxide in your nostrils, and with my will-power and my soul-science you shall tell me in your delirium what I want to know.'

'Why trouble yourself?' said Simple Simon. 'I can't answer for the Wilhelmstrasse, but I have certainly no secrets from you. Come, how can I enlighten you?'

'There is something very wrong,' mused the other; 'very wrong. But we must just try it out. Please step to this side!'

He began his examination in a low voice. He was answered simply, fluently, convincingly, without the least attempt at concealment or equivocation. The magician revealed a dozen secrets, any one of them enough to shake the world. Prince Joachim positively gasped. Simon Iff, in twenty minutes' conversation, had made him one of the fifty most powerful statesmen in the world. But once again his scepticism stopped him.

'There is something wrong,' he repeated ponderously, 'there is something behind all this. Why do you so willingly tell me these things, Mr Iff?'

'It is the Way of the Tao, Prince. You ask me, and I tell you. What can be more simple? Surely you can see that all the trouble in this world arises from not being natural, from raising artificial obstacles where none need exist!'

'Ah well, if it is mysticism, very good. Very good. That and the so much alcohol – and the drugs also – they have made the brain soft. I understand. Well, I know all now. What is the combination of your safe, please?'

'The word is Water. The strongest thing in the world, Prince, because it doesn't resist.'

'And will you write me a letter, so that I may visit your bank? I must have that little paper, Mr Iff.'

'Certainly, with pleasure. I am always delighted to oblige.'

He wrote the desired authorisation, and handed it to the Prince with a low bow.

'It is ended, then,' said the latter, with a change in his voice. 'I suppose you think, Mr Iff,' he continued impressively, 'that I am deceived by your foolish talk about the Tao. A fig! Rubbish! Rubbish! You say it to save your face. No, you knew that you were in my power, and hoped to buy your life by servile obedience. But, Mr Iff, it will not do. I tell you that it will not do. If I let you go, you might become dangerous again.'

'Let me enlighten you on one more point before I die. I was never dangerous to you. The defect of such minds as your own is that you always look for danger in the wrong place.'

'There is something very wrong,' reiterated the Prince. 'But it can do no harm to hurry with our programme. Mr Berkeley, you will please kill these good people, and we will go away and leave them to Mother Meakins to clean up.'

'I'm damned if I do,' answered Berkeley. 'Mr Iff has behaved like a gentleman. He has told you all you wanted to know, and I won't do your butcher's work. A girl into the bargain as well. No, I'm through.'

'You see where you go wrong,' said Simple Simon to the astounded Prince, who had expected anything rather than that such a well-tried tool should break in his hand. 'A broken gentleman is still a gentle-man, if you know how to remind him of it.'

The Prince found his voice. 'I must break my rule,' he said hesitatingly, 'and do it myself. And I shall include you, Mr Berkeley, in the butcher's work. Keep them covered, von Weibheim; I will do what is necessary without noise.'

The momentary silence that followed was broken by a resounding knock upon the door. The Prince sprang to the situation.

'Throw away those silly guns, Fritz, you fool. We must open. I knew there was something wrong. Open, Mr Berkeley. Will you try one of my cigars, Mr Iff?'

'Thank you,' said Simon, 'I am sure they are better than mine.'

As Berkeley lifted the latch the door was thrust violently inwards, and Mr Commissioner Teake with six armed detectives burst into the stable. Behind them, particularly cool and supercilious, sailed Dolores Cass. The three conspirators made no resistance to the police.

'Ah, Dolores!' smiled Simon, 'you must really let me introduce Prince Joachim von Arnberg.'

'I feel already as if he were an old friend. My father used often to speak to me of him.'

'So!' growled the captive.

'But that doesn't explain it at all,' interjected Simon. 'And I'm quite as anxious to know as the Prince is.'

'Know what?' came the sinister voice.

'How this lady got here, of course.'

'Why,' said Dolores, 'it was really very exciting. I had no idea whatever where to look for you. But I reasoned that if you had been lured away to be murdered by this very highly organised gang, it was probably to a place carefully prepared, with all the latest improvements for getting rid of bodies. But who knew where that was? The Prince was kind enough to provide me with a guide – the man who had just confessed to the shootings which I knew he didn't do. So he must have been a member of the gang. I went to Mr Teake, who has been very kind in every way and gave me a free hand.'

'So that swine squealed!'

'No, that swine did not squeal. I told him how we were on to the whole business; Mr Teake promised to send him to the chair on his confession unless he came across; we tried everything. But he was absolutely confident in the power of these people to save him.

'So I just sat in Mr Teake's car with him, and held his hand. His muscles told me when I was "getting hot" or "cold," as they say in the old game. At first it was rather difficult, but when he saw that I was gradually getting nearer all the time, his nerves gave out and he reacted splendidly.'

'Magnificent,' said Simon Iff.

'And so say I,' cried Teake heartily. 'But I guess I had better take these men; see you later.'

'Don't take Berkeley!' begged the mystic. 'He's all right; I want him to stay for a bit in a colony I founded for reformed Oxford men.'

'Quite your old form!' cried Dolores, delighted.

For the first time the Prince uttered a protest. 'What am I charged with?' he asked, a gleam of cunning in his eyes.

'It hardly matters, does it? Just a lot of tedious formalities – a terrible fuss to make over electrocuting anybody!'

'What are you talking about?' roared von Arnberg. 'Is this more of your foolery? What have I done?'

'Well, there's one thing I know of, myself. You listened to all that I told you. Curiosity killed the cat, don't you know?'

The man's face broke into a cold sweat. 'My God, it's true,' he cried in agony. 'I wouldn't let anyone live, myself, who knew all that.' His head fell hopelessly on his breast.

They led him and von Weibheim away. Berkeley followed. 'I'll call tonight,' he said to the magician humbly and gratefully. Iff shook his hand, and he went out.

At that moment Mollie gave way; the reaction took her. She fell trembling on Simon's shoulder.

He put an arm about her to support her. 'Take it easy,' he said, smiling. '*Cephas* means "rock", doesn't it?'

'Mr Iff,' said Dolores severely, 'I am exceedingly angry with you. If I had not turned up, you would most certainly have been killed.'

'But you did turn up,' he protested mildly.

Something in his tone caught her ear. She shot a quick enquiring gaze, which grew fixed.

'She held him with her glittering eye –
The wedding-guest was still,'

laughed he. 'It's very simple. As I told you before, the way to manage this business was just not to interfere, to let everything happen quite quite naturally.'

'Dig on!'

'Yes, my child, I judged that it would be in your nature to want to follow me, and to be able to do so. I felt perfectly safe, thank you.'

'You are a perfect Beast!' she cried angrily. 'If I'd guessed that!'

'I thought you might guess at least that as it was your case originally, I should not want to rob you of the glory of it. It was the natural thing to do.'

'Indeed, indeed, you are adorable!'

'Also, I am leaving America next week, and I wanted a final proof that the continent was in competent hands.'

Mollie woke up. 'What! you are going away?'

On the *Deutschland*. It's the safest boat, by a strange paradox; it would never never do for me to have an accident just now. *Cras ingens iterabimus aequor.*'

'You're going away! You're going away!'

'The *Deutschland* is quite a large boat.'

Dolores broke into a musical laugh. Mollie could only wail, 'You're going away!'

'We're going away.' He put his other arm about her and held her tightly. 'This little bunch of red mischief offered her life for mine just now, Dolores!' he said softly. 'I'm really and truly puzzled for once; so we had better go away for a little, and find out what it all means.'

'You silly man,' smiled Mollie demurely, perfectly herself again. 'It's no puzzle at all to me. It's the natural thing to do.'

'Perhaps it is,' said Simon Iff.

3

Simon Iff Abroad

DESERT JUSTICE

1

The sun broke violent over a harsh blue-grey line of hills, and his beam shot through a ragged gap to strike the face of Lord Juventius Mellor.

'Damnation!' cried the boy. He had overslept himself again. He might be the son of a duke, but he was also the disciple of Simon Iff; and there was Simon Iff quietly rising from the posture of meditation to greet the dawn.

'Hail!' he cried, in those great words that have come down to us from countless centuries of Egyptian kings and priests:

> 'Hail unto Thee who art Ra in thy rising, even unto Thee who art Ra in they strength, that travellest over the heavens in thy bark at the uprising of the Sun! Tahuti standeth in his splendour at the prow, and Ra Hoor abideth at the helm; hail unto Thee from the abodes of night!'

And Simon Iff had bidden him to be most particular not to neglect the dawn-meditation. Now it was already hot. Damnation!

But Simon Iff was busy kindling the fire. It was a great meal. The old man had got a gazelle on the previous evening, and there were steaks. There were dried dates, and Garibaldi biscuits, and fried rice; and there was real Turkish coffee such as no millionaires can buy. Moreover there was the best sauce – the best sauce of the proverb – for Simon Iff and his disciple had come eighty miles across the desert in two days. They had no attendants; Simon was just about to start on what he called a Great Magical Retirement, which involved finding a place where there was absolutely nobody at all, and that is not easy, even if you go to the Sahara. However, another twenty miles would bring them to Ouled Djellal, from which village they could probably find the road to Nowhere.

Breakfast was not a tedious festival; there were no newspapers to read. Only, while smoking 'the earliest pipe of half-awakened birds' as he sometimes called it, when feeling not so good, he traced various signs in the sand with a curious carved walking-stick which he was wont to carry.

'It will be a hot day, Ju,' he prophesied cheerfully. 'We meet a horse and an ass; we find a house. There is a woman; the day ends with trouble.'

'Already,' said Juventius, who had eyes like a hawk or an Arab, 'I see the horse and the ass.' Indeed, on the horizon appeared a cloud of dust, with a speck in front of it which might have been anything.

Simon Iff looked. 'There's a man on a horse,' he said.

'Probably,' remarked Lord Juventius quietly, 'the man is an ass.'

'Oh, discredit to your puff-adder mother, and shame to the burnt bones of your unknown father,' replied Simon with asperity. 'You can make a fool of the aged adept, but you cannot fool the Lord's Overseers who inspect the punch-clocks of young brethren. What, may I be permitted to ask, was the subject of the dawn-meditation?'

They were already well on their way. Simon Iff, as his vow bade him, recited continuously the Chapter of the Unity from the *Qur'ān:* 'Say thou, Allah is One; Allah is eternal; nor hath He Son, Equal, or Companion.' And after every recitation he bowed himself to the earth. He had to do this 1001 times a day, in 11 series of 91, because 91 is the numeration of the Great Name Amen, and is seven times thirteen; the eleven series made it efficacious, because Eleven is the Number of True Magick. This was merely his practice, medicine-ball stuff; when he settled down he would use what Mohammedan Sheikhs declare to be 'A Great Word to become mad and run about naked.' And when he had cried this without intermission day and night until the desired result had occurred, his disciple would look after him with unusual care till he came out of the trance, which was usually a matter of a week or two; and then they would go back swiftly to syphilisation, and plunge into secret diplomacy, with crime-detection as a diversion.

His first series was over. 'But who is this,' he cried, 'that cometh forth in the wilderness from the tents of Kedar? Is it the Sultan of the Ivory City, or the Lord of the Mountains of Bronze?'

'It is certainly a considerable cavalcade,' returned the boy, 'but the man on horseback looks to me like a missionary.'

'Another series should elucidate our bewilderment.'

'And alarm.'

But Simon had already started his eternal '*Qul: Huw-Allāhu ahad*' and the rest of it.

'The world's all rose and blue and yellow,' mused the boy, 'except ourselves, in white, and yonder rider in black. The universe needs its shadows, I suppose; let me see. Letter in Defence of the Clergy. How should I start? H'm. Analogy from Whistler, who used black as a harmoniser – black but comely – the Black Prince. Yes, by Jove, it is a missionary – and the Queen of Sheba, to judge by the camels.'

They came upon the man of God just as he halted for breakfast. It was a very different affair to Simon Iff's; four servants hustled in its preparation. According to custom, Iff gave the desert salutation, and would have passed; but the missionary was astonished to see two Europeans in Arab clothes, walking unattended.

'Here, you fellows,' he called in bad French, 'come here! Who are you?'

Simon Iff went across very briskly as if he were repelling an attack at the charge. But he spoke very humbly.

'This is Lord Juventius Mellor, sir,' he said, 'and I am his servant.'

'Delighted to meet you, your Grace,' cried the missionary, ignoring Iff, and running eagerly to the young man. 'I think I had the pleasure of preaching before your Grace's father, three years ago, at Bellows Falls.'

'Sorry,' returned the disciple, 'but that was not my father; it was Virgil Abishag Curtiss; they sent him up the river last year.'

'Dear me, how very, very sad! But won't you partake, your Grace, of the frugal hospitality of a poor servant of our dear Lord and Master?'

'We have just breakfasted, but we shall be glad to take a cup of coffee with you.' One must never refuse hospitality in the Sahara; to do so is a declaration of war.

'And are these all your camels?' asked Lord Juventius, after having falsely explained that he was consumptive and had come on this walking tour as his last chance.

'They are,' smirked the minister. 'The Lord has been pleased to bless my efforts greatly'

'Offerings of grateful converts?'

'Alas, the converts are but few. There seems a lack of understanding in this people: truly said Esaias.'

'They accuse you of multiplying gods, don't they?'

'Indeed, that is the substance of the difficulty. Only the Holy Ghost can prepare their hearts to receive our dear Lord and Master.'

'Have you three gods or five?'

'Ah, your Grace refers to the Papists! I am from the American Baptist Mission.'

'Splendid, splendid! I have often longed to meet one of you hero martyrs. Have you gleaned long in the Lord's field?'

'Twelve years in Africa, my dear young Grace.'

'You are going home now?'

'Only for a season. Candidly and frankly, I have heard the call of China. The teeming millions! The perishing millions!'

'That is a long way off.'

'For our dear Lord and Master, I would go further yet.'

'Indeed, I humbly trust it may be so,' interrupted Simon piously.

Juventius smiled sweetly and continued. 'But how many converts have you made here?'

The good man's face fell. 'As I told your Grace, there is a certain difficulty – an obstacle to the Grace of God, as it were, so to speak.'

'But you hope for better luck in China?'

'Indeed, yes; your Grace will observe that we have a means which we use with the Chinese; we find so many many slaves to the opium habit. And we cure them. That gives us a claim on their gratitude and so prepares the way for their salvation.'

'How do you cure them?' asked Iff, suddenly. He knew China as he did his own house.

'We administer morphia, in what seems to us suitable doses. That helps greatly, for of course only converts can be supplied with morphia.'

'Excuse me,' said Simon, 'but I knew a man who got left badly in China once. I hope you aren't going out there without a hard and fast contract with the drug ring.'

'Indeed not, my good fellow; I should guess not.'

'Quite right,' said Simon, rising – he had not tasted his coffee. 'Look out – there's a horned viper on the path.' Two servants had already seen the reptile, and were striking it with long sticks.

'That's a clumsy way to kill them,' he continued over his shoulder to the missionary. 'You should let them bite you.'

'Goodmorning and a pleasant journey and restored health to your Grace,' cried the missionary despairingly to the departing Juventius.

2

'This is pretty good *dawamesk*,' said Simon Iff in Arabic to the big white-bearded Sheikh who acted as patriarch to Ouled Djellal. (*Dawamesk* is a preparation of hashish, or The Grass, as the Arabs call it.) They were seated outside the little inn which is the principal building of the village.

'*Abu'd Din*,' returned the Arab (for Simon Iff was known all over the desert by this title of 'Father of Justice,' *Din* meaning Truth, Law, Faith, but above all Justice), 'it is good *dawamesk*. It is made in Djelfa by a wise and holy man who can balance himself upon one thumb, o thou who also art most wise and holy!'

'It is indeed The Grass, o Father of Lions, and I am refreshed in my spirit by its soft influence. Allah is munificent as he is great.'

'There standeth no man before His face,' returned the Sheikh, 'and not by *dawamesk* alone, though it be one-third hashish, shall man behold his glory.'

'Nay, but by right intentness, with an holy life.'

'But hashish doth indeed assist us who are weak in soul, and whose lives are defiled with iniquity.'

'There was a great king,' said the magician, 'in a country beyond Suleiman's, whose name was Nebuchadnezzar. For seven years did this holy man live upon Grass, becoming mad and running about naked. These things are written to encourage us. I am myself made bold to find a secret place in the sand where I may seek this blessing, for I have the Great

Word from a certain *ulama* of Al-Qahira, the most cunning reputed in all Al-Misr.'

The old man clasped the knees of Simon Iff in pathetic entreaty. 'O my father, wilt thou not reveal it to me? I swear by the Beard of the Prophet of Allah that I will not profane it.'

'Thou must first renounce all human ties and duties; wilt thou leave thy children to perish in the desert for lack of thy wisdom?'

The Sheikh sighed. 'My father, it is hard to wait for Paradise.'

'It is also a mistake,' said Simon, on whom the hashish was having a delightful effect, 'as in the case of Mohammed (Peace be upon him!) when he waited for the mountain to come to him.'

The Sheikh began to laugh uproariously; a mild blasphemy is much appreciated by the simply pious. Nor is judicious *dawamesk* any impediment to mirth. Iff took him by the arm.

'Let us go to the entertainment. Have you good dancing-girls in Ouled Djellal?'

'We have pride in Fatima, the Scorpion,' replied the old man with enthusiasm; 'she is like a young date-palm heavy with fruit. Her teeth are like pearls, but her bite is like a scorpion's sting, and hence is her *lakab*' – 'nick-name,' said Iff to Lord Juventius, aside – 'the Scorpion. She is like the air of the desert at dawn when she dances, and when she loves it is a *simoon*.'

'And the others?'

'They are soft like shadows upon the sand dunes in the belly of the desert, and she is the full moon.'

'I am certainly encouraged in my determination to see her.'

They were walking across the big square of the village. It was only a few steps; but the *dawamesk* made the way seem long and infinitely brilliant. The universe was stainless, ineffable, silent. The moon lit the world with incorruptible fantasy. All was white, even the sand, save only for the soft blue shadows, and the gold stars in the impenetrable indigo of Heaven. Only the low monotonous clang of cymbals stirred the night. Only the flitting forms of men, like ghosts, disturbed the shrine-like sanctity of the square.

Now they were at the dancing-hall, a long room with tables and benches, with a wide aisle and a dais at the end where sat the dancers and the musicians.

'There is Fatima,' said the Sheikh. 'Look how the eyes of Muley Husein are fixed on her. He goes to the south tomorrow to his own house; it is said that he will take her with him.' Muley Husein was an enormous negro, fierce and proud, with a green turban and an aigrette of uncut jewels to fasten it. Two Arabs, with their hands upon their daggers, stood behind him to guard him.

Simon Iff seated himself and drank the coffee brought by the attendant as he watched the dance. There is no fascination in the world like this: if you have enough coffee, and enough tobacco, and just the right amount of hashish, you can sit all night and every night and never wax weary of that splendid show. There is no question of a performance in the Anglo-Saxon sense of the word. It resembles nothing so much as ocean. There is no object, not even play. The dance simply existed, indifferent to all things. For those who can stop grasping the streams of event and float upon that ocean, it is very Paradise. If you expect something to happen, or want something to happen, it is Hell.

The girl who had been dancing sat down, without warning, as she had begun. In these Arabian Nights nobody takes apparent notice of anything. But there was a murmur as of the birth of some hot deadly wind when, after a pause, Fatima advanced to the front of the dais. She was tall and slim but sturdy. Her headdress, her necklaces, her amulets and her anklets were all of Napoleons strung on gold wire. As she stood and swayed, there were a couple of thousand dollars on her in gold currency. She was of rich yellow-brown skin, like an autumn leaf at its most golden. There were purple shadows, luscious as ripe plums. All blended admirably with the dull blue of her tattoo marks and the Indian red of the big sash which accentuated her hips. It was fastened with a huge brooch, circular, of rough pearls; and with her glances and her gestures her whole dance seemed to say, 'Look at my brooch!'

Simon Iff looked. His eyes left her body, that swayed just as a snake does when it hears music of the right kind, her head that jagged from shoulder to shoulder with an insanely impossible jerk, and came to the brooch. It rose and fell like the breast of a sleeping child; then it made circles, loops, whorls, sinuous and subtle, as if the moon were drunken on old wine; then with savage ecstasy it gave a series of strong jerks, straight up and down, and Simon thought that it could drag his soul to Hell, and he would love her for it. He contrasted her mentally with a fat hag from Tunis – Jewish and Greek, he thought – who banged a cymbal in the background. The flabby piece of paste!

The old Sheikh noticed the magician's glance wander, and told him that the object of his animadversion was Fatima's mother.

'Italian and Jewish from Malta the island is she by birth, and her name is Desda, which in that speech means desirable; but Fatima's father was a pure Badawi, a lizard of the sand. Dirty Desda, they call her, and Mother of Snot.'

'O father of fortunate warriors, is it the *dawamesk* which betrayeth my judgment, or is this Fatima indeed a *peri* of the Prophet? For such enchantment have I never beheld with these eyes.'

'It is the *dawamesk*, without doubt, o Lord of Judgments, for I also have not seen her in this flowering on any other night.'

The music seemed to hush itself to low muttering intensity as she danced. The night was stifling hot; in that airless barn, with its heavy candles, the smoke of oil, of tobacco, of kif, it seemed to Simon Iff as though time were abrogated, as though the fantastic movements of the brooch on the girl's belly were the geometry of some insane and sensual god. With one side-twitch he swooped down slippery wave-summits of glaucous air until he came nigh swooning; a circular heave, and he saw a billion universes set awhirl by lust; she shook her shoulders and he thought of God with his winnowing-fan, driving the light souls as chaff into annihilation. She slowed into bowers of night, and then – those fierce vertical jerks sucked the magician shuddering through aeon upon countless aeon of orgiastic ecstasy. He noticed that he was gasping strongly.

One of the many advantages of hashish is that the slightest call to action bestows the power, if one wills, to come straight out of the intoxication into a state of especially vigorous freshness. 'It is not the *dawamesk*,' he said to himself; 'the girl is really dancing as I have never seen anyone dance before. Then since it is not that, the Sheikh too sees her in abnormal state.' Abnormal states interest Simon Iff. Is it love?

'That Muley Husein is certainly a magnificent beast,' he said aloud, turning to his disciple. 'You observe the super-excellence of our young friend? What is it?'

The young man inhaled his cigarette deeply before replying. 'She is intensely concentrated; she has utterly lost herself. She is dancing on her second wind, if I may call it that. But she has done this at the cost of an infinitely fierce struggle with something in herself. She may have made up her mind to kill somebody, or more likely herself. Or she may be under the influence of some drug not hashish; or she may be going to be ill.'

'Time will show,' replied Simon, relapsing into his intoxication with complete indifference to all speculation. But before another minute had passed Fatima herself settled the point by staggering and then settling to the ground. Her mother went to her, lifted her into a chair and sent a boy to bring water. Another girl took her place, and the music clashed out anew with vital frenzy. No one appeared to notice the accident.

But the new girl did not interest Simon; she was an anticlimax; he kept his eyes on Fatima.

'Ju,' said he, 'your third arrow hit the mark. She is very ill. I will ask the Sheikh to give orders.'

In a few moments the girl had been taken to her room in the courtyard. Muley Husein loomed in the doorway over the little party. Simon Iff made his examination. Her skin was cold and clammy, her pupils contracted, her breath stertorous.

'All is well,' reported Simon Iff at length, after administering an injection from a small case which he invariably carried on long journeys. 'It is the will of Allah that she shall not die this night.'

The negro gave a fierce cry of joy.

'But I am bound to tell you that she has been poisoned.'

'It is not possible,' shrieked the mother, while Muley Husein roared with rage.

'It is possible, and it is true,' said the Sheikh, 'for the Father of Justice makes no errors.'

'Let me know the jackal that did this!' cried Muley.

The Sheikh was as indifferent as before. 'All things are known to Allah, the All-Knower' was his comment, which is Arabic for 'I don't know and I don't care.'

'Perhaps a small investigation?' suggested the magician.

'O Father of Justice and Perspecuity, the case is common. All the women are jealous of her beauty and of her fame, and all her lovers are in despair because they fear that Muley Husein will take her into his harem.'

'O Protector of thy People, it is written that the All-Knower bestoweth knowledge according to His will, for He is the Merciful, the Compassionate, and pitieth the ignorance of His creatures.'

'I will give a camel-load of ivory to the man who discovered this shame,' groaned the negro, whose emotion seemed to become more violent every moment.

'Bestow it upon her, then, for my wedding-gift; for I will make this door open, by the favour of Allah, and the help of our Lord the Sheikh Abd al-Kabir.'

'I shall help, as I may, far-seeing one!' said the Sheikh. 'But thy way is hidden from me.'

'Let Fatima be given much coffee, and made to walk seven times around the village, and then taken to thy house and put under guard. Then in the morning do thou assemble together all that are in the village, both men and women, everyone with his cooking-pot, and I will shew thee the magick of my country.'

'According unto thy word so shall it be.'

Fatima was now almost able to walk, and the Sheikh, summoning two men, had them support her. They started away at a brisk walk.

'That,' said Simon to Lord Juventius, 'will sweat the rest of the stuff out of her. She will be well in the morning.' Then he turned to Muley Husein: 'Our ways lie together, if it be thy pleasure to return to thy tents; for I am going into the desert that I may pray Allah for wisdom in this matter.'

The negro gladly consented. When they were outside the last houses, Simon Iff put a hand upon the man's huge shoulder.

'I will instruct thee, o chief of warriors, as a father to his son, for I am old and well-stricken in years. I have saved the life of thy gazelle, and I shall give into thy hands the chastisement of the poisoner. This is the justice of the desert, where Allah dwelleth with open eye. See thou to it that thou play the part that I assign to thee, seeking secretly afterwards for the thought concealed in my speech.'

The big man assented with a child's gratitude and a child's trust.

'Swear it unto me!' And he sware solemnly. They parted after Simon Iff had drunk his share of a bottle of champagne in the chief's tent.

Lord Juventius Mellor had slipped away to follow Fatima. He knew without being told that his master was apprehensive of a further attempt upon her life. He was consequently prowling around the Sheikh's house when the old magician returned to the village.

'Not a mouse stirring,' he reported. 'I've been thinking – trying to do what I call thinking, you would say, perhaps – and I can't imagine for the life of me how you propose to spot the criminal. As old Abd al-Kabir justly said, it's open to the whole village to have done it. Anybody can go to her room, whether she's there or not, and poison her food.'

'No,' said the other, 'this is your first journey in these parts, so I can excuse you, but it's almost impossible to poison food. They're always on the lookout for it; they cook it themselves, or have it done by trusty people who know well that an indigestion means suspicion and a beating, and serious illness quick detection and bitter retribution.'

'I should not have said food. Abd al-Kabir mentioned that a week since a seller of *dawamesk*, a son of Eblis, accursed, a father of calamities, passed through. It would be easy to change her *dawamesk* without detection. But the man is gone, no one knows where; and if we had him, he would deny selling the poison; much less would he say to whom he sold it.'

'Good as far as it goes, Ju, but as a matter of fact we have a very good line on the culprit. What, let me ask you, was the nature of the poison?'

'Symptoms suggested opium.'

'They did, but you couldn't mix opium in poisonous doses with *dawamesk* without changing its appearance. Hashish and opium are more or less physiological incompatibles. Mix 'em, and you get that very gorgeous jag in which she so enthralled us. But for the opium to bide its time, to conquer the hashish, to knock her out, oh a very big dose, boy!'

'Well, one could mix morphia with the hashish.'

'One could.'

'But morphia isn't known in the desert.'

'Exactly, and that is our clue. We have to find a person with a guilty conscience and a knowledge of European medicine – some small knowledge at least.'

The lad laughed. 'It points to that Baptist scoundrel. He was here yesterday. He may be a connoisseur in murder, or he may be trying to work up a market in morphine – a little preliminary practice before he gets busy with China's perishing millions.'

'Unfortunately, Ju, he was not here yesterday, or any day. His horse and his camels had crossed the *chott*; I saw the mire on their hoofs. And the Sheikh had heard nothing of them. No, it's someone in the village.'

'With a guilty conscience and some modern science – well, I'd love to see you get him!'

'Let us fortify nature by repose.' And they went off to the hotel together, and to bed.

3

At sunrise the next day the Sheikh had duly gathered the whole village in the square. Each had his cooking-pot, squatting behind it. Simon Iff asked the Sheikh to inform the people officially of what had occurred, and to propound an oath of innocence. They took it as one man; not a face there betrayed the slightest interest in the proceedings.

'Now,' said Abd al-Kabir, 'the Father of Justice will determine by his magick which of you is forsworn to Allah, as well as an assassin.'

Simon asked for a supply of camel's milk, which was at once forthcoming.

'Now,' said he, 'a little milk shall be placed in each pot, and the pot sealed. Then let all go about their business, bringing the pots here at sunset; and it may be that he who is guilty shall find the milk sour, while that of the innocent shall be sweet.'

This sounded good, something like magick! For milk in Ouled Djellal turns in a couple of hours. The people went about all day in suppressed excitement; nearly everybody felt guilty and nervous. It was a very critical moment when they reassembled in the square.

The Sheikh himself was to inspect the milk. What a sigh of relief went up from all hearts but one when the very first pot proved to be sour! The man was on his feet, leaping and protesting.

'Shut up!' cried Simon Iff, cowing the man with a fierce glance. Then to the Sheikh: 'Go on.'

The old man looked at the magician in mild surprise.

'There may have been an accomplice,' he explained. And the second pot was sour, and so were the third, and the fourth, and the fifth; the people began to laugh.

Abd al-Kabir wanted to create a diversion. 'My Father, the magick has failed. I am putting shame upon you.'

'I can bear it,' said Simon, 'but I will pray a little harder. In the meanwhile, pray go on!'

Simon Iff began to recite the Chapter of the Unity aloud, with many bows, and the people halted in opinion, thinking that there might be something else coming. Eventually he stopped.

'And what is the report, o great Sheikh?' he asked.

'Alas, all the milk is sour, save that which was in the pot of Fatima's own mother.'

'Ah, Madame Desda,' said Iff lightly, 'the effect of mother-love. Is that how you explain it?'

'These are all savages,' replied the pallid piece of salt pork, 'they have all murder in their hearts. I am not of them; I am also a Christian.'

'Also!' said Iff; 'ah yes, also.'

'And thus our Lord Issa protecteth us from even the shadow of evil.'

'Doth he, really? I should go into that again, if I were you. How did you find the Light?'

'I am not a common woman. I was in the American Baptist Mission in Tunis.'

'Infant baptism, by the dates,' murmured Iff.

'I teach in Sunday School.'

'Ah, that's where they taught you to sterilise milk?'

'No, no, no, I don't know how,' cried the trapped woman.

'Nonsense,' said Simon, 'everybody here knows enough to boil milk; but all the others trusted in my magick and their own innocence to keep the milk fresh; which did you doubt, Desda?'

'It is foolish, it is nonsense; it is my habit to boil milk; I did it without thinking.'

'Without thinking enough,' corrected the magician. 'Fatima was poisoned with morphia, which nobody here has; I was merely looking for a person with European knowledge and a guilty conscience.'

'I am satisfied,' put in the Sheikh. 'Surely this woman shall be put to death.'

'You can't touch me,' she screamed; 'you can't prove I had morphia; you can't prove I gave it. I appeal to the Commandant of the District.'

'She has you there,' said Simon cheerfully; 'you can't prove a thing. But this is all child's talk. Let me rather explain to you the Law. It is written: Do what thou wilt shall be the whole of the Law. And again: Love is the law, love under will. From this we learn that every one of us is justified in doing what he will. Woman, neither do I condemn thee. But – your will has been thwarted, since your daughter is not dead. Do you then wish to kill her, now, before us all? You are safe from the law which punishes – tell us, what was your will in poisoning Fatima? Had you no object beyond that?'

Desda saw that things were going her way. It was all very unexpected, but no doubt Christians must stand together. Her colleague was fooling these savages.

'I wish to be the wife of Muley Husein,' she said boldly, 'and Fatima was in my way.'

'See how simple and beautiful it all is,' said Simon Iff with enthusiasm and a ferocious glance at the big negro, who could hardly contain himself. Lord Juventius went over to Muley, and stood ready to check any move in case that glance failed of effect.

'Love! What a passion is love! How prove a great love better than by willingness to commit crime, to risk detection and the guillotine in order to satisfy it? Most certainly, Desda, you have deserved to win! Muley Husein, on your oath I charge you to receive this woman in your harem!'

His voice rang out like a trumpet. The people did not understand, but they saw the joke on the negro and roared with laughter. Lord Juventius gripped the man's arm with slender fingers, strong and brown. The magician threw a veil over Desda and led her to him.

'Remember your oath to the man who saved Fatima,' murmured the disciple.

Muley was shaking like a leaf with rage and shame. He turned furiously and stalked away to his tents, the old woman smirking and smiling and tossing her head, wallowing in his wake.

The Sheikh protested. 'Muley Husein is the guest of the village,' quoth he, 'and you have put him to open shame.'

'Then I am no more Father of Justice – the Father of the Desert?'

'My father, forgive me. I have been blind in this matter; it may be I am yet blind.'

'At sunrise tomorrow – may Allah grant thee sight!'

And at that hour the magician called upon the Sheikh. Muley Husein's caravan was crossing the square on its way to his home in the south. As the last of the camels passed, it was noticed that a short cord was attached to its near hind leg; the other end of the cord was tied to a very heavy iron ring, and that ring was soldered through the nose of Desda. Behind her, a carefree boy was trying his skill with a long lash of hippopotamus-hide, and from the stately litter of the negro Fatima's laughing face peeped out, until her husband drew it to him, and glued his mouth to hers.

The village was again in laughter, and the Sheikh in passionate admiration for his friend.

'It seems that substantial justice has been done,' drawled Lord Juventius Mellor.

'To me not so,' retorted Simon Iff, with cold fury. 'But if we could get the American Baptist Mission here, and some stakes and cord and molasses and red ants, we might make a beginning.'

IN THE SWAMP

1

The belly of the swamp was black. Thick stagnant pools of slime sweltered. Even the firm ground was but a mass of rotten trees and rotten undergrowth. Nothing lived here but things both obscene and deadly. A tangle of giant trees extending over thousands of square miles shut off the sun eternally from the earth. The rain falling in torrents upon this roof was caught and deflected by the vegetation so that it reached the ground in streams, as if spouted from countless myriads of gargoyles. It was impossible to see for any distance, not only because of the thickness of the forest and its abiding gloom, but because the air was misty with miasma, a foul hot sweat. Here and there it was made darker still by swarms of gnats, mosquitos and flying ants. The pools were hideous with reptile life. Malignant serpents and greedy crocodiles were masters of land and water, while the trees owned no lordship but that of the most obscene and savage gorillas.

Through this abominable morass, a path had been cut, or rather tunnelled. It was barely large enough for a man to pass his fellow. It wound inextricably among the trees, constantly seeking higher and dryer ground, and finding it not. Across the depressions it was only possible to go by taking the path to where some giant tree had fallen, and crawling across its slippery and infested trunk. Where one of the sluggish streams cut off the way from its general direction, ladders of twisted osier made a dangerous passage through the air.

In this jungle, even so simple a matter as the lighting of a fire is a serious operation. One keeps one's matches as dry as possible by enclosing them in a specially constructed airtight receptacle. But even when you've got your flame, it is only a beginning. You must cut some wood which is not hopelessly rain-sodden from a tree. Then you must split it into the thinnest chips, and when you have got a little heap of these alight, you must dry other wood above your tiny fire, constantly increasing the size of the pieces until, after about an hour's work, you can begin to think of cooking dinner. A big fire is necessary at night, partly on account of our First Cousin but principally because, though the heat may be stifling, the thermometer above 100 degrees Fahrenheit, there is yet a deadly chill in the very marrow of your bones. There is also the minor consideration that it is nice to feel dry, even if one is not dry, for an hour or so in every twenty-four.

By such a fire, which smoked lazily upon a small plateau which had been cleared sufficiently to allow a glimpse of sky here and there, stood a man. A man so thin and worn that he might have sat to Rodin for a statue of Death – but of Death on a hot scent! His arms were shaking with malarial ague, so that the rifle which he held shuddered passionately in his grasp. His teeth were clenched, his eyes fiercely glinting, his ear, so to speak, cocked. The silence of the forest is the silence of an ambush. Its noises are as the sounding of the charge.

Whatever noise he had heard, it stopped very suddenly. The man with the rifle did not relax his vigilance on that account. Whatever it was might have got away. But on the other hand, the sudden stillness might mean that it saw the fire and was preparing to attack. The man turned and signalled to his servants, sixteen immense negroes hardly less simian than the gorillas he had come to hunt, to throw more wood on the fire from the great stack which they had prepared, both to dry the wood and to serve as a rough barricade. A shower of sparks roared heavenward, defying the rain. The man and his servants leapt into the darkness beyond the bulwark and crouched there in grim silence. As active as any of them was the white man's *intombazane*, a young woman, half Dutch, half Zulu, from the Zambezi, who travelled with her husband (as marriage laws go in Africa). She was a sturdy muscular type with a flat face, a broad grin, pig's eyes, a turned-up nose and a shock of gold-brown hair. She was slightly pitted with the smallpox, and had a scar across her forehead from the great uprising.

The surprised party had no fear of talking; the fire was sufficient evidence of their presence. They discussed the cause of the disturbance.

'It sounded to me like the scouts of a war party,' said the Honourable Charles Sexton.

'No,' said the head-man, 'this noise stopped. Scouts would have gone back to warn the war-chief.'

'What do you think, Bill?' said the white man. The girl always answered to the name of Bill – it was short for Billiken, though she looked more like a regular West African idol.

'I don't think,' she said, 'I smell. There is a white man here.'

Silence fell intense like a pall on a coffin. Then from the top of a tree rang a firm voice which said:

'Do what thou wilt shall be the whole of the Law.'

The party looked up amazed. In the branch of a tree, at the end of the clearing, they could see the face of a small, spry, active old man wearing very ragged khaki and a smile which was not ragged at all.

'I wish you a very good evening, sir,' the voice continued, and with a light leap the man sprang into the clearing. As he did so, he was joined by a slim youth, exceeding pale. Sexton ran forward to greet them.

'Excuse this quite unwarrantable intrusion, my dear sir,' said the old man, 'and still more the alarm which we inadvertently caused you, but we had no means of knowing who you were. A thousand apologies to the lady,' he added, as Billiken came forward, all smiles, and took him by both hands.

'Permit me to introduce myself – my name is Simon Iff; and this is Lord Juventius Mellon'

'Glad to know you,' said the hunter, 'my name is Charles Sexton; and this is Billiken, better known as Bill. I hope you will take food with us.'

'You are very kind indeed,' returned the other. 'To tell the truth, we have been on quarter-rations for some time.'

'We have enough dried hippo meat and broiled monkey for a regiment, to say nothing of tins.'

They sat around the fire in a certain state, for the Honourable Charles Sexton always did himself pretty well. He gave the 'Colonel Elliot's chair' to his principal guest, while he and the rest seated themselves on such loads as had not been unpacked. Bill devoted herself to Lord Juventius, beginning a passionate flirtation by offering him a pellet of opium, which was the thing he most needed to combat his sickness and exhaustion. With this and a little more than his share of the champagne, he was soon able to sustain the combat.

'This is a most particularly fine cut of monkey,' said Simon Iff. 'I wish indeed that I had the secret of your cuisine.'

'The secrets are two,' said the hunter. 'The first is Bill, who can make parrot taste like Sole Mornay, and the second is Worcester sauce. But forgive my curiosity – where have you come from, and where are all your men?'

'We have come from Timbuktu,' answered the magician, 'after crossing the Sahara with the caravan from Biskra, and we have not any men because we thought they would be more trouble than they were worth; besides, it's more exciting.'

'I should say it was,' returned Sexton, 'but how in blazes do you find your way? Have you any idea where you are?'

'Pretty fair,' answered Iff. 'I have a sense of direction and a sense of distance which serve me pretty well. Besides, when we went into this delightful swamp twelve days ago, they told us that there was only one trail and that it led to the village of Mwala. They told us that Mwala was a terrible potentate, the offspring of a gorilla and a demon-king, that he was cruel, treacherous, bloodthirsty and a cannibal. As the very charming people who gave me this information were described in precisely the same terms by their neighbours to the north-east, I expect to find Mwala a modern Old King Cole.'

'We are two days' journey from Mwala,' said Sexton, 'but only about ten miles of it is this ungodly swamp. Beyond that there is pleasant upland park country with plenty of game. But as to Mwala, he was a pretty decent sort when I was here three years ago. Something seems to have spoilt his temper.'

'Have you had any serious trouble?' asked the magician.

'Well, there's a war on, for one thing. There's another king called M'Qob – we thought at first you were scouts of a war party of his – and somehow or other they've both got guns – strictly against the law, of course – and they've been itching to use them. The old man wanted me to lead one of his armies. Did you ever hear of anything so asinine? I told him that sooner or later the French would be down on him, but of course he said he was bound to defend his people from the assassin M'Qob. I am a Gallio in these matters, but they had quite a nice battle last week, with fifty or sixty killed on either side – village raided, cattle driven off and all that sort of thing.'

'What's the war about? The usual nothing?'

'Can't make out. The two kings were as thick as thieves three years ago. They had sworn blood-brotherhood, they had put down raiding, stopped human sacrifice, and generally had become the very best kind of nigger, than whom there is no more charming person alive. Now it's all upset. I hear that human sacrifice has been started again.'

'What's the ostensible cause of the quarrel?'

'Naylor can tell you more about that than I can; he's the trader out here. He is at Mwala's now. I hope you will join my party. We are going straight back. I have got three gorillas, two of them alive, as you see in the cage there, and I have had enough of this poisonous darkness.'

'I shall be very glad,' said Simon.

'Splendid,' cried the hunter. 'And now I am sure you want to sleep.'

'My body does,' replied the magician, 'and the beast has carried me so well that I begrudge it neither its oats – not even its wild ones – nor its straw.'

But long after the rest of the party was asleep, the magician, smoking a curved black briar pipe, gazed intently upon the fire. Perhaps he saw faces there. But one may doubt whether he saw any face so strange as that of the days that were to be.

2

Mr Naylor was an Englishman of the lower middle-class. He was conventional; and he was stupid; and he was cowardly: and the combination of these qualities had made him the regular British hero. One must earn one's living in the regular way. What better place than Africa? His stupidity and conventionality quite discounted his cowardice, for though he saw men dying all around him, he believed himself to be under the special protection of a deity called Jesus Christ by the Methodists, to whom he belonged, but to be carefully distinguished from a false god of the same name worshipped by Baptists, Wesleyans, Presbyterians, Congregationalists, Plymouth Brethren, Agapemonites, Lady Huntingdon's Connection, or other savage sects.

Intelligent men, such as the French or Germans, cannot colonise. The art needs a race too stupid to understand that it is being martyred. Empire is a dream, with nightmare passages. And men must be asleep to dream.

Mr Naylor was breakfasting in his compound at Mwala's village. The meal consisted of a little tea and a little banana and a lot of whisky and quinine. He was too blond and too fat to thrive in West Africa. Dysentery to him was almost a hobby. He had no imagination and counted his days dull, though hoemoglobinuria did its little best to add a touch of colour to his life. He cursed the mosquitoes in a way that would have shocked the Methodists of Birmingham. He was passionately devoted to Mr Joseph Chamberlain as a colonial administrator and empire builder.

Mr Naylor was particularly annoyed this morning, the second after Iff's arrival at Sexton's camp, by the fact that the Rev. Moses Rose had not seen fit, as promised, to join in his not very festal festivity. The missionary was somewhat aggressively 100% American; but some people, on introduction, ventured to speculate how long it was since Rose was Rosenbaum. Mr Naylor wanted to see him very badly because business was wretched. His stock consisted of things desirable in peace, and the war had completely upset his calculations. Everybody had denuded himself of his substance in order to buy the instruments of death. He hoped at least to do a little business with the good man, though he knew him of old as a very shrewd hand at a bargain. But more important still, he wanted to sound him on the situation, and to bribe him by offering him a commission to 'put the fear of God into the niggers' and get them to dig up enough rubber and other treasures to take the stock off his hands. But there was no Moses Rose to say Grace Before Bananas. He smoked his woodbine tremulously and determined to go around to the mission after breakfast.

His meditations were disturbed by the beating of innumerable drums and a very inferno of yelling. 'The damn fools are going out to fight again,' he thought. But no, the drums came nearer and the village itself broke into joyful clamour. Women and children ran forth gleefully.

'It is very good, sir,' said Mr Naylor's servant, a tall negro from Sierra Leone. 'It is a great victory – now they will buy everything.'

Naylor knew that the victor in any war is only one degree less unfortunate than the vanquished. This holds even in Africa, where the object of war is avowedly loot. However, victory was better than nothing. He walked feebly to the door of the compound to see the return of the warriors. But as the head of the procession passed, his negro Sam informed him (for of course he would not condescend to understand a word of the language of the people with whom he was trading) that it was not victory, but peace. The two kings had met on the previous day and talked to each other instead of fighting.

The interview, it appeared, had been engineered by a Roman Catholic missionary in M'Qob's village. Mr Naylor had never liked this man; both because he was a wicked Papist, which is worse than any other idolatry because the sinner has sinned against the light, and because he would never play Mr Naylor's little games for him by mixing up religion and business. But this time it seemed he had done him a particularly good turn.

Mr Naylor returned to his hut. The sun was already very hot. He did not want to see Mr Rose any more, just then. He had to calculate on how much he would raise prices on him.

Meanwhile the other inhabitants of the village abandoned themselves to unrestrained joy. Mr Naylor would put in an hour or two on his accounts, and sleep the midday sleep. In the afternoon he would see Mr Rose, and in the morning perhaps the people would be sober enough to do business.

His intentions were interrupted by the Hon. Charles Sexton, who came into the compound like a leopard, crying, 'Get your rifle, man, and bid your caravan stand to arms, there's going to be a fuss.'

Mr Naylor's terror thrust forward the accelerator of his remarks. In less than a minute the head-man of his caravan had placed a strong guard at every wall of the compound. But nothing happened. The streets of the village were deserted. Everyone had gone to the great space around the palace, to celebrate peace.

About one-half hour later the rest of Sexton's caravan filed in. Mr Naylor was in the last extremity of fear; for Sexton had explained matters to him, in an off-hand way, like a man describing a costume ball. It is probable that his stupidity grasped none of the details of the explanation; for when he visualised it with the arrival of the caravan, his teeth chattered like a monkey's. On a litter, in the midst of the procession, lay Mr Rose; and it was shockingly evident that he had lost a foot. His hands, too, were discoloured and disfigured, terribly swollen, and his face was almost shapeless with mosquito bites. Fear of torture and loss of blood had rendered him a hideous lump from which all semblance of humanity had nearly fled.

Simon Iff's eyes swept round the defenders of the compound. 'How far is the nearest white force?' he asked of Sexton.

'Probably not within a week,' replied the hunter.

'Then, assuming your messenger loses no time, no one can get here for a fortnight.'

'Just about,' said Sexton, 'though my man might do it in five days – perhaps four.'

'In that case,' returned the magician, greatly pleased, 'we have ample time for deliberation, which seems to me our chief need.'

'What we need is food,' said Sexton shortly; 'there wasn't too much of it before the fuss started.'

'I want to talk this business thoroughly over with Mwala. His ingenuity seems to me to run away with him.'

'You will have your chance,' said Sexton grimly; 'he will be here with about one thousand men in five minutes, after he hears of this.'

'And M'Qob's men, too,' bleated the missionary. 'Pilate and Herod have made friends.'

'Their guns are as good as ours,' continued Sexton, 'wherever they got them. Luckily they shoot more for the noise than for result.' This was a cheerful lie intended to encourage Mr Naylor.

'Mr Sexton,' said Simon Iff sharply, 'it is no use deceiving others; it teaches us to deceive ourselves. If your psychology and your facts are right, we can be stormed in an hour or starved in a week. What we need is thought. I don't see why you're so sure that this is a race-riot. If it were, why didn't they get Mr Naylor? Let me see. Are you able to answer a few questions, Mr Rose?'

The missionary nodded, with an effort.

'What time was it when they took you?'

'Just before evening service.'

'And where were you then, Mr Naylor?'

'I was dining here at home,' said the trader. 'I had no idea of any disturbance.'

Simon Iff puffed at his pipe. He was watching the face of Billiken out of the corners of his eyes. He turned to her sharply.

'Bill, my dear,' he said, 'you know something. What is it?'

'I don't know anything,' she replied stolidly. 'I smell something.'

'Well, what do you smell?'

'I smell magic'

'That's only me, my dear,' smiled Iff. 'I am myself something more than an amateur of the art.'

'Great!' she cried, and flung her brown arms round his neck, a gesture which she followed with a hearty kiss.

'Pray, do not say such things even in jest,' murmured the missionary; 'you mean a conjuror, of course. But out here in Africa magic is a dreadful superstition associated with the most revolting crime. My present state, my martyrdom, if I may say it, is evidently due to the personal action of the Prince of Evil. We are in touch with the powers of darkness – it is for my faith that I suffer.'

'Did they do the same to all your converts?' asked Iff.

'But they were all my converts,' wailed the missionary.

'Ah, back-sliders,' commented Simon.

'I can give you a terrible example of the workings of the devil. About six months after I arrived here, the tribe reverted to human sacrifice; and you will be astonished and appalled to learn that, abandoning their old method, they have blasphemously resorted to crucifixion.'

'I am not very much appalled and not at all astonished,' returned Iff. 'You convert these people, assuring them that all their sins, past and future, are forgiven, and this by a means of a story of a crucifixion, which to them is to the highest degree exciting from a sexual point of view.'

'I never thought of it in that way; but of course their morality is dreadfully low.'

'Strange,' said Iff, 'whenever I've passed, I have found the native code fantastically rigid. However, these people naturally want to visualise your stimulating story, and, being highly dowered with mimicry, they get busy.'

'I think that's about the psychology of it,' said Sexton. 'I've seen similar reactions in more places than one.'

'It is the Doctrine of the Vicarious Atonement that does the harm,' said Iff. 'Despite all Paul's special pleading, it is bound to destroy moral responsibility.'

'Mwala is coming,' said Billiken.

Simon Iff looked at the girl again, still more intently. Neither he nor any of the others could hear a sound; and if Mwala were coming it would be with the noise of a great army. She read the question in his eye.

'He is coming for a palaver.'

'Ah,' said Simon Iff, reflectively, 'I am more than ever convinced that you know something.'

'I don't know anything,' she said again. 'I smell it.'

'Her nose knows,' murmured Lord Juventius Mellor from the background.

'While he is coming, perhaps you will tell us about the magic you smelt,' said Simon Iff.

'I think there is an old custom,' she said. 'When a building is made, something must be killed or burned at one corner, or else it will not stand firm. So also is it when they wish to build a peace.'

'But,' objected Iff, 'Mwala is a man of quite advanced education – that mechanical arrangement by the river—'

'I taught him mechanics,' groaned the missionary. 'It only goes to show that the highest intellectual attainments are not incompatible with the depths of barbarism.'

'What did they actually do?' asked Mr Naylor.

The missionary dragged himself into an easier position.

'They lured me from the mission house, upon a pretext. They took me down to the river where you found me, and then without a word of explanation they hung me by the wrists to a projecting bough with an arrangement of weights and pulleys, so that the release of part of my weight would lower my body little by little.' He fell back fainting with the horror of the recollection.

'As I told you,' said Sexton, 'only you were too scared to listen, his feet were about a foot out of the water, and the crocodiles were jumping for him like puppies teased with a biscuit. He had been there all night. We were just in time to see the first successful dash. The curious thing is that the natives didn't stay to enjoy the effect. I'm beginning to think there is something very funny about this business.'

'Here comes Mwala,' cried Lord Juventius Mellor, whose quick ear had caught approaching footsteps.

'Admit him,' said Simon.

It was curious how instinctively he had taken command of the party. No one thought to question his good sense. But Mwala stood still at the gate of the compound. Behind him two men held a big umbrella over his head, and on either side marched two soldiers armed with spears. But it was evidently a friendly visit.

'Now, why won't he come in?' said Simon to himself. 'He isn't afraid, because we could shoot him where he stands. Some taboo, I suppose.'

Closely followed by Sexton, he advanced to the gate. The king greeted him very solemnly, in good English. Simon Iff replied with similar reserve and repeated the invitation to enter.

'No,' said the king, 'to me you are a stranger. I will explain. I am chief in this place. You are my guests. But when I look from my house upon the hill, I see you armed, on guard. Am I then no longer king? Or why do my guests distrust their host?'

'It's a trap,' whispered Mr Naylor, who had crept up behind. 'Remember Cawnpore.'

'I can't remember it,' said Simon, 'I've never heard but one side of the story.'

'It is I,' said the king, 'who should have been arming against you. You have committed a breach of my hospitality.'

'Yes,' said Simon curtly, 'I rather want to go into that with you.' He spoke to the king rather as a college professor might speak to a student suspected of some delinquency.

'I beg you to explain,' said he.

'You see, Mwala, we have a taboo in England against using men of our race – er – I mean – of – er – man, in short, in mechanical experiments.'

'This was not an experiment,' replied the king, with an air of one putting everything right with a word. 'This was the peace-sacrifice.'

The magician looked at the king with extraordinary intentness. He felt sure that something was hidden behind that simple savage speech.

'Mwala,' said he, 'the sun is hot. By your leave I will sit down for this palaver.'

The king bowed gravely, and they squatted opposite each other.

'What exactly,' asked Simon, 'do you mean by a peace-sacrifice?'

'It is an ancient custom of our nation,' replied Mwala. 'Peace must be bound with blood.'

'I don't see why you selected Mr Rose,' said the magician.

Mwala began to assert his dignity. 'I am king of this nation,' he said. 'I am the father of all. I rule with justice and benevolence. All that I do is part of that rule.'

'Not exactly the Golden Rule, in this case,' remarked Lord Juventius.

'Pray be silent, my lord,' said Simon, who never addressed his disciple in this way unless he was extremely angry with him.

'The Golden Rule,' he continued, addressing Mwala, 'interpreted in such a sense, would end all human justice. When man does not do unto others as he would that they should do unto him, somebody must teach him his error, by showing him that two can play at the game if he chooses to make it necessary.'

'It is a true saying,' answered the king. There came a pause. 'But what has this to do with this matter?'

'This much,' replied Simon, 'that your action has aroused a reaction in us, from whom, although you are our host, you also receive benefit. The question is whether you should be unkind to anyone, even in order to secure lasting peace.'

'I dispute the theory,' put in Sexton. 'I find myself in entire disagreement with the theory.'

'It is the practice that matters, after all,' returned Iff. 'Your majesty seems to me a person of very great intelligence; I may add, despite the facts, of excellent fine feeling. I am a stranger to you, but I have just come from the great desert in the north, and there they call me the "Father of Justice." May I propose then that you appoint me judge in this cause?'

The king rose, and plucking an ostrich plume from his headdress, handed it to Iff. 'This feather,' he said, 'is the symbol of my justice; the breath of man deflects it. I leave it in your hands.'

'Do I understand, Mwala,' said Simon, 'that you, as king of this country, appeal to this court to deliver into your custody the body of the Rev. Moses Rose, to be sacrificed to crocodiles with every circumstance of terror and bodily torture?'

'I do,' said the king, with the most frigid expression of stolidity.

'Call Mr Rose,' said Simon.

They brought the missionary in on his litter.

'Swear Mr Rose,' said Simon.

The sick man took the oath on a copy of the Gospels.

'Your name is Moses Rose?'

'It is.'

'Your business?'

'I'm a minister of Christ. I've been sent here by the American Baptist Mission.'

'Tell us your relations with King Mwala.'

'We have always been on friendly terms,' returned the missionary. 'Only a few months after my arrival, the Lord saw fit to bless my work by touching his hard heart. In a little while, practically the whole nation became Christians – nominal Christians, I fear, most of them, merely nominal Christians.'

'Did you consider Mwala's conversion sincere?'

'I did at the time. He was very friendly indeed, and has been until yesterday. He took the most active interest in our American discoveries and inventions – steam, electricity and so forth. I have rarely met anyone so eager to learn. Even at this moment I have saved him from his enemy. It is the black, bitter ingratitude of his conduct that wounds me most.'

'How have you saved him from his enemy?'

'I have warned him in season and out of season against M'Qob, a black-hearted Papist who was constantly plotting treacheries. It was I that ran the guns into the country so that he might defend himself adequately against him. And now, for some utterly incomprehensible reason, he has become leagued with that arch-ruffian.'

It did not escape the impromptu judge that Mwala appeared to be under the influence of some subdued emotion of a not unpleasant kind.

'Mr Rose, is it not against the law to run guns?' asked Iff.

'I must admit that it is so,' said Rose, 'that is, under ordinary circumstances. But here was my convert, my patron, my friend, and all his people in utmost peril. Could I have done otherwise?'

'Where did you get the guns from?'

'From Springfield.'

'It must have taken rather long to execute the order. You must have had moments of great anxiety. Surely it would have been quicker to have asked for the white garrison.'

'They would not have believed us,' answered Rose. 'You know what colonial officials are. We had nothing on M'Qob, either; it was merely my knowledge of the human heart, too terribly justified by the event.'

'Were these guns then a gift to the king?'

'I am a poor sergeant of the Lord; I was obliged to receive payment.'

'At a fair profit, I presume?'

'You may say, considering the risk, hardly a fair profit.'

Simon Iff had seen gun-trading in his time, gold weighed grain for grain against steel, gunpowder, brass, lead and nickel.

'Thank you, Mr Rose. You should go to the house for treatment. Call—'

But he was interrupted by the arrival of a swift litter borne by six sweating runners. It contained no less a person than M'Qob himself, followed by a small chubby person in a cassock and a broad black hat, whose eyes beamed eagerly.

'Are we in time?' he cried.

'You are,' said Iff, 'you are. Very much in time. Call Father – I haven't your name, sir.'

'I am Father Duval.'

'Call Father Duval. Swear Father Duval!'

'I don't understand,' said the priest.

'You will.'

Mwala and M'Qob had striven to outdo each other in cordiality.

'Your name?' said Iff.

'Abelard Cesar Duval.'

'Your business?'

'I am a priest.'

'You live in the country of M'Qob?'

'I do.'

'Do you know the Rev. Moses Rose?'

'I do.'

'Are you on friendly terms with him?'

'I have come here today to save his life; the moment I heard of this atrocity, I commanded M'Qob in the name of the Holy Church to add his great influence to my weak protests.'

'I must beg you to answer my question.'

'I am not personally well acquainted with Mr Rose.'

'No, then?' A pause.

'No.'

'You disagree with him on many points?'

'Naturally.'

'He is a heretic, of course?'

'He is in error, as I believe.'

'About practical policy here now. Do you differ with him about that'

'Really, the divergencies are – well, are not divergencies natural to all men? Please may I ask what this is all about?'

Simon explained.

'But it is impossible!'

'Only if we prejudice the case,' said Simon. 'Let us imagine it a purely abstract matter for the present. You delay, but do not divert, the purpose of my questions. Why did Mwala and M'Qob do this thing to Mr Rose?'

The priest paled.

'My evidence would be but hearsay, and it is under the seal of confession.'

'Thank you, Father Duval. Call King M'Qob.'

But this was not easy. Father Duval passionately objected to the course of procedure. M'Qob refused point-blank to answer anything.

'It really doesn't matter,' said Simon wearily. 'I have other witnesses of truth.'

'Mr Judge,' implored the little priest, 'I beg of you not to continue this travesty of justice.'

'I commit you for contempt!' snapped Simon. 'Tipstaff, take that man!'

The indignant Father was taken into custody by Lord Juventius, and handed over to two of Sexton's men. He bit his lip and remained silent.

'Before I call any more witnesses,' said Simon, 'I will explain the case. It is simple, because we have an absolutely unspeakable atrocity committed by people who evidently think themselves within their rights. That, as Bill here says, smells like magic. Compare the whole theory of the Bible. Now we have a very frank statement from Mr Rose, and (excuse me!) a very suspicious reticence from Father Duval. He comes running twenty miles to save Mr Rose, but he won't open his mouth to do it when he gets here. Why? He finds the situation changed; he finds Magick, the one worthy rival of the Church, in the seat of judgment. No doubt that must be it.'

A scarcely veiled sarcasm mellowed his tone.

'To proceed. The two kings are equally loath to testify. They stand upon their right of life and death. Delightfully antiquated of them! However, the motive is evident. M'Qob has heard that Mr Rose has warned Mwala against him, and makes it a condition of peace that Rose is offered as the sacrifice. A little strange, in either Protestant or Catholic. And infamous treachery and ingratitude on the part of Mwala. Shocking thing, sometimes, human nature! So, all's explained.'

Everyone but Mwala seemed decidedly relieved.

'But,' the magician continued, 'we must be careful not to generalise on insufficient data. Call Billiken! Swear Billiken!'

The girl refused any ordinary oath. 'My father was a hunter, and my man is a hunter,' she said, with an extraordinary grin. 'I must swear upon two rifles.'

They yielded to her whim. But two ordinary rifles would not do; one must come from one side and one from the other. So one of M'Qob's men and one of Mwala's obliged. Having been duly sworn, she refused to testify. 'I have already told everything,' she said with an impudent grin.

Mwala and M'Qob conferred together in agitation. Father Duval kept his lips firmly set in silence.

'The whole method of science,' said Iff, 'consists in putting two similar things together, and two dissimilar things apart. We need an expert witness. Call the Honourable Charles Sexton! Swear the Honourable Charles Sexton!'

The witness claimed to be an amateur explorer, hunter and collector.

'You are familiar with firearms of all sorts?'

'I am. I have actually worked in a factory, so as to be able to repair my own guns in case of accident; I was also in the Ordnance when I served in the army'

'What are the principal differences between these two rifles?' Iff caused them to be handed to him. The witness grinned, and was most sternly rebuked.

'My lord,' said the hunter, 'there is only one difference: this rifle is numbered F31876, and this one F32124.'

'Thank you, Mr Sexton; that will do. Bring Mr Rose back; he must hear the rest.'

By this time Mwala was itching to make a bolt for it. His dignity, and perhaps his sense of Fate, kept him statue-steady.

'King Mwala,' said Simon sternly, 'there is no justice without Truth. It is useless moreover to seek to hide from me what I already know; what everyone here, even Mr Rose, knows, unless there be some imbecile among us. And Bill, who only smells things! I tell you, King Mwala, that it is even bad policy, though you think otherwise so strongly – no doubt the cause of your stubbornness – to stick to this stupid story of the peace-sacrifice. Unless you speak, I break this feather here and now!'

The king rose violently, as if with some gigantic determination. He caught up the two rifles, and thrust them out over the head of the Baptist missionary.

'Father of Justice,' said the king solemnly, 'I said peace-sacrifice, and spake no lie. Three years ago M'Qob and I were brothers. Then came this Rose, and warned me secretly against M'Qob, and sold me guns, and at the same time warned my brother against me, and sold him guns. These guns came in the same consignment from America; three hundred and a score of my children, four hundred and two score of my brothers, are dead. To have a lasting peace, one must do justice on the maker of the war.'

He stopped dramatically.

'Mr Rose,' said Simon Iff, 'what have you to say to this?'

Not speech but inarticulate shrieks, bestrewn with hideous blasphemies, obscene curses, answered him. The missionary, in abject bodily pain, and utmost horror of soul, sounded every abyss of hell in a few minutes. Exhaustion silenced him at last.

'Your majesty,' said the magician solemnly. 'I restore to you your Justice.' And he replaced the feather in the king's headdress. Mwala signed to his man, who caught up the litter and began to carry it toward the river. He and M'Qob saluted the little party of whites, and walked together in the same path.

No sooner was Mwala's back turned than Father Duval cried out. 'You're judge no more, and Mwala isn't here. Let me go!'

'I purge you of contempt,' smiled Simon, 'and I wish you luck. But remember that you're a wicked Papist, worse than an idolater, in the eyes of Mr Rose, whose pupil is a strict Baptist, very severe in his morals, though I'm glad to say he keeps to native ideas of Justice. You've no influence with Mwala; Rose saw to that. The wicked are fallen into the pit that they themselves digged.'

'Mr Iff, I beg you to believe that I have long known that man for a bitter enemy of myself, nay, of God and of Man also. But I am responsible for the situation; I discovered what was being done, and I felt bound to bring about a peace. But I am going to force Mwala at the pistol's point to let him go; and I shall offer to take his place.'

'You are really the most immoral person I have ever met. It's awfully sweet of you, and all that, but you never had a pistol in your life; and if Mwala accepted your offer, well, really now?'

Simon Iff was quite pathetic; his speech had failed him. There was a great gulf fixed between the points of view.

'You mean, what good would it do? That a good man, as perhaps you ignorantly think me, should die to save a bad one? I can only call your remembrance to history.'

'My dear sir, I have yet to see what good that did, especially as I don't think it ever happened. But without the Resurrection, the Death is wicked, as Paul showed; and with it, the Death is a farce.'

'But the ensample! the ensample!' pleaded the little priest.

'Is a bad one. I admit it's made you a hero, but only because you are a better man than you are a theologian, and a stricter theologian than you are a moralist. I'm not sure that I ought not to detain you on a charge of attempted suicide. But, as you justly urge, I'm judge no more; so let me shake your hand, if I be worthy, and bid you Godspeed on your noble, bootless and unethical errand.'

The priest wrung Simon's hand in silence.

'It's most annoying' said Mr Naylor. 'I had counted confidently on Mr Rose to buy at least twenty pounds' worth of goods.'

THE HAUNTED SEA-CAPTAIN

1

The sixteen thousand tons of the triple-screw liner *Urquhart Castle* churned smooth-sliding seas with groaning monotony. She was over three hours out from Durban, bound for Colombo. Lord Juventius Mellor had been pulled down considerably by fever during his adventurous trip across Africa with Simon Iff, and the old man had thought that a long sea voyage and a month or two in the beautiful climate of Kandy would be the best treatment. Camilla Craig, the vaudeville headliner, had adopted the boy for her 'steady.'

The weather was abominably sticky, and in the recess of the magician's deck-chair stood an immense tumbler full of dry martini which he was sucking blissfully through a straw. In the chair on his right was Captain McVea, a genial salt at sixty, who bore the highest sort of reputation for all seaman-like qualities in the line on which he had commanded ships for over thirty years, with hardly a mishap so serious as to fail to reach port on schedule time. He had had his adventures, though, and at this moment was recounting one of the liveliest of them to an amused group of passengers.

This was by no means his first voyage with Simon Iff; the magician had travelled on his ships more than once. He liked the quiet, steady, capable, even-tempered seaman.

The captain had the great faculty of carrying his hearers to the scenes of his adventures; and the little gathering was watching a munition ship ablaze in Toulon Harbour when they were recalled to reality by a steward who entered the group with an envelope in his hand.

'Beg pardon, Captain,' he said. 'Wireless – personal.'

'Excuse me a moment, gentlemen,' said the captain, breaking off his story. He tore open the envelope and took out the slip. His jaw suddenly dropped; he rose to his feet; the paper dropped from his hands; he fell forward stricken by apoplexy. Fortunately, the ship's surgeon was a member of the party. The sick man was carried to his cabin, and the passengers were left to recover from their consternation as best they might. In presence of the terrific suddenness of the event, all were subdued but one man who, with more curiosity than delicacy, picked up the radiogram. His amazement was pathetic to witness.

'I say, you fellows,' he stammered. 'I don't get this at all. Listen to this; it's sent from Durban, and it isn't signed, and all it says is "A pleasant voyage to you!"'

Simon Iff rubbed his hands briskly together. 'Jolly, oh very jolly!' he chirped. 'And I was looking forward to a dull evening.'

Just at this moment the surgeon rejoined the group. 'He'll get over it all right, bar accident,' reported he. 'But he can't speak or write at present, and at the same time he is horribly afraid of something. He seems to want something done, as far as I can make out, but there's no way of getting at what it is.'

'That's as may be,' said Simon Iff. 'The first thing to do is to find out the events which have led up to this from the data at our disposal.'

'We don't seem to have any,' said the man who had read the radiogram.

'Oh dear me, yes,' said Simon Iff. 'This is a most illuminating document.'

'It doesn't seem to be anything much,' complained the surgeon, examining the slip.

'It isn't so much what it is,' said Simon Iff, 'as what it isn't. And as for its conventionality, the captain was disturbed emotionally in reading it. The apoplexy was but the physical echo of the mental thunderstorm. There is therefore no question of coincidence. The message meant something to the captain that it doesn't mean to us – at present.'

'Some sort of code message,' suggested the surgeon.

'Not so fast, my friend. We know something about the message before reading it at all. A message which can cause apoplexy means bad news. Either something has happened of a disastrous character, or something has become liable to happen. Now glance for a moment at the sender. He does not need to sign his name. He knows that the captain will understand the message.'

'That is, it is a code,' insisted the surgeon obstinately.

'By code,' said Simon Iff very soberly, 'we mean a prearranged system of communication between two or more people, who are at least on sufficiently good terms to arrange that system. This is no ordinary code of transpositions or ciphers or anything of the kind. The captain got its meaning at a glance.'

'Then,' said the surgeon, 'it becomes more a signal than a code.'

'That is a little better,' replied the magician. 'We can imagine that the captain, before leaving Durban, had arranged with someone to report on some occurrence, and communicate in these terms if the worst had happened. But I will ask you to consider what this theory implies. There is surely something sinister about a communication which requires such fantastically guarded secrecy as a signal couched in such conventional terms. Why not employ a single noncommittal word? The captain is on his own ship. There is no one to suspect anything wrong. Observe, gentlemen, we are already getting the idea of something wrong – morally and perhaps legally wrong; it is involved in our present theory. Another point is that if this were a prearranged signal, the captain must have contemplated the possibility of the occurrence which threw him into apoplexy. In such circumstances, he must surely have been in a state of extreme anxiety. We all saw him at dinner and since then. I think we may all agree that, if he was anxious, he must be a wonderful actor. He might have mastered himself; but I think we should have seen some touch of tremor, or hurry, or something of the sort, when he took the radiogram. I am sure that we did not; but I thought I noticed a very mild surprise when the steward said "personal," as if he were thinking, "Now who the deuce can that be?" Besides all that, if he had been expecting it, as he must have done if he were to understand it, he would surely have been steeled against the shock of the news. I think that we are therefore compelled to assume that our whole theory is wrong, and that this is the last message in the world that he expected.

'There remains, however, this possibility: that our signal was agreed upon a long time ago, and that the captain had forgotten the whole affair; had assumed that the issue had been closed. We have still, however, the difficulties suggested by the character of the message. We have to assume that McVea had almost conspiratorial relations with somebody at one time; and the whole of his career and character makes this unlikely. Now what can have happened in Durban? What, for the matter of that, can have happened anywhere? Captain McVea has spent his life on the sea; he has been a widower for twenty years and has no children; his fortune is safely tucked away in government bonds; his only love-affair is his ship; he is not mixed in politics or intrigues of any kind; he is one of the simplest men I ever met. It is difficult to conceive of anything that would upset him unless it were a threat. He might have left a sample of blood with the doctor at Durban, and the germ of sleeping-sickness or something pleasant have been found in it; but a physician would hardly communicate such intelligence in such ironic terms. Note how I have been compelled to bring in the word ironic. Irony is implicit in this message – I ought perhaps to have said so much at the start.

'Now already we know something more about the sender. He is not trying to break bad news gently – he is rubbing it in; in short, we have an enemy. How then does it happen that the enemy has no need to sign his name? How is he sure that McVea will understand his irony? Observe McVea's instant comprehension of the message. Words so conventional might come from anybody and mean what they say; yet the captain has no doubt whatever. We can, of course, imagine, since this is our evening for imagining, that the sender of the radiogram had at one time been a friend, and at that time arranged and so forth, as we hypothesised before; but that still involves the idea of conspiracy, and fails to explain the irony. I think we must put that hypothesis in the locker.

'Consider once more the character of the message. We have now decided that it was not a signal. I can only think of one other thing that it could be, and that is: an allusion. Those particular words must have some terrible association for the captain. Yet he must have heard those words thousands of times in the last quarter-century and more that he has sailed these seas, and he has not been having apoplectic fits on each occasion.

> It wasn't the words
> That frightened the birds
> But the 'orrible double ongtong.

Anybody writing a straight message would have added a signature unless it had been some romantic girl; and if so, why the apoplexy?'

Lord Juventius cleared his throat. Simon's glance flung a dagger, and he subsided.

'No, it's clear that McVea was not expecting anything of the sort, that it dug up something hidden very deeply in his life.

'Now, how could he be sure that an anonymous communication of this harmless appearance was in reality some shocking threat to life and honour? Only because he knew just what we don't know – the nature of the allusion. The message must be from some person or group of persons to whom these words mean something terrible. One can imagine secret societies in which they were the valediction to a traitor – a warning that he had been found out, and that they meant to execute him. But again this does not fit in at all with what we know of the captain's character. He never had fantastic notions – he has never been mixed up with anything shady. For the purposes of the argument, we are compelled to assume that McVea is a good man, and his enemy a bad one. Considering the effect of the message, its innocence becomes positively devilish. Now a man who commands a great ship has to be absolutely stainless, financially and in every other way. He is liable to make bitter enemies – to incur deadly hatred. A brave man, however, takes all this in the day's work.

'You will observe, moreover, that the message came from the port we have just left. One cannot imagine the message as meaning much more than that his enemy is in Durban. He has plenty of time to take precautions, one would think. But would one, if one thinks more deeply? From his anxiety to speak, to get something done, as Mr Eliot here reports, one could seem to suspect some danger imminent. It suggests that the captain is inextricably in the toils. This radiogram reads "malice and revenge triumphant." The man in Durban, rightly or wrongly, is sure that he has turned the trick, and cannot refrain from torturing his enemy with anticipation of disaster. But then again, what does the message say? We have eliminated the theory of collusion. It means this: There is a man who hates McVea. McVea knows this man and fears him. There is a passage in their lives when these particular words possessed so fearful a significance that their mere quotation is sufficient to identify the sender to McVea. What then is the information conveyed? McVea must have thought his enemy incapable of harm – he must have thought that he was dead or in prison. On no other hypothesis can we explain the shock. If he had been in prison, the captain would have been able to calculate when he would be at liberty, unless he had broken prison, which doesn't happen as often as one might suppose from reading story-books. Besides, if he had broken prison, McVea's course would have been quite simple: a wireless to the Durban police, describing the man, would stop his game. I think that we must conclude that the captain supposed him to be dead.

'You have all heard of the professor who could reconstruct an extinct animal from a single bone, and you may think that these deductions are rather tenuous; but, after all, the professor used to be right. We are then encouraged to go on a little more deeply into the significance of this message. Its sender is no ordinary man. He is a person big enough to make McVea afraid of him, and McVea is no chicken. We have a man of great intelligence. This impression is confirmed by the subtle simplicity of his method of declaring himself. Imagine him in Durban composing his message. He says to himself "I have a thousand ways of letting that swine know that I'm alive and on the job; how shall I put it so as to fix my fangs most deeply?" He decides to use nothing but this terrible allusion, these words which were a climax in the past. We have no means of knowing what these events were, save that they must have been such that the formula was burnt deeply into the captain's brain.

'One step further. We know that criminals, otherwise astute, often give themselves away through vanity, as in the case of the Gunpowder Plot – a weakness to warn some friend discloses a conspiracy; or, for one reason or another, the mischief-maker wants his victim to know what is going to happen to him, and who is behind it. But would a man of such subtlety as we have deduced share in such a weakness? How could he be absolutely certain that his blow would go home? He is apparently giving his victim every chance to take precautions. This consideration leads us to wonder whether the man is in Durban after all. He might have an accomplice on this ship. But would not that rather be inviting McVea to look around for an accomplice? Also, I don't particularly see this man trusting other people. One can have associations of people who are technically criminals, if they are banded together for what they deem a cause more sacred than law; but the real criminal is a lone wolf.

'I do not think this idea of an accomplice is in character. Suppose that he has bribed someone on this ship to kill the captain; his warning risks his success. It seems to me much more likely that he should leave a false trail. Nothing easier or less suspicious than to leave his message with a friend, an office-boy, for the matter of that, with instructions to dispatch it at a certain time. This would both frighten McVea, and put him off his guard. The first place that McVea would by no means look for him would be on board the boat. The idea naturally crossed my mind that this chap might be an anarchist who had planted an infernal machine on the boat, and timed it to explode shortly after the captain got the message.'

The company, who up till now had been partly interested and partly bored by this elaborate gossamer of thought, began to feel extremely uncomfortable. Iff hastened to reassure them.

'I am not very much afraid of this,' he said, 'because the explosion has not yet happened. He could not have foreseen the apoplexy, and obviously McVea's first act would have been to report all particulars to Durban. Besides, this man isn't an anarchist. Anarchists are earnest, God-fearing people with no sense of humour, and we have already decided that this chap is as intellectual and malicious as Goethe's conception of the

Devil. We have now established a very strong probability that he is on this boat. Question is "Where?"'

'We can eliminate the crew and the steerage,' said Lord Juventius Mellor, 'they are all good chaps. All the intellectual people are in the Second Class, and all the malicious ones in the First.'

'This is not a joke,' said Simon severely. 'The conclusion of your argument would be that no maliciously intellectual person could travel by sea at all. But I think that we should look for him in the saloon. He would have the run of the boat, and so easier access to the captain. Besides this, he would be less severely scrutinised. We must remark, however, that in coming aboard at all, he exposes himself to the risk of recognition by the captain. His personality and appearance must be branded deeply on our friend's mind, else how could so simple a message produce so tragic a result? We are therefore certain that he regards his disguise as impenetrable. It has already appeared that the allusion in the message must be to something in the past. This makes it look as though that past were somewhat remote. But we cannot content ourselves with this. We all know how, on meeting a man, perhaps hardly more than a casual acquaintance whom one has not seen for more than twenty years, there is, if not an immediate recognition, a puzzled feeling: "I know that face; I've seen that man somewhere." Sea-captains, with their keen eyes, don't miss much; certainly not a man like McVea, who has always been particularly smart in dealing with men. Is there anyone among the passengers who was changed so as to be utterly unrecognisable? The marks of such a change would be evident. They would amount to total disfigurement. In other words, we have arrived at a complete impossibility.

'It seems as if we were thrown back upon the idea of an accomplice – a person unknown to the captain – but we have already seen serious objections to this suggestion. The way out leads us into a yet more formidable darkness. This message becomes more terrible yet, if we suppose it to be sent by a person absolutely convinced that he is safe. Perhaps that person is dead after all, or at least neither in Durban, where the police could deal with him, nor on the ship, where we could deal with him. I seem to have come to the idea of a legacy of vengeance. We have the painful incident connected with the wording of the message. We see that the man concerned is dead or perhaps in prison, but he has arranged for somebody to execute his mission of revenge. This somebody is taking a long chance. We are not living in the days of the Venetian Oligarchy. Men do not execute the vengeance of others unless they are passionately moved by love for the wronged person, or incited by the hope of gain. It is possible that a man could command wealth from a grave or a jail, and though his hireling would be unlikely to think of the device of the radiogram, the sending of it might have been stipulated. But one could hardly arrange for this in a will, and if the original man is in jail, why should he trust his accomplice so deeply? The man would have every inducement and opportunity to double-cross him. Number 2 must therefore be honestly devoted to Number 1.

'Here is another impossibility. We have a satanically intellectual person risking his life, in all probability, to commit a crime with a motive of sublime love and self-abnegation! From this we arrive at the conclusion that whatever Number 1 thinks or thought, Number 2 believes that Number 1 has been infamously wronged by Captain McVea. We know something else about Number 2 – he is quite young; an older man does not act in so quixotic a fashion on behalf of another. We cannot suppose him to have been on the job for very long. This ship is the best-known of all the common objects of this part of the sea-shore. There would be no object in delaying to throw a scare into the captain.

'Now, how far have we got? We have a very young, enthusiastic person, with a passionate love of an apparently wronged person, and an almost insanely chivalrous attitude. But of course you will object that we have here another impossibility. I have spoke of an infamous wrong – nothing less would justify the action even of Number 1, still less of Number 2. Now since the radiogram had to be intelligible to the captain, he must know well what that wrong was, and he must fear revenge. But on the other hand, we who know him know that he is not at all the man to wrong anyone, even in the most trifling manner. Whatever the events were that are associated, in the minds of these people, with the words of the radiogram, we are bound to think that McVea's share in them was justified in his own eyes, and misinterpreted by Number 1. The captain, however, certainly knew that Number 1 had so misinterpreted that action, but he was unable to clear the matter up because the man was either dead, or thought by him to be so.

'I have made these remarks in public, not without apprehension that I may have bordered on indiscretion; but, generally speaking, it is safe to look for truth. And the conclusion has justified me. When I saw how my analysis was turning, I began to hope that Number 2 might be within hearing of my voice – he would want to be where he could watch the effect of the receipt of the radiogram. And in this sheltered portion of the deck we are not visible to anyone outside our little circle of a dozen persons. I will therefore ask Number 2 to talk to me privately before he proceeds with what I make no doubt to be his very admirable plan.'

The men looked at each other, wondering. The younger members of the party became exceedingly self-conscious.

'I think,' said Simon Iff, finishing his drink, 'that I will go and see the captain while you think it over. Perhaps he may be able to speak by now. Shall we run along and see, Doc?'

He took the surgeon's arm and they walked away, leaving the crowd in a very curious state of mind.

'I should really tell him,' lisped Lord Juventius Mellor. 'I know it will save an awful lot of trouble.'

Camilla Craig rearranged the pillows under his head, and stole a sly kiss in the shadows.

2

Except in German universities, it is held to be a decided disadvantage to a theory if it will not work. Nobody replied to Simon Iff's advertisement. The matter was quietly dropped. The captain had completely recovered, but it was understood that he did not care even for expressions of sympathy.

'He had recovered his speech, when we got there the other night,' said Simon Iff to his pupil, 'but all he would say was that there was no danger to the ship. His silence confirmed my general view. There is something in the past which the captain supposed closed forever; something whose revelation means tragedy for him. I cannot believe that he is to blame, and yet I'm sure that Number 2 at least would acquiesce in Bacon's definition of revenge as "wild justice."'

'Do you still think that Number 2 is on the ship?' asked the boy.

'The alternative is that he is waiting for us at Colombo, but I think he is on board, and if so, we need not look for violence. I am beginning to think of Number 2 as in some way or other legitimately armed. He does not fear the consequences of his act, whatever act he may have in contemplation. He may be a person absolutely wedded to his fixed idea. His subtlety may be a lunatic's cunning, but I don't think so. McVea knows something of my reputation. If it were possible to avert the fall of the axe, he would have asked me to help him. But he keeps silence – he does his duty like a haunted man. One can see that he is sinking under the anticipation of the blow. It is "the one thing as certain as death." That alone makes me certain that Number 2 does not propose to do anything illegal. Even a *camorra* cannot carry out every assassination with the punctuality of an omnibus service.'

The conversation was interrupted by Camilla Craig, who wanted Lord Juventius to play at the ship's concert and Simon Iff to tell one of his stories.

'I think not,' said Simon Iff. 'I know better than to challenge a supreme artist in the line which has made her famous throughout the world. What are you going to do, my dear?'

'I think I will try out a dramatic monologue,' said the girl. 'I haven't told it before – I should like to see how it goes.'

'Try it on the dog,' said Simon. 'You know we are bound to applaud, especially when every cheer means an extra sovereign for the Seamen's Home. I am really very anxious for that concert. Your devotion to Juventius has driven me to Pirate Bridge.'

'Well, it's not long till tomorrow night,' smiled Camilla, 'and twenty-four hours after that you will be eating curry at the Grand Oriental.'

'I wish I could do something to help that poor old boy,' said Simon, when she had gone. 'If he would talk – well, all things are possible – but I am certain that he doesn't deserve what's coming to him. I see only one chance. If I were present when the blow was struck, I might be able to parry it. Who knows – who knows?'

The following night, the saloon of the *Urquhart Castle* was crowded. By special request, the Second Class passengers had been invited to the concert. The purser was in his glory. Hardly anyone noticed how weak and ill the captain was as he sat in his chair on the platform, but people with a little psychology could read him easily: a simple, desperate man, knowing himself doomed, and determined to do his duty to the end. The concert went off more pleasantly than such functions usually do. Everyone acquiesced in the general mediocrity, content to wait for the treat in store for them, when Camilla Craig, with her red hair ravishingly emphasised by a frock of rich soft blue, would do her turn.

'I am going to tell you a story,' she began, and her inimitable smile flashed round the crowded saloon. 'It is called "The End of the Voyage." Once upon a time—'

Simon Iff suddenly stood up.

'We have with us tonight,' cried Camilla, 'a very distinguished gentleman who very wisely observed on the night that we left Durban that, as a general rule, it was safe to look for truth. I crave that gentleman's indulgence for my little fiction.'

Lord Juventius Mellor looked very swiftly at Simon Iff. Camilla's mouth had shut like a trap. The boy seemed to understand that a duel had been in progress; and he was amazed to see that his master, having tried to cover his movement by pretending to adjust his trousers, sat down again and folded his arms. Camilla's smile was radiant as sunrise on soft snowy mountains.

'Once upon a time,' she began again, 'it was just three and twenty years ago, a wealthy lawyer whom I will call James Smith, finding himself threatened with consumption, had gone to an island in the South Seas, which I will call Friendly Island.'

The audience shuddered. An incredibly bitter sneer was in the tone with which she pronounced 'friendly.'

'James Smith was accompanied by his wife and their infant daughter. Friendly Island is an earthly Paradise; only two or three Europeans live there, in the regular way. I do not mean that this circumstance alone would constitute a paradise. There was the inevitable missionary; there was a romantic German who sold stores; there was a rascally pearler who was always getting drunk and raising trouble; and besides James Smith, there was another stranger whom I will call William Brown. He had the appearance of a seafaring man, had William Brown. He was a man of good breeding, manners and education, and he was undeniably handsome. He had arrived there about six weeks after Smith had settled down. He had come from the port of the neighbouring island where steamers occasionally put in, in a small fishing boat, a boat with a big square sail easily handled by one man.

'Smith and Brown became the greatest friends possible. The lawyer was passionately fond of fishing, and would often go out in Brown's boat to an island some four hours' sail distant where were tall crags, within whose shadow lay a pool which enjoyed a tremendous reputation for big fish.

'Lawyer though he was, he had not lost faith in humanity. He never guessed that Brown would soil honour and betray friendship. It happened that Mrs Smith was a true woman. She told Brown to cease his insults, but she was too good a woman for this world. She ought to have warned her husband, and she did not.

'Brown pretended to acquiesce in the situation, but the Devil had entered into him. His guilty passion decided him to override all obstacles. Smith was in his way – then Smith must go. Most of us who sail these seas believe that there is something in the sun's heat which tends to intoxicate the passions. It is as if the brain boiled into madness. When Brown finally decided to put Smith out of the way, he was not content to choose a simple accident. He resolved upon a death by torture.

'One night, it had been arranged that Smith should sail over to the little island for the fishing. Starting at midnight, he would arrive comfortably at dawn, catch his fish, and be back in time for dinner. Mrs Smith had retired early to bed that night with a slight touch of fever. But Brown took his friend' (again the sneer rang out) 'to the boat. He pushed it off from the little wharf, waved his hand cheerfully to Smith and cried, "A pleasant voyage to you!"'

The audience sat as if hypnotised. Not one but was too appalled even to shudder.

'Drowsing at the helm, Smith sailed past a long, low key of coral, which extends some two miles eastward from the island. It lies almost flush with the water. It has neither a hut nor a tree, but it serves to break the freshness of the trade winds. Smith was hardly beyond the point, about two miles from shore, when he was awakened from his pleasant lethargy by the sudden fall of the mainsail. He jumped up, amazed, for the rope was nearly new. An examination revealed something absolutely astounding. The main haul had been treated with sulphuric acid – the stain was on Smith's fingers. I suppose he thought this was Brown's idea of a joke. He looked for the oars. They had been taken out of the boat. There was absolutely nothing for him to do but wait for rescue. It never entered his mind that this was a plot against his life. The sun came up; it began to be very hot – not a breath stirred. He began to be thirsty. He went to the locker for water – the bottles had been filled from the sea!

'"This is beyond a joke," he cried angrily to the unsympathetic universe. And then he laughed. There was a melon in the locker. He cut it open. A bright blue liquid flowed – copper sulphate! The melon was uneatable! An hour or two later, what with bewilderment, anxiety and torture, he began to wander in his mind. He had made endless efforts to rehoist the sail by cutting away the rotten part of the rope, but he was a poor hand at climbing, and he was not strong enough to take down the mast and fix the sail. Ultimately he drove a spike into the mast as high as he could reach and fixed the boom to it, so that he was able to get a little way on the boat. Of course he headed her for the nearest shore visible. But the breeze was very light, and he made poor progress. The heat of the sun was intense and his thirst maddening. In vain he scanned the sea for any sail.

'Then he discovered that smoke was rising from the forehatch. He hastened to investigate the cause. Again sulphuric acid! Three carboys had been placed upside down and stoppered with some material that would resist the action of the acid for a number of hours. The time had expired – the bottom of the boat was awash with vitriol, and the fumes began to choke him. He knew that to throw water upon it would only quicken the action of the acid. It was only a question of time, and a short time at that, before the sea rushed in. Swimming was out of the question – too many sharks. He might conceivably construct a raft, but that was not a very simple job for a lawyer, single-handed, with he knew not how few minutes to spare.

'As God willed it, however,' (Camilla's voice grew very solemn) 'he was not to die that day. Out of His treasury, the Great Father let forth a squall, a little local squall scudding across a tiny strip of ocean. It struck the sinking boat, lifted her almost out of the water, drove her furiously toward the key. She was not two hundred yards from land when she sank under his feet. He had seen his chance, and thrown off his clothes. He never knew how he did it, but he reached the shore. The squall had passed – he lay there naked in the blazing sun, a raving lunatic. Night calmed him. He began to crawl over the razor edges of the coral towards the village. He probably fainted from loss of blood, for the coral cut him cruelly. He said afterwards that he thought his mental and physical agony had made him dance in madness. He passed a second day upon the key – a shadeless day, a day of blazing torture – a day without water. But by dawn on the third day, he had reached one of the paths about the village. There he was found by some of the natives. They did not recognise him. His face was scarred by coral, and twisted by agony. He himself did not know who he was, but his wife and his child knew him. There was no one to suspect anything beyond the most ordinary accident. Brown exhibited the proper sympathy, and even renewed his abominable intrigues. But Mrs Smith, with her man wounded, was a lioness. She may or may not have suspected something wrong, but however that may be she told Brown – in front of the other white men of the island – to get out and stay out, which he did. A month after that, Smith came to himself with full clear memory of every incident. One thought was uppermost in his mind: revenge upon the fiend! A lawyer's idea of revenge is not to stick a knife into someone when he isn't looking, and trust to luck to get away with it; a lawyer knows a trick worth two of that.

'Brown was a pretty well-known person – a capable and ambitious man, a man easy to find, a man without suspicion that he was being hunted – and he was a man moreover on whom the law could put its grip. Smith went to work in a perfectly clear-headed way. He found it easy enough to establish the proofs of guilt. He got sworn statements from the trader who had sold Brown the acid; the pearler had been on the wharf when Brown arranged the provisioning. Even the missionary was able to contribute a detail to the case. He had been pleading with Brown, begging him to change his manner of life, and the sailor had replied, "I'll come to Jesus when Ella comes to me" – Ella being the name of Mrs Smith. The missionary had replied that he understood perfectly that Brown's evil passions were in his way, and Brown had replied, "Hell, no! Smith's in the way – but it won't be for long."

'Armed with these weapons, Smith and his family went to London to begin the search. All this took over a year, for Smith's activities were interrupted by continually increasing ill-health. A shock more terrible than all was yet in store for the unhappy man. They had not been a month in London before Ella Smith disappeared! No trace of her was ever found, though of course Smith set every wheel in motion. One must not say so, since one does not know, but one can have little doubt that Brown found some means to kidnap her, or perhaps to make away with her. The shock completely wrecked the brain of the unhappy lawyer. Two days after his wife's disappearance, he had to be placed in a private asylum for the cure of the insane. His little daughter was left in the care of her father's unmarried sister.

'Three years of treatment restored Smith to health. He returned to his house, and his daughter, who by this time was old enough to understand things, heard from him the story of his wrongs. He had prepared a long and formidable statement, supported by the affidavits of his wife and of the other people on the island. "Yvonne," he said to her one day, "there is a spot in my brain not quite healed. I can forget everything but one thing, and that one thing is Brown's Judas smile and false words – 'A pleasant voyage to you!' I think he must remember them too. They sealed the triumph of his malice. Now I will burn them in his brain. I will not have him arrested – not just yet. I'm going to change my name, and travel. I shall send him a copy of this statement and these affidavits, so that he may know that I have got him by the short hair, and whenever I find him starting on a voyage, for he is a sea-captain, I shall telegraph to him these words, 'A pleasant voyage to you.' He will know from whom they come."

'This programme was duly carried out. Smith and his daughter travelled in many delightful places of the earth. He took great pains to have her well brought up; but he himself was the only real influence in her mind. Almost from infancy she had been fed by day and night with this tale of infamy and horror. She began to have a fixed idea about it – almost as strong as her father; and he, poor man, was slowly sinking into chronic madness. He developed ideas of persecution; he lived over again and again those hours of agony on the boat; his mind gradually became confused. In his last years, he even ranged his wife among his persecutors.'

'Ah,' cried Simon Iff on a high note, 'what did I tell you? Or, more accurately, what should I have told you if I had had a chance?'

Captain McVea immediately asserted his authority; though, if he were a king, it was surely in some hell unthinkable. 'I must request silence,' he said sharply and angrily.

Simon Iff shrugged his shoulders and subsided, murmuring something about an obstinate man doing himself no good.

'I beg your pardon for being interrupted,' said Camilla sweetly. 'It proves how much I have been boring you.'

In point of fact the audience had been breathless ever since she had first pronounced the words 'A pleasant voyage to you!'

'To continue my dull story,' she went on, 'Smith sank slowly from depth to depth of melancholia. He still put off the arrest of Captain Brown. His only pleasure was to gloat upon the agony which that scoundrel must be suffering. And then, quite suddenly, he died. His sister sent Yvonne to a convent to put her wise to all the tricks of life – a very necessary education for one who was intended for the stage.

'My story is nearly at an end. In the excitement of life, she forgot about Captain Brown; but she always carried with her the proofs of his guilt. Recently, the matter was recalled vividly to her mind. She found herself booked to travel by the ship which Brown commanded. After all, justice is justice. Here are the documents in the case,' she cried, throwing a packet on the table, 'and I will conclude by calling upon Detective Sergeant Green, of the Durban police, to arrest John McVea.'

The detective proceeded to perform his duty. Blank silence reigned in the audience. Then somebody, more imbecile than his fellows, jumped up and shouted, 'It's all a joke, boys; it's part of the dramatic monologue!'

The spell was broken. Everyone laughed, stamped, shouted and cheered. For though most people present knew that the captain's apoplexy was no joke – which the theory of a joke would involve – yet when somebody gave voice to an explanation which let everybody out, they followed the bell-wether.

'Silence, pray, gentlemen!' roared Simon Iff above the hurricane of the emotion. 'Of course we can't let the lady sit down without a hand, but I want to make one comment on the story. It is utterly false, documents or no documents. Captain McVea never did this. We all know him. One can imagine him sufficiently provoked to kill a man in a quarrel, provided that he knew himself to be in the right of it. But that he is what Miss Camilla paints him is unthinkable.'

Loud cries of 'Speech' came from all over the saloon.

'I implore you to say no more,' said the captain, raising his manacled hands in a pitiful gesture. 'Let the law take its course. I make no defence.'

'Nonsense,' said Simon. 'I am the next item on the programme, with Mr Mate's permission. Who ever heard of a concert – above all, one in aid of the Seamen's Home – coming to a stop merely because the chairman is held for attempted murder?'

If the imbecility of the bell-wether had been infectious, how much more the buoyancy of Simon Iff! A way to the platform was made for him, and he began to speak.

'I only want to put in a word or two of criticism,' he said, with a queer grim puckering of his lips. 'But I want to say this much – that although we have the facts of the story, detailed in affidavits, the psychology of the story is all hearsay. Miss Craig was not old enough to know what was really happening on the island. This is a purely *ex parte* statement prepared by the man who fancies himself injured.'

'Fancies!' cried Camilla indignantly. 'I lived with him for years. I saw the scars upon his body; I watched the cancer eat away his mind.'

'You give your case away, Miss Craig,' returned Iff, expostulating. 'You force us to remember that this statement was drawn up by a lawyer who was also a lunatic, with ideas of persecution. You remember that, towards the end, he —'

His speech was interrupted by a hubbub at one door of the saloon.

'All this must stop,' cried a harsh voice. 'It has gone on too long.'

It was the captain who sprang to action. 'Turn her out!' he cried.

But Simon Iff put his hand on the mate's shoulder. 'You're in command of this ship, Mr Mate,' he said, 'and I think that we ought to hear what this lady has to say.'

An old woman was walking towards the platform. Every neck was craned to look at her. No one present could have doubted the truth for a moment. Her hair was white, though it showed that it had once been as red as Camilla's. But enough remained of fierceness in the eyes, of voluptuousness in the mouth, and of arrogance in the nose, to declare them mother and daughter. Instinctively the room was hushed.

'My name,' she said, 'was Clare O'Grady. I remember very little of my early life. My first clear memories take me to New Orleans. I lived in the Red Light District. On my professional cards was printed "The Little Red Devil," with an obscenely-worded invitation. One night, a party landed from an English ship. Two of the men were hot in argument. The youngest of the party, a bigger fool than the rest of them, you may think, was defending the women of the District. "It isn't their fault," he shouted, "they aren't given a chance. I could take one of these women right here, and make a damn fine thing of her." The others immediately took him up. They dared him to make his word good. "By God, I will," he said, walking straight to my door.

'The first words he ever spoke to me were, "Will you marry me?" Of course I never thought he meant it, and I joked with him. "Will you?" he insisted. "Of course I would," I answered. "Come to my ship at eleven tomorrow morning," he said, "and we'll get married right away. You may want to buy yourself some things," and he pulled out a one-hundred-dollar bill, and put it in my hand. You could buy something for one-hundred dollars in those days!

'He went on his way. Of course, he was drunk – in the morning he would throw me off the ship. But I would go nevertheless. Suckers like that are not born every minute. Well, the next day we were married. There sits my husband, John McVea.

'But the Little Red Devil was devilish still. I delighted in making my husband's life a hell. I deceived him almost to his face. I made drunken scenes. I stole his money; I pledged his credit. I assaulted him. He remained absolutely imperturbable. The most he would say was that a good ship should weather most storms.

'At first I had liked his kindness. I tortured him, strange as it sounds, because I loved him. But my inability to conquer him turned into hate and fear. We had – we have a daughter.'

It was the last stroke to Camilla Craig. She went into violent hysterics, and had to be taken from the room. The old woman would have continued her story, but Simon Iff checked her.

'Pray wait till Miss McVea comes back,' he said. 'You must finish, since things have gone so far; but she must be the first to hear.'

The silence lent great impressiveness to the scene. Each mind was busy with a thousand speculations. When Camilla reappeared, it was as if the curtain had been raised upon some famous tragedy, for the first time unearthed. Mrs McVea, pale with suppressed emotion, went on with her story.

'We had a little daughter, and she bored me. I hated domestic life. I wanted constant change of scene and people. I wanted drink. I had plenty of money to spend; I could do what I liked, but the moral force of my husband cowed me. I was never quite comfortable when I had done wrong, and as that was every day, I became wretched. I wanted power – I ruined men as some rakes ruin women, not for love but for vanity – and my husband was the only man I could not move. Among my many intrigues, I had conquered a lawyer, named Johnson. He was a very wealthy man, and I knew that I was cleverer than he. I would collect an independent fortune, and enjoy myself. One day my husband came back from a voyage to find the house shut up. Johnson had no need to practise his profession – I insisted on his taking me all over the world. We landed up at last on the island of which my daughter has told you. It was there that things began to happen. My lover was passionately devoted to me, but he did not trust me. He wanted to keep a whip of money over me. He would not marry me; he would not settle anything on me. I was no better off than before.

'One day, I saw an ad in the overseas edition of *The Daily Mail.* It contained these words: "Little Red Devil, nothing to forgive, when you feel like it."

'I hated my husband as I have never hated anything. I knew how his life was bound up with the child. I had taken her away – *nothing to forgive*!! I would give him something to forgive if ever he crossed my path, and just then, well, it was not paths crossing. But he caught up. He had taken a year's leave, and somehow or other he had tracked us down. He made no advances to me – he treated me as though he had never seen me before. I understood that he was there to be my husband if I were tired of Johnson. To me his attitude was a persecution. I lay awake night after night thinking how I could break his spirit. I wanted to soil him. I thought I would put a crime upon him. It was I who tried to murder Johnson. The other

Europeans on the island were all crazy about me – my puppets. I meant to see my husband hanged. And then the plot went wrong – Johnson came back. I held my hand, but I told my husband that I would not have him on the island. I could not bear the situation. If only Johnson had had the sense to die! But he came back to reason. He had regained my favour. I could make him a hideous engine of revenge against my husband.

'But after years, the taste even of revenge grows dull. I had managed to embezzle, I suppose you would call it, various large sums from Johnson's estate during his incapacity. The missionary on the island had forged a marriage certificate for me. When I couldn't stand it any longer, I quit the game. With my money and my magnetism, I was a queen in Paris, Vienna and St. Petersburg. I went on the stage – I became the favourite of emperors.

'And then again, Nature had her revenge. So insatiable was my temperament that I wearied even of the wanton bounty of my life. I was at the time very intimate with the Mother Superior of a very fashionable nunnery – a woman of princely family and income, and the morals of Satan himself. The nights that I passed under her roof were literally heaven to my world-weary mind. I craved to join them, but it was no use. I could understand their austerities as a sort of perverse pleasure, but I simply could not believe the nonsense of their creed. I think I must have been a little mad. Remember, I was more famous then than my daughter is now, and with worse reason. Oh, I was sick of it! I wanted a new sensation. I tried drugs – I wore them out. I couldn't even acquire a habit. There was one sensation left for me – the one we're all sure of – Death. The Little Red Devil should be game to the finish. I would make a splash. I was to appear on Christmas Eve at the Ellis Theatre in London. I had the lead in a new play. When I took my call, I would kill myself in full view of the audience.

'The night came. During the performance of a play I've always made it a rule not to see people in the house. It disturbs one's thought. I came to take my call, to make my little speech – I had the pistol in my sleeve. I had prepared my speech – it was to end by telling the audience that this play was the crowning triumph of my life, that now I was quite sure that I had everything the world could offer, and that I hated it, and so... I intended to finish the sentence with a shot. When I came out before the footlights, I saw my husband sitting in the stalls. I hardly remember what happened in my mind. It was a remorseless logic so clear that my dull brain cannot pick up the threads, but I went on with my speech, and I ended it by pulling out the pistol, putting it to my forehead, and dropping it to the floor. "I will come home with you, John, if you will be round at the stage door in half an hour."

'A tumult of laughter and applause was the passing bell of my life.

'My husband received me as if nothing had happened. But about one week later he said, "I've been watching you, Little Red Devil, and what you need is work. Another month of this, and you would turn loose again." He made me stewardess on his ship, and I have never left him since. We never found the baby; Johnson had hidden her too well – until tonight.'

'The case,' said Simon Iff, 'is one which appears to me to present all the features of an early reconciliation. I suggest that that, at least, might take place out of court.'

4

Simon Iff, Psychoanalyst

PSYCHIC COMPENSATION

1

Miss Mollie Madison was dressed in a cream-coloured frock. It was decidedly daring with her emeralds and her blazing hair. But it satisfied the eye of Simon Iff, and that was the great point at issue.

For a terrible disaster had befallen him. His colleague, Captain Lascelles of the British Navy, had fallen sick, and there was nothing to be done in the way of regular work till he recovered. He had therefore the option of going into a trance, or of finding some amusement. The words 'Satan finds some mischief still for idle hands to do' had come into his mind, and he, taking this as an inspiration, and reflecting that no mischief could be so mischievous as Miss Mollie Madison, had asked her to come round.

'Tell me anything but the Old Old Story,' he exclaimed, 'I'm bored to tears; don't you know any old thing like that Pasquaney Puzzle?'

She went to fetch her vanity bag, and proceeded to extract a letter.

'Dolores wrote me this the other day,' she said, and began to read.

> 'Darling Mollie,
>
> I *must* just jot down this while I *think* of it. Dearest, *don't* *don't*, *don't* make any *mistake*. They're *all* alike. It *bores* them – you know what I mean – now *don't* be angry, because it's *true*. So *prepare* yourself, darling, for the *very worst*. What you must do is to work up all the *unsolved mysteries* in the papers – the real ones, of course – and if you ever see *signs*, bring one out, and *tide him over*.
>
> Your *loving* DOLORES'

'The infernal genius of this cat!' cried Simon. 'How dare you flaunt your very trickery in my face? I must be a lost soul.'

She shook her finger, the one with the great cabochon emerald, at him.

'Do you wonder we're not truthful, when you talk like that when we are?'

'I admit that when a man understands a woman, he tries to put an ocean or two between them. However, you had better "tide me over." *Qualis artifex pereo*!'

'Listen to the tale of A. B. Smith of Potter's Place, Massachusetts. Four years ago, June 23, 1907, at precisely eight o'clock on a Sunday evening, came the climax. One week earlier, A. B. Smith had reached the fifty-third year of his age. During all that period nothing had ever happened to him, or to his. His parents were farmers, decent people in moderate circumstances, his uncle an Episcopalian minister. Potter's Place is a cross-road, of no importance or interest to anybody beyond the local worthies. There is a railway station, where the less fortunate or skilful trains occasionally stop.

'A. B. Smith inherited his father's farm and his uncle's library. He had a good education in Boston, and took a mild interest in butterflies. He married Matilda, the only daughter of Farmer Jones across the valley, when he was twenty and she twenty-one. Their union was blessed by two children, a son William and a daughter Mary. The birth of Mary had been a serious risk for the mother; she lay ill for months. Two operations were necessary to save her life, and she was never her own woman again, but sank rapidly into age and infirmity.

'With advancing years A. B. Smith became a substantial man. He had no energy or ambition; he just drifted into prosperity with the rest of the country. He became more absorbed in reading and in entomology and, leaving the farm in William's very capable hands, built himself a house on the side of a hill, a mile from the next dwelling. It is situated on a grassy slope, with hardly any trees. It is a substantial building, but not very large; Mary and her mother tended it without assistance. They moved to this house in 1899.

'Wlliam, assisted by a capable manager, lived on in the old farmhouse. He was thirty years of age in 1907; Mary was a year younger. Neither of the children had any more imagination than the parents. They had not even fallen in love, though William was supposed to be "getting acquainted" with the inn-keeper's daughter. That is, he called on her most evenings, and said nothing particular. On Sundays, meeting his family at church, he would invariably return to the new house for dinner. He would pass the afternoon in relating the news of the week – for his father rarely left the garden, which he was very fond of tending in an amateur way – and after an evening collation, walk home to the farm to bed. In fine weather his family would walk part of the way with him.

'A. B. Smith had suffered slightly from rheumatism, and now and then (though by no means always) walked with a stick.

'On June 23, 1907, this placid ritual had reached the point where they were all leaving the house. The evening was fine, warm and windless. They left the door open behind them.

'A. B. Smith, walking on his daughter's arm behind his wife and son, was just thirty-two yards from the door when he said,

"I think I'll get my cane, Mame," and went back. The others waited. They saw him enter the house. He never came out again; from that day to this there has been absolutely no clue or trace of him of any kind.'

'Is that all?' said Simon, seeing her fold up the paper.

'That's all.'

'Very uninteresting. You don't tell me a single pertinent fact. Where was the stick he went to get, in the first place? What about other exits to the house, for the second? Then – oh, there are fifty points I want to know!'

'I don't know about the stick. I saw the house, though. There is only the one entrance; the back door merely leads to the wood-pile. It is a long one-story building, cut into the hillside for shelter. It would take a very fine climber to get up the perpendicular shale behind the house, and nobody could possibly do it unobserved. The family naturally enough had turned to watch at once for the father's return; the old lady called out only a minute or so after he had entered, impatient of delay, and she sent Mary to look almost immediately afterwards, as he did not reply. She could not have taken a minute to fail to find him, in that small house; and she came out with awe and wonder already upon her to raise the alarm, within five minutes – I feel sure – of his passing within the door. There is no question of any distraction of their attention; they were all looking at him from the very moment of his leaving them, and watching for his return. It was like a Vanishing Lady trick on the stage.'

'There is certainly very little to take hold of in the case. There are of course millions of other facts quite as unimportant as those you have told me, and any of these might supply the missing key. But, on the facts as you state them, the main line of our solution is quite obvious. Tell me some more, though.'

'We went through the old man's affairs very carefully. There was no change in the routine of his business, had not been for years. He had very few visitors, and these were casual gossips. Mary was a plain flat-chested colourless woman, and had never had an affair of any kind or an offer of marriage, though she was a good match, for the district. There had been no quarrel in the family, barring the usual petty jarrings and scoldings from which I suppose no family is free. After the event they settled down into a new routine, undisturbed at least up to last week when I put through an enquiry. You see, there's no incident to take hold of, no motive—'

'Ah, but that is just where you fall down, my fairy skater! Cities afford us few of these inexplicable crimes, so-called. In cities, people are always in touch with the external world, with "reality." They need money, or they desire something connected with others, and by finding out their circumstances we find out them. But in the country where "nothing ever happens" the individual is thrown back upon himself. He learns to live in the "imaginary" world created by his own "psyche." He discovers (in and through symbolic form) the realm of the unconscious, as Professor Jung calls it, and his actions are determined by fantastic motives based on hereditary peculiarities, or in the accidents, so-called, of his physical and psychical constitution. Thus – I am perfectly serious – a man might murder a perfectly inoffensive stranger because of something that happened, quite unknown to him, two thousand years ago. This world of the unconscious is so vast, so unexplored, that its laws are hardly guessed. The little that we have discovered is in great part not yet accepted. In fact, we who accept it at all are still quarrelling about many fundamental principles, and attract the scorn of the pedant. However, we are proving our case – such as it is – in the good old way of science, by our ability to predict the future. Our present purpose, though, seems to be to explain the past, which is nearly as useful, and I am sure that a dark tailor-made suit will be less conspicuous than that adorable cream frock – in Massachusetts.'

Miss Mollie Madison was used by this time to unexpected terminations to the psychoanalyst's little sermons; so she rose quietly, and, remarking that she would be back in an hour with her travelling bag, waved an airy farewell.

'Good,' nodded the mystic, 'and tell Dobson to be round with the Napier.'

2

Dobson was an English peasant from Simon Iff's place in Yorkshire. He possessed all the impenetrable stupidity of the type, with its equally impenetrable subtlety. He was one of those people who, after a course of being swindled for several months by a particularly smart and unscrupulous Jew, would leave his oppressor wondering at exactly what stage of the transaction he had lost all his money! Before the age of the motor he had been a groom, dealing a little in horses as a side-line; and what he had once done to some inhabitants of Aberdeen is not a safe topic in that city. In particular, he had the art of drawing people out by the simple process of pretending to fail to understand them. They felt they had to prove it to him. In about an hour's conversation, he would extract the story of his life from the most taciturn of mortals, and leave his victim with the impression that he had told nothing, and been neither comprehended nor believed. Simon Iff often used him to pump people with whom he himself could not be seen talking without arousing comment. He was also useful to his master when it was necessary to do something that looked like an accident. On this particular adventure, it was his clumsiness with the car that was to blame for the breakdown at Potter's Place, and the determination of Iff, as a surly old grouch calling himself Dr Hodgson, to spend the night at the inn. Miss Mollie Madison was well remembered by the local yokels, but that couldn't be helped, for Simon needed her as a link between topographical and historical knowledge. She asked with just the desired degree of disinterested interest if any more had been heard of A. B. Smith.

Nothing could have been more unsatisfactory. The disappearance had left no more effect of any kind than a natural death could have done. Mary and her mother had indeed left the house on the hill, and gone to live with William on his farm; also, there was a rumour that the new minister was 'getting acquainted' with Mary, and he being an impetuous youth from Chicago, it was thought that a marriage might result in six or seven years. William himself was to marry the innkeeper's daughter in the fall.

Mary's age being mentioned, Simon Iff ventured to remark that it was strange that she had not been married earlier. It appeared that she had 'never been of any account.' She was quite a regular girl in every way, only without personality. She had the 'old maid's' temperament, even as a child. She had never given any trouble, or taken active part in any other person's affairs. She was considered a comfort to her parents, obedient, careful and agreeable. She had been a capital scholar, and was clever at reciting Longfellow and Whittier. Her prudence was the most notable thing about her; and though without love-affairs of her own, the young men and maidens sometimes came for advice in their own perplexities. But the disappearance of her father might be called the first thing that had ever really happened to her.

William was her equivalent in terms of masculinity, but he was more popular than his sister. He had been a good deal in Boston; he was a 'mixer,' in a mild way. He had the name of swallowing more whisky and showing less of its effects than any man in Potter's Place. He had been soused properly once, long ago, a debauch which ended in a fight, and his shame had taught him to manage his liquor.

So much the inn-keeper was able to contribute to the problem before Miss Mollie Madison retired to her room. Simon Iff went to smoke his pipe along the street, and was joined at the corner by Dobson. The latter had picked out a youth with a wicked eye, and struck what he considered a rich oil-field. His few boastful words about the naughtiness of New York had led the native to disclose that Potter's Place was the true Modern Babylon. Dobson didn't believe him. The youth went into details about sundry periodical excursions to Boston; and – oh, indeed, he could prove it – he had no less a partner in infamy than the respected William Smith. He wouldn't have told any inhabitant of Potter's Place, but this New Yorker had to be shown. Oh no! William Smith wasn't wasting his money; any fool could be wicked in Boston with a fat wad; but he and William were the Original Mephisto Troupe; the girls fell for them, sure thing, mister.

Simon Iff appeared more than gratified by this discourse, and he gave Dobson his heartiest goodnight. But it was a sad and sleepless night for himself. He knew it would be useless to go to bed; so he determined to walk to the house on the hill, now untenanted and fallen into disrepair. He explored the ruin with the aid of an electric torch. Everything confirmed the tale as he had heard it. He walked slowly back, smoking pipe after pipe; and even when he threw himself without undressing upon the bed, he continued that sedative occupation.

At breakfast he was silent, save to propose a walk to Miss Mollie Madison. She knew his mood better than to do more than nod. When they got clear of the village, he threw off his gloom with a wide gesture, as if it had been an actual cloak, and said: 'Mollie, my dear, I am going to have a very dull day. I almost envy you your exciting task of kidnapping the parson.'

'What on earth do you mean?'

'Yours, my poor child, is a long and sad story. Bereft of both parents at an early age, you became the ward of a wicked uncle – my detested self – and all your millions come to me if you remain unmarried at the age of twenty-five. For your parents, unhappy orphan, were conscientious Eugenists, and deplored Race Suicide. Your uncle has therefore cruelly kept you from the sight of men, and, in despair, you are about to marry Dobson if you can find a minister. Will this impetuous young parson from Chicago do the trick? It occurs to me, dear child, that he may be reluctant. He is a climber, or he would hardly be after plain Mary Smith. It may occur to him that millions instead of thousands, and beauty instead of plainness, and social elegance instead of bumpkin crudeness, may lie within a bold man's grasp. At this point you sigh and say, aside, you only wish it were not Dobson.

'Child, he will fall for it; for he too is a simple soul, or he would never have got to such a place as Potter's.

'Pillowed upon his manly breast, you proceed to point out the difficulties. You will prompt him to explain to Dobson that there is some hitch about the law in this particular state, so that the only way to do it is to steal the car and make a regular elopement of it. Suggest Scots law in Canada, possibly. Off you go, then, anywhere, anywhere out of Potter's Place. Dobson will find a way to put the Lord's humble servant out of the way of telegraph offices and such for one week, which is the extent of my little bet with myself, and you rejoin me this evening at the Copley Plaza. Register as Miss Carmichael. *Selah.*'

'The programme pleases. But what do I get?'

'The right to open the letter which I have mailed this morning to your New York address, seven days from now, at high noon, by the pale light of the full moon, aha!'

'I suppose you have found out about A. B. Smith, then?'

'Well, not altogether. The case is old; I have only one hope of explaining the past; this is a little prediction about the future.'

'What is it?'

'Innocent, innocent child!'

She could have bitten her tongue off for the indiscretion.

'I shall fall asleep shortly,' he went on; 'that will be your chance to escape.'

She nodded, all on fire with the idea of her inexplicable adventure. Half an hour later, in the parlour of the hotel, Simon Iff's pipe fell from his lips to the floor. She picked it up. He did not stir.

'Hush!' said she to the inn-keeper, who could see into the room from his place at the bar, 'don't disturb him. If he wants me, I've gone for a little walk.'

With much obvious stealth, calculated to the diplomatic atmosphere of Potter's Place, she found Dobson in the garage. Prey to a thousand fears, registered with all the exaggeration of a moving picture, they got out the car, and drove out to the parson's house.

Miss Mollie Madison had a very easy job of it. Her dazzling beauty with its frank yet delicate voluptuousness, her jewels, her distinction, would have turned the head of any man. She was not a girl to play any game half-heartedly; she swept him clear off his feet, told him that she loved him at first sight, proved it with a kiss and a hug that could hardly have been matched in Budapest, and had him safely in the car within half an hour. Dobson made fifty-eight miles an hour through the main street of Potter's Place, the awakened 'uncle' standing in front of the hotel and swearing like a Mississippi pilot. He got no sympathy from the romantic villagers. He rushed to the telegraph office, and dispatched frantic messages to the police of all the towns in the neighbourhood, except those on Dobson's route. Ultimately, after a very fine imitation of an apoplectic fit, he boarded the train for Boston, and screamed his wrongs aloud to everybody in the car.

At the Copley Plaza he was Simon Iff again, and slept till he was informed on the telephone that a Miss Carmichael wished to see him.

It was dinner-time; the evening papers devoted comic columns to the escapade. But Simon Iff was in his most serious mood. He talked of Life and Death, of Responsibility and of Justice. His theme was mainly that all actions bear in themselves their retribution for good or ill, but only in seed, so to speak. It was circumstance that made that seed increase, and bring forth fruit. Consequently, it was no crime to bring about the flowering of such seed. He recalled to her the case of the Marsden Murders – how he had put into the mind of the guilty lawyer the thought that would drive him mad with fear – the case of Phineas Burns, and that of Aminadab Spratt.

'Should I reproach myself?' he ended. 'Where the law cannot reach a criminal, I have no right to take that law into my own hands. But have I not the right to let loose the latent justice in that criminal's own soul?'

Mollie agreed easily, not comprehending any importance in his speech.

He suddenly flared out at her with two sharp words, and a flung-forth finger.

'Remember that!'

But she did not remember it. He came down the next morning to find her at the breakfast-table, a newspaper open before her, her face white and drawn, her big eyes dreadful with black rims, and the tears dried at their source with the excess of her affliction.

'Blame me!' he said, and shook her by the shoulder roughly, so that she winced. A dry sob answered him.

He did not need to look at the newspaper. 'That,' said he, 'was the purport of the letter I mailed yesterday.' Her wonder momentarily overcame her anguish.

'How did you know?' she cried, and covered her face. 'No! no! I don't want to know; but why, why, why did you make me do it?'

He sat down at her side. 'There are people about. Command yourself. Oh, but I am a fool. I should have known you would never understand the connection.'

'The connection?'

'Pull yourself together! Can't you see that this is merely the sequel to the A. B. Smith mystery?'

'I can only see that I have played a mad jest, and brought a woman to her death.'

'There's hope yet. I've been thinking it out, and I'm morally sure she hasn't burnt it.'

'Burnt it? Burnt what?'

'The story of the Mysterious Disappearance of A. B. Smith. Come now; I'll get the coroner on long-distance, and tell him to look for it. What does her note to him say, by the way?'

He picked up the paper. 'Ah, here it is.

> 'Sir,
>
> I beg you to pardon a most unhappy woman for the trouble to which she is about to put you.
>
> Respectfully,
>
> MAMIE SMITH

'Oh, this is more to the point. To her brother:

> 'Dearest William,
>
> In my will I have left to you all my share in the property. But I ask you to get the best publisher you can find in Boston to bring out my poems, in the manuscript volume in the cupboard over my bed. The keys are round my neck. Forgive me for this act, but I could not bear life any more. Kiss mother for me.
>
> Your loving but broken-hearted sister,
>
> MAME

'Hum! nothing about any diary – oho! methinks I smell powder. We must read those poems, you and I, Mollie. I have an idea. I will ask friend Mullins, who is most certainly all that is desirable in a publisher of *belles lettres,* to let me run up to Potter's Place on his behalf. Come, let us telephone; no matter for breakfast; we will catch the morning train.'

3

'I am bringing you into the next act,' said Simon, 'contrary to tact, to prudence, to good sense. There will be all kinds of a row when you appear, especially without our friendly parson, who, by the way, Dobson informs me, is quite reconciled to his sad fate. He has a nice little wad to console him, and, anyhow, he can hardly return to his flock, can he? Abduction is his Scylla, and laughter his Charybdis, if he goes back. So we eliminate him. But then why bring you up there? Why print a duodecimo edition of Hell, with plates, half-morocco, when it isn't in the least necessary? Because, o blue-eyed babe, I want all those naturally silent parties to go up in the air about it. I want excitement, and gossip, and the rest of it. We are still far from the solution of the problem of A. B. Smith. At least, we've got to prove our case to the hilt; otherwise, we're in a rather critical position. We've done – apparently – a lot of moral, and possibly a little bit of legal, wrong. We must do a good deal more than put up the argument which the enemies of the Jesuits falsely attribute to them: that the end justifies the means. Well, here's Potter's Place; for I perceive the noble Dobson at the wheel, amidst a crowd who are not quite sure whether to lynch him. How perfectly jolly!'

Dobson himself was as indifferent to the gesticulating people as if he had been blind and deaf. His aplomb, aided by that of the magician and the maiden, was triumphant. Nothing happened. A pleasant time was had by all.

Twenty minutes later the Napier drew up at the door of the farm of William Smith. Simon Iff rapidly explained his business, in the most formal terms.

The coroner was with Smith, who had spent the hour or so previous in abusing Mollie, whom he perceived dimly as the cause of the catastrophe. At the sight of her he broke out into a string of curses.

Iff stopped him with a commanding gesture. 'Curse me, if you will,' said he; 'this lady acted at my request.'

Smith was not a person of marked perspicuity; but he saw, even in his anger, that he had come suddenly upon an unintelligible motive, and his wrath fell instantly.

'What's the big idea?' he said, almost with indifference.

'Mr Smith,' said Simon, 'I am come to clear up the mystery of your father's disappearance.'

Something in his manner prevented the obvious retort of incredulity. This strange man, who had come so violently into his placid life, not only might, but must know something. Else, why should he have come? The pretext of publishing dropped out of sight without causing surprise or suspicion.

The magician was pleased; the reaction was better than he had expected.

'Come then,' he continued, 'let us get this famous manuscript. I will most particularly ask Dr Upton here to take note of what I shall have to say during the reading.'

The coroner nodded. 'Pleased, I'm sure.'

They went into the dead woman's bedroom. The body still lay where life had left it.

'She knew her anatomy,' said the doctor; 'a wound with a pair of common scissors, but as straight to the heart as the Mayos could have done. Never saw a neater job.'

He took three keys from the dead throat. The cupboard (in that distant simple place!) had a Yale lock. Within was a safe. Within the safe they found a second iron box, and again the key was of elaborate and expensive make. Everybody began to understand that such precautions must have been taken to guard something held of incalculable value.

But the second box, lined with cedar-wood, contained only a heavy sheet of rose-coloured silk, which was wrapped about a small book of the kind that very fashionable stationers sell to rich women for memoranda. The binding was of deep blue polished morocco, the paper hand-made.

Simon Iff took the volume in his hands with a certain reverence.

'Before I open this,' he said, 'I will prove my right to be here. We know that this book contains poems, and that Miss Smith valued them most highly. We know no more; but I will say more, for the satisfaction of Mr Smith.'

He turned to the brother. 'Your sister was careless and clumsy with the pen?'

'Yes, sir, she never liked the trouble of writing.'

'These poems will be found to be in the most careful and delicate calligraphy. She was a prosaic, matter-of-fact woman, very patient and humble, inclined to avoid notice?'

'Quite right, mister.'

'These poems will be found high-flown, passionate, romantic, and above all proud. Now then to the proof.'

He opened the book. The first page was his vindication. It was written with a crow quill, ornamented with flourishes which wandered, like strange vines, over the page, in such a fashion that the contour of the design was as it were a symbolic representation of the title itself. Simon read it out.

'*The Book of the Heart's Blood of the Lily of God.* Do you understand?' he asked.

'I was never one for this high-brow stuff.'

'Well,' said Iff, 'it means that she regarded herself as a being divinely pure, perhaps even uniquely pure, and that she had pressed out her sorrow, like rich wine, into this book. Let us go on.'

The second page bore the author's name, and a date: May, 1891. Beneath this, in brackets, 'My first poem.' Then the title "The Angel of the Sun.' Simon proceeded to read it.

'I am he the soul that dwelleth
In the Sun mine habitation.
I must cloke myself with glory,
Clouds of burning flame and glory,
Lest the people of the planets
See my face and die of terror,
Hear my voice and die of terror.
O be silent! O be silent!
Such a little slip might slay them,
Just a glimpse or just a whisper.
For I am the soul that dwelleth
In the Sun mine habitation.

'Now what is the meaning of this poem? Why does a girl of twelve or thirteen occupy herself with such ideas? She uses the first person, yet who is speaking? The most glorious being possible to imagine, so glorious that the photosphere of the sun himself is a thick mask upon his face. Yet this being is afraid! He fears that mortals might see or hear him, and die of terror.

'Now what does this really mean? Here is a child of unusual plainness, rather despised, feeling herself already an inferior person—'

'Why yes, she was never of any account.'

'So, being sensitive, she created a psychic compensation. She deliberately retired from reality, and identified herself with what is really little less than God. Probably she would have made it God, but that the idea of Him was bound up too closely with the minds of the people whom she hated, and so had become repellent. It was God, too, who had made her weak, plain, feminine; so she had to invent a "Saviour" of her own. She had to be very careful, too, not to let out this secret life of hers; so she invents a reason for her own shyness and reticence and fear of others. If those who tortured her guessed for one second Who She Really Was, they would fall dead with terror. Thus her social weakness is pictured as the virtue – she was taught to consider it as such – of compassion. Let us turn over.'

The next poem was entitled 'Knut Olaf' with a date two years later. It was in ballad form, quatrains, and began by describing the power of this great Norseman, how he slew the Dragon of the Sea, and made war on giants and kings. At last he comes to America; the Red Man resists him in vain. But he meets his Waterloo in the end.

'Now, listen to this particularly,' said Simon, who had been reading out only a few lines here and there to give a general idea.

'"Spare me," the father cried, "and I
Will give thee for thy bride
My daughter, the White Butterfly,
That is my country's pride."

"Nay, I will take her' gainst thy will,
For she is beautiful."
Knut Olaf swung his axe with skill,
And split the father's skull.

But then came forth White Butterfly
Dressed in her silk attire;
Knut Olaf laughed "Come here, and I
Will tell thee my desire."

She came, but oh! to end my tale!
Never a word she said.
She simply lifted her white veil.
The Viking fell down dead.

'Exactly the same idea as in the first poem; but we have a touch of the sex-symbol, as she is now of age to use it. Here is the incarnation of all might and violence, the world-conqueror, slain in an instant by the mere lifting of White Butterfly's veil. Kindly note the complete absence of any sense of humour in this passage! Note too, please, that there is a distinct feeling of satisfaction in allowing Olaf to split her father's skull. Let us go on.'

The third poem in the book was entitled 'A Dream.' It began, shamelessly enough:

> Here, where the forest primaeval once sheltered the tent of the red man.

and continued, less obviously,

> We may be thankful to see nice farms and churches and railroads,
> Yet, in the night there may come to those who are fitted to see them,
> People pure in the heart, like the moon, some dreams. And I dreamt one,
> And I cannot imagine at all why it seemed so exceedingly vivid.
> It was in the fall of the year, and the trees were losing their verdure.
> I went through the woods, and the leaves on the ground were all of them corpses.
> Then I came to the town where my father was selling a diamond,
> But nobody wanted to buy it; but then came a squab, and he took it
> Away in his beak to the woods, and buried it under the corpses
> And sat on it all through the winter, and then, when I wanted to know most

Of all what would happen, I woke, and I found that the
pillow was moistened
With tears. Ah, what did it mean? It was really
exceedingly vivid.

'I want only to call attention to the fact that in the first scene she is the one live being in a world of corpses; in the next, her father is trying to sell a diamond, a clean and precious jewel, unvalued except by a squab (or dove; connected in her mind, of course, with the Holy Ghost). She herself has really disappeared in this scene; in truth, she has become the diamond. And though she is sure that some glorious fortune is in store for her, the feeling of doubt enters, and prevents a triumphant conclusion to the dream, which therefore makes her cry.

'Hullo, here's prose. August 1895.

'diarfa saw ch LLA fo cm dcbbor sah rchtaf ym niatrcc si ti
llik ot hguone gnorts eb dluohs yeht tsel syob owt evah ot
eht meeder ot nesohc ma I live lla si nam suht mih
deyortsed eb lliw nam snaem siht yb ytinigriv yb dlrow

'She may have thought that a sentence with the words written backwards was undecipherable. Poe is unknown in America as yet. Now what is the next lyric? "The Waterfall."

'I loathe thy ceaseless clamour in my ears,
O waterfall! I would thy noisome flood
That speaks to me of evil and of fears
Were turned, as Moses turned the Nile, to blood.

Nay, I would rather have thee turned to glassy steel,
So to beat back the Sun in proud disdain;
For in thy motion and thy noise I feel

Only the threat of everlasting pain.

'In a dream or a fantasy, water usually means maternity. That idea is to her the climax of horror. Birth is the device by which nature perpetuates suffering – for to her the world now appears wholly evil. Of course, she did not know what she was writing. She thought of it only as a "poem." But to us who have the key the reference to Moses is highly significant. The blood is the safeguard. Yet there is still danger from which the subconscious mind shrinks. Nothing can really alleviate its anxiety but the cessation of the water altogether, its transformation into a glassy steel, which shall repel the assault even of the sun, the greatest of creative forces. It is a symbolic confirmation of the cipher, at least of part of it.

'Here's another lyric, same month: "The Sun."

'O father of all woe, I will not deign
To plead with thee for universal pain.
I will remind thee only that thy face,
Red robber, is no match for icy space.
The time is coming when thy race so rash
Is run, and thou a crust of cinder ash.

'Same story; the father has robbed her; she hates his energy, his superiority, his power; and she delights to think that he will die. And what is it that will overcome him? Empty space, cold, formless, infinite. She is no longer merely the angel of the sun, who wishes only to avoid striking men dead. She is space itself. She will strike the sun himself dead, and she rejoices in it.

'This change is brought about by her experience of the world. As a child she was still hopeful of acquiring superiority in the world of reality. Now she knows that it is hopeless. Her vanity-fantasy is not strong enough to compensate; she hates her torturers, and begins to concentrate that hatred upon her father, who robbed her, by one of those mysterious sex-magic tricks, of her right to be a boy.'

'But this is rubbish,' broke in Smith. 'Mamie was very fond of her father. And she didn't want to be a boy; she was always boasting of her womanhood.'

'I said so. Men were all evil to her. Yet she did want to be a boy before she invented these fantasies. Think now. Go back to your earliest memories.'

'That's so, by Gosh. I remember it all now. And then one day she shut up like a clam, and got furious when I teased her.'

'And she only developed the hate of her father when she was old enough to have all this subconscious stuff thoroughly suppressed. She would have been horrified if you had told her what those poems meant. And yet the cipher is plain enough. It was dictated by the neurotic's need of confession, and put in cipher by his parallel need of secrecy. Cheer up! I know it sounds mysterious and contradictory, and not a little unlike humbug; but I've a hunch that we'll come out to a Fact with a capital F before we're through this book. Come along; let's skip a little – suppose we find something about nineteen five or six. What's this? The title-poem! "The Lily of God."

'There is a lake – 'tis everlasting space,
And on its windless calm a lily flowers
Alone, no sunlight to insult her face,
No time to violate her with his hours.
Ages and ages ere she was a bud
God made her, then she could not well be less
Than he, and so she sucked away his blood,
And bleached it for the dye of her own dress.
Then she pressed out that purity to still
Her soul, for music also is a curse.
She wrote the triumph of her virgin will
Over the ruins of the universe.

'In this poem the fantasy has fulfilled itself. She has destroyed God, and remains sole and supreme; she even pretends to despise the record of her victory. Note also how definite is the conception; we shall find, perhaps, that in this year (1904 it is) she is more independent in reality. Possibly her father was actually sick.'

'Well, this is sure some stunt. Funny stuff, I call it. Dad had the grippe that winter, and laid up for a month. Never quite the same man, to my way of thinking.'

'Let us go on. Whew! Here's Buddhism!'

'Why yes, 'bout that time she was plumb crazy on Nirvany or some such heathen god.'

'This is her "Ode to Nirvana."

'O vast abyss! Engulf all seeming form
Within thine amphitheatre of ice!
Shield me from Life's inhospitable storm,
And slay me Mara's dazzling cockatrice!
O Nirvana! blest Nirvana!
Save me from the woes of Prana!

'Verse Two!' announced Simon Iff, with a savage look at Miss Mollie Madison, who was making things excessively difficult for his self-control, though (as she subsequently swore by all red-headed gods) she was doing her utmost to preserve propriety.

'O bliss of nothingness! Thy silence great
Hath swallowed moon and planet, star and sun;
With the inexorable Urge of Fate,
Thy Virgin Nought hath mastered Father One.
O Nirvana! Blest Nirvana!
Shila! Kshanti! Virya! Dana!

'There's a lot more, but we have enough here. It's the same thought, in a jargon of misunderstood Theosophy, and a great show of sham learning introduced to give her the sensation of superiority of knowledge or scholarship: more psychic compensation. But the main idea is this vast, formless, negative, icy sphere – she's compelled to the formula she hates, poor girl! – which swallows up the fire and energy of the father, not by construction but by annihilation. Observe, she is no longer content to have his skull split; she wants him to disappear without leaving the minutest trace. Oh we're getting near nineteen seven, be sure!'

William Smith had become strangely excited. He trembled continuously, and the sweat ran over his face.

Simon Iff turned the pages. The poems were more confident and positive as he proceeded. There was one that ended:

> The Curse, the Everlasting Curse,
> Swept beyond the Universe.

Another was on sympathetic magic, as if she had been reading *The Golden Bough*. One verse read:

> Every boy that fills a cup
> Winds eternal mischief up,
> And every girl that breaks a rod
> Throws his malice back to God.

'Something of Blake in that, somehow, eh? Never mind; it shows she was thinking of doing a magic ceremony. Just as you can raise a wind by blowing in some ceremonial fashion, so you could blot out the infinite evil if you could blot out some person whom you took to symbolise the cause of evil. In this case, the father. Now – come to the critical year – hullo! This is great. Words no longer seem adequate to the conception. So we find a symbolic picture.'

It was a very simple drawing, entirely crude and untutored, but with a curious fascination of evil such as one often sees in 'automatic' or 'spirit' pictures. The whole page was covered with stars, and the Milky Way ran through it like a snake. Part of this group was thickened into the likeness of a shark, on whose head was set the crescent moon. With open jaw it was rushing upon the sun, to whom the artist had given not only features, but thin arms and legs. In one arm he was brandishing a stick. The picture was full of movement; a most skillful artist might have been less successful in this respect than this untrained woman.

At the bottom of the page appeared the earth, a hilly landscape with clouds masking the sky. There was a house upon a hillside, and between the house and the hill a rude bridge of planks. Under the bridge was a small black circle, and in the air above it a broken stick.

Simon Iff did not take long to read the message.

'Here,' said he, 'we see an attempt to picture the relations between heaven and earth. The shark Nirvana, with the chaste moon for his crest, is going to swallow the sun with his symbol of authority and paternity. The corresponding facts on earth concern this house on the hill. Mr Smith, was there a plank gangway to the back door of the house?'

'Why yes, Mr Iff. There was a shallow cave in the shale where things were kept for coolness. The planks saved one from walking over the rough shale, which was pretty wet, too, most times, from a spring somewhere.'

'Then if you will get into my car, I will take you to the grave of your father.'

Smith, like a man in a trance, followed, with Miss Mollie Madison and the coroner to bring up the rear. He had a new shock of terror when Dobson produced pick and shovel from beneath his seat. He perceived that all had been understood and foreseen.

The planks of the gangway were already rotted. They broke at once under Dobson's vigorous blows.

'Dig a six-inch channel,' said the magician, 'it won't be very deep.'

He was right. The loose shale flew high as Dobson shovelled. Less than a foot beneath the surface he struck a hard smooth surface. It was cement. A few strokes disclosed a circular plate of this material. The chauffeur took the pick, and broke it. He stopped, and flung the loose pieces to one side. A broken stick, all rotten, lay upon the skeleton of a man.

It dawned suddenly upon William Smith that this whole operation had been designed to trap him. He trembled. He read something akin to his own apprehension in the eye of the coroner, who was regarding him askance.

'I swear by God,' he cried solemnly, 'that I had not art nor part in this.'

'My dear man,' returned Simon, 'I never supposed for one moment that you had. Your alibi is perfect.'

'Alibi!' stammered Smith, more alarmed than ever. 'I don't know what you mean. I was here.'

'A moral alibi, friend Smith! Your mind was not on sharks and suns; you were cantering away to Boston, having a glorious time with the girls. You had conquered reality; you did not need any psychic compensation for a sense of inferiority.'

He extended his hand; Smith took it, with tears in his eyes.

'Understand, please,' said the magician, 'that I knew this whole story, all but the location of the body, before I had been three hours in Potter's Place.

'It was certain that your father had met with foul play; his psychology was all against a voluntary disappearance. And how could he have avoided the family? And why should he not have disappeared in some simple way, by going off to Boston, and crossing the Atlantic, for instance? Besides, he had touched no money for such a journey. It was then clear that one of the family was responsible; perhaps two, or even all three. But the active agent must have been Mamie; it was she who followed her father into the house, and was alone with him for five minutes or so. She could easily arrange the details: a place of concealment for the body, possibly a temporary affair like her trunk. Anything would serve, since no one would think to look for a hidden corpse, but only for a living man. She had then merely to hide his stick, so as to detain him in the house, and give her an excuse to go back and do the murder. More likely still, she may have hidden the stick as a symbolic gesture, and simply seen and taken the opportunity, despite her conscious will, when it presented itself. Some casual word of the old man may have fired the hidden train of gunpowder.

'But why should she take so extraordinary a means to cope with her secret anguish? One could only see an answer by invoking the Psychology of the Unconscious. I began to probe the persons concerned. Mrs Smith was clearly guiltless. She had not the physical strength or adroitness; besides, she was not there. Unless all three were lying, Mamie was alone with her father. And all three were not lying; if they had been, they would have invented some commonplace story of accident.

'So we contemplate Mamie, the plain, flat-chested unconsidered nullity, not wanted save for household drudgery. It was she, surely, who, if she became neurotic, as she was almost certain to do, might accentuate her compensating fiction to the point of attacking the social condition which oppressed her in the person of its representative, the "Father-Governor." He, too, was personally responsible for most of her misery, since he had begotten her female and not male, or (as she put it in that cipher) had robbed her of manhood. Also, he was – in the eyes of her unconscious self – "the Man"; that is, she was as an infant unconsciously in love with him. The incest-barrier (as we call it) baulked her here; and as, when she came to the experience of sex-need, she was not able to obtain other men to represent the Father, she threw back on him the responsibility for her emptiness.

'Now then, was William Smith her accomplice? At first sight – or rather hearing, for I got all this, so far, in New York from this lady's account – it seemed probable, for material if not psychological reasons. But when I discovered that he was expressing himself freely and fully as the "superior male," capable, ambitious, enjoying himself without restraint in Boston, I absolved him. Morals are the cause of madness. Unmoral people never go mad, except in the case where insanity is a symptom of some disease like tuberculosis. Madness is caused by a conflict in the will. Immoral, as opposed to unmoral, people often go mad; for their "conscience" reproaches them – Satan divided against Satan. And moral people go mad too, for their suppressed desires reproach them; and this is worse than conscience, because conscience is a factitious thing, an Intruder on Nature. Do what thou wilt shall be the whole of the Law. The penalty of disobedience is insanity.

'So this book of poems, which the writer herself never properly understood, fully and wholly, leads us to this grave. Here is the stick, the symbol of authority, broken by the blow which shattered the skull of its living parallel, the Father. Now we are ready to continue our reading.

'The next few poems are short and joyous. The magic has succeeded. But look here! Nineteen nine, April. Isn't this strange? "The Pipes of Pan." Last verse.

> 'O Syrinx, we were glad indeed
> To hear thee, changed into a reed;
> Thine, losing Pan, was all the loss,
> Thou female Jesus on the Cross!

'Still no sense of humour! But are not these strange words from the Chosen Virgin? No; for her father's murder has been successful. She feels that she has conquered reality; so she faces it at last. The murder is only a substituted satisfaction of her real need; but it has given her confidence. The idea comes into her mind: "I may be able to fulfill myself sexually after all." Now watch this idea grow. Here are poems passionate, even sensual, one after another. "The Night is Short," "My Dove," "Abelard," and so on. She still wants to triumph over man, but now it is in the normal way. All this means that she sees a chance to marry. But with this comes the note of doubt, of lack of confidence in herself. In the world of her psychic compensation she had conquered completely; but in this real life she was still unproved. We are near the end now – ah look!'

The poems had all been fair copies in her superbly delicate calligraphy; but this last page was a hurried scrawl, with blots. It was as if she wished to symbolise, even by means of external form, the sudden ruin of her life. The poem was entitled 'Red.'

'O flame of hell! how I have hated thee,
Thou God, thou Father, thou creative curse,
Red robber, red smutch on virginity,
Red energy of this vile universe.
I conquered thee, I blotted thee quite out,
Abolishing thy presence like a dream,
But when I came to try my triumph out,
Again I found the accursed red supreme.
O vile! O serpent! I had crushed thee firm
When I destroyed, annihilated Man,
But thou, disguised, o execrable worm,
Hast by a prostitute upset my plan.
Thou art the Sun, thou God and Father, thou
Red-Headed Harlot, scarlet Babylon
That took my triumph. O, I see thee now

> And him thy red mouth, harlot, fixes on.
> I see thee pass me in a flash of light,
> The chariot of the Sun. Then what's to do?
> I will die virgin, for my soul is white,
> Spilling the red in me, my fault all through!'

Simon Iff hesitated a moment, as if puzzled.

'Excuse me, sir,' said Dobson, 'but I can explain one bit of that. She was in the village as we raced through. Miss Madison didn't see her because (begging your pardon, Miss) she was all over the parson, kissing him, with her hair down.'

'I have never been accused of lack of thoroughness,' cried Mollie, her shame taking refuge in pert effrontery.

'I think it's all clear now,' said Simon Iff, very sadly. 'At the last moment Reality defeats her by that very symbol of Red which she thought she had destroyed. Then the true horror was revealed to her as by an angel: the Red was in herself all the time. The "Virgin" compensation was a fraud, after all; the red blood was in her heart. Ah well, that could easily be cured.'

He closed the book, and put it into the hands of William Smith. Then he locked his hands behind his back, and went with bowed head out of the house.

They followed him. He ignored the car, and went slowly towards Potter's Place, none daring to speak to him.

Smith and the coroner, walking some fifty yards behind with Miss Mollie Madison, saw that she was crying. Smith tried a stammering word of consolation.

'Oh! Oh!' she said trembling, 'there was never a man like Simon Iff. His soul is one fierce flame of love for humanity, and he – he – sees – too – much.'

STERILISED STEPHEN

1

'Take an arm-chair, young lady,' said Simon Iff genially. 'Every man and every woman is a star. Dobson, tell Nankipoo to bring the drinks and gaspers.'

The woman addressed sank into a chair rather than took it. She covered her face with her hands and began to wipe away the tears with a corner of her ragged, gaudy skirt. Iff scrutinised her in silence.

'Explain the Law,' said he, when Dobson returned from his errand. 'After that, leave us alone.'

'It's this way,' said the chauffeur, 'as I understand it. Mr Iff says that we are all really sort of gods who have disguised ourselves as men and women for the sake of the experience; and life on earth is always so painful and hideous that we are all first-class heroes simply for getting ourselves born. We ought all to respect each other for what we really are and for what we have done. It doesn't make any odds what particular rig we've got ourselves up in. Sit up and smile, lass, and talk to Mr Iff as if he were your own twin brother.'

'That'll do, Dobson,' said Mr Iff. 'I *am* her own twin brother.'

The girl lifted her head. The bitter years had taught her to read strange men at a glance. She saw respect and sympathy in the magician's face. There was no hint of patronage or anything else that could wound the most sensitive spirit. She smiled timidly. Dobson left the room as the Japanese servant served the refreshments.

'Not bad stuff. May I fill your glass again?'

The girl nodded. The stimulant had given her courage.

'Righto,' said Simon, 'tell me the whole trouble, young 'un.'

She began to stammer. 'I don't know how I'm here,' she managed to get out at last.

Iff answered her. 'Simple enough, my dear. It's one of Dobson's duties to keep his eyes open for beauty in distress. Whenever he spots anyone in need of any kind, he helps them out; and if he finds the job beyond him, he brings the business to me.'

'I thought he was your chauffeur,' said the girl, as if the magician's statement were somewhat surprising.

'So he is,' cried Iff. 'But then, what is a chauffeur? Doesn't the word mean one who warms things up? He saw you shivering in this cold world. That's all.'

She still seemed puzzled. Simon sighed.

'Alas, I see that you have been taught to think of a servant as somehow inferior to his master. Dobson is my colleague, a star whose business happens to be to shove another star along the streets.'

The wine was beginning to work in the girl. She began to recover from the obsession of her surroundings. She had never imagined the possibility of so gorgeous a room as Iff's. The sober splendour frightened her. She connected it instinctively with wealth and power, and to her, wealth and power meant only the hidden horror behind the police – that monster, many-armed, that might pounce upon her at any moment without reason and without warning.

'What kind of a star am I?' she asked, and trembled at her own audacity.

'It's my business to find out,' said he; 'to find out why you happen to be in this particular disguise; to put you on your proper course; to free you from the forces which have dragged you off it.'

She shook her head very slowly and sadly but with decision. Iff eyed her narrowly. She sat up straight, gripping the arms of her chair. There was something like a sneer on her lips, something like contempt in her voice.

'Looking for lost sheep? That game's no good. I'm a goat, and you can't get mutton from me.'

'Great,' cried Iff. 'That's the spirit I like. I'm a bit of a goat myself. Goats will be goats. Did you ever hear what one of the greatest poets and prophets that ever lived said about goats? "The lust of the goat is the bounty of God."'

The girl's animation increased. It was a new experience for her to be addressed by an apparently respectable member of society except in one of three ways: either it was the coarse familiarity of casual admirers, the sanctimonious severity of professional philanthropists, or the savage menaces of the police. Iff understood.

'Why in hell should I want to reform you?' he laughed. 'I suppose you've had a streak of bad luck. I prescribe a new dress, a new hat, some gloves and silk stockings, with change of scenery. I admit that 8th Avenue, with all its charms, may seem monotonous in the long run. Help yourself,' he concluded, tossing his bill-fold into her lap. 'Try what the Broad Walk will do for you.'

To his surprise, the girl sprang up as if his action had broken some spell that had bound her. She crossed the room like a queen, and handed back the case. Then she burst into a torrent of tears which shook her slight shoulders with tempestuous violence.

Simon Iff took her back to her chair and soothed her. As soon as she was calm, he spoke with curt authority.

'Tell me the whole trouble.'

His tone made her mistress of herself.

'All Morgan's millions wouldn't help me – you don't understand. How could you? I've got used to every kind of suffering. I've been sick, I've starved, I've been in gaol! I haven't a friend – I've nothing before me but death – I'm sliding; no one can save me. I don't want to be saved. Thanks for the money – at least for the thought in your heart. But a glimpse of joy would only make my wretchedness harder to bear. I haven't cried for five years.'

The natural question shot through Simon's mouth. 'Then why were you crying today?'

'Not for myself – I'm too hard and too proud. Look at this paper.'

Her trembling hands fumbled in a shabby plush bag. She handed a slip torn from the columns of an *Evening Journal* to Simon. It was a police report. It recorded the conviction of Stephen Adams, aged twenty-three, assistant cashier in the office of a well-known firm of stockbrokers. The charge was 'theft' of a number of Liberty Bonds. Few details were given; but the method of the robbery had been the abstraction of a number of bonds from a packet, detection having been postponed by replacing them by Bolshevik-manufactured forgeries.

The sentence had been draconic. Even the employers had asked mercy on the ground of the boy's previously good character, and the element of doubt as to his guilt caused by the failure of the prosecution to trace either the disposal of the stolen goods, or the way in which the Russian bonds came into his possession. But the judge was 'determined to stamp out that sort of thing,' and put on his heaviest boots.

Simon returned the paper to his guest with a gesture of enquiry.

'Stephen's my brother,' she said.

'And you are very fond of each other?' asked Iff.

She hung her head dejectedly. 'He cast me off when I went wrong. I haven't seen him since.'

Iff's respect for the girl increased once more. Why should she take so much to heart the punishment of the Pharisee? Her intuition read his thought.

'I was like a mother to Stephen,' she murmured. 'I'm seven years older. Mother died when he was born, and Father two years later. Aunt Dorcas, his sister, brought us up. She did her best for us both. She was ever so kind, but dreadfully strict. I was always bad at heart, I'm afraid. I wanted my own way, and it brought me to what I am. But he was a dandy kid, clever and good as anyone could possibly be. He seemed to take naturally to all her ideas. He was the model boy of the whole town. I'm sorry to say, I despised him for his goodness. I thought he was a sissy; maybe that's why I mothered him so much. I was twenty when Aunt Dorcas died. She left us all she had – it wasn't much, just over two thousand dollars. We stayed on in the flat. Stephen finished his schooling; but I couldn't send him to college, though he was such a splendid scholar and took heaps of prizes. I might have worked it if I hadn't run wild. But as soon as I found myself free, I was like a crazy thing, and before I knew it I had gone wrong with a boy who came down our way fishing for the summer. He knew all the tricks. When he knew what he had done, he wouldn't marry me, but he sent me to a wicked doctor. I was sick for a long while, and somehow they found out in the town what my trouble was. When I tried to get back to my old job, I was thrown out. It was the same everywhere. I came to New York and begged my boy to be decent; to help me out about Stephen. He got him a job in his father's office.

'As for me, he was tired of my troubles. He wanted pleasure without paying for it. I got work, and found it wouldn't keep me from starving. I and another girl decided to do the usual thing. We went for the high lights on Broadway, and year after year we were driven further and further to skulk in the shadows.'

She swallowed a lump in her throat. Iff seemed to be looking, not at her, but beyond her. His eyes glowed with angry bitterness. He was thinking of the stupidity of society.

'Don't you feel any resentment against your brother?' he asked tonelessly.

'Why should I? I'm proud that he is good. He's right to disown me.'

'It seems that we are likely to quarrel,' snorted Iff. 'I prefer your career to his. You only obeyed your nature – your misfortunes come from other people's meanness – while Stephen, with every chance in his favour, turned thief and stole so stupidly that I haven't a spark of sympathy for him. His virtues make him viler.'

The woman flared up in fury. 'But he isn't guilty!' she shouted. 'How dare you?'

Iff was impressed. 'I suppose you are so sure of him because you know him so well. But let me tell you that it never surprises me to find puritanically virtuous people coming a cropper, especially when they are so well aware how good they are, and when they prefer their respectability to natural human feelings.'

She remembered a good many similar cases. Her faith staggered for a moment, and then asserted itself with augmented certainty.

'Not Stephen,' she cried. 'He was always genuinely good. He never had the idea of revolt.'

'My dear girl!' said Iff, 'I admire you tremendously, but can't you see that you are simply arguing against yourself? Stephen, as you describe him, is simply a straw man, a weakling with no will of his own. Temptation would knock him over like a nine-pin.'

'Oh, how I wish I could show you how wrong you are! He wasn't merely obedient, he loved goodness for its own sake. He was active and eager to be better than he was asked to be. You know how dirty boys are; they seem to enjoy mud. Stephen could never endure a speck of dust on his clothes. His linen, his hands, his shoes – you couldn't have found dirt on them with a microscope. A boy can't do that just by passive trying to please. After Aunt Dorcas died, instead of getting slack and being influenced by my own carelessness, he got almost crazy about keeping himself clean. He read lots of learned books about germs. He was always disinfecting everything, from sauce-pans to door-knobs. He wouldn't kiss me for fear of germs. He always wore gloves, even at night, because of a story in a Sunday paper about the danger of infection from fingernails. He was a joke in the office – they called him Sterilised Stephen.'

Simon Iff had been twisting his mouth as if a curious flavour had touched it. He cleared his throat as he rose from his chair.

'Look here, young woman,' he said, standing over her, 'I doubt very much whether your sublime confidence amounts to anything; but you interest me enormously, and so does Stephen in a rather whimsical fashion. I'll look into the case for you and do what I can; but don't be silly enough to hope too much. Don't worry yourself; face the facts. Believe in yourself. Take these bills from Stephen's brother and yours; trot off to Atlantic City and let the breezes have a chance at your lungs. Come back here in a week, and perhaps I may have something to tell you.'

He jotted down the name, and that of the brokers, and took her to the door himself. They shook hands. Her grasp was so steady and so firm that he felt, in spite of himself, that her faith was something more than the passionate protest of the bigot against the blasphemer who overthrows his idol.

2

The next morning Simon Iff called on the stockbrokers. Mr Lubeck, the senior partner, was a middle-aged man whose natural kindness of heart had not been destroyed by the racket of the Street. He shook his head when Iff explained his errand. It was evident that he thought it quixotic. But Stephen Adams had been a special favourite, and Lubeck would have done much more to restore his belief in the boy than Iff required. He explained the circumstances briefly and clearly.

'Adams worked in a compartment shut off from the main office, with the cashier Hobbs, who had been twenty years with the firm, and another assistant, Jackson, of about Stephen's own age. On the day of the theft, Jackson had been absent – suffering from influenza. A packet of bonds had been handed to Adams that he might inscribe their numbers in the appropriate register. He was then to hand the packet to the messenger for delivery to the customer, after having placed them in an envelope and sealed them. The bonds were handed to Adams at exactly a quarter to twelve. They had been carefully checked by one of the partners on taking them from the safe, and examined by another partner. Both were absolutely sure that none of the bonds were forgeries. The forged bonds, incidentally, were poor imitations; besides which, all dealers had been warned by the Treasury that systematic attempts were being made to circulate them. Everybody was, in consequence, very much on his guard. It is thus certain that Adams had received the genuine bonds, and moreover, he had entered the numbers conformably to the record of the bank which had issued them.

'Adams had himself sealed the package and handed it to the messenger, who had locked it up at once in his satchel, and gone straight to the customer. This latter had taken the envelope at once to his bank, where the cashier broke the seals, and discovered at once that all the bonds except two, those at the top and the bottom, were forgeries. The bank telephoned to Lubeck, who called in the police. It was proved that nobody had entered the cashier's office except Hobbs, who had been out on some errand in the building, and darted hurriedly in for his hat and coat, and out again in less than half a minute. His haste had indeed attracted general notice. Detectives found him at his usual restaurant talking volubly and excitedly to a friend. He explained his unusual conduct as due to sudden and severe trouble in his family; enquiry confirmed his statements. He had no discoverable financial anxieties, and was an old and trusted servant of the firm. It was not possible for him to have substituted the forged bonds in full view of Adams, who was actually engaged upon them. Hobbs swore that in his hurry he had taken no particular notice of what Adams was doing – yet he was conscious of a vague impression that his sudden entry startled his assistant, and that there was a sort of shuffling among the papers.

'Adams had gone to lunch immediately after handing the packet to the messenger. The clerks noticed that his face was grey as if with fear, and that his hands were trembling.

'He returned an hour later, still agitated, as if he had partially failed to conjure the peril that awaited him. He had spent the hour, not at lunch, but in a crazy dash uptown to his boarding-house, where he had stayed less than ten minutes.

'It being physically impossible for any other person to have committed the theft, he was tackled outright. He met the charge with stubborn denial. He admitted the logic of the situation fearlessly and firmly. He confessed that he could not suggest any alternative to the obvious conclusion. But he stuck stoutly to his statement. It was very striking to observe that his agitation ceased instantly when he heard the accusation. He was frightfully pale, but the calmest man in the office. "I can't excuse it; I can't explain it. I didn't do it. It's beyond imagination. I am in the hands of God." They walked him off on those words.'

Simon Iff mused a while over this story. He recognised, despite the wide divergence of form, the almost fanatical faith and firmness of the sister in that of the brother. Her integrity in her infamy was the same as his in his innocence; and the certainty of her candour as a sinner induced him to put confidence in his as a saint!

'This is your first robbery, by the way?'

'Why, no!' cried Lubeck, suddenly troubled without quite knowing why. 'We've had more than I care to think about, right along for years and years. The fact is, Mr Iff, I'm what they call an easy mark. I like to trust people; Wall Street is wasted on me. I can't seem to learn sense – the truth is, I guess, that I won't. I'd sooner be a sucker than sour on humanity.'

'Mr Lubeck,' said Iff, his eyes very bright, 'you're a pretty good man of business, from my point of view. You've had the good sense not to sell your soul to save a few dollars; the power to love and trust is a man's best asset when he balances the books of his life.'

'That's about the way I feel,' returned the broker, simply. 'Do you see any way out for Stephen? I'd give more than a cancelled coupon this hadn't happened.'

'May I look at the office?'

'Sure; this way.'

'Don't hope enough to hurt yourself,' Iff warned him; 'I can't see one spark. Yet I feel a sort of feeble flutter somewhere, as if something might turn up. Is that the scene of the crime?'

'Yep,' answered Lubeck, his hand on the knob of the door.

They went in. Hobbs and Jackson were busy on the books; they stood up respectfully as their employer appeared.

Iff swept the room with his glance. Its walls and roof were of opaque glass, framed in varnished oak. All was spotless and orderly, from the desks to the safe. There was no way to enter the room save the one door; the window had not even a sill, and opened on a sheer smooth wall ninety feet above Broadway.

Lubeck, following his guest's eyes, volunteered that on the day of the theft the window had been closed, as a bitter wind was blowing, with sleet.

'Not a place for a rabbit to hide,' remarked the broker, sadly.

'Unless in some conjurer's hat,' laughed Simon, touching a derby that hung from a peg behind the door. A thought seemed to strike him; his eyes darted from the hat to the two men.

The second hat was of soft felt, old and much worn but well-kept, while the derby, though nearly new, bore marks of grease. One might have fancied it begging to be brushed!

There was no need to enquire which of the men owned it. Jackson was dressed in shabby shoddy; it shone where the nap had been rubbed smooth. But the trousers had been carefully pressed, and the cuffs of the cheap cotton shirt were protected by paper.

Hobbs, on the contrary, with far better clothes, was careless about them. His whole appearance was that of some eccentric recluse, too much absorbed in study to pay attention to externals.

Lubeck introduced him as the best cashier in 'little old New York.'

'He lives for his work; we have to wake him up to go home.'

Iff recognised the eyes of an enthusiast; the man evidently itched to get back to his books. But the magician was not interested in the merits of Hobbs; he was looking for something out of the common, something that nobody had noticed. A trifle might tell him more than a treatise, just as the almost imperceptible aberration of a planet indicates some invisible influence more significant than all the rest of its orbit.

There was only one object in the office which seemed superfluous in that ideally efficient and economical arrangement. Everything was planned for three people, from the chairs and the telephone to the blotters and the hat-pegs. The third man being out, the third peg was vacant; and Iff, as he mentally recorded this instance of the fitness of things, was reminded of a minute matter that meant nothing, that had not aroused any augmented attention. In a recess on the wall near the window there was a fourth hat-peg. Simon swerved sharply from the door, and inspected this intrusive superfluity that insulted the threeness of the furniture. He pointed an enquiring finger at it as he noted that it looked newer than its rivals for the rapture of being garnished with head-gear and overcoats.

He heard Hobbs chuckle, and Jackson giggle, over his shoulder.

'A painful subject,' said the cashier. 'I hate to think of it. That hook was put up to humour a fad of poor old "Sterilised Stephen." I guess you've heard the story. Goldurn it, I'd give a month's pay to think we all got it wrong.'

Jackson was angry with himself for having laughed, and murmured something about how horrible was temptation.

'Temptation, hell,' growled Hobbs; 'must have known he'd be spotted straight off. My belief is he went plumb crazy, didn't know what he was doing. Seems to me that fool fad of his about dirt and germs was a sign he had bats in his belfry. Wouldn't hang his things up with ours, what d'ye know about that?'

Simon Iff had turned to face the speaker.

'Mr Hobbs, let me thank you most heartily for your remarks. I believe in my soul that you have thrown very full light on the case. I must go off now, but I hope to see you again very soon – perhaps to thank you for helping me to get an innocent lad out of prison.'

Five minutes later, Simon Iff was on his way to apply for a permit to visit the convicted cashier.

3

It was three days later when the magician stepped from his automobile across the threshold of the gaol where Stephen Adams was serving the first weeks of his sentence. He had taken unusual pains with his toilet. 'Mollie, my dear, I must look as if I had sprung out of a bandbox,' he had insisted, and Mollie had been made to assure him over and over, with the most terrific oaths, that she had removed the last obstinate staphylococcus from the last square millimetre of his coat.

His first act was to hand the governor of the prison an order to permit an investigation of the mental condition of the convict Stephen Adams.

'It would be charming if you and the prison doctor would agree to witness my little experiment,' he purred. 'It's a bit out of the usual line.'

The governor assented cordially enough, and sent for the medical officer. The three men found Adams in his cell. He appeared exhausted as if by severe mental strain, but stood up readily enough at the summons.

'I prefer not to explain the object of my enquiry at present,' began Iff. 'I merely beg that you gentlemen will make careful notes of the prisoner's reactions to what I say or do.'

He then approached the convict and began a conversation with him, cheerful in tone and trivial in subject. As he talked he made violent gestures, touching the boy several times. Once he dropped his notebook; it was instantly picked up and returned to him. After some ten minutes of this, Iff turned suddenly to the witnesses and asked if they had remarked anything unusual. Both shook their heads. They seemed surprised that Iff showed no disappointment.

'Perfectly sane? Perfectly normal?' Iff asked.

'As any of us.'

'Quite perfect,' came the answers.

'Every faculty in full free function?'

'Certainly,' the governor nodded.

'Much above the average all around,' affirmed the doctor.

Iff turned again to the prisoner, and resumed the thread of his previous remarks. His manner was in all respects unchanged; yet after a few seconds Stephen started back, as if he had received a blow. His face paled; his eyes glared in horror; he shrank back trembling from the magician as if he saw a ghost. He struggled to answer Iff's questions but did so at random, either misunderstanding what was said or replying irrationally. The magician worried him twice round the cell, and then left him shuddering in a corner. He next proceeded to execute a fantastic war-dance, with howls, ending in a double somersault. He then returned to the door, and requested the doctor to ask Adams to describe what had taken place.

The convict made a powerful effort to control himself. As he spoke, he recovered little by little. He gave a more or less connected account of the conversation, but omitted to report the majority of Iff's actions. The doctor prompting him, he acknowledged with apologies that he had 'somehow forgotten,' but he denied positively that the final dance had ever taken place.

The officials signalled their bewilderment.

'What does it mean?' cried the governor.

'May I tell you in your room?'

The governor nodded; the visitors retired, Iff waving his hand to the prisoner, and bidding him count confidently on being out in a month at most.

'First of all, gentlemen,' said Simon Iff, settling himself in a huge leather chair, 'I may assume that you have no doubts as to the genuineness of the behaviour of that boy?'

'Barring your having put him up to it, which is absurd, it's impossible. It would be senseless.'

'He had no idea of your object,' chimed in the governor; 'nor, for that matter, have we!'

'Next,' pursued Simon, 'will you please examine me closely? Am I in any way altered since I was last in this room?'

Inspection gave negative results.

'Tut,' cried Iff, 'your old gaol wants a wash! Just look at my coat! These cuffs were clean this morning! How did that spot get on my shirt? My nails are simply disgraceful!'

Apologies were forthcoming, of course.

'Excuse the digression. What could it have been that transformed that intelligent youth, that patient, clear-minded, observant person, into panic-stricken bewilderment that destroyed both intellection and observation for the time being?'

'Search me,' laughed one, to conceal his sense of shame.

'Modern psychology offers numerous alternative explanations of the phenomenon,' pronounced the other, to smoke-screen his ignorance.

'All I ask you to do is to write a report of the facts as you saw them, and send it to the District Attorney. You'll hear the results in a few days. Excuse me, won't you – now, I'm hot on a trail – and ever so many thanks for your kindness and assistance.'

He bowed and smiled himself out of the gaol, and told Dobson to 'step on it' all the way back to Gotham. A telephone call secured him the company of Mr Lubeck at dinner, where he proposed a programme which pleased, even while it puzzled, the kind-hearted old broker.

4

Stephen's sister came back from Atlantic City with colour in her cheeks instead of on them; Simon Iff wasted no time in telling her the results of his week's work.

'The hard half has been done, my dear; we know Stephen didn't do it, and we know who did. We know how it was done, what's more, and for that we must blame – you'll never guess – your Aunt Dorcas!'

'Aunt Dorcas!' echoed the girl blankly.

'Nobody else. Let me tell you the whole story as it happened. Here's a boy, kept away from danger (damn the fools) till he is afraid of every mortal thing he hears or sees. It's sin or sickness, hell or hospital, lying in ambush for everything he does! He is never allowed a chance to find out for himself that most of these horrors are bogies. He never faces his fears; they occupy his whole outlook; he devotes himself heart and soul to dodging them. As it happens, he reads a lot of exaggerated rubbish about germs, and his mind is obsessed about them. He becomes "Sterilised Stephen." The approach of "infection" terrifies him clean out of his wits, so that he is unable to see what is in front of his eyes. A cowardly thief is cunning enough to make a plan to take advantage of this. He threatens to touch the boy with some unusually dirty object, knowing that his senses will be paralysed with fear; while Stephen is in this state, he substitutes forged bonds for genuine in the packet on the desk. Your brother sees nothing; ten seconds, and the thief is away. Stephen picks himself up, still dazed, with no thought, no reason to think to examine the bonds. He seals up the packet—'

The girl's teeth were clenched with rage; her breath came hissing through them.

'But why did he bolt uptown?' she asked as Iff paused.

'I suspect he went to his coat for some patent disinfectant he favoured – and that the thief had stolen it, judging that Stephen would rush home for more. He's a good psychologist, the skunk; it all panned out according to schedule.'

'How can I ever thank you? I feel frightfully bad about it.'

'Nothing done yet, my dear, I'm sorry to say. The last half looks a pretty tough proposition. It's not a soft job to put one over on friend Hobbs – and that's where you come in!'

'I? How?' cried the startled girl.

5

The gift – or the achievement – of concentration upon the work in hand is a two-edged sword. Having deliberately shut oneself off from full attention to one's surroundings, there remains a penumbra of vague consciousness of what is presented to the senses. As long as everything passes normally there need be no disquietude, still less disturbance; but when the routine of nature (as it seems to the worker) is disorganised, a very curious and distinctly unpleasant phenomenon takes place. One cannot remain perfectly absorbed in contemplation of the 'bright spot in one's mind' – so to call it. At the same time, the habit of concentration persists, and prevents one from turning one's search-light upon the moving shadows of the background. One realises dimly that something is going on which is unusual and demands immediate attention, but one cannot awake sufficiently – unless the disturbance is very serious indeed – to feel sure that one's impressions are justly apprehended. The feeling of uneasiness is on such occasions not that which we associate with straightforward doubt as to what is happening; there is a touch of some equivalent of 'a bad conscience' connected with it. One feels that one ought to be able to describe events accurately, as one could in normal conditions, and the inability to do so takes the form of a sort of timid reproach to the observer. He feels himself somehow an inferior – to himself as he naturally is. Against this the will to concentrate reacts, often with violence: knowing (as one thinks) that whatever it is cannot be of any real importance, and therefore ought not to be allowed to interfere at all with one's work, one pushes it away with tempestuous anger as a weakness. The degree of concentration habitually attained in any case determines the degree of success in this process.

Now Mr Hobbs was a man of very considerable development in this great art. Shouting in the street – even a shot – would be dismissed automatically from his mind as none of his business; and if questioned subsequently, it would be hard for him to say whether he had heard it at all; much less, just what he had heard.

Events in his own office would affect him more nearly. His two assistants might go in and out all day, as part of their regular duty, and he would not raise his head. He would be subconsciously aware of the approach of Mr Lubeck, and adopt instinctively the proper degree of alertness to greet him. The footsteps of a stranger would arouse him completely, provided that the moral attitude of that stranger, as witnessed by the manner of his tread, might suggest some strikingly unusual interview *in posse*.

Bent over his books, therefore, he did not consciously notice the return of his two assistants from lunch; for that was the daily occurrence. But when, twenty minutes later, they both rose quietly and left the office, his attention was attracted to the unusual character of the event. And somehow, he got the impression that they were both dressed in the deepest mourning – as they certainly had not been before lunch. But why should they be in such a costume? He worked it all out even as he went on with his figures. They must have lost a relative and obtained permission from Mr Lubeck to attend the funeral that afternoon. Strange, though, that he should not have been notified. At this point his will indignantly protested. It was no business of his, after all, and – well, he couldn't swear that they were in black, now he put the question directly, though reluctantly enough, to himself. With a final effort he put his foot down, and swept the whole matter out of his mind.

At that moment he heard the approaching step of Mr Lubeck. 'Coming to explain' he registered briefly, half-annoyed at the additional distraction. Then he noticed, with genuine alarm, that the well-known tread of his superior was slower and more ponderous than its wont. As the door of the private office opened he lifted his head, as was customary with him, and his face went suddenly white. It was not Mr Lubeck at all, but a police inspector in uniform. 'Nonsense,' he cried internally, 'I know his step among a million.'

'Are my ears or my eyes at fault?' suddenly clamoured the sentinel of his mind. Testing his eyes by a direct gaze as he rose to greet the intruder, he was brought up by an 'impossibility' of the most astounding order. Despite the uniform, it was Mr Lubeck after all!

He growled at himself furiously. He simply could not believe that he was hallucinated about the uniform – and then the memory of his vague impression of seeing the two clerks in mourning unsettled him. Was it then someone with an astonishing resemblance to his chief?

That theory died a sudden death, for the new-comer sat down quietly opposite and began to speak to him casually in the perfectly unmistakable tones of Mr Lubeck.

Before half a dozen sentences had been spoken Hobbs' sentinel was, so to speak, shouting and firing off his rifle. He found it utterly impossible to attend to the slow, deliberate utterance, as his duty and habit was.

His mind had already been badly distracted, and his senses were storming at him to account for the appearance of his chief in that absurd uniform. He was so alarmed, psychologically, about his state of mind that he was praeternaturally on the alert for any new deviation from the normal. And what assailed him was so subtle and so abnormal that it preoccupied his mind completely. He did not hear a word of what was being said. What he noticed – at first vaguely, then with keen curiosity, and finally with terrifying accuracy of recognition – was a most strange, though negative, phenomenon. Outside, the clang and hubbub of the street continued as ever. But there was something missing. Imagine a man lying awake with nervous insomnia – at an inn by a waterfall. He is unaware of the ticking of his watch under his pillow. But the watch stops. He is instantly alarmed. It is some time before he is able to make out what has disturbed him.

Just so with Mr Hobbs: he realised slowly – after what seemed to him endless hours – that he was missing the perpetual clack and hum of the outer office. Had work suddenly ceased? – and why? What connection might that not have with the vague vision of the clerks in mourning, and with Mr Lubeck's incredible masquerade – or his own hallucination?

He dared not make sure of the alternative by appealing to the sense of touch to confirm his eyesight, or by asking his chief point-blank about it. It might be as much as his job was worth; he might be thought to be going insane. And Mr Hobbs had the very best of reasons for avoiding the slightest word or gesture which might in any manner give him away, might sow in Mr Lubeck's mind that he was not altogether the steady, sensible, even stolid cashier that he had manifested to enquiring eyes for twenty years with such unvarying success.

At this point in his meditations Mr Lubeck startled him by a sharp change of tone.

'Hobbs!'

The cashier sat up almost as if he had been struck.

'Are you listening to what I have been saying?' asked his employer, severely.

Mechanically, Hobbs repeated the instructions which had just been given. His conscious memory had recorded them perfectly. He was to take certain bonds – he had examined, verified and entered their numbers in his ledger during the interview – to Mr Simon Iff's apartment, take his receipt, and any further instructions.

'All right,' said Lubeck more gently, as if relieved. 'Excuse me, Hobbs, but I actually fancied for a moment' – he gave a little laugh – 'that you were actually not paying attention. Of course' – the broker assumed a soft, almost pitying tone – 'it's only natural if you should be a little distraught, as it were. You saw it at the lunch hour, I suppose?'

Hobbs assented, still mechanically. What was he supposed to have seen? He felt somehow that it would be a dreadful mistake to ask about it.

'Well, then, seal the packet,' went on the other. The cashier's fingers were nervously employed in thrusting the bonds into a thick office envelope. Hobbs complied.

'Now then,' went on Lubeck with an intensified seriousness, 'that is not quite all. Please give me the whole of your attention; every detail of what I am going to say is of vital importance.'

The cashier, putting the packet on one side, bent over to catch the low voice. It seemed as if secrecy, even in that empty office, was in some danger. At the same instant he paled once more. A footstep was again approaching; familiar somehow, and yet Hobbs was sure he had never heard it in his life – no, he knew it only too well – no, impossible. Keenly introspective, he evoked the '*sens du déjà écouté*' to explain.

'Come, come!' said Lubeck reproachfully. 'I quite understand. Go home when you are through with Mr Iff – and take a day off tomorrow. I wouldn't have asked you at all, but you're the only man I can trust on a business like this!'

The cashier, by a violent effort of will, fixed his eyes on those of his employer and put his whole conscious being under control. But do what he might, he could not help hearing the footsteps in the outer office, or feeling in the marrow of his bones that their maker was no other than Stephen Adams.

The door opened. Stephen! No! Of course not. Frightfully, ghastlily like him, though. But it was a girl? He looked heavily at Lubeck: not a flicker of an eyelid gave any sign that he was aware of the entrance of the new-comer.

The girl took off her overcoat and derby and hung them on the pegs sacred to his ex-assistant. His eyes started from his head: she was in convict clothes. She sat down calmly at Stephen's old desk, opened the books, and began to write.

Mr Lubeck gave no sign; instead, he laid his hand, kindly enough, on the cashier's trembling arm. 'I don't want to ask you for the third time,' he said compassionately, 'to give me every last particle of your attention.'

But this time Hobbs' whole mind revolted. Come what might, he must clear up this insane mystery.

'The girl in the chair!' he gasped. Mr Lubeck repeated the words, in blank amazement.

'What girl? What chair?'

'There! there!' cried the cashier, releasing his forearm and pointing.

'Where? Are you plumb crazy?' answered his chief, with irritation. 'Really, Hobbs, this isn't like you.'

Hobbs still pointed; the girl quietly rose, put on her hat and coat, and left the office.

'My dear man, I don't see any girl!'

'No – didn't you see her go?'

'Tut, you must be seriously ill, man,' cried Lubeck, with great concern in his voice. 'Are you rehearsing the supper scene from *Macbeth*?'

The unhappy cashier subsided into his chair and sat, panting, holding with nervous agitation to its arms and gazing blankly upon the other's wondering face.

There was a long silence. At last: 'I was dizzy for a moment,' stammered Hobbs. 'Headache – couldn't sleep last night – something at lunch—'

'More beauties of Prohibition?' laughed Lubeck, as if to reassure him.

'No, no, sir; never a drop!' cried the other, seriously upset at such a suspicion. 'Just indigestion – fancied I saw something for a moment – better now – beg your pardon, sir, most sincerely.'

'Good man, if you feel all right now, get along. We mustn't keep Mr Iff waiting.'

'No sir,' replied Hobbs miserably, and began to undo his waistcoat to put away the packet in the special pocket which he used for such purposes.

With a brief nod, and a cheery word, Mr Lubeck walked out of the office.

But the cashier, having buttoned up the packet safely, sat lost in the deepest thought. Was this fantastic adventure a joke? – unthinkable. A plot of some kind? He could not imagine his employer party to anything of the sort. Hallucination then, after all? The idea worried him very badly. He knew just enough of medicine to think that one sure characteristic of any such delusions would be that the victim could not possibly suspect them to be anything but real. His mind began a zig-zag logical sorites on the problem: every time he came to any conclusion, some detail or other would pop up again and reverse the probabilities once more.

'Whew,' he muttered, wiping his forehead. 'I'll think more clearly in the fresh air.' And he flung out of the office; in his state of mental disturbance, he forgot to take his hat and coat.

In the outer room he got a new shock. It was, as his ears had told him, empty. He looked at his watch. 'Too absurd,' he muttered, in acute annoyance. He walked across; just then he heard the closing of a ledger, in Mr Lubeck's private office.

'I'll go and see about that uniform and settle that once and for all.' He would have been positively relieved to find his chief disguised as a Zulu warrior. No such luck! He was sitting in his ordinary business clothes, very intent on his work. No trace of any masquerade.

'Well, what is it, Hobbs?' The chief did not look up.

'I beg your pardon, sir, did you say I might take tomorrow off?' was the best excuse he could invent.

'I did,' replied Lubeck, with a peculiar intonation which somehow struck terror into his inmost marrow, though he could not have said why. He went out like a man in a dream.

The elevator, the hallway, the street all reassured him that his senses were intact. But then—? In a way, that made things rather more serious than ever. It was curious, too, the way in which people were looking at him – at least – were they?

'Damn it, I'll square this!' he cried, as he pushed his way into Park Place. 'Here's a sane man; I'll test myself by him.'

He went up to the traffic cop. 'Would you mind telling me what that building is, officer?' he said, pointing to the Woolworth.

The man knew the cashier by sight well enough; he had seen him pass there four times a day for years. Why hadn't he his hat and coat? And why did he look so agitated? And why – of all things – ask such a foolish question? He decided that there was a joke or a bet in the background.

'Yes, Sir Ethelred, beg pardon, my lord,' he answered saluting. 'That there edifice is Grant's Tomb.'

In any other circumstances the psychology of the moment would have been clear enough to Hobbs, and reassured him finally that he was sane; but as things were, the answer shook him badly. He suppressed an inclination to howl and run off; he stood a moment, dazed. The policeman began to suspect something wrong and would have interfered, but the sense of routine duty came back suddenly to the cashier in the complete ruin of the superstructure of his mind. He hailed a passing taxi, called out the address of Simon Iff, and sank back with a sense of luxurious relief. It seemed to him, though – he had no idea why – that he was safe at last, that he had stumbled out of the nightmare as mysteriously and suddenly as he had stumbled into it.

Every detail of the journey uptown, familiar and restful, restored him almost wholly to himself. He was able, by an effort, to distrust the unsolved problem of the past half hour, and was sufficiently himself by the time the car drew up to realise that he was hatless and coatless.

'Why, of course, that explains the whole thing,' he murmured joyfully – not seeing in the least any explanation of even any one part of it. It was his subconscious self, alarmed for his sanity, that had been subtly reassured by the fact that events, generally speaking, had resumed their normal tone. There had been an accident of some sort, as the lack of hat and coat declared, but it was over now; it had not been serious, and as soon as he learnt the reason for his neglect, the nightmare features of his 'attack' – so he now called it – would become explicable.

'Amnesia, that's it!' he concluded happily, as he paid off the chauffeur with that proud delight that the half-educated experience on finding themselves in bed with a long Greek or Latin word which is often in the newspapers and must be therefore perfectly respectable.

6

The embarrassment of Mr Hobbs about the absence of his hat and coat completely dominated his mind between the taxi and the door of Simon Iff's apartment. He had quite satisfied himself that whatever had happened at the office was over and done with. It was therefore a terrific shock when the door was opened by that very replica of Sterilised Stephen in feminine flesh and felon attire that had flitted through his office an hour earlier. He was struck speechless. But the girl addressed him without a trace of surprise.

'Mr Hobbs from Lubeck and Lewison,' she said. 'Come right in, Mr Iff's expecting you.'

Despite his conscious paralysis, something in his mind registered the fact that the girl's accents were not Caucasian or Semitic; it was the precise and pretty, soft and slurred English of a Mongol. The effect was to bewilder him completely. His subconscious good sense told him surreptitiously of a possible point to the farce in the office, but there was no rational connection to be traced in this, and it led him back to the state of uncertainty as to whether his senses were not playing him tricks. He suddenly remembered Simon Iff's reputation as a magician. As the girl led the way to the door of his study he felt rather like a character in an Arabian Night, doubtful as to what dreadful or horrible experience might be lurking behind the door.

Ushered into the study, he was immediately reassured. There was nothing in any way abnormal. He began to look for the big envelope which he was to deliver, but Iff stopped him.

'I thought if you had the time, Mr Hobbs, we might go down to the bank together. The bonds will be safer where they are. But I see you are a little out of breath. Will you take a cigarette and a cup of coffee with me? As you see, I am just finishing lunch.'

He filled a cup for the cashier and a liqueur glass of old brandy. He lit a match for Hobbs' cigarette and the two men smoked in silence. Somehow or other the calm impersonal gaze of the magician had the effect of making Hobbs extremely ill at ease. He felt himself – he had no idea why – in the presence of a god – very gentle, yet very terrible, one who saw through him without even seeing him. And there was born in his mind an almost over-mastering impulse to lay open his soul. His instinct of self-preservation held him back, and he satisfied the impulse by appealing to the magician for an explanation of the extraordinary events at the office.

Simon listened without surprise.

'This sort of thing is fairly common,' he said, and went into a little technical sermon on hallucinations and their causes.

'It is only natural,' he concluded, 'that you should be mentally upset. You were quite all right before lunch, weren't you?'

'Quite,' said Hobbs.

'Exactly,' continued Simon. 'Your hallucinations are simply due to what happened during the lunch hour.'

'But nothing happened during the lunch hour,' objected Hobbs.

'What! Didn't you see it?' cried Simon, with the utmost surprise.

'See what? I don't know what you mean!' stammered the cashier, thoroughly alarmed, he knew not why.

Iff struck a hand-bell at his side, and the cashier almost jumped out of his chair.

The girl appeared at the door. Simon addressed her volubly in Japanese and she answered briefly in that language, with a low bow, and disappeared.

Hobbs could not contain himself. He told Iff how things looked to him.

'What, Togo in stripes?' cried Iff laughing, and then checked himself and looked at the trembling man before him with the most serious commiseration. 'Strange, strange,' he said in a meditative voice. 'I could understand it if you had seen it.'

'Seen what?' cried Hobbs, his voice rising to a scream. By his elbow was the girl in stripes. She was handing a copy of *The Evening Mercury* to her master.

Iff ran his finger down the columns. In the stop press was only one paragraph. It stared loudly from the blank of the rest of the column.

SUICIDE IN SING SING

> Stephen Adams, recently convicted for theft of bonds, hanged himself in the prison early this morning.

The finger with which Simon directed his attention to that bald statement seemed to the guilty man like the finger of God. He was struck speechless. His face went blank as a sheet of paper. Iff took no notice.

'If you didn't see that,' he said slowly, 'I don't see what upset your mind so seriously as to make you see things. You don't drug?' he asked sharply.

Hobbs tried to frame the words 'never in my life,' but his articulation refused its office.

'Can it be?' mused Simon Iff – and rose suddenly from his chair. 'Never mind the cause,' he declared vigorously, 'the cure is the thing. Business before pleasure. Attend to duty and never mind the tricks our eyes sometimes play us. Let's get down to the bank. Here, swallow this.'

He poured the cashier a stiff drink of brandy, which pulled him together physically but left his mind in a blank passive state. He was quite fit to do anything, but deprived of initiative, of the power to think, in all but the most superficial sense of that phrase.

He followed Iff out of the room and was not in the least surprised to find Togo looking like a quite ordinary Japanese servant. Simon asked him about it.

'You see,' he said, 'you're better already.' But when they got to the outer entrance, instead of Iff's motor-car he saw a prison van. However, it did not seem so apparently to Simon, who said, 'I think it'll do you good if we walk down to the bank this day. Nothing like fresh air to blow away the cobwebs.'

Hobbs assented mechanically, and Iff addressed the uniformed driver. 'I shan't want you this afternoon, Dobson,' he said, 'but be back for the theatre after dinner. Amuse yourself as you like till then.'

'Yes, sir, thank you, sir,' replied the man, saluting; and even distressed as he was, Hobbs could not fail to observe that the man's accent was utterly remote from anything American.

He began to analyse his perceptions. He tried to look at his experiences in perspective. It seemed in particular that his ears were somehow at war with his eyes. No, that didn't account for everything. He began to realise that almost all the inexplicable perceptions had something to do with Stephen and the police. Were they then phantasms created by his conscience? If not, was he suspected? Had a comedy been staged to frighten him into confession? Knowing himself safe, he brightened instantly at the thought. And yet, when he considered the matter, it seemed impossible. There would not have been time to prepare so elaborate a scheme, for Stephen had only hanged himself that very morning. And then he realised for the first time the import of that fact. It was he that was responsible for the boy's death. He had not thought of that before. He had hated Stephen as a coward and a prig, and despised him as a crank. He had felt no remorse at his imprisonment. But that he should have killed himself was another story. Why had he not foreseen that such an issue was inevitable, given the ultra-neurotic character of the boy?

Hobbs had never believed in the supernatural, but now it seemed to him as the only rational explanation of events to suppose that, by some mysterious sympathy, a dead man was somehow able to revenge himself by throwing the mental machinery of his murderer out of gear. There were plenty of well-authenticated stories of the sort.

'I must pull myself together,' he thought, 'whatever I do, I mustn't give myself away. I must ask for a holiday and go to a safe place till I've got over these fancies.'

And he began to make plans, but they were always interfered with by a vision of his victim hanging from a bar of his cell window.

'Here, wake up!' said Simon Iff, who had not spoken all the way to the bank. 'Here we are.'

Hobbs took stock of his surroundings. Again his eyes were playing him false. An automobile was drawn up at the door of the bank and in it were two fashionable ladies, almost extravagantly dressed. There was a little crowd around the car, which the porter was trying to keep back. And the motive of the crowd was evident, for the chauffeur was the girl in stripes.

Then did other people share his hallucinations? Slight as the matter was in comparison with what had passed, its incongruity brought to the ground all his previous theories and left his mind more completely bewildered than ever. It couldn't be hallucination if other people could see that accursed girl, and it couldn't be a comedy staged for his benefit, for that fact would knock the house of cards to pieces.

He followed Iff to the receiving teller's desk and pulled out the sealed envelope. The teller opened it. The man's face changed.

'There's some mistake here, Mr Hobbs,' he said. 'Except these two, these bonds are forgeries.'

The cashier found himself unable to utter a word. The teller gave a signal, and two of the plain-clothes men in the bank immediately slipped their arms through those of the terrified Hobbs. History had repeated itself. A glaring light broke in upon his mind.

'It's a conspiracy,' he shouted, 'and I know exactly how the trick was done.'

'Yes, you might tell us about that,' said Simon very gently.

Hobbs no longer knew what he was saying. 'I'm not guilty,' he cried, 'Adams can clear me.'

'Isn't it rather for you to clear Adams?' suggested Simon Iff, and then the cashier remembered that Adams was lying dead in prison.

'I never meant to kill him,' he went on. 'I never thought he couldn't stand—' and once again he broke off short, appalled.

He saw that he had no chance to clear himself. He had sealed up the envelope and it had been in his possession till that moment. He knew too well that it had been changed by the girl in stripes while Mr Lubeck was talking to him, but he couldn't tell that story to a jury – he couldn't tell it to his own attorney. They would only say that he was shamming mad to get off. He had been trapped, and instinctively he turned to Simon Iff to save him.

'I didn't steal the bonds,' he whined. 'I want justice.'

'Then you must do it yourself,' answered Simon. 'Come, let us go into the president's room, and tell us the whole story.'

Completely broken down, the cashier complied. Iff had accurately divined the method employed to scare Sterilised Stephen. Hobbs had led up to the critical moment by teasing Stephen about his fears, and threatening that one day he would bring down a culture of virulent bacilli and shed them over him. He had, in fact, squirted a little dirty water on Stephen's person, and taken advantage of his distraction to change the bonds. Hobbs ended his confession with an appeal for mercy.

'It shall be granted,' answered Simon, and sent for a copy of *The Evening Mercury*. It was the same edition as the copy in Iff's apartment, but the stop press column contained no reference to Stephen Adams.

7

Simon Iff had been absent from New York for some weeks attending to the matter (elsewhere recorded) of Col. Van Schuyler. On his return he found a letter from Mr Lubeck, who concluded his congratulations by inviting the magician to dinner to meet Stephen Adams and his sister Violet. The boy had been released immediately on the confession of Hobbs, and the dinner-party was intended not only to celebrate the victory but to plan future campaigns. The stockbroker's original interest in his aseptic employee had been revivified by the sympathy he felt for his tribulations.

The good man blamed himself quite unjustly for his reluctant contribution to the catastrophe. But Simon Iff was in his most cantankerous mood. He would not admit that any catastrophe had taken place. He blamed Lubeck, not for prosecuting his clerk, but for having encouraged him in his iniquity.

He had no kind word for Stephen that night. All through dinner, in defiance of every rule of politeness, he treated the boy with savage contempt. He lost no opportunity of sneering at everything he said; he criticised his personal appearance in absolutely unpardonable terms. There was never such a bear at any dinner-party that New York had ever seen. Only with Violet did he preserve the commonest form of politeness.

Not until dinner was over did Simon unmask his really heavy artillery. He attacked Sterilised Stephen with callous brutality, so that Mr Lubeck, seeing how acutely his guest was suffering, unable to defend himself because his enemy was also his saviour, ventured a word of protest.

'My dear man,' retorted Iff, 'have you no common sense? Can't you see that this rag of humanity is on the way to getting worse torn than ever? What's his whole attitude? That of a deeply injured man who has been justified. His punishment begins now.

'You had Dr Braithwaite examine you three days ago?'

'Yes,' stammered Stephen, 'and he told me I was perfectly healthy.'

'That's what he told you,' sneered Iff. 'But here's his private report of the scraping he took from your throat.'

He took a paper from his pocket-book and passed it to Stephen. The gesture was as if he had stabbed him. The boy read the slip. It appeared that his throat harboured the germs of influenza, diphtheria and typhoid, and some half-dozen lesser diseases.

It was necessary to apply restoratives. At last, he mastered himself sufficiently to stammer something about his death-warrant.

'Now look here, my boy,' said Simon. 'That's all nonsense. All our throats are full of those germs all the time. But none of us get any of those diseases except under special conditions, the chief of which is a lowered vitality. Now, nothing lowers vitality so much as fear. Look at yourself. The doctor declares you in perfect health, and yet you nearly faint when I pass you a scrap of paper. I've travelled a bit in the tropics and seen plague and cholera sweeping away whole townships as a storm scatters the leaves from trees in autumn. I thought even in America everyone knew that the one sure way to get an epidemic disease was to funk it.'

'That's right,' put in Lubeck. 'I was in Panama in the old days, and the people who got Yellow Jack were not the people who took the big risks, but the people who brooded on the danger.'

'There's another point too,' pursued Simon. 'When fear, which is a definite pathological condition, a disease far more deadly than tuberculosis, attains a certain degree of intensity, it deprives a man of the use of his five senses. Did you ever read that essay of Sullivan's on Human Testimony?'

It appeared that nobody had.

'Well, you should,' proceeded Simon. 'However, I'll quote you, as nearly as memory serves me, one remark.

> 'During the war it was noticed that the evidence of soldiers freshly wounded was often of the most fantastic description. They would testify to the details of catastrophes which had never occurred; they would assert that so-and-so had been decapitated in front of their eyes, and so-and-so buried by an explosion, when, as a matter of fact, nothing remotely resembling these events had taken place.'

'Is that possible?' asked Lubeck.

'Well, you ought to know,' retorted the magician. 'You've had the case of this wretched invertebrate here, and a much more striking example, under your very nose.'

'Yes,' said Lubeck; 'of course. Do you know, I've never really understood how you got away with that absurd business of Hobbs. He wasn't at all the nervous hysterical type, and he hadn't been freshly wounded.'

'Fishing for compliments,' laughed Simon. 'I've already congratulated you on the goodness of heart which inhibits so effectively the operation of your cerebral cortex. Hobbs had lived for years with the worst kind of fear: that of being found out. It wasn't pathological in the sense of being irrational, but on the other hand, he had no protection whatever against it. He couldn't fly to antiseptics whenever it became acute. He couldn't even relieve his mind by talking about it. He had to be perpetually sitting on the safety-valve; and any form of suppression always tends to turn normal instinct into pathological channels. I didn't expect to break him down by the scene in the office. I saw to it that he was freshly wounded.

'I staged the comedy to prepare him for the wound. I wanted to evoke his fear from the hell of the unconscious self in order that it might shake his confidence in his own critical judgment, in his sense of reality.'

'But no one would really believe that his eyes and ears had gone wrong so suddenly and to that extent. He must have suspected that we were laying a fantastic trap for him, and that should have put him on his guard, rather than induced him to betray himself.'

'True enough,' admitted Simon. 'But the things he saw were, so to speak, phantasms of his hidden fear, connected vaguely with Stephen through Violet's likeness to him, and the circumstances of the plot, assuming it to be one, were all so wildly improbable. The result was that a mere trifle of absolutely genuine evidence, as he supposed, believing (as people of his class do) in the newspapers, was enough to wound his guilty conscience. It never occurred to him that I had had that paragraph specially printed in my copy of the *Mercury*, especially as we had both prepared him for it by attributing his experiences, which we both assumed to be hallucinations, to something which we pretended to suppose that he must have seen during the lunch hour.'

'Yes,' said Mr Lubeck thoughtfully, 'but Hobbs was hardened by years of crime and utterly callous of the consequences to others.'

Simon looked at him very sadly. 'Surely you understand,' he said slowly, 'that such callousness is the very measure of the intensity of his own fear. The thought of prison was so intolerable to him that he did not dare to allow himself the luxury of the faintest human sympathy for his victims. But he had not contemplated death. He saw in an instant, taking him at his worst, that to be found out might drive him to kill himself. As a matter of fact, he was not as bad as that; he suffered genuine remorse. The psychological resultant was however the same. What he lost on the swings, he made up on the roundabouts. In any case we were sure of the main object: to render him incapable, at the critical moment, of the normal reaction. He saw himself caught in the identical trap which he had sprung on Stephen. He saw instantly, with every particle of his instinct of self-preservation, that this fact proved his innocence, that he was the victim of a clever scheme, so that in his anxiety to prove his innocence, he exclaimed jubilantly that he knew exactly how the trick was turned. In his normal state he would have perceived the implications of the statement. Suppose a man has been swindled by the three card trick; he could not have been swindled if he knew exactly how the trick was done. His explanation proved previous knowledge. We cannot be sure of the deep workings of his mind at this point, but this at least is evident: that the series of shocks had quite abrogated his conscious control. He probably recognised his blunder in some stratum beneath clear consciousness; for he instantly completed it by the appeal to Stephen to clear him, very much as a man in certain conditions will run his bicycle into the very object which he is trying to avoid. The realisation that Stephen was dead crowned the edifice with ills, as Euripides says. His unconscious stood before us all, stark in its horror of malignity and fear. The one relief which he had so long denied himself – confession – became the over-mastering passion, and he reeled off the list of his iniquities with something really not far from gusto. He had to get rid of twenty years of silence in a single outburst.'

'Well, I must say,' remarked Mr Lubeck, 'it has been a most masterly demonstration of psychology.'

'I'm not very proud of it,' replied Simple Simon. 'The method was far too elaborate and complex to please me. It ought to have been managed in a quiet conversation. My excuse is that I had really no access even to the person of Hobbs. He was guarded in every way but one, and I had to arrange a scenario which would cut short all ways of escape. It was necessary that all explanations of events were equally untenable.

'However, enough of the past. Our business is to *un*sterilise Stephen. The bacillus of self-esteem finds him a most favourable medium? I doubt if he understands even now how I despise and loathe him. My chief satisfaction in getting him out of gaol is that I have saved his fellow criminals from the contamination of his example. I cannot even make him angry,' growled the mystic. 'If he had any self-respect, instead of self-esteem, he would have walked out of the house an hour ago.'

The outraged youth began a homily on gratitude.

'I don't want your gratitude,' howled Iff. 'That's only another clean collar, and what you need is to play in the mud. You were brought up with a host of virtues, so-called; so many painted masks to hide the face of a coward. You even despised your sister, and where would you be now without her? You've got to chuck all that. It's all a mass of iniquity, a monstrous growth in a thousand hideous forms of the original fear which was drilled into you by that accursed old hag, Aunt Dorcas, who, I hope, is roasting in hell at this minute. However, you've had your medicine, and I'm going to give you a chance.'

His hand went back to his pocket and he produced a letter which he handed to Lubeck. The good old man's eyes grew dim as he read it. He went over to Stephen and laid his hand on the boy's shoulder.

'I am glad I prosecuted,' he said with humorous brusqueness. 'I couldn't have done as much for you as this if you had stayed with me for ten years.'

'Dear Mr Iff,' he read aloud,

> 'I think this is about what you want. Send Adams to me at four o'clock next Monday. He can manage our new branch at Fu Ling above Hankow.'

Stephen only understood that he was appointed to a position of great and absolute responsibility, carrying a very great increase on any salary he might have hoped for for many years to come. He sprang to his feet. But Iff checked him with a gesture.

'Fu Ling is a glorious place,' said he. 'I was there a few years back. The only European in the place was the Customs Collector. He was just getting over a couple of bullet wounds in the riot when the missionary was killed, thank God. That's why he wasn't there. It's a delightful old town – on the top of a mound about seventy feet above the plain; not a natural mound, of course – the solidified refuse of centuries. There is no sanitation as we understand it, not even in a European's house, and I hope you will notice that everyone is healthy as anywhere else. The death rate is about the same as in this country.

'Of course,' he said as if by an after-thought, 'there are lepers.'

Stephen's hair had not yet grown long enough to stand any straighter than it did.

'I shouldn't worry,' went on Iff remorselessly, 'there's no influenza, no cerebro-spinal meningitis, no sleeping-sickness, no consumption, no cancer, no rickets, and better still, none of those hydra-headed imaginary diseases which afflict us weekly in the Sunday newspapers. The risk of being murdered is a good deal less one-half per cent of what it is in Memphis, Tennessee. The risk of Hobbs is nil.

'You have to learn courage and self-respect out there,' he went on, 'and you will also lose your self-esteem, for you have to face reality every hour of the day and night – and in reality,' he concluded, on a full diaphragm, 'every man is a hero and every man is a god.'

Something broke in the brain of Sterilised Stephen. He strode forward impulsively, head erect and sparkling eyes, to clasp the outstretched hand of the magician, but all he said was 'I'll go,' though his lips were as white as his cheeks.

Simon Iff collected Violet with his free hand.

'Observe, my child,' he said. 'He says he will go. And is not going the sure sign of godhead? Old artists represented the Egyptian gods as bearing a sandal-strap in token that their function was to go, to go through every phase of existence untouched by anything they chanced to meet. Did you never hear the saying "Every man and every woman is a star"? And what does a star do but go, and give light in its going?'

The eyes of the girl were fixed upon him with the soft yearning look of a dog for its master.

'Yes, my dear,' he smiled, 'you're going too. Your job in life is to look after your brother. You've seen all the worst side of life? Your experience is just what he needs.'

He sat down in a big arm-chair and lighted a proportionate cigar.

'The trouble with respectability,' he said, 'is this: that for the most part it doesn't exist at all. It's a phantasm created by fear. For this reason, every cunning scoundrel can use it to cloak his misdeeds. But when you've got rid of the sham, the genuine good of humanity comes; and Violet here knows how much lovelier were the lives of the harlots and criminals with whom she has lived for years than those of people like Aunt Dorcas, who practically condemned her to starve to death for following a natural impulse, or the boy who persuaded her to it and left her to sink. Which is the better man, the thief who stands you a meal and a drink out of coarse comradeship, or the cop who blackmails you out of half your earnings on Broadway? You'll find an honest set of values at Fu Ling. You have never done anything in your life that wasn't perfectly decent and straightforward – in itself, I mean, dear girl – apart from the artificial restrictions of society. You failed financially through ignorance of the low cunning and the hypocritical tricks of your neighbours, and the poison of their vileness is so strong that they actually persuaded you that they were right to despise you. That's why you're going to Fu Ling with Stephen. For another thing, you would never recover in this mephitic atmosphere. Out there, you will be a royal personage by right of race, and they will all look up to you because you won't look down on them – as missionaries do, God burn their rotten souls in hell, that the smoke may be for a sign.'

The essence of Violet's nature was to love and trust, to protect when she felt strong, to appeal when she felt weak. At the moment it was as if she had been suddenly hoisted on to a throne, and a moment's fear passed over her face, the noble fear that she might not live up to her task. She murmured something about the strange ways of those strange people.

'They won't be strange to you,' the mystic said. 'Mankind is just the same all over the world. The differences between civilisations are the differences between shams, for the most part. The primal needs of all men are alike, and those needs form the basis of all their funny little ways. You have been at grips with them all your life, and you will make no mistake in dealing with people as long as you love and understand.'

There was dead silence in the room. Simon Iff suddenly discarded his prophetic manner and became the conventional guest.

'Goodnight and goodbye for a while,' he said. 'I must return to my sheep.'

When he had gone, the silence lasted for a long while. Each of the three was lost in his own thoughts. When Violet thought it time to retire, Lubeck took them to the door himself, and as he shook hands, jerked his head over his shoulder towards the number on the door.

'Goodnight, my children; remember your father's address.'

8

Fifteen months later a serious riot in Fu Ling was aborted by the moral and physical courage of Violet and Stephen. He had learnt that the only germ he had to fear was the germ of fear in himself. And to that, a year in China had made him immune.

For more details and a full list of titles:

visit https://www.hachetteindia.com/home/yellowbacks

WELCOME BACK TO THE GOLDEN AGE